AT LONG LAST LOVE

"So go," Lilli said.

Zane looked at her and laughed. "Just like that?"

He looked into her eyes. They both knew it was his love for her that kept him from his dream.

He kissed her. He breathed love into her and inhaled it back into himself as if it were the only nourishment he'd had for months. He pulled her into his arms and held her close.

Suddenly Lilli was truly frightened. She could see the future as clearly as if she'd taken a snapshot. Zane would eventually leave Texas and she would be left behind. She could almost hear the wrenching of her heart.

Yet if she truly loved him, she would have to let him go . . .

Other Avon Books by
Catherine Lanigan

THE WAY OF THE WICKED

CATHERINE LANIGAN

AT LONG LAST LOVE

AVON BOOKS ◆ NEW YORK

AT LONG LAST LOVE is an original publication of Avon Books. This work has never before appeared in book form. This work is a novel. Any similarity to actual persons or events is purely coincidental.

AVON BOOKS
A division of
The Hearst Corporation
1350 Avenue of the Americas
New York, New York 10019

Copyright © 1994 by Catherine Lanigan
Published by arrangement with the author
Library of Congress Catalog Card Number: 93-91668
ISBN: 0-380-76948-4

First Avon Books Printing: February 1994

AVON TRADEMARK REG. U.S. PAT. OFF. AND IN OTHER COUNTRIES, MARCA REGISTRADA, HECHO EN U.S.A.

Printed in the U.S.A.

RA 10 9 8 7 6 5 4 3 2 1

This one is for Bill,
my own childhood sweetheart

ACKNOWLEDGMENTS

I have been blessed with wonderful and caring friends who, as usual, have come to my aid during the writing process. I am grateful to them all for making *At Long Last Love* a special story.

Much gratitude to my editor, Ellen Edwards, the other half of my brain—the genius half.

Many thanks to Joyce Meadows of Houston, Texas, for her professional expertise and knowledge with the archaeological aspects of this book.

Much appreciation to Lynette Prowler of Houston, Texas, for sharing her experiences and success in the antique jewelry business with me.

To my mother, Dorothy Lanigan, I am ever grateful for her patience (I wish I had more) with the endless proofreading of this story.

For his invaluable help, I thank Dr. Howard Sussman of Houston, Texas, for sharing his amazing "stories" about his fifteen years of experience as the host of a radio program on UFOs and aliens.

To Judith McNaught, my friend, thanks for holding my hand during the dark days.

For aid with the financial aspects of the story, I relied again on my brother, Robert Lanigan, who keeps hoping one of these days I'll get it . . .

And to my sister, Nancy Porter, for loving me and making me laugh.

Special Appreciation

My list of cheerleaders has grown over the past year and I am ever grateful that God continues to send me so many angels.

On the top of my list is Karen Paterson at Barnes & Noble, Inc., Ceneta Williams at Waldenbooks, and John Sutter at Crown Books.

Since my move to Indiana I dearly miss my friends at East Texas Distributors, Doug Mote and Kathy Akins; Nancy Reiner of Waldenbooks, Houston, Texas; my ICD representative, Chris Dunham; Dorothy Jones of Randall's Food Stores in Houston; and lastly, the whole gang at B. Dalton's in Town and Country Mall.

Denis Farina at Avon Books in New York and my Avon Book representatives Ken Trout in Texas and Ron Wilson in Maryland have helped me so much.

Special thanks to Paul Kilber, my ICD representative in Chicago, and Cathy Kadek at Levy Home Entertainment here in Chicagoland.

Much gratitude to Majerek's Reader's World in La Porte and in Michigan City, Indiana, and to Bernadette Csanaky of Brennens' Book Store in New Buffalo, Michigan. To all my new friends at Waldenbooks in University Park Mall and Scottsdale Mall in South Bend, Indiana, my thanks.

God bless you all.

Part
One

Prologue

May 1986
San Diego, California

*L*illi Mitchell was exhausted by the time she drove over the San Diego Bay to Coronado and checked into the historic Hotel del Coronado. She loved places like this that had retained their charm from an earlier age. She had always felt a link to things of another period, another time. To Lilli, this sprawling wooden hotel with its red shingled roof, huge round turret, two thousand redwood doors, and nearly twenty-four hundred windows was a fantasy castle by the sea. Just standing in the Victorian lobby still decorated with the original light fixtures and the chandeliers designed by Frank L. Baum, the writer of the *Wizard of Oz* series, made her feel as if she had been transported to another world.

She handed the reservation manager her American Express card and inquired about the dining room while the bell captain placed her bags on a trolley and informed her that he would meet her in her room. Lilli turned away from the desk and followed the bell captain and as she did, she passed by the cluster of upholstered Victorian chairs in the lobby, where drinks were being served to the guests. A pianist played a love song reminiscent of the thirties. A Billie Holiday tune, she thought. As she passed one of the massive dark wood columns that separated the bar area from the reception area, she detected the faint scent of sandalwood, the cologne that Zane McAllister used to wear.

Lilli stopped dead in her tracks. A flood of memories washed over her, stilling her senses and igniting her emotions. She remembered the summer of '77, making love with Zane under the moon and stars in the hill country of West

3

Texas. He was the first love of her life, a teenage crush that had not faded with time.

I can feel him, she thought. Sense him, somehow. How can that be? Zane is on the other side of the country, in New York. Worse, I'm a million miles from his thoughts. God! What am I doing to myself? I'm twenty-four years old. Surely, surely I'm over him ... beyond him. Past the pain and the heartbreak.

Lilli felt her stomach tighten as the sandalwood fragrance seemed to surround her. Her heart skipped a beat as she whirled around, totally forgetting about the bell captain taking her bags to her room. She wished she could fight this reaction, but she felt overwhelmingly compelled to follow the scent.

She approached a group of three men dressed in summer suits who appeared to be concluding a business transaction. One of the men looked at her quizzically and paused, as if awaiting her cue.

But Lilli's eyes were focused on a tall, well-built man with blond hair and blue eyes. When he saw her, he beamed, and energy seemed to crackle in his eyes.

"Lilli," he said, his happiness evident in his voice. He separated himself from the group and walked toward her.

Lilli wondered fleetingly if Zane McAllister was only an apparition. One that would appear then vanish just as quickly.

"Lilli? Is that you?"

"Zane." She said his name with a rush of excitement and fear. Lilli felt as if she'd been catapulted back into time. This wasn't real. This couldn't be happening.

He was impeccably dressed in an understated Italian suit that must have cost him well over a thousand dollars, Lilli thought. His shoes were expensive soft kid leather, his shirt was linen, and his cuff links were lapis lazuli. Not only was he doing well for himself, he was obviously free enough of the guilt he'd harbored when he first left Texas to enjoy the fruits of his labor. Zane had learned to be good to himself, and Lilli admired that. However, she couldn't control her surprise; she had never expected to see him again, and certainly not in California.

"What a twist of events this is," she said.

Zane moved next to her. "God, you look great, Lilli. I

didn't think it was possible for your eyes to look more violet, but that purple blouse ... with your eyes ..." His words trailed off, as if he had been about to say too much. Then he asked, "How are you, Lilli?"

"Fine. I'm fine," she lied. She felt suddenly sad, as if all her days without him were meaningless. What kind of fate is this, she wondered, to fall in love with only one person in my whole life? You've got to get over him, Lilli. You must.

But the truth was, she didn't want to forget him. Couldn't forget him. He was her Zane. Nobody else's. She still wanted to hope.

"What are you doing here in California?"

"Well, I—I—business," she finally said.

"Yeah, me, too," he said, smiling and staring at her so hard that she began to feel uncomfortable. "Gosh, you look beautiful."

"Thank you," she said softly. "You look pretty terrific yourself."

"Thanks," he said with that West Texas accent that eight years in New York City had not erased. "I'm really happy for you, Lilli, that everything has turned out so well. Your business and all ..."

"It keeps me busy."

"Not too busy, I hope," he said.

Lilli knew that Zane, in his modest way, was pressing for information about her personal life. God! she thought. Is he hinting about my love life? "Very."

"Hey, Zane!" the man who had regarded Lilli said. "I hate to break up your reunion, but Masterson is waiting." He smiled apologetically at her. "Sorry."

"I understand," Lilli said as she extended her hand to Zane. "It was great to see you."

"Yeah. Same here," he said, although she noticed that he was reluctant to let go of her hand. Then he walked away with his business associates.

Lilli watched him leave, still aware of the scent of sandalwood and pine. The room became crowded with her memories of him. "Bad timing," she said aloud. "That's always been our curse." She wondered if it would always be that way.

One

*L*illi carefully swept the dirt away from an eight-hundred-year-old human skull. Although she was only fourteen, she'd been on enough archaeological digs in the British Honduras, Mexico, Peru, and Chile to know that one used a fine-bristled whisk broom to flick the dust particles off ancient artifacts and skeletons so that the precious patinas or coatings, which would give clues about the cultures, would not be disturbed.

Her father was not interested in skulls or bones, but Lilli was. A clump of dirt fell away from the base of the skull, and she could tell that this Mayan had been decapitated. She assumed it was a man, since his skull was larger than the female skulls they had found in the area. Also, the jaw was more pronounced than one belonging to a female, and the nasal crevice was wider and longer. "He must have been some sort of sacrifice," she said to herself, knowing that Mayan religious beliefs greatly valued human sacrifice. The previous year she had accompanied her father to Chichén Itzá, where Mayan high priests had hurled sacrificial victims into a cenote, or sacred well, in order to obtain rain from the rain god. Too often Lilli had seen artistic depictions of these sacrifices: of hearts being cut out of the victims, of beheadings, or of skeletons marked by hundreds of arrowheads. She still had a difficult time dealing with man's inhumanities in the name of religion, so she told herself that such injustices were part of the past and had nothing to do with the present.

"How're you doing over there, Lilli?" John Cameron Mitchell yelled across the expanse between the temple and the jungle.

Lilli's father, J. C. Mitchell, was more interested in the monetary value of the pre-Columbian artifacts they found than in the archaeological value. He sold them to anthropologists and other archaeologists who were eager to spend long hours decoding hieroglyphics and deciphering the meaning behind ceremonial pottery, jewels, and headdresses. Lilli, however, didn't know about her father's motivations for his digs; she was simply glad that he always wanted her to accompany him.

"Fine," she said, working more quickly since she knew that they were racing not only against the setting sun but also against the rainy season. They had been lucky this year. The rains nearly always began the first of June, but they had been able to squeeze two extra weeks out of the gods. In that extra time they had culled numerous treasures.

At a dig not far from the "ball courts" in Copán, where they were currently foraging for more bounty, J.C. had discovered jade beads, similar to ones used in Mayan necklaces. Jose Peron, their guide on this and the last four Mesoamerican digs, had found two "eccentric flints"—those intricate chert sculptures that revealed the genius of Mayan craftsmanship. Lilli's co-workers, Miguel and Ricardo, had found hammered copper disks they believed had once adorned a headdress.

The ever-darkening skies pressed upon Lilli. She wanted to know who this person had been. What had been his hopes and dreams? Had he had brothers or sisters? Lilli was an only child and she had often thought about this. Had he ever fallen in love? Recently she had developed a crush on a boy from school. Paul Newsome, newly arrived from Ohio, was incredibly handsome: black, wavy hair, sparkling hazel eyes, and a smile that could melt butter. His parents were renting a house in the West University district of Houston, where she lived, and they both went to the Windmere School, although she was going into ninth grade and he was in tenth. He didn't know Lilli existed, yet she'd done everything in her power lately to impress him.

She'd tackled him four times in the last neighborhood Saturday-afternoon flag football game, hoping he would look into her eyes when she was sprawled halfway across his body. But Paul just shoved her aside and scrambled to his feet and never looked back. Sometimes after school she raced home and then watched, from her second-story bedroom window, as he passed her house. Sometimes she would go only halfway home and stop at Mrs. Barker's house and pretend to be inquiring about her gout, then drink a glass of lemonade on her screened-in porch and wait until Paul passed by. Then she would gulp down the lemonade, say her good-byes to Mrs. Barker, shoot out the door, and pretend that she had just seen Paul that moment, walking down the sidewalk.

Lilli supposed Paul was being a good sport about her overtures. He didn't exactly reject her. He didn't come right out and tell her to buzz off, the way Jerry Ackerman, the only other love interest in her life, had when she was seven. No, now that she thought about it, Paul had been pretty cool about her. "Cold is the word for it," she mumbled with a frown as she swept the dirt from the eye sockets of her Mayan friend.

The fact of the matter was that Lilli was a tomboy. Well, she thought, more than "just" a tomboy. She was an adventurer, like her father.

Lilli adored her father. He was the most interesting, intelligent, knowledgeable, and exciting human being she knew. Or ever cared to know. She was proud of the fact that he didn't work some boring nine-to-five job like Paul's father for one of the oil companies. J.C. was bigger than life to Lilli. She had only been four when they went on their first dig, slight though it was, in Arizona and turned up nothing of importance. However, they had spent a whole week together. She had slept under the stars in a sleeping bag next to her father. "I'm right beside you," he would say and reach out to touch her cheek. He comforted her during the lightning storms, told her fascinating stories about the Hopi Indians at the campfire, and showed her that her efforts, no matter how insignificant they seemed to others, were important to him. J.C. never let a day pass without both telling and showing Lilli that she was loved.

Lilli had always attended a private school, not because her parents cared so much about the education—although Arlette thought Lilli would meet a "better class of people"—but because the school was lenient about letting Lilli out of classes for her archaeological digs. J.C. Mitchell was a charmer, and he knew just how to manipulate the principal. He always promised a free lecture to the students upon his return, and often he accompanied his request for Lilli's excused absences with a donation to the school.

This was the third year in a row that Lilli had been excused from taking her final exams with the rest of the class and given until the end of June to complete her courses. She always promised herself she would study while they were on their digs, but she never did. She always ended up studying on the airplane on the trip back to Houston while her father slept. Yet she always made perfect scores. School curriculum was easy for Lilli, too easy.

In truth, Lilli worked twice as hard as most young people at her education, but she never saw it that way. She spent hours in libraries and at home reading her father's books and magazines about lost cultures. Her father often said she had a curious mind.

It was that same curiosity that made her want to delve more deeply into Paul's feelings. Why didn't he like her? She was pretty. Her father had told her that a million times. Even her mother, Arlette, who never complimented her, had actually told Lilli that she was beautiful. "A dead ringer for Elizabeth Taylor when she was your age. I wish to hell you were interested in acting instead of old bones and dirt, like your father is. I could make a bundle on you, baby."

Unfortunately, that was her mother's way of complimenting someone. She perpetually seemed to find fault with Lilli no matter what Lilli did to please her. Lilli thought her mother was a complicated person. She had absolutely zero interest in her husband's work. She seldom went to his retail showroom except when he invited her to lunch, and then she would insist they go to some very expensive restaurant, and usually J.C. would acquiesce. Lilli knew that her father loved her mother. But she wasn't so sure her mother loved him back. Lilli wasn't sure if her mother loved anybody at all. She loved things. She loved pre-Columbian art when it hung on the walls of the homes of her River Oaks friends. She loved shopping at expensive boutiques on Post Oak Road, and she loved giving parties. J.C. loved Arlette for giving the parties that brought him more clients to buy the unusual artifacts that his showroom, Antiquities, was known for. They

were a funny family, Lilli thought, but she liked the life she
led. In some ways, she hoped it would never change.

Lilli knew she was different from the other girls at school,
and for most of her life she had liked being an individual. It
wasn't until recently, when Paul had entered her life—or
hadn't entered it, depending upon which way she looked at
the situation—that Lilli began to criticize herself.

She hated wearing glasses and had asked her mother several times for contacts, but her mother always said no.

One afternoon, just before the trip, Arlette had come into
Lilli's bedroom. They had gotten into an argument about the
clothes Lilli wore, that she never wore anything "feminine."

"I like wearing jeans, Mother, and shorts and hiking boots.
I don't need skirts and dresses for digs."

"Those damn digs," Arlette retorted. "They're just an excuse for not looking better."

"It's a fact," Lilli retaliated from behind her silver-rimmed
glasses, knowing she looked especially superior when she
raised her black, finely arched eyebrows.

"Don't you glare at *me*, young lady! And push those glasses back in place."

"I can't."

"You mean you won't." Arlette constantly battled for control of her daughter, no matter how minor the battle.

Lilli put her hands on her hips. "Mother, how many times
do I have to tell you that my glasses will not fit close to my
face because my eyelashes are too long and they brush
against the lenses? It bothers me."

"Then cut them off!"

"The glasses?" Lilli purposely baited her.

"Your damn eyelashes!"

"This is one of my flaws that is correctable, Mother. I want
contact lenses. Everybody in school has them."

"I don't care what everybody else has. The doctor said
they don't make contacts for your kind of astigmatism. The
glasses stay."

"I called Texas State Optical and the woman there told me
they do indeed make the kind of lenses I need. They just cost
a little more. Then I called Dr. Pearson, and he verified that
information for me. *And* . . . he told me you knew this and
that you told him you refused to pay any more than the 'spe-

cial' they had going last month." Lilli remained standing, arms akimbo, watching her mother's face flame. She knew her mother was struggling to hold back the curse words that couldn't wait to shoot out of her mouth. Lilli made bets with herself on which one her mother would use first. The redder her mother's cheeks became, the more foul her mouth grew.

"Four hundred fucking dollars he wants! Do you have four hundred dollars, Miss World Explorer?"

Lilli made a mental note to deposit five bucks in her silver-duck bank for winning the bet with herself. "No. Where would I get it? You're the parent . . ."

Arlette threw up her hands. "Go ask your father. He gives you anything you want anyway." She stormed out of the room and slammed the door so hard, Lilli's poster of Central America, on which she had marked the digs she'd been on, fell to the floor.

Lilli asked J.C. for the contacts, and she got them two days later. That same night she eavesdropped on her parents, who were arguing. She discovered that her father had given her mother the money for the contacts months earlier, but that her mother had spent three hundred dollars on new clothes. She had lied to Lilli.

Lilli made a point to remember the incident.

Now Lilli believed that her only flaw was that she had only recently started to "develop." Maybe that was what Paul was looking for. Her mother said she was a "late bloomer". . .

"Lilli!" she heard her father's voice calling, bringing her back to the present.

"Yeah, Pop!"

"Let's wrap this up," he said as he struggled up the temple.

"But, Pop, I can't! I might have found something else." As she had been thinking about Paul, she had continued digging.

"Like what?" J.C. asked, coming closer. "Gold? Jade?"

Lilli looked down at the arrowhead she held in her hand, the fine, dry dirt still sifting through her fingers.

"No gold. But here's an arrowhead."

"Good." J.C. nodded and picked up the arrowhead, then turned to Miguel. "Set up the tarp, Miguel. Night is coming. Maybe the rains."

"Sí, señor," Miguel answered and set to his task.

Lilli took a last look at the skull. She wished she had left the Mayan to his sleep. Her father wasn't interested in him, anyway.

She went to her father, who held out his outstretched arm. She put her arm around his waist and hugged him. They started walking away from the excavated area. "Was it a good day, Pop?"

"Never as good as I hoped."

"You expect too much," Lilli said.

"I know it, but I can't help it." He laughed. "Jose is setting up camp. If it doesn't rain tonight, the stars will be glorious. This close to the summer solstice . . ."

"I know. You can almost feel the ghosts of the Mayan astronomers."

"Yes, I can. And you know what else?"

"No, what?"

"It's when I'm here amid the ruins that I feel I'm so very close to something—but I just can't quite figure out what it is."

"You mean like the meaning of life?" she asked expectantly.

He threw back his head and laughed. "I wouldn't dream of being so presumptuous. No, I meant . . . there's some information here that I'm always just missing. I can feel it in my bones."

"Pop, I think all archaeologists feel that way."

"I suppose you're right." He put his arm around her shoulder again. "So what do you say? You pop the cans and I'll pop the cork."

"Tuna and beans. Coming right up! And Miguel's wife's tortillas, too. A feast tonight!"

Lilli had never asked her father why they kept the campfire so low on this trip. She guessed it was because the flame was already hot enough to melt rubber. They ate much of their food directly out of the cans, which she then smashed with her foot and deposited in a vinyl-lined knapsack she used for all of their waste. Lilli prided herself on the fact that they could come and go in the rain forest, barely leaving a trace that they had been there.

That night, however, Lilli prepared the flour tortillas that Miguel's wife had made by hand. After warming them in a flat skillet over the fire, she filled them with frijoles negros and tuna fish. They had finished off the last of the cheese two days before. If the rains held off, they still had enough food for three more days.

Jose left to go to the latrine, and Miguel and Ricardo kept to themselves as they gobbled down their tortillas. When they had finished eating, J.C. turned to Miguel and inquired in Spanish why Jose had been gone for so long. Miguel and Ricardo shrugged their shoulders but then glanced at each other and began laughing. They whispered to each other in rapid Spanish so low that Lilli was unable to decipher the joke.

"What's going on?" she asked her father.

"Beats me. But I have a feeling that as soon as Jose gets back, I'll find out."

Jose was gone for over forty-five minutes. The first thing that Lilli noticed when he sat down on his serape across the dying fire from her was that his wineskin was bulging.

Lilli pointed to the wineskin. *"Agua?"*

"No," Jose replied, stone-faced.

"Vino?" J.C. asked as Jose shook his head. "Can't be wine. Where the hell do you buy wine in the rain forest?"

"Tequila?" Lilli guessed.

"No."

"Café? Sopa? Soda? *Coñac?"* Lilli rattled these off and Jose started laughing and kept on shaking his head. "Okay! I give up. *Qué?"*

"Balche!" Jose replied.

Miguel gasped. "Balche?"

"Sí!"

"Huh?" Lilli looked at her father.

"Oh, shit." J.C. slid his hand over his face and peered between his splayed fingers at his daughter. "We're in trouble."

That was the night Lilli found out about balche. Brewed from honey and tree bark, balche was given by the ancient Maya to their sacrificial victims before they were killed. After nearly every ceremony or festivity, there was much balche drinking. Jose told Lilli that balche was intoxicating. She listened to his warning but paid it little heed. This was not the first time she had tasted alcohol. She'd had her first glass of wine when she was only eight—on an archaeological dig with her father, though unbeknownst to him. The previous year she'd done shooters with the workers when they'd gone to Teotihuacán. She knew she would never, ever touch tequila again. When J.C. found out she'd gotten drunk, he blasted her with a twenty-minute sermon. The next night, he himself slammed down fourteen shooters and could barely move the next day. He apologized for the sermon. "It'll never happen again."

J.C. had always treated Lilli more like a boy than a girl. She guessed that was why she was a tomboy, but she didn't care. Over the past year, she'd shared a Dos Equis with her father, a glass of champagne at one of those charity "dos" when her mother wasn't looking, and once she'd had a margarita. Lilli decided that her father considered her occasional drinking to be nothing alarming and, in fact, a kind of bonding between him and his child.

However, neither J.C. nor Lilli had ever experienced balche.

"I don't think you should drink this, Lilli. I've heard stories . . ."

"Rumors. Myths. Isn't that what you always say to me? Let me at least taste it."

J.C. was thoughtful for a minute. "Well, okay. But we won't ever tell your mother."

Lilli's violet eyes narrowed, and then she grinned. "Have you no faith in me? This is between you and me."

"Right," he said, taking the wineskin from Jose.

The balche was thick at first, nearly like Jell-O and overly sweet. J.C. filled his mouth and let the dark golden liquid slide down his throat.

"Well?" she asked. "What do you think?"

"Tastes like honey to me."

"Gimme," Lilli ordered, sticking out her hand impatiently.

He handed her the wineskin. Since she knew she was only going to get this one chance to drink balche, she made it a good one. She was still squeezing the wineskin when her father said, "Enough!"

Lilli gulped the balche. "Yuck! It tastes like horehound cough drops. Remember those horrible things Grandma Mitchell used to give me?"

"Yeah, I do. I think . . . you . . . ahwr . . . weeeeelllly

wight ..." J.C.'s speech was slurred. "The stuff is fuh ... *hic* ... funny."

Lilli handed the liquid to Miguel, who drank deeply, then passed it to Ricardo. By the time Jose finished and her father was drinking the balche again, Lilli's head was swimming.

She had intended not to drink any more, but in order for her father to pass the wineskin to Miguel, it had to go to her first. She stared at the wineskin for a long moment, then stole a glance at her father through her lowered lashes. She saw him laugh, slap his knee, then turn to Jose. Lilli stole another drink.

This process continued for four more passes, until all the balche was gone.

Lilli fell back onto her bedroll and serape. She slapped a mosquito and then dug into her knapsack for her can of Off. She sprayed the air around her but missed her exposed neck and face completely. It took her four tries to replace the plastic cap. She stared at the glowing stars. It was the first time in her life that she could make out the designs of the constellations the way the ancients had seen them. She marveled at how different the sky seemed here than it did in Houston, where the city lights destroyed the celestial magic. She wondered if Paul ever looked at the sky. And if he did, would he ever see it the way she did, filled with mystery? The Mayans had been right to think that there were answers in the sky.

Lilli fell asleep.

That night it was not Paul who came to her in her dream; it was someone else.

This man was tall, blond, blue-eyed, with a compassionate smile. He was older than Paul—maybe twenty, she would guess—and he was holding her in his arms as she cried. She didn't know why she was so sad, but in the dream she felt as if her world had just ended. A deep pain radiated from her heart. She didn't know if this man had hurt her, for he seemed too loving, too affectionate, to have been the villain in her dream. Then, just as he was about to kiss her, she woke up.

She stared at the bright stars for a long time, trying to separate illusion from reality. At that moment she felt suspended in space and time. It was a feeling she'd never experienced

before. How could it be that her dream was more real to her
than her waking state right now? The man was eerily real to
her. She could smell him . . . it was a soft mixture of sandalwood and pine, as if he'd just gone hiking in the Colorado
woods where she skied with her parents at Christmastime.
She had touched him and she remembered that his forearm
was very muscular. Maybe he lifted weights or played a lot
of tennis. She could feel his heart beat as he held her in his
arms. She felt as if she knew him and that she should be able
to say his name, but nothing came to mind. He seemed to be
a part of her, a part of her experiences, although she didn't
know how that could be.

"It was so real . . . as if I were really there . . ." she mut-
tered to herself. Perhaps the balche had been some kind of
hallucinogenic. Nothing else could explain the weird dream
she'd had.

Just then, Jose came crashing into camp. He woke J.C. and
spoke frantically to him. Then he went to Miguel and Ricardo
and kicked their feet. *"Amigos! De prisa!"*

J.C. bolted to his feet. "Quickly! Lilli! We have to go." He
scrambled around and gently placed the huge knapsacks filled
with precious pottery, jade, and flints over his shoulder.

Lilli rolled her serape over her arm and picked up her
knapsack and the bag of garbage, then kicked the remains of
the fire out. She glanced back to the area where they had
been digging for three days. "Shall I get the tarp?" she asked
her father.

"Leave it. There isn't time," he replied and bolted to the
west, through the thickest part of the rain forest. Everyone
was moving so fast, Lilli didn't have time for questions.

At first she assumed the rains had already come to the
north of them where Jose had been positioned as lookout. But
as they ran, the rains did not come. Lilli knew they couldn't
be that lucky. She glanced back at Miguel and Ricardo as
they followed quickly behind her. She noticed that their ex-
pressions were fearful. They were running from more than
just the bad weather.

A huge banana-tree frond obstructed her view of her father,
who had taken the lead position, and she pushed it aside,
hearing a loud snap as it broke from the tree.

J.C. craned his neck around and glared at her. "Quiet, Lilli," he cautioned.

"Pop, what is it?" she finally said, gasping for air. "What's back there? And why are we going this way . . . deeper into the forest?"

"Later," he said and pulled out his machete and whacked off a wide, low-growing palm frond, then pressed ahead.

Lilli could hear Miguel and Ricardo jabbering in Spanish as they came up from behind. She knew bits of Honduran dialect and parts of words, but mostly she heard the anxiety in their voices. She distinctly heard the words *"ladrón de tumbas,"* but she didn't know at the time that those words meant *grave robber.*

Two

June 17, 1976

*L*illi cranked her neck back as she looked at the ceiling's *sombrilla,* which resembled an Adamesque medallion, in the dining room of the home of June Wallace-Taylor. On the plane back to Texas, her father had told her that they would be stopping in San Antonio to bid on several prized Spanish antiques owned by the newly widowed June Wallace-Taylor.

Lilli had expected an elderly woman, draped in the black mantilla and widow's clothes of many old-world Spanish wives. Instead, they were greeted at the door by a young, very young, woman with hair so blond, Lilli knew in an instant the woman bleached her hair herself. This seemed odd to Lilli, since the woman could obviously afford a hairdresser. June was dressed in skin-tight jeans, a Western shirt she had unbuttoned to reveal deep cleavage, and black-and-white "pony" boots. Although Lilli seldom paid attention to jewelry, this woman's diamond ring was hard to miss. It was the kind of ring her father would label "vulgar" and her mother would call "generous."

June spoke with a thick West Texas accent that revealed little education and a lot of time in honky-tonks. "You all like the Carlos chairs?" she asked, referring to the white Carlos IV bench chairs that surrounded the table.

Lilli eyed the new, cheap peach velvet upholstery. She gave her father a look of scorching disapproval.

J.C. cleared his throat as he looked away from Lilli and back to June. "What else do you have?"

"Why, whatever you-all want, honey."

"In the way of antiques," J.C. corrected her.

18

Lilli watched her father nervously run the back of one hand across his forehead. She muffled a laugh, spun on her heel, and went over to the Aureliano de Beruete oil painting of the Castilian countryside that hung on the far wall. Lilli loved the Spanish Impressionists. J.C. made a bid on it. Next June moved to a Ramon Casas, then to a Santiago Rusinol. Again J.C. made bids. Lilli wondered if this woman had any idea of the value of these paintings. She had heard her father state that the Spanish Impressionists had not been rediscovered as yet, but he was buying them up at bargain prices, betting that his instincts would pay off in the future. Lilli had accompanied him on many private buying trips such as this one.

She heard the woman's high-pitched affected giggle. Lilli didn't know whether June was flirting with her father in hopes of getting a better deal, or if she was really interested in him. Either way, Lilli felt like telling this woman she was wasting her time. Her father was interested in making money, not romance.

June's heels made a hollow tapping sound on the expensive parquet floor. Lilli had learned from her father to notice everything when in the home of a potential seller or buyer. Now she looked at the floor and saw that it needed waxing. The unwaxed floor told her that this woman probably could no longer afford a maid to keep the house in prime condition. Lilli guessed that the woman was selling her husband's antiques collection because she desperately needed money.

"Come with me," June said as she led the way into the living room filled with overstuffed burgundy-and-gold brocade sofas and chairs.

Lilli couldn't believe that this crass woman possessed the good taste and sense of old-world style it took to put together such a beautiful room. "This is a wonderful room," Lilli complimented June as her eyes took in the sixteenth-century friar's chair, Castilian wood-carved fireplace, and *vargueños*. There were seventeenth-century gilt lanterns, Imari vases from Japan, and a seventeenth-century Brussels tapestry of a hunting scene.

"Do you think so?" June drawled. "I've always hated this room. Too stuffy. Too old." She fluttered her lashes at J.C. "I'd be ever so grateful if you-all would take it off my hands."

J.C.'s eyes gleamed. "I don't have a problem with that, Mrs. Taylor."

"June, please," she said and giggled.

"June," he replied, turning away from her and jotting notes in the little white notebook he kept in his breast pocket. "What about the La Granja mercury glass collection on the bookshelf?"

"Of course," June said.

"And the eighteenth-century repoussé silver urn and writing box—are they from the factories at Granada or Salamanca?"

"Granada," June said.

She's not as dumb as she makes out to be, Lilli thought. June knew exactly what she owned and, no doubt, how much money every object would bring. However, Lilli still would have bet that the woman needed to sell everything—and sell quickly. And by flirting, she was hoping in some screwball way to play on J.C.'s sympathies and get a better deal. Well, Lilli thought, it wouldn't happen. Her father was too smart for that.

J.C. made more notes. He inspected the intricately carved writing desk and Spanish chair that sat beneath the Joan Miró painting. He took a more studied approach to every lamp, rug, bronze statue, and leather-bound book in the room. Nothing missed his intense probing.

Lilli feigned ignorance about the objects in the room, almost to the point of pretending to be the impatient brat. "I'm getting hungry. How many more rooms, Pop?" she asked with a whine that her father knew was affected.

"I don't know, Lilli. June, are there more?"

"Yes. The master suite." She turned and walked out of the living room.

Lilli looked at her father, grinned, and shrugged her shoulders. They followed June up the curved staircase, which was covered in a deep crimson floral carpet. Lilli noted that the handrail of the wrought-iron banister was covered in Spanish leather.

They did not linger long in the master suite. J.C. took quick notes on the seventeenth-century Spanish armoire, the eighteenth-century Santa Barbara tapestry, which represented the royal arms of Philip V of Spain, and the elaborately draped mahogany four-poster bed, which had been made in England in the 1820s.

They went downstairs in silence. J.C. retrieved his brief-case and pulled out his adding machine, then plugged it into the wall near the writing desk. June watched him nervously. Lilli could feel the tension mount. Finally, J.C. pulled the tape from his adding machine and looked at June.

"I'll give you two hundred and twenty-eight thousand for everything, except I don't want the bed upstairs."

"That's preposterous!"

"I'll drive my rental car directly to the bank and have them draft a cashier's check against my account in Houston. I'll ar-range to have my associate flown in today to begin packing."

"I'm afraid not, Mr. Mitchell. These antiques are nearly priceless. I was expecting three—four times that amount."

J.C. put his adding machine back in his briefcase. "These antiques need a great deal of refurbishing. Also, the market for Spanish antiques is very low right now and you know it. I deal in them because I have a list of private clients who will take them off my hands. However, they're the kind of people who are always looking for a bargain. You can come with me to the bank. Take it or leave it." He watched June closely.

The woman paused for a moment, then said decisively, "I'll get my purse." She left the room quickly.

Lilli's astonishment rang in her voice. "Just like that?"

"Yes. Just like that."

"You conned her."

"What I said was true. The market is down and she knows it. She was hoping I wasn't as smart as I was and I was hop-ing she would be as desperate as she is."

"You're the greatest, Pop," Lilli said as she hugged J.C.

"I hope you always think so," he replied.

Lilli and J.C. took the eight o'clock flight to Houston. By nine-thirty they were walking through the front door of their home on University Boulevard.

Arlette was waiting for them in the living room. "I've been expecting you for hours. Where have you been?" she de-manded.

Lilli shook her head. Why was it that her mother did not run to her husband with open arms? There were no hugs for

Lilli, no breathless inquiries about their trip or the mysterious objects they'd uncovered in the Honduran soil. "Don't tell me you were worried about us." Lilli knew her tone was sarcastic. She'd meant it to be.

Arlette threw her a quelling look but did not respond. She was a firm believer in ignoring tantrums. She'd told Lilli that a hundred times, or at least every time Lilli's anger at being slighted reared its ugly head. Lilli wished she could learn to bite her tongue, but sometimes the words just popped out.

"Sorry," Lilli said.

"You should be," Arlette retorted.

She walked over to her husband and placed her ruby-red lips next to his. When she pulled away, she left a smudge of lipstick on his mouth that made him look silly, Lilli thought.

Lilli had to hand it to her mother, she did look smashing. She must have spent the whole day at Galmiche's, Lilli thought. Her brown hair had been blond for years now, but today it was three shades lighter and her makeup was flawlessly applied. She wore a new white sharkskin nautical jumpsuit with red enamel anchor-styled earrings on her ears. Lilli noticed that the red pumps she wore were new, too.

Lilli looked down at her own multicreased cuffed shorts, dirty khaki-colored socks, and brown hiking boots and then back at her mother. "I think I'd like to change," she said.

"Good idea." Arlette nodded. "Those clothes are disgusting. You'd better take a bath, too. What's it been . . . a week?"

"Something like that," Lilli replied and dragged her knapsack filled with dirty clothes behind her. " 'Night, Pops."

J.C. stopped her by placing his hands on her shoulders. "I love you, Lilli. Sweet dreams."

"Thanks," Lilli said as she went toward the stairs.

Before she reached the top of the stairs, her parents had already begun to raise their voices to each other. Lilli stopped, crouched next to the railing, and listened.

"Why do you do that to her, Arlette?"

"Do what?"

"Make her feel like shit."

"I'm not trying to make her feel like shit. I want her to feel, dress, and act like a girl. She *is* a girl, you know, J.C."

"I'm well aware of that."

"Really? I doubt that seriously."

"Oh, ho! You've spent so much time with her! You know her innermost secrets."

"I know a lot more about *our* daughter than you think," Arlette replied smugly.

"Like what?"

"Like last month she had her first period."

"Do we have to talk about this?" J.C. said, revealing his discomfort.

"You see? This is exactly what I'm talking about. One mention about womanly things and you turn off. You can't stand the fact that she *is* a girl and pretty soon nature is going to turn her into a woman and you'll have no choice but to give up this fantasy of yours that Lilli is still a kid and that she's your son."

"I need a drink."

"That's right—run away from me again, J.C., just like you always do. You don't want to talk to me about anything. Not Lilli, not your business—"

"My business? My business! When have you given a fuck about my business? All you care about is that I fund your bank account each month."

"That's not true!" Arlette declared.

"It's not? Then tell me what your number-one priority is, Arlette."

"This family. You and Lilli."

"Bullshit!" J.C. lifted the stopper from a Waterford crystal decanter and poured himself two fingers of scotch, started to put the stopper back in the bottle, thought for a moment, and then poured another deep splash into his glass.

"It is important to me that Lilli not be confused about who she is," Arlette said.

"She doesn't look confused to me."

"Did she tell you she's in love?" Arlette crossed her arms over her full bosom. "Did she?"

"No," he said, looking into his glass and not at his wife.

"Well, she is. His name is Paul."

"That new boy down the street?"

"That's the one."

"I don't like him."

"Why not?"

"I saw him riding by the house on that motorcycle. He was wearing a black leather jacket."

"Oh, for God's sake. The motorcycle is his father's. Lots of kids have leather jackets."

"He's only fifteen, Arlette. He's too young to be riding a motorcycle." J.C. slammed his glass down on the marble-top console. "Jesus Christ. She's only a baby."

Arlette could not stifle her smile. "She'll be fifteen in July herself. She's growing up, and I want her to start behaving like a girl. Her manners are deplorable. She has no idea how to dress, style her hair, or wear makeup. She's . . . she's practically a heathen."

"I suppose that's all my fault."

"Yes."

"Thanks a lot."

"You're welcome."

J.C. suddenly sounded extremely tired. "It's been a rough trip. I'm going to bed."

Lilli bolted to her feet and dashed quietly down the carpeted hallway to her bedroom and closed the door. She sprinted for the connecting bath and turned on the water full force. She listened at the door for her father's footsteps. She watched beneath the door and saw his shadow as it stopped at the bathroom door for a moment and then moved on down the hall.

Lilli sighed deeply.

She peeled off her sweat-stained camp shirt, unlaced her boots, yanked them off her feet, and dumped tiny piles of Honduran sand onto the tile floor. She peeled off her socks and then her shorts, took off her Lollipop underpants, and stepped into the hot water. She slid down beneath the water line and wet her hair. She reached for her shampoo, squeezed out a handful, and massaged it into her scalp.

"Ugh!" she groaned when she realized exactly how sweaty and smelly she was. She left the suds in her hair as she lathered the bar of soap against a clean white terry washcloth. She scrubbed her skin until it turned pink. Then she dunked under the water again and washed most of the suds out of her hair. She turned on the tap and finished the job with clean warm water.

After drying herself she went to her antique gilt chest of

drawers, which was said to have come from the bedroom of Ferdinand VII, and pulled out a clean cotton nightgown.

"This is new," she said, looking at the Neiman's label in the summer gown of printed pale pink rosebuds. It smelled like roses, Lilli thought as she pulled the gown over her head. She glanced inside the drawer and spied a tiny chintz potpourri bag. She lifted it to her nose and inhaled the rose scent.

"Mother thinks of everything."

Lilli went to her white iron bed, which reportedly had come from a French orphanage outside Paris. She pulled back the eyelet comforter and slid between the white cotton sheets. She let her head sink slowly into the down-filled pillow.

Then she crossed her arms behind her head and stared up at the slowly rotating ceiling fan. She ignored the first tear that trickled out of her eye. The second tear was a bother, but the third was accompanied by a burning lump in her throat.

"She promised she wouldn't tell . . ." Lilli swiped angrily at the increasing flow of tears. "Why do you do that to me, Mother? I didn't want Pop to know . . . not about the period, not about Paul. Why? Why?"

She turned her head and let the pillow muffle her sobs. "I never want Pop to think he's not number one with me . . . I want to be his number one. If I become a girl like Mother, I'll lose him. I know I will."

Lilli tried to hold back her sobs, struggling valiantly not to behave like a girl, but she failed. She cried and sobbed and cried some more. Her world was changing, and she didn't like it one bit.

Three

July 4, 1976

*T*he bicentennial of the United States of America was a major event in Lilli's life. She found it astounding that she was alive when history was being made—or at least marked. She hoped it wouldn't be the most historically remembered event in her life, but just in case it was, she intended to make the most of the day. She bought a leather diary at a stationery shop in the Village in which to record her observations. After all, she thought, the Maya wrote their events on the walls of their temples and tombs. What if someday she were to die beneath an active volcano and centuries later dug up like the people in Pompeii? Lilli's daydreams often bordered on the extreme, a trait her mother discouraged and her father nurtured.

However, Lilli's daydreams about the bicentennial were fed by national preparations for the big day. Nearly every major city in the country planned a parade of some kind and plenty of fireworks. New York's gala, including the parade of brightly festooned yachts and boats into New York harbor, the entertainment by many noted celebrities, and the million-dollar fireworks display, was to be televised nationwide. Houston's parade was not nearly as grand, but there were open-air concerts, fireworks, and traditional family parties that would rival any Thanksgiving festivities.

In the Mitchell house, Arlette had planned her Fourth of July party for six months. She had begun with a complete redecoration of the kitchen. Gone were the lime-green-and-yellow wallpaper and white wicker furniture that both J.C. and Lilli loved. In came the newest cranberry, Williamsburg blue, and cream wallpaper exacted in an Old

26

Williamsburg motif. Four Queen Anne chairs surrounded a cherry pedestal table next to the new fireplace Arlette had designed herself. It had a red brick interior and facade and a wood mantel painted in the same colonial blue-gray as the moldings and wood trim in the room. The French doors lost their bamboo shades and now wore cream café curtains edged in dark cranberry to match the linens on the table. Everywhere Lilli looked were artifacts of Colonial America: wood bellows, black wrought-iron fireplace tools, splatter pitchers, and dried flowers. Wooden toys marched across the mantel, and colonial candles, which looked freshly dipped with their long wicks, were tied to a long iron rod.

At first Lilli had hated the renovations, things American never having had much appeal to her, so she was surprised to find that by the morning of the Fourth, she had come to like sitting in the cozy kitchen. Fresh cherry pies were baking in the oven, or at least being warmed, since her mother had bought them already baked at Randall's. Outside the French doors, her father was smoking a brisket of beef and thick slabs of baby back ribs in the smoker that looked like an oil drum.

"Lilli, would you fill the jugs with water and start the sun tea?"

"Sure," Lilli replied and set about unwrapping the tea bags she would float in the clear glass gallon jugs that she would then place on the steps outside.

Arlette filled a huge glass bowl with potato salad, also made at the deli at Randall's, and then began whacking a zigzag pattern into a monstrous watermelon. Lilli knew that her mother did not like to cook, but her friends did envy her "watermelon boats." Arlette would shape the watermelon into a basket complete with a handle and then scoop out the insides with a melon-ball tool. Then she would add raspberries, strawberries, blueberries, honeydew melon, apples, raisins, almonds, cantaloupe, mango, cherries, and pineapple. Arlette's secret ingredient was honey mixed with a touch of apricot brandy, which she would pour over the fruit. To finish off the basket, she would dip green and red grapes in egg whites and roll them in superfine sugar, then intersperse the clusters of grapes with sprigs of fresh mint around the edges of the watermelon.

Lilli found the fruit too tempting. She picked up a plump

strawberry and dipped it in the pure golden honey sans the brandy.

"Lilli! Those are for the guests!"

"I know. That's why I wanted to get mine before they get here."

"You're incorrigible," her mother replied.

"I don't know what that means."

"Go look it up."

Lilli swiped a raspberry. "Naw, I don't think so. I have a feeling it's not good."

"It's not," Arlette said, slipping her knife around a tricky corner. "Did you clean your room?"

"Yes," Lilli lied. "You never told me—" She stole another raspberry, which her mother did not see. "Who did you invite?"

"Oh, absolutely everyone important." Arlette was concentrating on her creation.

"Okay. Who's actually coming?" Lilli knew her smirk was apparent, but she couldn't help it. Sometimes the most fun she got out of life was baiting her mother.

Arlette whipped the knife out of the watermelon and into the air. "Don't you get smart with me, Lilli."

Lilli knew she had gone too far. "I just wanted to know," she said apologetically.

"The Laniers. Oscar and Lynn—the Wyatts," she said proudly, "are stopping by, but just for a bit. They have so many invitations. Lynette Proler, the Mecoms, the Cullens, Denton Cooley, and Betty Moody, to name a few."

"What about Paul's family?"

"I doubt they would fit in," Arlette replied, giving Lilli a look that warned her not to press further.

Lilli rarely paid heed to warnings. "I'll bet you haven't even welcomed Mrs. Newsome to the neighborhood. Maybe they would like your friends."

"Lilli, this is all very complicated to explain to you right now when I have a lot to do before my guests arrive. I suppose a girl your age is naturally obtuse. Anyway, the Newsomes are not coming. Besides, your father doesn't like this infatuation you have with Paul. I'm simply following his instructions. Now, please check the tables in the garden for me. Those two girls I hired from the domestic service company don't seem very bright to me. I'll bet they don't know on which side of the plate to put the fork."

"The left," Lilli said and popped another strawberry into her mouth.

"Lilli, puhleeeze!"

"Okaaay. I'm going."

Lilli opened the French door that led to the eastern patio and was blasted with a cloud of mesquite-smelling smoke. Coughing, she pummeled the cloud with her arms. "How's it going, Pop?"

"Excellent." He beamed at her as she put her arm around his waist and stared at the thick coat of barbecue sauce on the ribs. He was quick to see the frown on her face. "What gives? You look pretty glum."

Her eyes searched his face. "Did you tell Mother not to invite Paul's family?"

"Not in so many words."

"Pop, how come you're being this way about Paul? You don't even know him. He's nice."

"I'm sure he is, Lilli. But I also think you're too young to be interested in boys. There will be plenty of that when you're older."

Lilli didn't know whether to be shocked or to thank him for at least being honest with her. What she couldn't tell him was how much his disapproval of her desires had wounded her. She always wanted him to think that she was doing the right thing. "How'm I supposed to know when I'm ready?"

He shrugged his left shoulder in the awkward way he had. Lilli thought it made him look broken on one side. "You'll just know." He stared at the meat on the grill. "I'll know . . ." he mused.

"How?" Lilli demanded. She had a bad habit of wanting answers, the clear and precise kind, instantly. Trouble was, she was discovering as she grew older that there didn't seem to be any answers to anything anymore, much less clear ones.

"I don't know how to explain this. Maybe your mother would do a better job—"

"I doubt it," Lilli interrupted.

"I do know that what you feel for Paul is just a crush. Puppy love, we used to call it. He's not interested in you, we both know that, and I think you're simply fascinated with the challenge of him. He seems remote to you, a treasure to be uncovered—just like on one of our digs. When you meet the right man, someday when you're older," J.C. added tersely and quickly, "you'll feel a connectedness—that's the best way I can describe it. There will be a kind of communication between the two of you that you don't have with anyone else. You'll share things. Important things. You'll like the same things."

Lilli frowned in confusion.

"I'm not making myself clear, am I?"

"Not really. But go on."

"He'll want to be with you. And you'll want to be with him. You'll tell him your dreams. He'll tell you his. Things like that."

Lilli nodded and watched as he stuck the long-handled fork into the juicy ribs and flipped them over and then closed the lid to the smoker. He took off his gray oven mitts.

"Did your mother tell you who was coming today?"

"Yeah." Lilli looked down and kicked a fallen mesquite chip with her sneaker. "Bunch of people I hardly know."

"What?"

"It's not going to be much fun for me. That's for sure."

"But your Aunt Vicki is coming with Faith. And I believe that Zane McAllister is about your age. Well, come to think of it, Hannah did say he was almost seventeen now." J.C. put his hand on Lilli's shoulder. "Hannah is having a rough time of it right now. Her husband is at M.D. Anderson, undergoing tests. He's been sick for a while."

"What's wrong with him?"

"The doctors don't know yet. That's why they're doing tests. You might be extra nice to Zane. He won't know anyone here."

"Gee, Pop, that's too bad. I liked Mr. McAllister when I met him at the store. Mrs. McAllister, too. Do they still live in Bandera?"

"Yes." J.C.'s face was darkly contemplative, as if he were facing his own mortality.

Lilli hated the idea of death even more than her father did. She couldn't imagine what it would be like not to have her pop around. She gave him a quick squeeze. "Don't you worry, Pop. I'll make sure Zane has a good time."

"Thanks, Lilli," J.C. said and kissed the top of her head.

Just then Arlette opened the French door. "Lilli? Did you check on those girls for me?"

"Righto!" Lilli said and rushed to the backyard before her mother could scold her.

Lilli found that the maids were quite competent. The half-dozen round tables had been covered with red-and-white-checkered cloths. On each table was an arrangement of tiny American flags, red carnations, white daisies, and blue asters. At the top of each blue-and-white metal splatter plate was a blue votive candle. The red cotton napkins were tied with white ribbons from which small wooden replicas of the state of Texas dangled. Japanese lanterns were strung through the oak trees that interlaced their long limbs, forming a cool arbor over the small yard. Lilli noticed that the landscaper had planted a border of red begonias against the back wooden fence. Huge Mexican clay pots filled with red geraniums and white vinca had been placed on the corners of the tiled patio. A temporary bar had been set up by the garage, and a huge American flag had been hung on the side of the garage as a backdrop. A tall, black-haired man in his twenties was busy filling the frozen-margarita machine with tequila, ice, and margarita mix. Every detail had been attended to, Lilli thought as she looked up at the red brick, two-story house. She wondered again why it was that her mother perpetually outdid herself whenever it came to her socialite friends, yet seldom did the same for J.C. and herself.

Arlette's hands were shaking as she put the final garnishes on a flower she'd carved out of an enormous red onion. She was petrified that something, anything, would go wrong. It was imperative to her that even the smallest detail be perfect. It wasn't just because the majority of her guests were J.C.'s clients or that she wanted, no, needed, desperately to be accepted by them. It was because this party was a test. Arlette despised tests, but invariably she set herself up for them even without thinking. Arlette believed that everything in her life, every turn in the road, was a test. She remembered her childhood in Louisiana and the times she had always failed . . .

1943
Near Grand Lake, Louisiana

Arlette had grown up in the backwater bayous of Louisiana. Her father, Bobby Joe Herbert, was an uneducated tyrant, who wielded his monstrous ego over the heads of his wife, Marie, and six children like a lion tamer uses a whip. He threatened his family with his power, both emotional and physical. Arlette's most vivid memory of being beaten was when she was five. She had felt like a caged animal as he came toward her snapping his long leather razor strap. She remembered the smell of the old leather and the stale whiskey on his breath when he railed at her. She had pleaded for mercy but he only laughed at her. Until that laugh, that menacing, raspy, uncontrolled laugh, she had cried and begged. But then something inside her head clicked, freeing her thoughts, making her situation crystal clear. Her tears dried instantly. Anger shot through her like sparks beneath the metal wheels of a train when it brakes on the rails.

"Papa! Stop."

"Shut up!" he shouted and rained spittle on her face.

She glared at him in defiance. She didn't feel little anymore, although she should have. She knew he could kill her if he wanted to. He could pick her up and break her in half, but she didn't care. Her hate was gargantuan at that moment. She felt like that young boy, David, in the Bible story her mother had read to her. She was facing a monster, not a father.

He raised the leather strap and it made a whizzing sound as it sailed through the air. Arlette raised her arms to protect herself and the strap landed on her forearm. It stung worse than the bee she'd stepped on earlier that summer, but Arlette did not cry out. She lowered her arms and glared at him again.

"I hate you!" she screamed.

Bobby Joe was stunned at her defiance. "I'll teach you!"

"No!" Arlette screamed vehemently.

This time when he raised the strap she realized that his eyes were glassy and he was having a difficult time maintaining his stance. Quick thinking saved her. She crouched down, scrambled between his legs, bit his ankle in the soft spot in the back, then shot to her feet and ran out of the shanty.

"Jesus Christ!" Bobby Joe yelled and whirled around, his razor strap raised again. But Arlette was gone.

Arlette raced through the moss-hung oaks and across the sunburned grass and dried mud ruts where the family truck had made deep impressions in the earth the previous spring. She shot down the dirt road that led from the highway to their shanty and took a secret path toward the bayou that she thought only she knew about. She was careful not to disturb the scrubs and reeds, just in case she was being followed. She promised herself over and over as she trudged through the mucky water that she would never, ever go back home.

She found her favorite water oak whose trunk had been hollowed out by years of rising waters and subsequent drought. She climbed up into the tree, chipping off pieces of the hundred-year-old bark as her bare feet slipped on the dry wood. One of the bark pieces sliced her foot, but Arlette paid no attention. It was a small price to pay for freedom.

She huddled inside the womb of the tree, protecting herself in the shadows. She watched the water slip silently past her and listened for the sound of human voices. She heard only egrets, herons, brown pelicans, and the sounds of minks and muskrats as they scampered through the woods. Arlette waited. She waited for an hour before her heart quit pounding. Still, she was prepared to run again, if need be, for she was guided by an instinct to survive that transcended age.

Arlette didn't know much about the outside world, since there were no newspapers in her area of Bayou Teche. Or at least her family did not read them. She knew there was a war in Europe, because on their trip to New Iberia in July for her birthday, there had been newsreels at the movie house about the war. Arlette's parents did not talk about the war, but her mother did keep mentioning something about the "draft," and Arlette noticed that each time she did, her father would fly into a rage.

Arlette did not know how she was going to get away from her father, but she was determined to do so. She had no money, but she thought she could get to New Iberia and maybe a nice lady would hire her to clean house and work in the garden the way she did for her mother. Arlette had seen a lot of "nice ladies" in New Iberia. They wore pretty pastel summer dresses that were new and not faded from years of washing. The women smelled like flowers, not sweat, and their fingernails were polished in bright red colors. Arlette wanted to be like them and did not understand why her mother didn't want to be like them. She had thought her mother was pretty until that trip. But after seeing the women in New Iberia, and especially after seeing the fancy ladies in the movies, Arlette realized that her mother was plain and woefully uneducated. But as far as Arlette was concerned, the worst of it was that her mother didn't care about her looks or how the family lived or the kind of man she shared her life with.

Arlette had come to realize that her mother didn't care about her. The reason Arlette's father was able to beat her anytime, anyplace, and without recrimination was because her mother didn't care. That was the truth of it, Arlette thought.

Arlette knew she was only five, but she was determined to find a way out of her situation. She had two older sisters and three younger brothers. She was stuck in the middle and no one gave a fig about her. She had not been to school yet and could not read or write, but her mother had taught her how to pray. She knew the Hail Mary and the Our Father by heart. Her mother had always told her that if she prayed to the Blessed Virgin, her prayers would be answered.

"Oh, Blessed Virgin Mary," she prayed as she squeezed her eyes shut and pressed her tiny palms flat against each other, "please, Mother of Baby Jesus, kill my father! Oh, Blessed Virgin, ask your son to kill my father. Jesus can do anything, Blessed Virgin. Mother of Baby Jesus, I pray to you and beg you to kill my father."

Arlette continued her prayer as the sun sank behind the Spanish moss draperies. Darkness fell on Bayou Teche, but Arlette was not afraid. She had her prayers to occupy her time and a new hope that one day, one day very soon, she would be rid of her father and his evil, mean-spirited ways.

The following morning, the sun had barely popped up over the eastern horizon when Arlette heard her sister Angelique's voice. "Whatcha goin' and doin' in thar?"

"Hidin'," Arlette replied.

"From Papa?"

"He hurt me."

"I know." Angelique was the oldest at ten. Arlette thought her sister knew everything and was very wise, but then

Arlette discovered that Angelique had never been to a picture show until New Iberia, too. Arlette was not as swayed by her sister as she had been in the past. Angelique stuck her hand into the interior of the tree. "C'mon. Let's go home."

"Noooo!" Arlette slapped her sister's hand.

"Hey! Whatcha doin' that for?"

"I ain't never goin' back thar."

"Is you plum crazy? You cain't escape Papa. None of us can."

"Stay with me, Angelique. I'm goin' to run away. To Lafayette if I have to."

Angelique started laughing. "You're only five! The gaters'll get you first."

"I ain't scared of no gaters. They ain't any worse than Papa."

Angelique's eyes clouded with sadness. "Papa can be awful mean, that's for sure. It's t'other mean things that're real bad . . ."

Arlette looked at her sister quizzically, but Angelique turned her head away. She was proud of her ability never to be sentimental or a crybaby, and she did not want Arlette to see her tears.

"You gotta come home. He'll be missin' you."

"I don't care!"

"Arlette, honey, please come home. I can tell him you was home all last night. He'll never know. He was drunk, is all. Just drunk. He'll forget all about it."

"No!"

"Jesus, Arlette. It was just a lickin'. Quit bein' so ornery."

"No. I'm runnin' away."

Angelique was finally tired of negotiating with her younger sister. She swept her arm inside the tree and pulled a twisting and kicking Arlette out of her sanctuary. "I'm tryin' to help you, Arlette. Cain't you see that? You gotta come home. You gotta eat."

Arlette was crying by now. "Don't make me."

"I'll tell you what, baby. If you come home with me, I'll help you get away from him. Only this time, we get money and food and we do it right."

Arlette's eyes grew huge. "You'll help?"

"I'll go with you."

"But we cain't tell the others?" Arlette asked as a test.

"No."

Arlette gazed at her sister. She compared her with the ladies in New Iberia and then with the beautiful ladies in the movies. Angelique had white skin that turned the color of a boiled crawfish in early summer and stayed red, raw, and peeling all summer long. Her brown hair was thin, dull, and dirty. She was wearing one of her father's old armless undershirts and a pair of her mother's old shorts that had been stained, ripped, and repaired. Arlette wondered if those shorts would be hers to wear one day. Angelique was not a pretty girl, and it frightened Arlette because she realized she herself might not be pretty enough either to be accepted as one of the "nice ladies" in New Iberia.

"We'll help each other," Angelique said.

"Okay," Arlette agreed and took her sister's hand as they walked through the swamp back toward the shanty.

Arlette found that her sister was right: their father never remembered the day before. He knew nothing of Arlette's escape and her night in the swamp. He left that morning with a headache, jumped into the family jalopy, and said he was going to fetch supplies.

The girls stood on the shanty porch with their mother and watched the jalopy disappear down the dirt road. Then their mother told the girls to tend the laundry.

Angelique stoked an outdoor fire and filled the washbasin with water from the well just as poor Southern women had been doing to wash their clothes for nearly two hundred years. There were no modern appliances in the Herbert household, and so even the most rudimentary tasks required a half day to execute. While Marie tended to three-year-old Billy Joe, two-year-old Joey, and six-month-old Bobby, Arlette stirred the boiling laundry while Angelique ironed their father's shirts with a heavy iron outside on an old kitchen table they covered with a blanket and a stained cotton sheet. Seven-year-old Antoinette used wooden clothespins to hang sheets, towels, and underwear on the clothesline that was strung between two old oak trees.

"I'm goin' to church t'morrow," Antoinette said proudly to Angelique.

"Yeah? Y'know good damn well Papa ain't drivin' you

anywheres on a Sunday mornin'. He's too hung over. And from the looks of things when he left, he ain't gonna be in any mood to cater to none of us."

Arlette remembered that Angelique had told her that because Antoinette was named after some queen of France, she could get real uppity sometimes. Arlette leaned forward over the hot tub to make certain she didn't miss a word of her sisters' exchange.

"Know what, Angelique? Sometimes you're just plain stupid. While you been lollygaggin' your summer away pinin' over that Boudreaux boy, I been figurin'."

"Figurin' what?" Angelique's voice was defensive, and Arlette noticed that she did not deny the accusation about Henry Boudreaux.

Antoinette stuck a clothespin in the waistband of Bobby Joe's boxer shorts and walked over to her sister. The sun filtered through the oak trees and seemed to drip off the ends of the leaves, leaving puddles of golden light on the ground. The late-summer breeze had picked up and flapped a yellowed cotton sheet across Antoinette's pathway, surrounding her in gold light, making her look regal. Arlette was prepared to believe anything Antoinette told her.

"I figured out that one of the reasons, maybe *the* reason, we're in this pickle is 'cause Ma and Papa are Catholic."

"What?" Arlette felt instantly afraid. After all, if she was wrong about the Catholic Church, then that would mean that her prayers to the Blessed Virgin that her papa be killed would all have been said in vain.

"I've thought of that," Angelique replied, nodding her head.

"You did?" Arlette was really worried now.

Antoinette motioned for Arlette to come closer. "It's like this. Lucette McMurphy's family is Baptist. They believe in Jesus, but she's the only child. She has plenty of food and new dresses all the time. And she says it's 'cause her mother uses birth control."

"Oh, yeah? What the hell does Lucette McMurphy know about birth control? I know a whole lot more about that kinda thing than she does. She's only eight." Angelique would not allow her position of eldest and most worldly to be usurped.

"I may only be seven, Angelique, but I believe her."

"Test her, Antoinette. Ask her what *kind* of birth control they use. That'll put her in her place."

"I already did," Antoinette announced proudly. "She told me they use rubbers."

"She didn't."

"She did."

Arlette's head swung from one sister to the other so fast that she thought her neck would snap. "What's a rubber?"

Angelique and Antoinette looked at Arlette at the same instant. They blinked at each other and then slowly, smiles spread across their faces. "You think we should?" Angelique asked.

"I sure do. Better she knows now than later."

"So tell her, Antoinette," Angelique pressed, hoping to prove that Antoinette didn't know what she was talking about.

"Okay," Antoinette replied and went into a long and very detailed description of sex and rubbers that almost sounded as if it had come out of the medical book Doc Carpentier carried with him when he traveled into the bayou country.

"I understand," Arlette said, blushing crimson. "But what's that got to do with us bein' Catholics and the McMurphys bein' Baptists?"

Angelique needed to reestablish her domain as the font of wisdom in the Herbert house. "I'll tell her," she said quickly to Antoinette. "Catholics have too many babies, Arlette. Not that me and Antoinette don't love you, we do. But see, it would be easier if there was just me or just me and Antoinette. With you, it makes for less food. Less clothes. We could've been goin' to New Iberia to the movies every weekend if it weren't for you . . ."

"What about the boys?" Arlette demanded.

"Especially without the boys!" Antoinette chimed in.

"That's right. Them boys done put us on the back burner for sure. Papa caters to them. And Mama, she's got all she can do just to keep them fed. Hell, it's just a bad thing to be Catholic. It's all the Church's fault, that's for sure. They make Catholic wives make babies. Even if you're gonna die, you gotta have more babies."

"But not the Baptists?" Arlette asked.

"Not the Baptists," Antoinette answered. "That's why I'm convertin'."

"Me, too," Arlette said firmly.

"Me, too," Angelique said. "Let's make a pact. We all become Baptists this Sunday. Papa won't care 'cause he don't believe in God anyway, except the part about havin' babies. And Mama, she's too damn tired to go to Mass. Antoinette? You think the McMurphys will let us ride in their truck to church?"

"I don't see why not. As long as Lucette sits inside with her parents. We could ride in the back."

"You know anything else about these Baptists?" Arlette asked.

"Just that we gotta wear nicer clothes than we wore to Mass. Baptists are pretty picky about that kind of thing."

Angelique looked at her sisters. "We'll just have to do the best we can."

Sunday found Bobby Joe drunk and still passed out. Marie told the girls they could go to church but they had to take Billy Joe with them. She would keep Joey and the baby with her. She helped the girls with their faded gingham dresses and put rubber bands around their washed braids and gladly sent them off to the McMurphys.

Billy Joe slept in Arlette's lap as they rode in the back of the red Ford truck to New Iberia. Arlette couldn't believe that her brother could fall asleep at a time like this, but he was only three and didn't know much.

The Baptist church was built of wood with a tall steeple and one stained-glass window. It held one hundred and fifty people. At least, that was what Lucette told Arlette as she held her hand when they climbed the wooden steps into the little church. Lucette made a big production of bringing her friends to her church. The minister (Lucette explained that this man was not a priest, which was the only type of clergy Arlette had ever known) made mention of the presence of the Herbert visitors. Everyone turned to look at the four children. Arlette enjoyed the attention. She had never felt so special in all her life. However, Antoinette and Angelique kept staring at the minister, their faces stonelike.

After the service, Arlette followed her older sisters out of the church. She noticed that they spoke with other children their age about going to Sunday school. Arlette was told she was too young to go with Lucette, Angelique, and Antoinette. Suddenly she felt quite unspecial again.

As the girls were hurrying off to Sunday school, Arlette noticed that Mr. and Mrs. McMurphy called Lucette back to them for a moment. Then she heard Mrs. McMurphy say to Lucette, "I'm proud of you, dear. It will be such a feather in your cap to convert the shanty children."

Lucette smiled and then raced off to her class.

Arlette was very young, but the words "shanty children" were seared into her psyche. She realized she was special, all right. She was a freak. Not only did she have the bad fortune to be born a Catholic, but she was a *poor* Catholic.

The McMurphys were being nice to Arlette and her sisters, but only because they had to be, or God would send them to hell for not helping the poor shanty children. Arlette squeezed Billy Joe's hand so hard he yelled, but it helped her keep back her tears. She didn't want anyone to know that she was ashamed of who she was.

She wished things could be different for her. And she knew that they could be if only she could get away from her parents. She wanted to remember that it would be important for her to become a Baptist and then, later, to use rubbers. She didn't want to have too many children like her mother did. She wanted to be more like the McMurphys.

"Would you like to get some ice cream, Arlette and Billy Joe?" Mrs. McMurphy asked.

"Whose birthday is it?" Arlette asked.

"Oh, you poor, dear thing," Mrs. McMurphy said. "Is the only time you have ice cream when it's somebody's birthday?"

"No. We eat ice cream lots of times," Arlette lied.

"I'm sure you do," Mrs. McMurphy said.

Arlette couldn't help but think Mrs. McMurphy was honey-coating her words.

"Tell me these other times and remember, dear, Jesus is watching you."

Arlette looked around her. She didn't see Jesus anywhere. She couldn't understand what He had to do with the lie she was going to tell Mrs. McMurphy anyway. "Christmas and Easter just this last year we had ice cream." Arlette was happy with her answer. She didn't want Lucette's parents to think that she was a nobody. And she didn't want to be treated like the charity families at her Catholic church. She remembered those children, the ones who wore potato sacks

with pieces of rope for belts until it was time for them to go
to school. Arlette thought their hand-me-down clothes
weren't much better than the potato sacks, though.

"Well, we're going to get some ice cream today while we
wait for your sisters to finish their Bible lessons." Mrs.
McMurphy held out her hand to Arlette to cross the street.

They waited for nearly a whole minute for a black Buick to
pass and then an old Ford. In that space of time, Arlette noticed
how soft Mrs. McMurphy's hand was. She had the softest skin
in the world, nearly like the underside of a squirrel, Arlette
thought. It was smooth and smelled like flowers, although
Arlette only knew the smell of magnolias and camellias. She
liked the touch of Mrs. McMurphy's hand, and even as they entered Tibideaux's Pharmacy, she would not let go of it.

"Would you like to sit at the counter or in a booth?" Mr.
McMurphy asked.

Arlette had never been allowed to eat ice cream at the soda
fountain. She had remained in the truck with her brothers and
sisters while her mother bought vanilla ice-cream cones for a
nickel for each one of them. Arlette realized now that her
mother was ashamed of her many children, just as Arlette
was ashamed of their poverty.

"I can stay outside," she answered quietly as she hung
back.

"We'll have none of that. Now, come along. I think the
counter is the most fun for children," Mr. McMurphy said,
picking up Billy Joe and placing him on a stool.

Arlette followed suit. She didn't want Billy Joe to have the
first experience at something to which she was not also entitled.

"That's good!" Mrs. McMurphy said. "Now, what would
you like? A chocolate malted? A soda? A root beer float? A
banana split? Although I do have to admit, the latter might be
a bit much for your small tummy. Hmm?"

Arlette looked at Mrs. McMurphy as if she had come from
another planet. Arlette didn't know what she was talking
about. What was a soda? Or that other thing . . . banana
something, she'd said. "Ice cream," Arlette replied simply.

"I know that, dear. But how would you like your ice
cream?"

Arlette's face must have revealed her ignorance. Before she
could ask a question, Mrs. McMurphy had taken Arlette's

face in her hand and squeezed it so that her cheeks were all scrunched up into a "fish face." "You've never even had a soda, have you, dear?"

Arlette did not like the pity she heard in Mrs. McMurphy's voice. She wanted to be treated like Lucette. But she also wanted to know more. She needed to know what a soda was. It was obvious to her that *all* rich people ate sodas. Arlette swallowed her pride and said, "No."

"I knew it, Thurston! What did I tell you? I'll bet they've not had ice cream half a dozen times in their lives."

Arlette quickly counted her ice-cream encounters. She hated it that Mrs. McMurphy was right. She hung her head.

"I'll order for you and your little brother," Mrs. McMurphy said. Then she signaled to the boy who was filling orders behind the counter. "Young man, we'd like a chocolate soda with vanilla ice cream for the young miss here, and for her brother, a hot fudge sundae. I'll have a cherry Coke—and, Thurston?"

"A banana split," Thurston McMurphy said.

When the order came, Arlette's eyes widened and she clapped her hands together with glee. "I've never seen anything like this before!"

"Wait till you taste it, dear."

Arlette had to kneel on the stool to reach the tall soda with the straw. There was white, fluffy stuff on top they called whipped cream, and a cherry, and when she sipped the drink through the straw, she tasted liquid chocolate, water with bubbles in it, and creamy vanilla ice cream that she remembered from her birthday jaunt to New Iberia. Arlette sucked and drank and sucked some more. She dipped her spoon into the sweet whipped cream and then let the cream dissolve on her tongue. She ate the ice cream slowly, and as it melted and blended with the seltzer water and chocolate, she thought she'd never in her life find a more divine drink. Chocolate sodas had to have been made in heaven, she thought as she finished the last of the drink. She almost, but not quite, felt sorry for her sisters, who were meeting new friends at the Sunday school.

That fall and into the winter, the two older Herbert girls went to school and then began taking small jobs at the homes of the people they met at the Baptist church. At first Marie objected to the girls' new obligations, since they were around less to help her with chores—until they came home and gave her the money they had earned. Five cents for laundry chores; ten cents for baby-sitting; five cents to iron a shirt; fifteen cents to tend gardens. Marie pocketed the money and made the girls promise not to tell Bobby Joe about the money. She in turn let up on her demands on the girls.

The smaller household chores and some of the more diffi-cult ones fell to Arlette. It was hard for a five-and-a-half-year-old to wash dishes, iron, and clean, but Arlette knew that Angelique was working hard to get money so that they could run away together. Angelique had told Arlette that she only told Marie about half of the money she made. Angelique didn't tell Marie that she kept half, and sometimes more, for herself.

Angelique, true to her word, saved her money. She talked about the day when Arlette could have all the chocolate sodas she wanted and Angelique would be the one to pay for it all. She was going to be the dream maker. Angelique persuaded Arlette to give her the odd change she found in Bobby Joe's trousers on laundry day. If there was more than a few cents, though, the money would have to go to Marie because she knew that Bobby Joe never remembered his change after he'd been drinking all night.

Marie kept the money in a mason jar behind the outhouse. She never told Bobby Joe, but she told Arlette that someday *she* was going to run away from him, but that she was going to take all the children with her. Arlette looked at the half-filled jar and knew that her mother was going to have to wait all her life to get them all out of there.

Arlette knew she would have to look out for herself.

Christmas seldom had any fanfare, and the only thing that made that particular Christmas memorable was a prayer that Arlette heard Angelique say shortly before she went to bed. Angelique thought that her sisters were sound asleep when she went to the grease-smeared window and gazed out at the winter sky. "God, if you're up there, I sure do need deliver-ance from this house. If You make me stay, I'll like to kill Bobby Joe. Please, show me a way to get outta here. I'll do anythin', Lord. Just help me out."

Arlette had never heard her sister beg so earnestly, not

even to Bobby Joe when he was beating her. Arlette watched with a half-opened eye as Angelique climbed back into bed, but she did not stir. Angelique slept fitfully that night and for many nights thereafter, which told Arlette that Angelique was probably not relying on God to be her deliverer, but instead was relying on herself.

Arlette believed that there was nothing Angelique would keep secret from her. They had both arrived at the same conclusion at nearly the same time and they both knew they would have to plan an escape. Throughout the month of January, Arlette kept waiting for the day when Angelique would come to her and tell her the plan.

One day near the end of the month, but before the February groundhog was to make his appearance, Angelique left with all the money she had promised to share with Arlette.

The act of betrayal was like a knife in Arlette's back. She had trusted her sister to care for her and include her in running away, but Angelique had thought only of herself.

Arlette knew she'd saved over five dollars herself from Bobby Joe's pants pockets. She had willingly and stupidly given the money to her sister.

That day Arlette learned not to trust anyone but herself.

That same morning, the police came for Bobby Joe. He was arrested for making and selling moonshine and for robbing the Bennetts' General Store. Bobby Joe protested he'd been drunk and was just "funnin' " the Bennetts, but the two deputies didn't see it that way.

Arlette watched her father being hauled away by the deputies. She watched her mother's emotionless face as the police car drove off into the denuded forest. Bobby Joe was gone, but the effect of his life, his thinking, his actions, hung over the shanty.

Prison, Arlette thought. Her father was going to prison, but all her young mind registered at the time was the fact that her father had run away, just like Angelique. Arlette was stuck in the backwoods of Louisiana and she was afraid she'd never get away.

Four

*A*rlette lived in fear of her father's return, but the years passed uneventfully. Marie eked out a meager living by taking in laundry—labor that fell to the girls, since Marie was too busy with the babies. Marie learned that handmade quilts brought a good price and she started stitching odd rags and pieces of old cloth together and sold them at church auctions in New Iberia. The monies brought in were never enough and Marie wrung her hands constantly out of guilt and despair.

Arlette learned many things during that time. She learned from her mother that Angelique had run away because their father had been molesting her. Marie had never wanted to believe the "filthy lies," but when the deputy told her that Bobby Joe had confessed to "more monkeyshines than moonshine," Marie finally had to face the truth. She told Arlette that Angelique had been placed with a foster family, but never elaborated further. Arlette knew nothing about "foster families" and so she tried to imagine that Angelique was suffering as much as she.

Arlette also learned that being pretty brought rewards. The highlight of each week was her Sunday school class at the Baptist church. She was in the second grade now, and her natural beauty had begun to show. Slowly, both at school and at church, people began to notice her. She learned well from Angelique's betrayal never to trust. She had to look out for herself because she knew that no one else would. But as her beauty gained attention, she found that she could use it to talk fellow church members into trusting her. She needed them for baby-sitting jobs, laundry, mending, and cleaning work, for which they paid her in cash. She gave small amounts to her mother, so that she wouldn't grow suspicious about the amount of time Arlette was spending away from home. But most of the money she hid. She was determined to use it to get away and get revenge.

In the months after Bobby Joe's arrest, Arlette still dreamed of running away, but as the months turned to years and Bobby Joe never returned, Arlette found she gained even more acceptance in the community by spending her money on herself.

She bought a dress at the J.C. Penney store in New Iberia to wear to Sunday school. She found that people talked to her more openly, smiled at her more freely, and when she added new black patent leather Mary Janes, she was even invited to a birthday party. Money bought friends.

Arlette worked harder and bought more things. She saved all of her baby-sitting money in the third grade to buy a new winter coat, sweaters, and wool skirts. She found that her new clothes kept the winter rains from invading the inside of her bones. Money bought warmth.

Money also bought revenge.

When she was eleven years old, she asked her mother for Angelique's address. Reluctantly her mother gave it to her. Arlette wrote to her oldest sister, asking her to come home for a visit. Angelique wrote back saying that she was still afraid Bobby Joe would come home at the same time and find her. She knew that her father would carry his grudge against her to his grave. Instead, she sent Arlette a bus ticket to New Orleans. Arlette was shocked at Angelique's generosity and nearly succumbed to guilt pangs until she read that the ticket had been paid for by Angelique's foster parents. Arlette felt no remorse for the hatred she'd harbored toward her sister.

When Marie watched Arlette open the letter and saw the bus ticket, her eyes filled with tears. Arlette had no idea her mother missed Angelique, since her mother had seldom mentioned Angelique's name in the years since her departure. For a long time Arlette wondered if her mother blamed Angelique for Bobby Joe's arrest, even though they all knew he was guilty. But the subject was never brought up.

Arlette wanted desperately to see her sister, and the last thing she had on her mind was to give her treasured bus ticket to her mother. But when her mother turned her back on

Arlette, who was sitting at the battered kitchen table, and
went to the sink to hide her sobs in the creaking sound of the
water pump, Arlette turned around in her chair.

"You want to see her, Ma?"

"Yeah. Maybe. I dunno."

"Why not?"

"It's better not to think about things you cain't have."

"Is that what you do, Ma? Don't think about it?"

"Not much. No."

Marie still had not looked at Arlette, but this was the usual
practice in the Herbert shanty. They hid their feelings and
their thoughts. They acted, sometimes, as if they barely knew
one another.

"I want to see her, too, Ma. I don't want to give you my
ticket."

"I don't want it. Go. But when you come back, don't talk
about her around me. Okay?"

"Okay," Arlette answered low.

Marie filled the sink with cold water and began scrubbing
the chipped dishes. She never said another word about the
trip. When it was time for Arlette to catch the bus, however,
Marie drove her to New Iberia.

Wanting to be alone with Arlette, Marie had left all the
other children at home. But once they were alone on the
country roads, she had little to say beyond reminding Arlette
to wash her hands and keep her mouth shut unless she was
spoken to. Arlette had never thought much about the fact that
her mother was a simpleminded woman, but as she rode next
to her in the old jalopy, Arlette started seeing her mother for
what she was. And she did not like what she saw.

Arlette didn't know one thing about her mother—not her
likes, her dislikes, her sorrows or dreams. Marie was the kind
of person who was sleepwalking through life. Arlette wanted
never to be like her in any way.

Once on the bus, Arlette peered out the dirty window and
waved to her mother. As the bus moved away, she watched
her mother's careworn face disappear from sight. At that moment Arlette wished she would never have to go back home
again.

* * *

New Orleans was hot, sultry, and it stank. The open canals smelled putrid to Arlette, who was used to the clean country. It had been arranged that Angelique and her foster parents would pick Arlette up at the bus terminal.

When Arlette got off the bus, she was looking for a ten-year-old Angelique still dressed in a faded calico print dress, but what she found instead was a beautiful blond teenager wearing a floral sundress and red leather flats. Arlette walked right up to the pretty girl who bore a faint resemblance to her sister and said, "Angelique! You've bleached your hair!"

Arlette was so stunned by the changes in her sister, she quite literally forgot about her hatred. "And your clothes! I've never seen such clothes!" She touched the soft cotton skirt of the dress. "And you have nylons ... and a charm bracelet!" Arlette's eyes were wide with surprise and wonder. She could not fathom how her sister could afford such luxuries.

Angelique hugged Arlette. "I'm so happy to see you, too," she said earnestly. "You've changed a lot—grown up, I mean." There were tears in Angelique's eyes. "You were only five and a half when I left ..."

At that moment Arlette remembered the reason she had come to New Orleans. She remembered the pain Angelique had caused when she left. She remembered the pangs of betrayal. She turned narrowed, cautious eyes on her sister. "That was a long time ago, Angelique. A lot has happened to both of us since then."

Angelique's delight over seeing her sister clouded her perceptions, and she did not notice the misgiving in Arlette's voice. She put an arm around her sister. "Come on. I want to introduce you to my new family." They walked over to a brand-new red Cadillac where a tall, good-looking, dark-haired man stood next to his pretty blond wife. Arlette guessed they were old, at least over forty. As she drew closer, she noticed that their clothing was impeccable. They both wore summer-white linen suits, his with pants and a jacket and hers with a long, pencil-slim skirt. He carried his summer hat in his hand; her hat was small and veiled and fit snugly over her short blond hair. Her summer gloves were lace, her purse was fine, soft leather, and her matching shoes were unscuffed and brand-new. The woman smelled of expensive perfume, and when she spoke, her words were refined and polished, and her voice was soft.

Arlette had seen the way that the people in New Iberia dressed, but she'd never seen anyone this rich. No wonder Angelique had never come home. Who could blame her?

"Mom, Dad, this is my sister Arlette." Angelique introduced her old and new family.

Arlette shook hands with the man, thinking his hand was softer than her own. "James Michon," he said with a heavy New Orleans accent. "And this is Betty." He indicated the woman standing next to him.

"I'm so pleased to meet you," Betty said with a smile Arlette thought was as bright as the summer sun. "Angelique has been counting the days. Haven't you, dear?"

"Crossed each and every one off my calendar."

"Well, let's get your bag in the car," James said, taking Arlette's battered tan-and-brown suitcase, which did not latch properly and which she'd tied with a clothesline to hold it together, and placed it in the trunk.

"You ride in back with me," Angelique said, possessively grabbing Arlette's hand and pulling her into the back of the Cadillac.

The ride toward the Garden District was a revelation for Arlette. She saw tourists and locals shopping, going to Saturday afternoon confessions, eating at old Creole restaurants, and exchanging stories in shop doorways. The Cadillac inched down the narrow streets of the French Quarter, where Arlette could hear honky-tonk music mingle with sad jazz tunes that Angelique called "the blues." Arlette glanced above her and saw a beautiful dark-haired woman leaning over a black wrought-iron balcony. The woman was laughing and looking at Arlette. Then she leaned over and plucked a rose out of a vase and tossed it down to the Cadillac. The woman's laughter was deep and throaty, and rang through the streets.

"Pay her no mind, Arlette. She's just trash."

"What was she doing? I mean, throwing me a rose?"

James patted his wife's hand, a signal that he would take over the situation. "She was just havin' a little fun—at your expense, of course."

Arlette looked up at the woman, but the Cadillac pulled

away from the stop sign and continued down the street. Fun? she wondered. Arlette glanced back and saw the woman throw her a kiss. It made no sense to Arlette, but as she turned toward Angelique, she realized that her sister knew exactly what the woman's gestures meant. There was wisdom in Angelique's eyes.

Arlette shrugged. "I don't understand."

"I know," Angelique said. "I'll tell you later."

The Michon house was in the heart of the Garden District, across from Audubon Park. It was a whitewashed brick, three-story house with huge white columns in front, a small lawn superbly landscaped with azaleas, magnolia trees, round and conical-shaped yews and evergreens, and a wide brick drive that circled in front of the house. Arlette was speechless as she gazed up at the double leaded glass doors with their shiny brass handles and knobs. The sun reflected off the glass and shattered into tiny pools of colored lights. Arlette thought she'd just walked through the looking glass. She was in Wonderland. No doubt about it.

The interior of the house only proved to Arlette that she was right. The entry floor and the stairs were white marble, a material she was certain could only be found in heaven. The flowers were exotic . . . orchids, roses, and lilies, none of which Arlette had ever seen. The house smelled of unusual spices mixed with lemons and limes and peaches. Angelique called it "potpourri," which Arlette decided must have been something else that came from heaven.

Angelique carried Arlette's suitcase up the celestial staircase and then down a hallway with such thick carpeting that Arlette thought she'd sink to her knees in it. "This is my room," Angelique announced proudly as she opened a dark-stained wood door.

The sun filtered through lace curtains, which cast patterns of roses and lilies on the walls and Aubusson carpet. A huge mahogany four-poster bed was canopied in white lace. The bedspread, pillow covers, and dust ruffle were all made of expensive, delicate lace. Against the wall between the two windows was a dressing table with a mirror and at least a dozen bottles of perfume and cologne. Next to a blue floral chair stood a phonograph and a box filled with records. There was a pennant that hung on the wall above the chair that said Tulane.

"You live here?"

"Yes."

"In this room?"

"Except when I'm at school, yes."

"Only princesses live this good."

"That's what Dad calls me."

"But he's not your real father."

"I don't care about what went before. This is my home now. This is my life. He is my father." Angelique went over to the dressing table, sat down on the stool, and began brushing her hair.

Arlette walked around the room, touching things, taking in the surroundings. Then she stopped and looked at her sister's reflection in the mirror. Arlette's face screwed up with curiosity, just like it had when she was five. "Why did that woman throw me a rose?"

"She liked you."

Arlette didn't care for the flat tones of Angelique's voice. "Lots of people like me. They don't play jokes on me, though. Who was she? Do you know her?"

"No. I don't know her, but I know women like her. She's a whore. I would have become a whore if it hadn't been for the Michons. They saved me. Papa would have kept on me all my life."

"What are you talking about, Angelique?" Arlette hated it when Angelique talked in circles.

Angelique turned and faced Arlette. "Rape. That's what I'm talkin' about. Papa raped me. Not once or twice but a lot, Arlette. He would've raped you, too, if I hadn't had the courage to speak up. I didn't want what happened to me to happen to you or Antoinette. I knew I was strong, or at least I thought I was ... Sometimes I'm not so sure now. I get kind of lonely by myself in this big house. I really missed you."

"You did?" Arlette was incredulous and suspicious. "But you have so many things. And beautiful clothes. Just look at—"

"It doesn't matter," Angelique interrupted. Tears filled her eyes. "I still missed you and Antionette and the boys. How are they?"

"Fine." Arlette still couldn't believe her sister. Not fully. Angelique had everything she wanted. She even had freedom. "If you missed us so much, how come you didn't come to see us or send for one of us until now?"

"My doctor wouldn't let me."

"Are you sick? How bad? Why didn't you say something?" Arlette was instantly ashamed of herself.

"I'm not physically sick like you think. I'm sick in here," she said, pointing to her heart and then her head.

"I don't get it," Arlette said.

"I'm seeing a psychiatrist. Dr. Mills is his name. He's helped me a lot. I had a lot of anger toward Papa . . . toward Mama. In a way I hated you—because you were so young and these bad things had never happened to you."

"You hated *me?*" Arlette couldn't believe her ears.

"Yes." Angelique hung her head. "I'm ashamed to say I did. But I don't anymore. Will you forgive me?"

Arlette stared at her sister. She blinked when Angelique extended her arms, wanting, needing, forgiveness. But Arlette didn't move. Suddenly she felt the dam around her own heart burst open and a flood of emotion escape. "But I hated *you,*" she said.

"Why?" Now it was Angelique's turn to be shocked.

"Because you left me. You swore you would give me some money so I could run away. You swore you would take me with you."

"I did, didn't I?"

"Yes." Arlette breathed out the word in a near whisper and wondered why, now that she'd said them aloud, her accusations had lost their fiery temperament. She raised her eyes to Angelique and watched the sun as it danced in her sister's golden hair. Her eyes were filled with empathy and caring. Her tears were of pain and regret and sorrow so deep, Arlette prayed quickly to Jesus that she would never experience her sister's sadness. Angelique looked like the angel she was named for.

"I'm so sorry, Arlette. I never wanted to hurt you. I only wanted to save you. Can you forgive me?"

"Oh, yes!" Arlette ran to her sister's arms and let Angelique's embrace fill her with strength. How wrong she'd been to misjudge her sister. How horrible those nights in the shanty must have been for Angelique.

"You were so little, Arlette. How could I tell you the truth? It's hard for me to explain it now. What does a five-year-old know of rape? I wanted to save you, because I loved you."

"I'm so glad I came," Arlette said, feeling her sister's strength infuse her own spirit. "I could have gone all my life hating you."

"I'm glad you're here, too, Arlette. I wanted you to know the truth."

Arlette looked over Angelique's shoulder at the room, reflected in the mirror. It was so beautiful here. And for the first time in her life, Arlette realized there was someone who loved her and that love came from the most unlikely of sources . . . her enemy. "I wish I could stay here forever."

"I wish you could, too, Arlette. I wish that with all my heart."

But Arlette couldn't stay in New Orleans with the Michons. When she wrote to her mother and begged to stay, Marie replied with the next post and told Arlette she had to return to Bayou Teche to help her care for the other children. Arlette's heart sank. Suddenly she wished she had never come to New Orleans. She wished she'd never seen the splendor of the Michon home or the graciousness they showed to each other and to her sister. Arlette found herself fighting onslaughts of jealousy. It wasn't Angelique's fault that she had captured the brass ring in life, no more than it was Arlette's fault that she was faced with returning to her desolate life in Bayou Teche. It was God's fault, Arlette concluded, and she hated Him for it.

Angelique was sympathetic to Arlette's situation, and so were the Michons.

"We'll simply have to make your stay a most memorable one in any case," Betty Michon said.

Then Betty did the worst thing she could do to Arlette. She led her to the edges of the Promised Land and revealed to her the incredible life-style that money could buy. Betty thought she was helping Arlette. Despite her young years, Arlette knew it was torture.

The three women shopped at Maison Blanche for new

school clothes for Arlette. She bought shoes in bright colors and pretty pastels to match sweaters with pearl buttons and pleated wool skirts. Betty took Arlette to her favorite hairdresser near Lake Pontchartrain and had Arlette's brown hair cut in a precision pageboy and conditioned with a miraculous concoction of avocado and turtle oil that made her hair glisten. She had a manicure and a pedicure. She bought peach-smelling soaps and lotions, lemon-scented shampoo, and a cologne that was called English Rose. They ate escargots and shrimp remoulade at the Court of Two Sisters and then browsed in the antiques shops on Royal Street in the French Quarter. Betty explained fine furniture, the grains of woods, the craftsmanship of the wood carvings, and the filigree of brass drawer pulls, all of which seemed to mean so much to her. Arlette saw bronze and crystal chandeliers that were over two hundred years old. She saw gold gilt chairs from Napoleon's court. She saw marble tables and consoles with ornate legs and pedestals that once belonged to the Hapsburgs of Austria. She marveled over gold-filigreed Viennese mirrors and Chinese porcelains and hand-painted screens. She saw Fabergé jeweled eggs that were once owned by the Russian czar. Arlette learned more history in one afternoon shopping with Betty than she had in the whole of her schooling in Bayou Teche. She felt woefully inadequate and said very little, but she noticed that Angelique hung on to every word Betty spoke. Arlette realized that half the battle of existing in this new world of the rich was knowledge. She needed to learn many, many things.

When they returned to the Michon house with all their purchases, Betty instructed the girls on the proper way to set a table. She showed Arlette the difference between sterling silver, silver plate, flatware, and tinware. She made each girl place the crystal on the table for dinner, making certain the white wines, the red wines, and the cordials were properly aligned.

By the time the day had ended, Arlette was exhausted.

"I never knew being rich was so much work!" she said as she threw herself down on the huge four-poster in Angelique's room. "Is it always like this for you?"

"Yes. And more. But it's worth it, Arlette. I am going to

learn everything I can, and soon I'll be ready for my coming-out party."

"Your what?"

"The debutante ball. The Michons are a very old and re-spected family in New Orleans. They know only the best people. Influential people. Mother says I'll make a good marriage and will become one of the leaders in New Orleans society."

"But you aren't one of them."

"James has so much power here, so much influence, other people will accept me. They already have, actually. I have tennis lessons every Tuesday. Golf lessons are on Thursday. Piano, ballet, and tap are crammed into a long Saturday, but I manage. I've got top grades in my classes . . ."

Arlette observed the determined bent to Angelique's face. She was cramming her sister's new purchases into an already overstuffed closet. She seemed almost angry.

"Do you mind the work it takes?"

Angelique turned incredulous eyes toward her sister. Arlette thought she could see white-hot hatred simmering behind the pupils. "It's worth every second. I will never, ever be Angelique Herbert again. If it's the last thing I do, I swear, as God is my witness, that I will wash the taint and sin of Bobby Joe from my life. I will never look back again. Never!"

Arlette was speechless. She'd never seen such bitterness, except when Bobby Joe was drunk—maybe. And even then it was different. When she finally spoke, her voice was a thin whisper. "And you don't really want to see me, either."

Angelique walked over to her sister and put her hand on Arlette's shiny hair. "You're my sister. But seeing you reminds me of where I came from. It's hard. But it has nothing to do with you. You have to believe that. I just want to forget. I wish I could wipe it all away."

Arlette pondered her sister's words for a long time. She knew that having been raped was a demon that Angelique would always have to fight. But still, to Arlette's way of thinking, all this money, the education, the society people Angelique was meeting more than made up for their father's sins. To Arlette's young mind, money cured every ill, especially the mental kind. After all, it wasn't like Angelique had lost an arm or a leg, was it?

"I understand," Arlette chose to say instead. She wanted to remain empathetic toward her sister. Angelique was a person she wanted to keep close to her. The Michon money had already changed Arlette's life. Maybe they could change it even more in the future.

By the time the visit was over, Arlette had endeared herself to Betty and James Michon. She hugged them both when she left and promised that she would come to spend Christmas with Angelique. As she waved exuberantly to the Michons and her sister at the bus station, Arlette was already dreaming of the mountain of glorious gifts the Michons would buy for her.

She leaned back in her seat and knew that her own future was a hundred, no, a thousand times more secure than it had been before this trip. The Michons would help her where God had failed.

The Christmas visit that Arlette awaited for nearly five months never materialized, because Angelique chose to break all ties with her family. She wrote a note to Arlette begging for forgiveness and explaining that she could not endure the nightmares of their father's cruelties toward her. She lived in abject fear of the man's return, and for her, the only way she could handle it was not to see any member of her family, including Arlette.

Arlette believed that Angelique had betrayed her again. The sound of the door closing on their relationship reverberated in Arlette's mind for years. She despised her sister for shunning her and for taking the Michon money and her own future with her.

The day that Arlette received Angelique's note, she stood at the dinner table and wiped the pork grease off her hands. "From this day on, I want you all to know that Angelique is dead to me. I will never speak her name. Neither will you mention her to me. I have disowned her."

Arlette walked away from the silent table and never thought of her sister again.

Five

J.C. Mitchell met Arlette Herbert when he was twenty-
three years old and drunk. He stumbled into the Avalon
Pharmacy at nearly midnight, dressed in a black tuxedo,
black tie, and black patent leather shoes. He never looked or
felt so bad in his whole life. He went to the counter, hoisted
himself onto one of the green plastic-covered swivel stools,
and pounded on the counter. The aluminum napkin holder
jumped and moved a quarter inch to the right of the Heinz
catsup bottle.

"Service!" he demanded.

Arlette had her back to J.C. when he walked in, but she'd
heard his shuffling feet and mumbled to herself, "Not another
one." She pretended not to hear his demands and continued to
fill the coffeemaker with water, then flipped on the switch.

"Are you going to wait on me or not?" he questioned with
a little less force.

Arlette turned slowly around and walked toward him.

J.C.'s vision was failing him. He squinted his eyes, trying
to make out the features of the beautiful, sultry creature moving toward him. "Ava? Is that you?"

Arlette smiled pleasantly at him. This one is really in bad
shape, she thought. She bent slightly, picked up a coffee mug
from under the counter, and placed it in front of him. She
filled it with hot coffee. "Who's Ava?"

"You are. Ava Gardner. I thought you . . . you . . . *hic*! . . .
only worked in the . . . movies," J.C. said through his hiccups.

"I'm not Ava Gardner, honey. But I will be if you'll be a

good boy and drink this coffee." She got him a glass of ice water. Then she took a teaspoon and filled it with sugar from the tall, silver-topped sugar dispenser. "Here," she said, shoving the teaspoon of sugar at him. "This will cure those hiccups."

J.C. tried to focus on the teaspoon of sugar. "Whazzat? Poison? It should be poison. Hic! I'm dying. Hic!"

When he opened his mouth, Arlette shoved the sugar into it. "Swallow!"

J.C. did as he was ordered.

She handed him the glass of water. "Now drink ten small sips and then one long gulp. Let's see if you're sober enough to do that."

Again J.C. followed orders. He finished the water off, and when he put the glass down on the counter, his depth perception was off, and he mistakenly slammed the glass on the tiled surface.

The two other customers, both truck drivers, stared at him.

J.C. smiled back at them sheepishly and lifted his hand in an apologetic gesture. "Sorry." He looked back at Arlette. "Sorry, Ava."

"I told you, I'm not Ava."

"You sure look like her." He paused. "Hey! My hiccups are gone!"

"Drink the coffee, honey. I think I have some aspirin in my purse. Then I recommend a very large order of toast, hash browns, and scrambled eggs."

"I'll take it," he said, finishing off the black coffee.

Arlette wrote down his order and then placed it on the pass-through to the kitchen for the cook. She dug out a bottle of aspirin from her black purse. She poured J.C. a second glass of water and another cup of coffee. She handed him the aspirin.

"What's your name?" he asked, becoming more sober every minute.

"Arlette."

"I wasn't all that far off . . . but you look like Ava Gardner," he said as his eyes fell to her voluptuous breasts. He noticed that she wore a white nylon uniform like the other waitress, and a white apron, but Arlette had unzipped her uniform just an inch more than was appropriate for a waitress.

He gulped the second cup of coffee, wanting very much to erase the effects of the champagne he'd been drinking that night at the Cork Club. As Arlette served him his order, he noticed she had one of the smallest waists he'd ever seen, and nicely curved hips. She had dyed her hair almost black, he could tell, because it was not natural-looking. Her face was heart-shaped, and she had a delicate nose, high cheekbones, and smooth, though overly powdered, skin. She had dark, sultry eyes that she'd lined with black eyeliner, just like Ava Gardner and Marilyn Monroe. He was intrigued with this gorgeous woman who tried to look cheap.

"Where are you from, Arlette . . . ?"

"Herbert," she answered easily, pouring him a third cup of coffee. "New Orleans," she lied just as easily.

"How long have you been in Houston?"

"Six months. I came here to go to school. I'm taking fashion."

"Is that right?" He moved his elbows out of the way of the plate in front of him. "So you're a fashion designer?" he asked, starting to eat.

"No. I want to be a fashion buyer. I was told that Foley's pays real good money for that kind of job." She leaned over conspiratorially. "I'll tell you a secret."

"Okay."

"I'm really only nineteen, but I told them at the school that I was twenty-one."

"Does that make a difference?" he asked. "I mean, I went to Rice University myself—"

"You did?" she interrupted excitedly. "My God! I heard you have to really have a head full of brains to get in there. I could never get into a school like that. My school is just a . . . well, a trade school, you know? I don't know if it's a big deal—about my age, I mean. I just figured that the older one is, well, that's more experience, and since I don't have much experience . . . well, you know what I mean."

J.C. indulged her. "Yeah, I know what you mean," he answered, knowing that at least he'd discovered the reason for the heavy makeup and dyed hair. But there was something about her that he liked. He peered at her and realized that her eyes were the color of smoky amethysts. He'd never seen eyes like that. She smiled at him like a little child and yet she was all woman. Maybe too much woman. J.C. had spent the past year resurrecting his father's antiques business and trying to mesh his anthropological background and his father's business to suit his interests.

When J.C. had told his father he was majoring in anthropology at Rice University, his father, a marketing major and lifelong businessman, nearly gave up on his son. By the time J.C. graduated, he had shown his father how he could incorporate pre-Columbian art and artifacts with Louis XIV chairs and settees. Growing up in the world of antiques and importing, J.C. had a distinctive flair and style that in high school had won him the "young designer's award." He liked things with a past, but he also liked putting furniture and art together in new and untried ways.

J.C. was just about to prove himself to his father when his father had a heart attack and died. J.C. and his sister, Vicki, had lost their mother when they were very young. Now they only had each other. J.C. did not deal well with grief. Sometimes he drank too much. Other times, when he was lucky enough, he would lose his emotions on an archaeological dig. The rest of the time he put his grief into making Antiquities, the new name for his father's old store, Mitchell Antiques, the most successful and innovative gallery of its kind.

J.C. was creative, talented, bright, and curious. Even though he was only twenty-three, he was on the verge of having great commercial success. Growing up in Houston, he knew everybody who was anybody, and a lot of nobodies, too. He ran with the Cork Club crowd, who vacationed in Palm Beach, skied in Vail, and flew to Los Angeles to rub shoulders with movie stars. He exchanged ideas with his pals from Rice and he sought knowledge from world-renowned archaeologists and anthropologists he'd met on digs over the past eight years. J.C. believed he had the world by the tail.

As he ate, he looked up at Arlette and thought he saw that same kind of ambition in her eyes. He couldn't tell if he was still drunk or not, but she seemed to be the determined sort to him. He liked the way she took charge of him, cured his hiccups, and was eager to please him and impress him. He liked that . . . a lot.

"You want some more toast or something?" she asked.

"No, thanks, I'm fine." He felt nearly sober now. "Tell me, Arlette Herbert, have you ever been to the Cork Club?"

Lights pirouetted in Arlette's dark eyes. "At the Shamrock Hotel?"

"That's the one."

"Never."

"Would you like to go there sometime?"

"Sure."

"With me?"

Arlette placed her hands on the counter and leaned down in front of him so that he could see the full blossom of her deep cleavage. Her dark ruby-red lips parted in a sultry pout, and she licked her upper lip while she pondered his invitation.

J.C. felt beads of sweat sprout on his forehead. He felt the bulge in his pants. Never had his hands itched to touch a woman in the way he wanted to touch Arlette's breasts. His mind felt as if it were suspended between earth and sky.

"Well . . ." His voice croaked as his sexual need suddenly seemed to fill his body and strangle his words.

"I have to think about it," she replied in deep, throaty tones that made him want her all the more.

"P-Please?"

She leaned closer to him. Her face was so close to his that their noses nearly touched.

J.C. knew his body temperature had soared. There was definitely no trace of alcohol left in his body now. It couldn't have survived the heat.

She pursed her lips, nearly brushing his mouth with hers. "Next time you're here, we'll discuss it. I'd like to know you when you're sober."

"I-I am . . . sober, I mean."

"Sure, honey." Using first one arm and then the other to push herself slowly away from him and at the same time making one breast twitch at a time, Arlette stood erect and looked down at him as if he were the lowest form of life.

He gaped at her. She had made the rules. She was the goddess. He was the worshiper.

She put her hands behind her back and untied her apron, then turned away from him and vanished into the kitchen.

"Hey! Wait!" J.C. scrambled off his stool and in his hurry, he tripped and fell clumsily to the floor.

The two truck drivers at the end of the counter who had been watching him burst into laughter.

"You better watch it, pal! She's a killer!"

"Ha! Stop now before that dick of yours does more than just trip you!" the driver in the red Western shirt said as he slapped the counter good-naturedly.

J.C. waved their warnings aside and raced behind the counter, still pursuing Arlette, but she was gone. The cook tried to stop J.C. with his pancake turner, but his weapon was useless.

"Get out of my kitchen! She's gone. Besides, she'll be back tomorrow night. Now get outta here!" He shoved J.C. back through the door and into the restaurant area. "Jesus Christ, I don't know what she does to you fancy-pants guys. Now get outta here!"

J.C. left a twenty-dollar bill for his meal, which had cost one dollar and eighty-five cents, instructing the other waitress to give the money to Arlette. "Tell her I'll be back."

"Sure, honey," the thirty-five-year-old redhead said. "That's what they all say," she added, placing the change in her own pocket as J.C. walked out the door.

Over the next three months Arlette told J.C. her saddest stories, from her father's abuse to Angelique's betrayal. She told him some truth and mostly lies. She never told him exactly how many brothers and sisters she had, and she told him that everyone in her family was dead. She told him she loved him and she made him want her.

J.C. fell in love with this beautiful and lost woman. To him she was a rare and exotic treasure that had been overlooked for ages. He wanted to "save" her; he wanted to make her happy. He believed in the illusions she spun and he believed she could make him happy in return. He bought her a brand-new diamond ring because Arlette liked things new, not antique.

When he proposed at the top of the Warwick Hotel in the glass-surrounded dining room, he expressed his loyalty to her and his love for her as he placed the diamond on her finger. "This is for life, Arlette. You've lost your family, and I've lost most of mine. For now, we'll be each other's family, and someday we'll have children and create a bigger family."

Arlette swallowed hard. "Children? How soon do you want children? And how many?"

J.C. laughed good-naturedly. "One or two would be nice. And I'll take them in God's good time." He kissed her tenderly. "You do want a family, don't you?"

Arlette smiled and nodded and then quickly drank her champagne. She had spent her life running from family. The mere mention of the word sent chills down her spine. It was just her luck to trap a man who wanted kids. Well, she was smarter than that. She could figure out how to dodge the motherhood bit for quite a while. She did like the part where he thought he and she were family, though. She needed him to believe they were sacredly joined, because in her own way, Arlette believed it, too.

Six

July 4, 1976
Houston, Texas

*L*illi thought that the parade of celebrities and jet-setters who streamed through her house that afternoon was much more exciting than any Fourth of July parade she could have seen downtown. These were the crème de la crème of River Oaks, Memorial, Tanglewood, and West University society. They were the movers and the shakers. She was especially impressed with the women. They were the wives of oil barons, bankers, oil executives, real-estate tycoons, and commercial builders. Some were old money; most were new money. These were the women who were married for their family names or their looks or both. They intended to cling to both until the day they died. Plastic surgery was only whispered about, but new noses had already shown up on several of Arlette's friends. They talked of their recent visits to the Greenhouse in Dallas, where they were pampered like princesses while they starved off excess pounds. Three of the women were discussing their newest masseuse, who they swore could beat cellulite off thighs and buttocks with half the pounding of their last masseuse. They were creamed, steamed, buffed, and puffed by the most expensive facialists in town, and none of them cared about the cost or the time. It was worth it. None of them had lost a husband to a younger woman yet.

Lilli was very aware that she was the only brunette in a sea of teased, sprayed, bleached blond heads. Texas "big hair" was in vogue, even though Lilli's fashion magazines declared the look "dead" back in 1968, but none of that mattered to these women. Lilli often thought that Houston hairdressers

must have the best biceps in the profession from all the blowing, back-combing, and spraying they did.

Lilli hated how these women came up to her and petted her
as if she were a poodle. Or worse, they acted as if she
weren't even there.

"Isn't she darling?" one wealthy young woman said, who
had just married a much older man.

"I hope she doesn't set her sights on my husband in a few
years," one buxom blonde in a tight-fitting jumpsuit drawled.

"Honey, you-all aren't still runnin' around Mexico with
your daddy, now, are you?" asked another woman in her late
thirties, who then turned to Arlette. "You are enrolling her in
a finishin' school, aren't you, Arlette?"

"Yes, of course," Arlette answered firmly.

"What?" Lilli's eyes nearly bugged out of her head. "Aw,
Mom!" She wanted to stomp her foot but knew it would do
no good.

"We'll talk about it later, Lilli. Now, go out and check on
the barbecue. Your father has probably gotten into some conversation with John again and my barbecue is probably
ruined."

"I think he can handle some ribs, Mom," Lilli said sarcas-
tically, although she was grateful for the reprieve. She was
about to gag on the cloud of perfume these women bathed in.

The French door banged shut behind Lilli as she stalked
outside. She walked straight over to her father, picked up his
arm, and put it around her shoulder while he continued his
discussion with two oil tycoons. Without looking at her father, she reached for the Corona he held in his hand, put it to
her lips, and took a deep swallow. She put the bottle back in
his hand. J.C. never missed a beat of his conversation, but he
acknowledged her presence by stroking her arm. She smiled
at the other two men, but they barely noticed her, they were
so enraptured by J.C.'s story.

"I'm convinced I can find it. I've gone over records. I reread Bernal Diaz del Castillo's *Historia Verdadera de la
Conquista de la Nueva España,* about the Aztecs' golden
wheels and the silver cartwheel that resembled the moon they
gave to Cortez."

"But, J.C., we all know that those things found their way

to Spain. Do you really think there's anything left here? Now?"

"I do. Too many tales of El Dorado still exist. I think the city of gold is deep in the Andes Mountains. I've been keeping up with my contemporaries, and there are new bodies of thought, new theories now. It wasn't the Aztecs or the Incas who actually mined the gold back then. It was the more ancient Toltecs, who go back fifteen hundred years before Christ. Maybe even more. There is so much to discover right now. I feel we're on the verge of something truly incredible in archaeology . . ."

"Oh, hell, J.C.," a tall, potbellied man dressed in jeans and ostrich-skin boots said, "we've all heard you say this shit before. I don't give a good goddamn what they find besides the gold. Now, are you gonna do this deal or not?"

John Cameron Mitchell did not hesitate for a second, which was one of the attributes Lilli loved most about her father. "I'll go, as long as you're writing the check, George." He smiled at the tall man, shook his hand, and winked at Lilli. With his other hand still on Lilli's shoulder, he pulled her closer to his chest and gave her a half bear hug. "What do you say, Lilli? Would you like to go to South America with me?"

"Would I?" Her voice rose with excitement. "You bet I would, Pop!"

"Then it's settled. Lilli and I will find your gold, George."

"See that you do," George answered.

Zane McAllister sat at one of the tables in the yard, watching the outrageous young girl who his mother told him was named Lilli and who was J.C. Mitchell's only child. He knew she was younger than he, probably about fourteen, he guessed, since her body showed few signs of having passed through puberty. Zane knew all about puberty, since he was already seventeen. It seemed like centuries since he'd been Lilli's age. Still, he thought as he watched her impudently include herself in her father's discussion, none of the men seemed to mind her presence. He also noticed, with some chagrin, that she drank her father's beer openly in front of her parents' friends, and neither her father nor the other men in the group so much as blinked an eye.

"Unfair!" Zane grumbled. He could not even think of drinking alcohol in front of his parents, much less doing so with the self-confidence that this girl displayed. Who was she? And what kind of parents were these people who were not disciplining her on the spot? The more Zane observed Lilli and her casual interaction with her father, the more he knew he didn't like this girl one bit. No siree, she was a hellion. He could tell. She was the kind of "bad girl" his Bible-reading mother was always warning him about.

He disliked the blue-jean cutoffs she wore, the bandanna print blouse, whose tails she'd tied around her midriff, and the fire-engine-red Ropers. She looked like a little girl playing at dress-up. He could tell she was trying to be sexy, but he thought she looked foolish.

Her body was much too straight and long-legged, with none of the curves of the older girls he knew at his small country high school in Bandera, where he was going to be a senior. Zane liked girls who acted like girls and who looked like girls. And yet, as he stood up and moved closer to the side of the house where he could peer at Lilli unobtrusively, he was aware that he had never seen a more beautiful face in his life.

Her face looked like a delicate valentine, heart-shaped with flawless white skin and cheeks the color of peach nectar. Her mouth was perky and drawn into a bow. But it was her eyes that held him spellbound. At first he thought they were an intense blue, until the sun came out from behind a cloud and he could see that her eyes were deep violet. Her thick black lashes shaded them and cast long shadows on her cheek. Just then she looked past the tall man across from her and she saw Zane. Her gaze was intense and curious. She gave him a slow, pleasant smile, and for a moment he thought she held her breath as she continued to stare at him. The violet eyes were filled with a knowing he did not understand. Suddenly he felt as if she were the one who was older and wiser and he was the child.

Zane was fascinated.

Lilli excused herself from her father, never taking her eyes off the handsome blond boy who was staring at her from around the corner of the house. She walked right up to him and asked, "You're Zane McAllister, right? How come your parents called you Zane?"

"Excuse me?" he said, still startled by her beautiful violet eyes.

"Is your mom a Zane Grey freak or something?"

"My dad, actually." Zane felt as if he'd just awakened from a deep sleep. "How do you know who I am?"

"My pop told me about you," she said, sticking her hand into her cutoffs pocket and pulling out a pack of chewing gum. "Black Jack. Want some?"

"No, thanks. I hate licorice."

"I love it." She rolled the stick into a ball and then popped it into her mouth. "So how come you don't like me, Zane McAllister?"

"What?" Zane had never met anyone who caught him so off guard. He was proud of his sharp wits and quick reflexes. After all, he was captain of the basketball team at school. But he didn't know how to handle this girl with her straightforward questions. "I never said I didn't like you."

"You've been looking at me like you just swallowed a lemon. So I'm asking. I need to know these things."

"Why?"

"Pop told me you were almost seventeen. You must know a lot about girls and the way boys feel about girls. Stuff like that. I figure you can help me out with my boyfriend." She looked up at him with an angel's face.

"You have a boyfriend?"

"Sort of."

"How can you sort of have a boyfriend? Either you do or you don't."

Lilli watched the sun as it danced in his wheat-colored hair. She liked his sky-blue eyes with flecks of gold near the pupils, and the way his long blond lashes swept slowly up and down when he was trying to make sense of what she was saying. She liked keeping him one track off the road, just to see his reactions. It was a game she played whenever she met anyone new. But there was something about Zane that was different from the other boys, different even from Paul.

Zane seemed familiar to her somehow, but she couldn't place him. She already knew from her discussions with her parents that she had never met him before, even though their parents were well acquainted. Maybe they had met a long time ago, and her parents had forgotten about it. Maybe she'd seen him somewhere. No, she thought. It was something else. She had a feeling about Zane that she could not label. It was as if she were different when she was near him. She felt suddenly safe, as if she'd just sailed out of a storm and into a cove where the water was calm and the winds could no longer threaten her.

You're just being dramatic again, she told herself. She wasn't in trouble. She'd just been asked to go on another expedition with her father. She was going to make sure she saw Paul at the fireworks tonight. Life couldn't be better. She had no reason to seek comfort from this boy who seemed to be judging her every action and word.

"I'm going to the fireworks with him tonight."

Zane gave her a superior smile. "No, you aren't. You're lying. I can always tell when someone is lying."

"Oh, yeah? How's that?" Lilli put her hands on her hips.

"I just know, is all. My mother says it's a gift of the righteous to discern good from evil, lies from the truth."

Lilli's right eyebrow shot up. "And you think you are more righteous than I am?"

"Of course I am," he said sincerely.

Lilli's jaw dropped. "Of all the conceited, egotistical . . ." she sputtered. "I think I've heard it all now! I've got to tell you, Zane, you are one for the books. I bet you're one of those football jocks—"

"I play basketball," he interrupted.

"Shit."

"Profanity is not necessary."

Lilli couldn't think of a thing to say. She was totally aghast at Zane's superior attitude and his judgmental attitude. She couldn't believe he was the same person she'd been feeling so close to only moments before. She had to remind herself not to make snap judgments about people. One thing was for sure: meeting Zane had taught her not to make assumptions about people until they opened their mouths. Test their mettle; that was what her father had always told her.

She decided to take a more cautious tack. "So your mother told you all this. What else did she tell you?"

"She knows a lot of things. She reads the Bible to me every day. Every single one of life's rules is there in the Bible. It has all the answers to every problem a person will have to face in life."

"It does?" Lilli replied, thoroughly unconvinced. "What does your father have to say about all this?"

Zane looked away. He didn't want to tell her about his father's illness.

"I'm sorry, Zane," Lilli said. "We can talk about something else." She purposely dropped the conversation. She was smart enough to realize that she had to wait for him to share that confidence with her.

Zane could feel Lilli's compassion as if it were a tangible gift. It was more than strange to him, because he had never been the recipient of honest sympathy. He didn't know if he should trust Lilli or not.

There was something about Lilli that reminded Zane of the sorceresses in the Bible. They were women who were supposed to be able to read men's thoughts. Zane couldn't be certain, but he thought Lilli could be a sorceress of some kind. She looked like a kid, but already he found himself drawn to her. She was like a child/woman he'd read about in the Bible. He wanted to ask her to spend more time with him. He wanted to sit by a lake somewhere with her and tell her all his problems. Even though she was so young, something told him she could help. His hand itched to touch her silky hair. He wanted to know what her favorite foods were. Which singers did she like? Which rock groups? Did she like to dance? Would she dance with him? He wanted to hold her and be held by her. Most incredibly, he found himself wanting to kiss her. She had hardly any breasts yet, but his mind was already whirling with thoughts of touching her. He couldn't understand what was happening to him. He had never reacted to a girl like this.

Hannah McAllister had not let Zane date girls until he turned sixteen, and he'd abided by her rules, although it nearly killed him. Girls were always on his mind. He'd gone out with Jenny Martin, the head cheerleader, a half dozen times since school had let out, and although she let him kiss her, he never felt quite like this around her.

His feelings for Lilli were something altogether different. Lilli was a child, he told himself, and yet he imagined doing things with her that only married adults were allowed to do. He tried to push the images out of his mind, because he knew that God would punish him for these bad thoughts. As he gazed down into Lilli's violet eyes, Zane knew he could never tell his mother what he was thinking ... and God, well, he'd just have to deal with Him later.

"My father and I don't discuss much," he finally said, thinking he'd successfully rid himself of his licentious thoughts.

"Why not?" Lilli's eyes probed deeply into Zane's.

"Why are you asking me these questions? I don't really know you—and these are private matters ..."

"It's okay." Lilli reached out her hand and touched his arm. Zane snatched his hand back.

"Jesus! I didn't burn you. All I did was touch you!"

"I'm sorry ..." Zane felt like a caged animal, he was so uncomfortable. Something was happening to him he did not understand, and he wanted to get away from Lilli—fast. "I think I'll go in the house and get a Pepsi."

"I'll get it for you. You wait out here," Lilli offered and sprinted toward the house. She rushed inside and raced to the new side-by-side refrigerator. She grabbed a Pepsi and slammed the door shut. When she whirled around to open the junk drawer for the bottle opener, she came face-to-face with the only woman at the party who had not used one and a half cans of hairspray.

"You *must* be Zane's mother!" Lilli blurted out.

"Yes, I am. How did you know?"

Lilli rolled her eyes. "I'm a good guesser." She stuck out her hand and shook Hannah McAllister's hand. "I'm Lilli Mitchell. You've got a fine son there, Mrs. McAllister," she said, sounding more like J.C. than J.C. himself.

Hannah gave a light, tinkling laugh, the kind Lilli hated, since it revealed a tendency toward timidity. Lilli was afraid she was not going to like Zane McAllister's mother. And that was too bad, she told herself, because Zane was going to be important to her someday.

"Thank you, Lilli. I'm very proud of Zane. He's one of God's finest. I don't tell this to many people, but he reminds me of an angel. Sweet and so devoted to our dear Lord."

"He is," Lilli agreed.

"I hope my Zane is not monopolizing all your time, Lilli. If he does, you just let me know. I understand that you have other guests to see to."

Lilli noticed that when Hannah smiled, her lips were tightly pulled over her teeth, and the corners of her mouth twitched ever so slightly. To Lilli, those involuntary actions were a sign that Zane's mother was lying. Lilli couldn't help but wonder why. "I'm fine, Mrs. McAllister. Zane isn't bothering me and I don't have other guests. This is my parents' party, not mine."

Hannah's smile vanished and her eyes became serious. "Just the same, I don't think he should take up all your time," she said adamantly.

Lilli couldn't help pushing just a little more. "I'd better get back. I told Zane I'd get him a Pepsi." She started toward the door. "Gee, Mrs. McAllister, Zane is such a great-looking guy." Then she rushed out the door.

Zane was waiting for Lilli beneath the wisteria arbor. She handed him the soft drink. "So, now. Tell me about your father."

"He's sick." Zane took a deep, long drink of the Pepsi, then continued. "That's why we're here and he's not. He's having some tests done at M.D. Anderson Hospital. We aren't staying long. We have to get back to see him."

"Zane, I'm so sorry. I hope it's nothing serious. Really."

Zane looked at her and realized that she was sincere. He allowed himself the luxury of gazing into her eyes. Once again he felt as if he were falling under a spell and he wasn't sure he wanted to recover. "Thanks," was all he could say.

"If you ever want to just . . . well, talk, you know you can call me."

"I'd like that," he said.

"Zane!" Hannah's voice rang out over the heads of the guests who were seated at the tables. "Oh, Zane! There you are!" She flapped her arm at her son.

Lilli watched the light vanish from Zane's eyes. His shoulders drooped. There was something going on between Zane and his mother that made no sense to Lilli.

Zane gave his mother an unenthusiastic wave. "Hi, Mom."

"Zane, I believe that you've taken enough of your hostess's time." Hannah turned toward Lilli, and with a chill of chastisement ringing through her words, she said, "We'll be going. Nice to meet you."

Hannah grabbed Zane's hand as if he were two years old and started across the lawn. To save face, Zane snatched his hand back, but he kept up with his mother. Then once they were on the other side of the yard, he turned to look at Lilli.

Lilli couldn't help but think he looked like a young Greek youth of mythology. Not a god like his mother thought, but one of those healthy athletic types who trained all day and then sat around on cushions listening to words of wisdom flow from Homer's lips.

She knew instinctively something had happened to them that day in that tiny stretch of time that had not happened to her with Paul or any other boy. She felt connected to Zane on a level that went as deep as her soul. They both had years of growing up before they would know who they were and what they wanted, but Lilli knew as she stood beneath the wisterias that Zane was worth waiting for. She hoped he felt the same about her.

He raised his hand to her and smiled. It was a crooked smile filled half with sadness and half with a touch of wickedness that did not fit Hannah's description of her "angel." Lilli could only imagine Zane's difficulties with his overly righteous mother. She returned a confident smile, and then he turned and walked away.

Suddenly it hit her. Zane was the blond man she'd seen in her dream while at Copán.

Seven

*L*illi crossed her arms behind her head and watched the summer night sky as the first of the bicentennial fireworks shimmered over Houston. Showers of gold, green, red, blue, and silver lights burst into fountains, stars, and spinning pinwheels, but Lilli was barely aware of their beauty. Her mind was filled with Zane McAllister.

Smack! Slap! Smack! Faith Geary, Lilli's cousin, swatted at the mosquitoes, killing only half the blood-sucking invaders. "Damn! I hate mosquitoes!" Faith dug in her yellow-and-white-striped canvas tote bag for her can of Off! She began spraying her exposed arms and legs, her neck, and even the air around her. She sprayed the blanket she shared with her cousin and accidentally squirted Lilli in the face.

"Hey! Watch it with that stuff!" Lilli said, waving the fumes from her eyes.

Faith frowned. "How come you never get bitten?"

"Mind control, Faith. I don't believe in mosquitoes. It's a trick I learned from Jose on a dig."

"That's bullshit!"

"Yeah? Well, they don't seem to be bothering me. I never get mosquito bites."

Faith tossed her long honey-colored hair over her shoulder and raised her chin in a haughty gesture. "I think you're full of it, Lilli. I think you get bitten just as much as I do. You're just too stubborn or proud to admit it."

"That could be true, too, Faith. However, wearing shorts and a sleeveless blouse to the fireworks like you did was not a wise move. What were you thinking?" Lilli prodded Faith mercilessly. Faith would be sixteen in August and she was everything that Lilli was not. Faith was blond, whereas Lilli was brunette. Faith was all girl and loved girl clothes and girl talk, whereas Lilli would rather talk about her near escape from an anaconda in the Bolivian forests. Faith had never performed a single athletic feat in her life, because she believed that "only boys do those things." Faith's one and only goal in life was to become a wife and a mother. The only reason she would even consider going to college was because she'd heard from older sisters of her high school friends that colleges were filled with men. She was already talking about going to SMU, where the ratio was three boys to one girl.

Faith admitted defeat. "You have a point."

Lilli laughed softly and patted her cousin's arm affectionately. "You're okay, Faith. You don't mind so much when I tease you. I've got to give you credit for that." She looked away from Faith and back to the sky.

Faith settled back on the blanket and watched the sky. "Have you seen Paul lately?" she asked.

Suddenly Lilli remembered that she had not seen Paul all day. Her mind had been so filled with thoughts of Zane that there had been no room for Paul. She wondered what he had felt, if anything, when he'd seen the line of cars in front of her house. Had he even cared that he and his parents were not invited? Did he have other plans? Had they chosen to go out of town for the holiday?

What is happening to me? Lilli wondered. Yesterday she would have defended Paul to the death, and today she'd forgotten he existed. For the first time she put her relationship, or lack of one, with Paul into perspective. Paul did not care about her. She was not important to him. It wasn't that there was something wrong with her or that she annoyed him; it was simply that Paul had his mind filled with other things. She was not important to him. And it was okay. It was *okay!*

Lilli couldn't believe what she was thinking. It was okay, she said to herself again. The reason it was okay was that in her own mind she'd replaced Paul with Zane. Her father had been right when he'd told her that Paul was just a crush, an infatuation. If she could so easily replace him, then he must not have been important.

Lilli watched the fireworks fill the sky with color and then descend. She was sure that the lights would fall on her, but at the final moment they extinguished themselves. It was like being lost in the stars, she thought.

Lilli was not sure if her reasoning about Paul was accurate or not, but she did know that what she was feeling for Zane was far more powerful than anything she'd felt about Paul. Her small inner voice told her that Zane felt something for her. It wasn't anything he'd said or done, but there'd been a particular knowing in his eyes that made her believe she had made an impression on him. Lilli ignored the silvery shower of lights above and turned her head toward Faith.

"Faith?"

"Yeah?"

"Do you think love has to be returned in order to be experienced?"

Faith dropped her jaw, then slowly smiled and closed her mouth. "Where did you hear that?"

"I don't know. I think Pop read it to me once. Shelley, I think. Maybe Browning. Anyway, what do you think?"

Faith's smile was warm and sincere. "I never thought I would hear you, of all people, ask that question. But yes, I don't think it's love unless somebody loves you back."

"Why is that?"

"Because love is supposed to be exchanged. Like Christmas gifts. It's more noble to give than to receive, but what's the fun in that—all the time, I mean."

"Have you ever loved anybody and they didn't love you back, Faith?"

"Sure. Most of the time."

"I don't get it. You're pretty and boys like girly girls like you."

Faith looked down and smoothed the blanket. "Boys can be very cruel sometimes, Lilli. Sometimes they tell you things and then change their minds. They see another girl and they want her. Then another and another."

Lilli touched her cousin's arm. She let her hand rest on the smooth, suntanned skin. "Is that why you broke up with Billy?"

Faith nodded. "Know what I think?"

"Uh-uh."

"I think girls can keep a boy only until he finds someone better. And they always find someone better. It's just a matter of time."

Lilli was sure that Faith was not telling her everything. "That's bullshit, Faith."

"Lilli, must you always swear?"

"Yes, goddamn it, and so do you. You're just changing the subject."

"I know."

"Why? You're acting like a wimp, Faith. You act like all a girl is supposed to do is live for a boy, any boy, to come along. Jesus! What *kind* of boy do you want? Haven't you picked one out, just for yourself?"

"Well, yes, I have, but ... but ..."

"But what? What's the goddamn problem, Faith?" Lilli was growing agitated. She sat up Indian-style on the blanket and confronted her cousin. "Well?"

"I sorta have."

"What's 'sorta' mean? Either you have or you haven't! It's as simple as that."

Faith sat up and assumed the same position. "I wish I could make life as simple as you do, Lilli. You always think there's an answer to everything."

"There *is* a goddamn answer to everything. Some answers are tougher to get, but they're there."

Faith reached out and touched her cousin's cheek. "You're very young, Lilli."

"You're only a year older, Faith," Lilli retorted.

"I know. But I hope that life always remains this simple for you."

"It will," Lilli replied, crossing her arms over her chest resolutely.

"It won't." Faith looked down at the blanket again and then back up to Lilli. "I've been seeing Paul Newsome."

Suddenly the sky was illuminated with one giant firecracker going off after another. It was the finale. Usually Lilli loved this final extravaganza of light and sound. But now the explosion seemed to come from a dark place in her brain. She felt her body go numb. She watched as the brightly illuminated face of her favorite cousin turned into a scaly monster. She felt cold, then hot, then cold again as waves of hate, pain, and anger rode over her. All that she was seemed negated. Trust and love, those thick, heavy bonds she and Faith had built since childhood, unraveled in a flash.

"Lilli, I had to tell you," Faith said tentatively.

Lilli continued to stare at Faith. She quickly rewound the tape of their conversation and then played it again. She wanted to know the instant of the betrayal. However, as Lilli thought about it, she realized that only moments before Faith's revelation, she herself had put Paul to rest.

Lilli had to admit that she was not in love with Paul. In fact, she felt a great deal for a boy she'd met only that day. She realized that she was jealous of Faith for many things. She was jealous that Faith could make Paul fall for her in a way that Lilli did not understand. She wanted to hate Faith because of what she'd done, but she couldn't. After all, it wasn't as if she were dating Paul. He'd never shown the least bit of interest in her romantically. Lilli had to admire Faith's honesty, if nothing else.

"How long?" Lilli simply had to know.

"Well, we haven't even had an official date yet. I saw him at the library at the end of the school year and he's called me a few times. Then he came over last week and we watched *M*A*S*H* together. I told him I had to talk to you first before we went any further."

"Oh, shit, Faith!" Lilli slapped the side of her cheek. "You didn't! Tell me you didn't really say that!"

"Not exactly in those words."

"Exactly in what words?" Lilli asked pleadingly.

"I just told him I had something to clear up." Suddenly realization flickered in Faith's eyes. "Oh, I get it! You didn't want him to know you liked him."

Lilli shook her head. "You're slow sometimes, Faith. But yeah, I would be real embarrassed."

"You've got to believe me, Lilli. I would never do anything like that to you."

"Thank God."

"So do you hate me terribly? I don't want you to be mad at me, but . . . I really do like him, Lilli, and I think he likes me."

Lilli realized that Paul was already a great deal more important in Faith's life than he had ever been in her own. Her life was filled with so many different goals, hopes, notions, and needs. She was already thinking about her next dig—South America. She had a lot of reading and research on the

Incan Indians to do this summer to prepare herself. And there was this interesting new boy she'd met . . .

"It's okay," Lilli finally said.

Faith heaved a deep sigh. "Thank God! I was so afraid. I know what a crush you had on him . . ."

"That's been over for a while," Lilli said, brushing the edge of the truth.

"Honestly? You're not just saying that to make me feel better, are you?"

"No. Actually, I've met somebody else."

"You're kidding."

"No. Really. And you know, Faith, it's all very strange how it happened. I mean, I sort of gave Paul up tonight, before you said anything about him, I mean. And it was because I met Zane. He's very different. But I don't know how." Then suddenly Lilli laughed. "He must be different—he likes me!"

Faith playfully punched Lilli in the arm and laughed along with her. "Now look who's being insecure!"

Lilli sobered for an instant and then looked up at the sky. The fireworks were gone save for long trails of black smoke where the lights had once been. The crowds were rolling up their blankets and taking their folding lawn chairs back to their cars. Only the stars remained in the sky. Some were brilliant, others dim and small. "The fireworks are over."

"For this year, yes," Faith said wistfully.

Lilli continued to gaze out into the galaxy. "I guess in a way we're all insecure, huh, Faith?"

"Yes, we are. It's just a matter of degree that separates us from the gods."

Lilli turned toward Faith. "Where did you hear that?"

"I don't know." She shrugged her shoulders. "Why?"

Lilli moved closer to her cousin and put an arm around her shoulder, and then they both looked up to the stars. "To be honest, it sounded too smart to come from you."

"Oh, Lilli." Faith laughed.

"Oh, Faith."

July 22, 1976

Lilli awoke on her birthday to the sound of her mother's voice.

"Lilli. Lilli, wake up."

Lilli was dreaming that she was being lowered down the center of a Mayan pyramid. There were snakes and skeletons all around her. She could hear her father's voice as he yelled instructions down to her. Lilli clung tightly to the hemp rope with one hand and held a Coleman lantern in the other. She had never been so frightened. Just as she was about to put her foot down on an interior staircase that ran up the far side of the pyramid, the dream began to fade. She heard her mother's voice.

"What are you doing here, Mom?" Lilli asked, sitting up and rubbing her eyes. She opened her eyes, blinked, and then looked at her mother. "How did you get here?"

"Where?"

"In the pyramid . . ." Lilli looked around her and found she was in her bedroom. She smiled sheepishly. "I was dreaming, huh?"

Arlette did not smile back. She was in a hurry. She checked her new Rolex. "I've got to go or I'll be late for my luncheon at the River Oaks Country Club."

"Lunch? Isn't it a little early?"

"You overslept. It's eleven-thirty. But since it was your birthday, I thought I'd let you sleep." Arlette smoothed the skirt of her summer Adolfo suit. She carried a new cream-colored leather purse with a long gold chain. "Anyway, there's a phone call for you," she said a bit testily. "It's Zane McAllister."

"Jesus, Mom! Why didn't you say so?" Lilli shot out of bed and stumbled over the books she'd dropped on the floor beside her bed.

"Lilli, please don't swear." Arlette followed her down the stairs, taking them one by one while Lilli nearly flew. "I want to know all about Zane when I get back." She wagged a finger at her daughter.

"I'm sorry my call disturbed you, Mom," Lilli said, picking up the receiver in the kitchen and giving her mother a quick peck on the cheek.

Arlette raised an authoritarian eyebrow. "I mean it, Lilli. When I get home . . ."

"Okay! Okay!" Lilli said and waited until Arlette was out the door.

"Hello?" Lilli told herself the rapid pounding of her heart was from her run downstairs, not from the anticipation of talking to Zane again.

"Happy birthday, Lilli," Zane said.

"You knew it was my birthday?"

"Yes. Why else would I be calling?"

To talk to me. To tell me how you are. To tell me where you've been for the past three weeks. "How did you know? Did I tell you this?"

"No. Your father told me. So I thought I would surprise you."

"You did that, all right," she replied. "When did you see Pop?"

"Last week. I had some work to do for my father. One of my jobs was to see your father at Antiquities."

"How is your father doing?"

"Better. It was cancer, you know."

"No, I didn't," she said softly.

"It's better now. He's taking chemotherapy and some radiation treatments. It makes him really sick. He can't do much about the business this summer, so Mother and I have our hands full."

"I guess you do. What kind of business does he have?"

"Antique jewelry. That's why I needed to see your father. I was thinking. Since I have to come to Houston today to show some pieces to one of your father's clients, I was wondering if you'd like to have dinner with me. I know that since it's your birthday, you probably have some big party planned . . ."

"Actually, I don't. No plans at all."

"You're kidding. You had such a big blowout for the Fourth that I thought—"

"That was different. That was a social thing. My birthday is highly unsocial. Mom doesn't get into birthdays too much. Besides, I'm only fifteen. It's not a big deal like being sweet sixteen or anything," Lilli said with a caustic edge to her voice. "And I've already told her I don't want a sweet-sixteen party next year. The only reason she'd throw one would be because her society friends think it's the thing to do."

"I'm sorry, Lilli."

"It's okay. I'm used to it. Anyway, we celebrated last night. Pop took us to Tony's for dinner."

"Is that a big deal?"

"Was for my mom. She spent half the night waving to and smooching her friends. Pop and I talked about making some more trips together. He wants to go to South America someday, but we're definitely going to Mexico in the spring."

"I'd love to hear all about it. So you can see me tonight?"

"Sure!" she said enthusiastically. Then she hesitated for a moment. "Can I ask you something, Zane?"

"Anything."

"Are you asking me out because I'm the only person you know in Houston?"

Zane laughed. "Well, that is true."

"That's what I thought."

"Lilli, I wanted to see you again. Okay?"

"Okay," she replied softly. "I'll see you tonight. What time?"

"Seven, if that's okay. You pick the place. Just remember I only have twenty bucks. And afterward I have to drive back to Bandera. I have to be here in case my dad needs me."

"Seven is fine, and I understand about your dad," Lilli said.

"I know. That's what I like about you, Lilli."

Zane drove a black Ford pickup that was caked with Bandera dirt and dust. He pulled up in front of Lilli's house at precisely seven o'clock. Lilli checked her watch. He was not a second too early or too late.

She went to the door and opened it.

He was dressed in Western-cut Levi's and a white, blue, and gray plaid long-sleeved shirt. He wore brown-and-tan boots, a Western belt with a silver buckle, and a black cowboy hat. The minute the door opened, he whisked his hat off his head. Lilli had never seen anyone her age make that gesture. She smiled at him and he beamed back at her.

"Evenin', Lilli," he said in the hill country's drawl.

"Come in, Zane," she replied.

When he walked past her into the foyer, she could smell his sandalwood cologne. He seemed to have grown taller since she'd seen him, but that was impossible, she thought. It had only been three weeks. Then she realized that his boots had two-inch heels. Still, there was something different about him. Were his shoulders wider? Was his stance more assured?

"You look good," she said appreciatively.

"Hey, that's my line," he said with a smile that was much too charming for Lilli to trust.

Lilli was unused to boy-and-girl games, except for flag football, and she was uncertain about her next move. Suddenly she realized she would rather be his friend than his girlfriend if it meant they couldn't be honest with each other. "I'd better tell my mom we're leaving."

"I'll go with you," he offered.

"Nah. It's okay."

Lilli left Zane and went to the kitchen, where her mother was showing the new maid how to sauté mushrooms. Her father had just pulled into the driveway and was entering the house through the French doors in the kitchen.

"Pop!" Lilli exclaimed and ran to her father, who gave her a hug.

"How's my girl?" He kissed her cheek. "I saw Zane's truck out front—"

"He's here?" Arlette interrupted over the maid's Spanish chatter. "Lilli, I told you to tell me the minute he got here."

"Geez, Mom. You said you were busy. I thought you had that big thing tonight."

"We do. But I *have* to show Maria how to make this cooked salad for the luncheon I'm giving tomorrow."

Lilli rolled her eyes. "Not another one."

Arlette patted a stray hair back into her chignon. "You would do well to meet some of these women, Lilli."

Lilli kissed her father's cheek. "I've got to go. Zane can't stay in town, and it's a long drive back to Bandera tonight."

"J.C." Arlette addressed her husband with the spatula still in her hand. "Go make sure that boy knows all the rules. I don't want him keeping Lilli out too late. And make sure he knows not to drive too fast."

J.C. patted his wife's shoulder. "Don't worry. I gave him the routine this afternoon."

"You've spoken with him?"

"Yes, Arlette. After all, he came here to sell some jet and platinum pieces to one of my clients. He's definitely not here to deflower our daughter."

J.C. put his arm around Lilli's shoulder and walked with her into the foyer. Lilli knew that her father was trying to ease her mother's mind, but somehow his words made Lilli feel less special.

"Zane!" J.C. shook Zane's hand heartily, as if they were long-lost compatriots. "Remember what I said today. If you have any other intact sets of the quality you showed me, I think we can do a great deal of business together."

"I certainly hope so, sir."

"I must say I was impressed with your knowledge about stones. You have an uncanny eye for quality. It's unusual for someone your age."

"My father says he's taught me all he knows. I believe he's an expert in his field."

"He is, but I find it interesting that he never did anything more with it." J.C. stopped himself. "I didn't mean that the way it sounded. It's just that, well, I've been dealing with gemologists and gem dealers in New York, Dallas, and Houston all my life, and I've never understood why your father didn't move to New York to work."

"My mother wouldn't let him," Zane said frankly.

J.C. looked at Lilli and then back at Zane. "I see. Well, you two have fun. Happy birthday, sweetie." J.C. hugged his daughter again.

"Thanks, Pop," Lilli said and then turned to lead Zane to the door.

Zane pulled the truck up to the third order stand at Prince's Drive-In. He turned off the ignition, leaned back in the seat, and looked at Lilli, a baffled expression on his face.

"This is your favorite place to eat?"

"Yes."

"You can't be serious."

"I am. My parents would never bring me here. Mother would have to take me to Tony's or Rudy's. Pop would always opt for Molina's or Ninfa's. But I just felt like a hamburger, and this is the best in Houston. Besides, it's fast, and you said you've got to get back to your father."

"That's true."

"So quit bellyaching and order." She laughed.

Zane continued to stare at Lilli for the longest time. It was so long, in fact, that Lilli grew self-conscious.

"What's the matter?" she asked.

He gave her a bemused smile. "Nothing. I was just wondering how it is that you can be only fifteen, and yet when I look at you, you seem much older to me."

Lilli looked down at her chest, which had not grown even a quarter inch since she met Zane (she knew because she'd measured), then lifted her face to his. "I don't think so."

"It's your eyes, Lilli." Zane lifted his arm and stretched it out on the back of the seat. He leaned closer to her, although there was nothing aggressive in his move. "Since the day we met, I haven't been able to get you out of my mind. I know this sounds really stupid, you being a kid and all."

"Hey! I'm fifteen today!"

"I know. There's a big difference between fifteen and seventeen, which is what I'll be one month from today. Don't you think it's weird that we're exactly two years and one month to the day apart?"

"Not particularly. No."

"Well, I do." He looked down at her hand and picked it up. He held it for just a moment, rubbing his thumb along the side of her index finger. Then he gently replaced her hand on her lap. "Do you believe in destiny, Lilli?"

Lilli had no idea where Zane was leading with all these strange questions. Why wasn't he asking her about her favorite rock groups? Did she like jalapeño pizza? Was she any good at swimming or scuba diving? (She was.) Didn't he want to know about her likes and dislikes? She'd read every issue of *Seventeen* magazine for two years and they always said that was how you kept the conversation going on a date. Didn't he know anything about the rules?

"What kind of destiny, Zane?"

"Like the kind they talk about in the Bible. That certain things are meant to be, and no matter what you do or don't do, they will happen to you."

Lilli's face betrayed her bewilderment. "I wasn't raised in

any religion, Zane. And I go to a private school. We aren't exactly into reading the Bible."

"You do believe in Jesus Christ, don't you?"

"Sure."

A look of relief crossed Zane's face. "Good. That's real important to my mother."

Just then the carhop came to take their order. "What'll it be, sir?" the redheaded girl asked.

"I'll have a cheeseburger, fries, and a chocolate shake. What do you want, Lilli?"

"The same."

Lilli waited while Zane finished giving instructions to the waitress about his condiments. She couldn't help wondering what kind of relationship he had with his mother. He seemed like a fairly normal boy, but then he came out with these weird religious comments that made no sense to her.

Lilli had been raised by a father who pushed her to probe, question, rethink, and analyze not only the present and her place in the present but also history, ancient civilizations, and their mores and religions. J.C. constantly told Lilli to use her own mind and never to take his word or anyone else's word for gospel. He said that every great thinker on this earth, including Martin Luther, asked on his deathbed, "What if I was wrong?" Lilli always remembered that, and it helped her to think about other people and their perspectives. J.C. said it was her best quality. It made up for the cursing.

"Are you and your mother close, Zane?" Lilli couldn't help but ask. That one time she met Mrs. McAllister, Lilli had thought she was very controlling.

"I guess so. Yeah. I would say that. Not as close as my dad and I, though."

"Tell me what your mother does that you like best."

"She's a good cook . . ."

Lilli playfully slapped him on the arm. "Not *that* kind of thing. I mean qualities—things that really help you out."

Just then their food arrived. Zane paid the bill, then handed Lilli her burger and fries. Lilli dipped each French fry into the chocolate shake before eating it.

"Ugh! That's disgusting!" Zane said. "Do you always eat your fries like that?"

"Not in front of my mother. As you've probably guessed,

my mother and I don't get along. Sometimes I can't wait to get out of the house. I go on digs with Pop and we have great times. We see things *you* can only dream of, Zane McAllister. But my mom and me, we butt heads all day. She doesn't think like me and Pop. She's just different, and if I tried to be like her, I'd go nuts."

"But she's your mother. You have to do what she says and love her. It's your duty."

"Bullshit!" Lilli said and instantly slammed her hand over her mouth when she saw Zane's shocked look. "Sorry," she said. She sank her teeth into her cheeseburger and chewed quietly.

Zane said nothing for a long time as he munched on his fries and cheeseburger. He'd never met anyone like Lilli. She was one contradiction after another: she was at once a child and a seductive temptress; she had the eyes of a vixen and the body of a boy; she was irreverent and yet logical; she cursed, but her voice was like that of an angel.

Lilli took his lifetime of perfectly formed rules and commandments and chucked them out the window. She made him think and reflect. With only one or two sharply phrased questions, she had unearthed more of his inner self than he was willing to examine.

"I don't care if you're mad at me, Zane," Lilli finally announced with false conviction.

"I'm not mad."

"Oh. Well, then. I'm glad about that."

"You are?"

"Yeah. I like you, Zane. I think you should just think about yourself a little bit more. Maybe you should be thinking about what you want to do, not what your mother wants you to do."

Zane winced. Lilli had a knack for getting to the heart of a situation. But he didn't want to talk about his mother, and he quickly changed the subject. "You're so smart. What are you going to do with your life?"

"Me? I'm going to be an archaeologist. I'm going to make a great discovery that will help mankind figure out what the hel—heck he's doing on this planet. That's what."

"Oh, you are?"

"I am," she said, smiling confidently. "My pop is going to show me how. I'm learning a lot all the time."

Zane wiped his hands on his napkin and then tossed it onto the tray that was attached to the driver's side window. He moved closer to Lilli. "I like it when you talk like that, Lilli."

"You do?"

He nodded. His blue eyes had grown smoky, she thought, or was it the lack of fluorescent lighting at this end of the drive-in? "Uh-huh," he said and took her empty milkshake container and papers and put them on the tray. "You're learning a lot very fast, aren't you, Lilli?"

Lilli was losing her assurance as he edged even closer. His arm moved to the top of her shoulders. His face was very near hers. Zane was going to kiss her, she thought.

"Has anyone ever kissed you before?" he asked as if he'd read her mind.

"Sure. Lots."

"Good," he said and pressed his lips to hers.

It was a soft kiss, a friendly kiss, without any of the passion Lilli had dreamed would accompany her first kiss. She'd seen enough movies and soap operas to know that there was supposed to be a lot of heavy breathing and both parties were supposed to act as if they were eating each other alive. But this was different. She felt as if she were floating and moving to another realm. She liked the feel of his lips against hers. She liked it very much.

He put both of his arms around her and held her, although he didn't pull her close. It was as if he were securing her to the spot, letting her react on her own and yet still making certain she would not run away.

Lilli's lips tingled, and then suddenly the tingling sensation shot through her body. She pressed her lips into his. She slipped her hand around his neck and let her fingers settle into the silky hair at his nape. She began feeling unfamiliar palpitations deep inside her that frightened her. She found that as her body came alive, her mind appeared to die.

Suddenly he pulled away.

She blinked at him.

He smiled. "You liked my kiss," he said triumphantly with a twinkle of male roguishness in his eyes.

"I hated it!"

"What? How can you say that? You were kissing me back."

Lilli crossed her arms over her chest. "Just as I figured. You haven't been kissed all that much either, Zane McAllister."

"I most certainly have. I've done it hundreds of times."

Lilli's violet eyes flamed. "Whoever has been kissing you isn't all that good, I can tell you that," she said with a self-satisfied pout.

Zane didn't know which would explode first, his mind or his body. On the one hand, he wanted to kiss Lilli's beautiful mouth all night long, and on the other hand, he wanted to show her that he didn't want her any more than she wanted him.

He slid back to his side of the pickup and without another word turned on the headlights so that the carhop would remove the tray. As soon as it had been picked up, Zane turned the key in the ignition and backed out of the drive-in. "I should have known better than to kiss a child."

"I'm not a child."

Zane kept his eyes on the road as he turned the corner and raced through the yellow caution light. Part of him wanted to take her back home and never see her again, but he knew that was impossible. If it weren't for J.C. Mitchell, Zane could not raise the money he needed to pay his father's doctor bills. Zane was going to see a lot of J.C. in the coming months. He needed J.C.'s contacts, clients, and expertise to pave the road for his own future. But all that aside, Lilli haunted him. He dreamed about her. He thought about her. He struggled to get her face out of his mind. But nothing worked. He had wanted to kiss her since the day he met her. Now that he had, he could honestly say that the experience was incredible. Maybe she was nothing more than just another girl, but then again, maybe she was part of his destiny.

He was bewildered by the fact that her criticism of him cut him so deeply. He'd had other girls turn him down for dates and it never mattered. He could not understand why Lilli was so important to him. The only course of action that made any sense to him was to run. Fast.

They were both silent on the ride back. When Zane pulled

the truck to a stop in front of Lilli's house, he said, "I'll walk you to the door."

"Don't bother!" Lilli said and jerked the door open.

Zane reached out and grabbed her hand. "I'm sorry, Lilli. I didn't want it to be like this. I-I—"

"You what, Zane?"

"I want to be your friend."

"You've got a funny way of showing it!"

He continued to look at her and as he did, Lilli felt her anger dissipate. He smiled timidly. She smiled back. "Maybe you were right, Zane. Maybe it's because I'm still a kid. Maybe we're just supposed to be friends . . . nothing else." She squeezed his hand.

He nodded reluctantly, knowing that wasn't the answer, either. "Yeah."

"Next time you come to Houston, let's talk. Okay?"

"Okay," he agreed, and she leaned over and kissed his cheek. She let her lips rest for a moment longer than friends do, which made him want to kiss her again. He fought the impulse and let her leave.

Lilli went inside and bounded up the stairs to her room. She did not turn on the light, but went to the window and pulled the curtain back. Zane had not left, which she knew somehow that he wouldn't. He was watching her window. She lifted her hand and waved to him. She wasn't sure, but she thought he returned the wave. The truck pulled slowly away from the curb.

Lilli stood at the window watching him go. She was only fifteen years old, but she knew that she had fallen in love that night. They still barely knew each other, but she believed that he felt the same way about her. Their timing was off this time, she thought. Yes, that was all that was wrong. Timing. But that would change.

Eight

Fall, 1976

*T*hroughout the fall, Zane and Lilli wrote to each other weekly. Lilli kept all Zane's letters tied together with a piece of braided leather from Mexico her father had given her. Lilli made it her "job" to retrieve the mail every day before her mother came back from lunch in River Oaks or a shopping trip with friends. Lilli could count on her mother to be gone from the house nearly every day until four or five o'clock. Thus, Arlette was unaware, as was J.C., about the existence of the letters from Zane McAllister.

In her letters to Zane, Lilli felt free enough to tell him about her dreams of becoming a great archaeologist. She told him about her unusual reading list, which included everything from von Däniken's works to specific articles in *National Geographic* and the *Smithsonian* magazine. Lilli read numerous books on the Mayan Indians, the Anasazi, and the Hopi. She was fascinated by Indian lore and rituals. She understood the Indians' bond with nature and the environment because she herself felt more alive when she was outdoors. Like her father, Lilli understood tales of water spirits, the voices in the wind and trees, and the vibrations in the earth. She wrote to Zane about these deeply felt beliefs of hers, but she noticed that he seldom commented on them other than to state that he loved her "natural qualities."

Zane's letters to her often mentioned his desire to go out into the world and seek his fortune. She didn't want to read these sections, and many times she passed them over, but soon tiny seeds of doubt about her future with Zane began to take root.

Dear Lilli,

I found a terrific article in the latest issue of Forbes *about the great potential in the antique jewelry market. I've noticed that even my dad's best clients are now from New York, when only a year ago they came mostly from Dallas or Houston. I think it would be so neat to see New York. I think it would be even more exciting to live in New York. What do you think?*

School is going great. But my dad isn't doing so well. He seems really tired these days. I'm afraid it's the cancer, not the chemotherapy.

I miss you. I'll try to call you Saturday night for our "date."

Love,
Zane

Lilli's reply to this letter and others like it was from the heart.

Dear Zane,

School seems slow and kind of dull to me this semester because all I can think about is going to Mexico with my pop in the spring. He's got such an exciting trip planned for us. I'll tell you about it over the phone, since the details would take forever to write down.

About this New York thing. Don't you think it's kind of dangerous there? I've heard all kinds of stories about that city. It's too big for my taste. But I suppose it's the kind of excitement that would make you happy. Me, I'm different. I really like being in wild and remote places. Places where modern man hasn't gone for hundreds of years . . . even thousands of years. I like discovering things that nobody would even think to look for. I guess I get that from my pop. I bet if you ever went on a dig with me and Pop, you'd like it, too. What do you think?

I miss you, Zane.

Love,
Lilli

Although they didn't realize what was happening, both Lilli and Zane were struggling to influence the other. They both were too individualistic and too young to know how to blend their dreams into one. Neither of them could see the pitfalls in front of them.

By late fall, Lilli had prepared herself for the dig at Yaxchilán, near Guatemala. New information about the Maya and their glyphs was coming to the surface. No longer did archaeological experts believe that the glyphs dealt exclusively with the mechanism and mythology of time. During the late fifties and through the sixties, Mayanist Tatiana Proskouri-akoff, at the time with the Carnegie Institution of Washington, D.C., found patterns in the glyphs that suggested a record of milestones in the lives of individuals. Once this hypothesis was tested, it proved itself out.

Suddenly the race was on to decipher the Mayan hieroglyphics. What had once been the largest puzzle uncovered by modern man was now being solved. The process was a slow and painstaking one.

J.C. was going to Yaxchilán to assist on a dig sponsored by the University of Pennsylvania, the National Geographic Society, and the Royal British Museum. J.C. had spent weeks on the telephone with experts in the field. Never before had Lilli heard the names of famous archaeologists being uttered in the Mitchell household so often: William R. Coe, John Howland Rowe, Dr. Joseph W. Ball of San Diego State University, a ceramicist whom J.C. greatly respected, and Dr. E. Wyllys Andrews IV of Tulane University.

Lilli didn't know what was happening to her father, but suddenly he'd become more intense about his work. He slept at his desk many nights waiting for phone calls from London. He started talking in riddles and half thoughts to Lilli when she would probe him for answers. Sometimes she thought he did not want her around, but that wasn't so. He would entreat her to read in the burgundy leather chair near the window in his study, but he seldom talked to her the way he had the previous summer.

"We're on the verge," he would say to himself while taking notes from his reading.

"The verge of what?" Lilli asked.

"Of it all." J.C. would not raise his head from his notations, but continued reading and marking maps. He was so absorbed in his work that Lilli noted he would not bother to eat the sandwiches she brought in or drink the Coronas she poured for him.

When she commented about his behavior to her mother, Arlette would shrug her shoulders and say, "He's always been like that, Lilli. It's just that now you're old enough to see it. You're seeing him with the eyes of an adult and not a child. All J.C. has ever cared about is his damn Maya. Dead people. What good are they?" Then Arlette would dash out the door, hop into her Cadillac, and rush off to another afternoon of shopping.

Lilli felt like an outsider in her own home. Worse, she felt rejected by her father. Lilli, as usual, believed the only way to solve the problem was to meet it head-on.

"Pop, you have to talk to me," she said one afternoon. She sat down on the chair in his study.

"About what?" he asked, glancing at her over the rim of his reading glasses.

Lilli knew he'd been spending too much time on this project, because he never needed reading glasses unless he was very tired. J.C. had not been out in the sun for a round of golf since August, and his tan was gone. But his eyes were on fire. His mind was working overtime and it was the zeal in his eyes that she responded to.

"What are we after, Pop? I've never seen you so concerned about a dig."

He peeled off the reading glasses and massaged the bridge of his nose. "I know. This one is important." He sighed heavily and she noticed the raspy, wheezing sound in his throat that reminded her of the time she had had bronchitis. She knew he detested her fawning over his health as if she were the parent and he were the child, and so she said nothing.

"Things are coming to light that I never imagined. The Mayan codes are being broken daily, and there are so many discoveries that I can hardly keep up with them. I'm torn between keeping Antiquities going and making history. It's fascinating. Truly."

"I know, Pop. I love it, too."

J.C. dropped his head and laughed lightly. "You're just a child, but you are so much like me, aren't you, Lilli?"

"You bet, Pop," she said proudly. "I can't think of anybody else in the whole world I'd want to be like . . . except maybe Joan of Arc."

He leaned back in his chair and gave his daughter a deeply scrutinizing look. His eyes widened. "Say, when did your hair get so long? And is that . . . lipstick I see?"

"Just some gloss, Pop. I was trying out a few things." She rose and walked over to him.

J.C. watched her move. He'd been wrong. Very wrong. Lilli wasn't a child anymore. What had happened to her over the past four months? She must have grown at least two inches and gained ten pounds. There was a curve to her hips he'd never seen before, and she definitely had sprouted breasts. What had he been doing that was so important that he'd missed the day his daughter had walked across the threshold of womanhood?

Suddenly he was nervous and found he could not formulate what he said to her as easily as he had twenty minutes earlier. Should he treat her differently now? Would she still want to go on this dig with him? Would they still have fun the way they always had? Would she still love him and call him Pop? How long would it be before all that, too, changed? How long before she left home, went to college, found a boy to love instead of him, and married? He was going to lose her, he could tell. She was growing up, and he didn't like it one single bit.

"Lilli," he said with determination to control the passage of time, "I want you to go with me to South America, some day. That has always been my dream," he said wistfully.

Lilli's eyes were as wide as saucers. "South America? I thought all this studying you've been doing was for our trip to Yaxchilán in Mexico."

"It is. But it goes further than that."

Lilli knew her father. He had a design, a well-thought-out plan to everything he did. "But why South America?" she asked, hoping he'd reveal more of his closely held secrets.

"I want to take a look-see. Not now, but sometime in the next two years. George withdrew his funding, so I'll have to find some other sponsors."

"You're after something, Pop. I know it," she said, staring into his burning eyes.

He leaned forward and met her gaze. "I am, Lilli. I'm pursuing something I never thought I had the courage or the time for. There are a great many things I've done that I'm not proud of, but maybe I can make up for it."

His remark completely baffled Lilli. As far as she was concerned, her father could do no wrong. He was J.C. Mitchell, after all. Everyone in Houston adored him. His business was very profitable . . . it had to be. Look at the way her mother spent his money. Lilli always wondered why her father never spent any money on himself. He didn't have a sports car or designer suits. He did buy a lot of books, but that was part of his business, she guessed. Her father was a noble man, Lilli told herself, and she wanted to be just like him.

"I think you're doing a super job, Pop. And of course I'll go to South America with you, whenever you want to go. But I'm really excited about our trip to Yaxchilán. We'll find all kinds of gold and stuff this time."

"No, Lilli. Not this time. I'm looking for other things. Clues to my theory. We'll look for the gold another time. Besides, I think the city of gold that Cortez and Pizarro were seeking is to be found in South America. I think it's in the Andes Mountains. All signs seem to point to it there. It's just a guess, but a well-educated one."

Lilli's violet eyes were earnest when she leveled them on him. "You really think there's a city of gold, Pop?"

"More than ever. And before I die, I'm going to find it. I think that one of the problems is that the academic community has closed its mind to many options and clues about the city of gold. I think too many of my learned colleagues aren't seeing a big enough picture. They're finding more incredible wonders that were built and formed by these ancient peoples like the Olmec, and instead of searching, really searching, for the answers by not ruling out any possibilities whatsoever, they're running down blind alleys. And then they say things like, 'Well, those ancients sure had a way of doing things. It's a mystery.' "

"Not good enough, huh?"

"Not at all. We're going to do it, Lilli. You and I," he said enthusiastically.

Lilli placed her hand on top of his and smiled warmly at her father. "Yeah. We sure will."

* * *

Lilli left the study and was headed toward the kitchen when her mother came down the stairs and stopped her. Lilli couldn't help thinking that her mother's face looked as if it had been cast in quick-set cement. The cold glint in her eyes told Lilli she was in trouble.

"I want to talk to you," Arlette commanded.

"Sure, Mom. What about?"

"About this!" From behind her back she produced an envelope that was addressed to Lilli. It was from Zane, and it had been opened.

Lilli's anger roiled inside her and she was unable to stanch its flow. "That's *my* letter." She pushed the words out between her clenched teeth. She kept her eyes on the letter. Until today she'd been successful in meeting the four o'clock mail delivery. Most of the time she was treated to disappointment, however. Zane was busy caring for his father's business, going to school, and spending time with his dying father. By now he'd fallen into a pattern of writing to Lilli every ten days or so. She wrote him two letters to his one. Her letters from Zane were sacred, and her mother had violated her privacy.

"How long has he been writing to you, Lilli?"

Lilli couldn't take her eyes off the mutilated envelope. "You broke the federal law," she said, still managing to keep her anger under control.

"Don't put this off on me. I asked you a question, young lady. What has been going on between you two?"

Lillie's violet eyes burned with anger. She was losing control. "You read the goddamn letter. Why don't you tell me!"

"I'm warning you, Lilli," Arlette snarled.

Lilli's arm shot out, and she snatched the letter from her mother. "Don't you ever, ever steal my mail again!" Lilli thundered up the stairs and slammed the door to her room.

J.C. came running out of his study as Arlette was staring up the stairs.

"What the hell is going on here?"

Arlette glared at him. "It's your precious daughter. It seems that she and Zane McAllister have grown quite close."

"What's the matter with that? Lilli is growing up, or haven't you noticed?"

Arlette put her hands on her hips. "I've noticed plenty. I caught her wearing one of my bras last week. And one of my cashmere sweaters. She's not a child anymore. And that's what worries me."

"So now you know what it's like to have the shoe on the other foot. Just last summer you were telling me that I was the one who was holding her back. She wasn't being enough of a girl for you."

"I meant she should acquire some manners and taste. Not a lover."

J.C.'s eyes widened in shock and his face went white. "She's been to bed with him?"

"Well, perhaps 'lover' was too strong, but it's very clear this Zane likes Lilli a lot."

"I don't blame him," J.C. said. "I think you're making too much of this, Arlette. Why can't you just let Lilli be? She can never do anything right for you. If she didn't have a boyfriend, you'd be upset about that. Now that she does, you're even more upset."

J.C. turned and started back toward the study; then suddenly he stopped and looked back at his wife. "I wonder . . . Maybe you're reacting like this, Arlette, because for the first time you can see that not only is Lilli going to be more beautiful than you, but she's really loved by many people. Maybe you should take a good look at yourself instead of prying into her life."

Arlette watched J.C. walk calmly into his study. "Bastard," she said, but her voice had lost its strength and the word died before it reached her husband's ears.

Dear Lilli,

I came to Houston yesterday and I tried to see you, but the maid said that you had gymnastics practice. How come you never told me about that? I think that is really great. I'll bet you're really good at all that tumbling and cartwheels and stuff. We've had some pretty stiff basketball practices already. Right now, most everybody in school is consumed with football fever, though.

I miss you, Lilli.

I can't believe I wrote that. When do you think you

can sneak away and see me next? It seems like forever since we went to Molina's last month. It has been a month! Wow! I've done a lot since then—at work, I mean. I've been working with a jewelry designer in Kerrville who is teaching me how to melt gold and design molds and then make the mountings for stones. I keep combing the area for buyers for my dad's antique jewelry collection, but in a way, my heart isn't in it, because I have this feeling that if I were in some place like New York, I could get a lot more money for these pieces.

I would love to show them to you. In fact, I have a favorite amethyst necklace set in old gold that would be really great on you. Every time I look at it, I think about your eyes.

I hope I get a letter from you soon.

> Love,
> Zane

Lilli reread her letter three times before getting up from her bed and putting it with the small packet of letters she'd received from him in the past three months. She retied the letters with the piece of leather and then put them inside her red Roper boot. Lilli kept moving her hiding place, not wanting her mother or the maid, who was a terrible snoop, to find them.

Lilli hated the fact that her mother had discovered her secret friendship with Zane. She wanted something that was all her own. It wasn't fair that her mother had not only found her letter but had opened it. And this was the first time Zane had ever said anything mushy to her. He said he missed her! Lilli couldn't believe it.

She missed him, but she assumed that was only natural because she was a girl, and especially now that she was rapidly developing into a woman, it only made sense that she would miss him. But he missed her back!

She wondered what that meant exactly, coming from a boy. Did he think about her the say way she thought about him? Or was it something else? She kept getting those funny feelings in her lower abdomen whenever she thought about him. She wasn't altogether sure if it was passion or not, but whenever she thought about Zane or conjured his face in her day-dreams, those zinging twinges down deep, deep inside her were pretty much a sure bet to show up.

Something was happening to her, and Lilli believed it was womanhood.

What Lilli didn't understand was her mother's reaction to all these changes. For years—no, for*ever*—her mother had nagged Lilli mercilessly about being a tomboy. Now that her breasts were growing at the speed of sound and she was forced to "borrow" her mother's bras because her own no longer fit, her mother was throwing tantrums.

What was Lilli supposed to do?

In a quandary, she finally consulted the only accessible or-acle she knew. She telephoned Faith.

In less than two minutes, Lilli had explained her dilemma and Faith was already dispensing wisdom.

"Tell the battle-ax to bug off!"

"That's easy for you to say!"

"My mother never opened any of my mail and I would be mortified if she did. However, what's done is done. I will tell you this, Lilli, Mothers go bonkers when we start maturing. Everybody knows how fast girls mature, but I think our mothers kind of forget that they went through the same thing. Did you remind her of her own adolescence?"

"She never talks about it. Remember? This is the 'woman without a past.' I've never seen any of her family. All she says is either they died or they moved away."

"I've always said, Lil, that your mother is weird. A real case and a half."

"I know. I wish I had your mother."

"I'll share her any time. Say! Maybe you should come over and talk to Mom. She's a Mitchell, though. Tells it like it is."

"That's what I like best about my family."

"So tell me, cuz. What did the letter say? Anything incrim-inating?"

"Not really. But he did say he missed me."

"He *did?* He really said that? I never had a boy say some-thing like that. I think I would fall down in a faint if Paul ever said anything like that to me."

"How is Paul, anyway?"

"We went to the dance after the football game, but he still hasn't kissed me."

"Don't give up. His birthday is coming up pretty soon. You could give him sixteen kisses for his sixteenth birthday."

"Hmm. I'll have to think about it. I'd better get back to my homework. Cheer up, Lilli. Your mom will come around in time. See, mothers aren't ever ready for their kids to grow up. It's hard on them. They just don't understand."

"You really think my mother will change?"

Faith paused for a very long time.

"Faith, this isn't a rocket science test."

"You're right, Lil. Aunt Arlette is a tough nut. Better you should just stay out of her way like you've always been doing. Some things never—"

"Change. I know," Lilli interrupted. "Thanks for the advice, cuz."

"Don't mention it."

" 'Bye," Lilli said and hung up, then sat looking at the phone. "Some help you are."

Now thoroughly depressed, Lilli resorted to an old habit of reading her books on the Maya and Incas when the real world became too much for her to handle. Immersed in lost lands and civilizations, Lilli looked for clues that would lead her to the lost city of gold. She read legends and myths of temples of gold and jewels. These tales had been passed down for so many generations that even modern-day descendants of the ancient Incas still believed these treasures were yet to be found.

Lilli knew her father believed some of these tales. He was still searching for maps that would lead him to buried treasure.

Lilli didn't know what all they would be searching for on their next trip, but she was going to look for maps. She promised herself that this winter and even next year in school she was going to minor in Spanish. She wanted to know what the natives were saying when they conversed among themselves. Lilli wanted to know so many things these days. She wanted to know more about the changes taking place in herself. She wanted to know more about her mother and why she was so closemouthed about her teenage years. Why, Lilli didn't even know how J.C. and Arlette had met. Why were they so secretive about such things? And she wanted to know more about Zane and his life. She wanted to know not only *what* he was thinking and planning to do with his life, but *why.*

Lilli had more questions than she had time, and the more she discovered about life and people, the more questions she had. It seemed to her that there were an awful lot of things going on in her life on many different levels, none of which she'd been aware of until the past summer. Life was changing rapidly for her, and even though she knew she had no choice but to meet it head-on, there were times like this when she wished it would slow down.

"It's all so complicated." She sighed as she dug under her bed and picked up the book by Erich von Däniken she'd begun over the weekend, entitled *Chariots of the Gods?*

"Time to give my brain a rest."

Nine

Spring, 1977

Lilli had never been on a dig on which her father was not in charge. She watched how he graciously accepted menial tasks from the dig supervisor, Dr. Daniel Rubenthal, prior to their leaving Houston. He never imposed his will or his theories on the learned doctor, nor did he complain about his reduced status. Lilli was used to the J.C. Mitchell form of conduct on a dig, so she was surprised when she discovered that her own presence was not looked upon favorably by the other dig members.

"Now remember, Lilli, keep your mouth shut. As far as these people are concerned, you've never been on an expedition before. They don't need to know about the times and places where we've gone on our own."

"How come, Pop? I know some things about the Maya myself."

"I know that, but these people have a certain protocol, and we need to abide by their rules. We're here to get information."

"What kind of information?"

"Anything that will help me . . . well, verify my own theories."

"You mean about the city of gold, huh?"

"Yeah."

"And they don't think one exists?"

"No. Dr. Rubenthal's reputation is based on his accuracy and precision. He does not cater to whims and fancies."

"You mean like that book I read by von Däniken."

"Von Däniken or any of his ilk would never be invited on a Rubenthal expedition."

Lilli grimaced. "You're right, Pop. I wouldn't have much to say to Dr. Rubenthal."

"Keep it that way, honey, and we'll do just great. I'm here at their invitation." J.C. patted Lilli's shoulder affectionately. "It's just a better way of doing business. You're too young to understand all the ins and outs, but there are some things that are supposed to remain secrets. You and I have our secrets, that's all. Okay?"

"Okay, Pop." She smiled adoringly at him.

They flew to Guatemala City on a 747. A taxi took them down Sexta Avenida, the main thoroughfare, to the hotel, where they met up with a driver from the Rubenthal expedition who had driven into the city from the site. The driver was a none-too-cheerful fellow by the name of Eugenio, who tossed Lilli's duffel bag into the back of the Jeep with little respect. Lilli frowned. Even the driver considered them second-class citizens. It wasn't a good sign.

They took the Pan-American Highway west out of the city, not north to the dense Guatemalan rain forest and further to Mexico's Yaxchilán.

J.C. turned to Eugenio. "We're going the wrong way," he said in Spanish.

"I know English and Spanish," Eugenio said contemptuously. "I know where I am going. The professor has planned a side trip."

J.C. was instantly uneasy. "To where?"

"Palenque," Eugenio replied flatly.

"That's well over two hundred miles from here," J.C. objected. "That's more than just a side trip. Why Palenque? I thought we were spending all our time in Guatemala, not Mexico."

Eugenio shrugged his shoulders and kept his eyes on the busy traffic. "Who knows?"

From the bewildered look on her father's face, Lilli could tell that he truly had no idea about this change in plans. What she didn't understand was his obvious apprehension.

By the time they reached Palenque, the sun had nearly set. Lilli jumped out of the Jeep and looked up at the Palace of Palenque. It was easy to see why this was the westernmost city of the Maya. There were artificial lights within the crumbling palace walls and tower, but at this time of night, when the moon and sun were both visible and the light on earth had an eerie gold-and-silver glow, Lilli felt as if she had been transported back to the seventh century, when the Mayan culture had hit its zenith. In those days the palace had towered over a dazzling city. Astronomers developed a calendar and a system of tracking time that was as precise as the most sophisticated contemporary time systems. They invented the most advanced writing system in the New World, and to Lilli's mind, and to many noted archaeologists, their art and architecture were some of the greatest the world had ever seen.

Lilli could see nine-foot-tall figures in the palace's eastern courtyard. She had read that the figures' hand-to-shoulder depiction was a gesture of submission. One figure had his arms bound behind his back filled with scars, which many thought was a form of self-mutilation that the Maya considered pleasing to the gods.

As Eugenio showed them the way to the informal camp, Lilli pondered the tall figures.

"Pop, why do you think the Maya thought they should scar themselves for their gods?"

"That's one of a thousand questions we'd all like the answer to."

"It seems to me," she said, picking her way over rubble, "there are always too many questions and not enough answers. But I guess that's what makes this work so fascinating. At least to me."

"I know," he said seriously. Then he gestured toward the hillside mausoleums. "Have you noticed that in this area, the design of the tombs and elevations of the buildings look strangely like the Valley of the Kings in Egypt?"

Lilli followed his gaze and realized that her father was right.

"On the winter's solstice, the setting sun will appear to plunge into Pacal's pyramid tomb over there, as if through the gateway to the underworld. Legend says that it is a tribute to the king's divinity."

They walked on to the camp just as the last vestiges of sunlight were fading. The temporary camp was not what Lilli had expected. She was used to sleeping bags and a campfire. This grouping of elaborate tents, folding tables with tablecloths, chairs, and Coleman stoves and grills looked to her like a small city.

J.C. walked up to a rotund man dressed in khaki shorts and a tie-dyed T-shirt and shook his hand. "Hello, Dr. Rubenthal."

"J.C., glad to see your plane was on time," he said with a voice that warbled. He looked at a round-faced watch he wore whose huge fluorescent numerals Lilli could see from her position two yards away and in the dark. "Good job, Eugenio," he said to the driver, who unceremoniously plunked Lilli's bag down at her feet.

Lilli frowned at the driver, but he ignored her.

Dr. Rubenthal peered over the top of his wire-rimmed glasses and scanned Lilli from head to toe, inspecting her as if she were one of his Mayan treasures. His head stretched forward on his neck and then back again, like a turkey's, as he continued his assessment.

Lilli felt as if he'd never seen a teenager before. She didn't like his creepy stare. She wanted to stick out her tongue at him, but she couldn't do that sort of thing anymore because she was grown up now and it would embarrass her father.

"This must be your daughter," Dr. Rubenthal finally said.

"Yes. This is Lilli," J.C. said proudly.

Dr. Rubenthal's thin lips were tight when he said, "See that you don't cause any problems and we will get along fine."

"I won't," Lilli said, unable to hide her defiant tones.

J.C. hurriedly changed the subject. "I was surprised at the change in the itinerary. What brought you here?"

"As you know, normally the tomb of Pacal is barred, but Professor Kelley is here again from Canada's Calgary University and he's going down into the tomb. I didn't want to miss it."

"Nor would I," J.C. said, his voice filled with awe.

Dr. Rubenthal's eyes narrowed. "I *can* trust you to stay with the others while Professor Kelley and I inspect the ruin, can't I?"

"Uh, yes. Of course."

"Don't be too disappointed, J.C. Many are called but few are chosen."

Lilli didn't like the snicker she heard in Dr. Rubenthal's voice and she didn't understand what this fat man was inferring.

"We've had a long day here. Everyone has retired early, so I'll make the introductions tomorrow, if that is all right with you. I'll have your supper sent to your tent, which is the last one in that row," he said, pointing to the fourth tent.

Lilli could barely discern it since it was not lit from within like the others and was nearly engulfed by banana trees and thick palms.

Dr. Rubenthal waved to the man who was walking toward them with a metal coffeepot and three coffee mugs. Then he turned his round face back toward J.C. "Won't you join me for a cup of this marvelous coffee? As you know, Guatemalan coffee is the best. The coffeehouses of Vienna would have to fold up if the Guatemalan coffee-growers here ever went on strike." He laughed, but Lilli detected menace in the man's voice.

Lilli sat on her duffel bag and waited while the "waiter" poured her a cup of coffee. From a drawer in the small table next to him, Dr. Rubenthal pulled out a covered tin camping dish in which he kept sugar cubes. He offered them first to J.C. and then, reluctantly, to Lilli.

She sipped the hot, robust coffee, wondering why Dr. Rubenthal didn't like her or her father.

J.C. and Dr. Rubenthal conversed for fifteen minutes about the interior of Pacal's tomb, which the doctor was going to witness the next day. Lilli didn't like his condescending manner. After they finished their coffee, they were dismissed by him like a king dismisses his servants.

Lilli trudged off to their assigned tent. She waited until they were inside, the Coleman lantern lit and their supper delivered, before she spoke to her father. "I don't like him, Pop."

"I could tell." He laughed and gave her a quick hug. "He doesn't like either one of us."

"Why not?"

A shadow fell over J.C.'s face and he turned away from Lilli and began unpacking his duffel bag. He withdrew soap and a washcloth. "He's an odd duck, Lilli, but he's highly respected. He's backed by the best foundations and universities. He knows everybody. He can get into places I would never see."

"Humph! A lot of good it did us to come here. He's not going to let us go down there, is he?"

J.C. turned back to his daughter with his most charming grin. "Ah, but that's where he's wrong, Lilli. I think we owe it to ourselves to see Pacal's sarcophagus, don't you?"

Lilli's eyes lit up. "You bet, Pop!"

"That's my girl," he said and caught her in his arms with a big hug.

The next morning the sunlight warmed the backs of the group as its members climbed the steep stairs of the Temple of Inscriptions, the mighty Mayan King Pacal's tomb. Lilli and J.C. had met the others shortly before departure. There were two young male assistants, Benny and Art, from the University of Pennsylvania, and a thirty-three-year-old woman, Maria, from the University of Mexico.

At the top of the temple, Lilli found herself out of breath, more from the amazing view of the plaza and green country-side beyond than from physical exertion. She was surprised to realize that she wished she were seeing this with Zane. She wondered if he would be as awe-inspired as she was by the view. She wondered what he was doing that morning. She had a sudden need to hold his hand, but she didn't know why. She guessed that he was with her in spirit, if that were possible.

She turned away from the beautiful vista and entered the temple proper, where she passed a glyph-covered wall. Lilli could not read any of its messages and was instantly struck by a feeling of inadequacy. If only she knew more. If only she'd read more about the Maya before this trip. Suddenly she was filled with a need to know things that she'd never dreamed would be important to her.

For weeks Lilli had sensed this trip would be even more meaningful to her than the ones that had preceded it. Her instincts had been right; something had happened to her. She was seeing the Maya and their history from a new perspective. She was not sure what had occurred to make this change, only that it had. She had always been curious, but this was something more. This was a true desire to know all the answers.

She noticed that her father was different, too. Maybe it was simply that she was picking up his vibes. Maybe it was his mind-set that marked the tone of this trip.

She noticed that he said nothing about finding jade or gold. He made no mention of scavenging for artifacts the way they had on previous digs. He had told her he was looking for clues to the whereabouts of the city of gold. She was supposed to keep her eyes and ears open.

I know so little, she thought as waves of inadequacy wafted over her. She reached up to touch one of the glyphs.

Instantly, Maria walked over and slapped Lilli's hand away. "Keep off!" Her brown eyes sparkled at Lilli. "Child!" she huffed in heavily accented English. Then she walked away to join Dr. Rubenthal.

"Geez!" Lilli snarled back, hoping to quell the pangs of rejection she felt. Obviously, she thought, Dr. Rubenthal wasn't the only one who was suspicious of her presence on this expedition.

Professor Kelley was expounding on the very first dig in 1949, when Dr. Alberto Ruz Lhuillier, the famous archaeologist and expert on the Maya, noticed the round holes in a slab set into the floor. Upon lifting it up, he had discovered a secret staircase. Though clogged with rubble and earth, this passage led to the heart of the pyramid. At the bottom Dr. Lhuillier discovered five skeletons and a chamber. He removed a triangular slab from a side wall and then found a large vault. Along the walls stood stucco figures with elaborate feather headdresses. Inside was a huge sarcophagus.

"We are going down to study the rectangular slab above the sarcophagus. The complexities of this inscription have long baffled us," Dr. Rubenthal told the group.

J.C. winked at his daughter before he spoke up. "I request that all of us be allowed to visit the sarcophagus with you."

"Impossible!" Dr. Rubenthal blurted out.

Professor Kelley eyed his overweight colleague. "I don't see the harm," he said congenially.

"But . . . the child. She could deface something. And we have already discussed Mr. Mitchell," Dr. Rubenthal said in a near whisper, thinking he would not be understood. Of course, Lilli heard every word.

"You are my invited guest. Let them see and contemplate."

Lilli thought her father looked as if he'd already discovered his lost city. His face was positively beaming.

They started down.

Lilli forced herself to ignore the tension she felt around her and the obvious power plays going on within the group. Instead, she concentrated on the tomb itself. She decided to let the experience be one of impressions without any regard to conscious analysis. She wanted to "feel" Pacal's tomb.

Tiny beads of moisture glistened on the limestone passageways as they descended farther into the pyramid. The stairs were steep and wet, and Lilli slipped on one of the steps. A piece of stone broke off and rattled down the stairway.

Lilli was struck by the incredible silence, as if time had stopped or was whirling so fast she couldn't keep up with it. This was where the body of the king had been sealed into eternal darkness, a place where equinoxes and solstices made no mark. Farther inside, Dr. Kelley shone a flashlight on walls that glowed red with cinnabar, the color of dawn and rebirth. Lilli saw the remains of a skeletal foot.

They all took off their shoes so as not to disturb any markings. The carvings in the rock might be defaced by hard soles, which could cause incalculable damage, for even the finest detail could give translators precious information. Flashlights and portable lights lit the portraits that were carved by ancient hands into the walls. The one in the center Lilli guessed to be Pacal. It looked to her as if he were being ushered into heaven.

J.C. turned to Professor Kelley. "It looks as if Pacal had a club foot."

Maria and Benny began investigating the other foot in the sculpture. "See, the artist's chisel slipped and broke off a piece of the other toe," Benny said.

The others then came to investigate.

Professor Kelley examined the foot. "That's a split toe, a congenital defect. I have it myself." He then peeled off a sock and compared his toe with that of Pacal's.

Lilli heard the murmurs from the group. They spoke of the verification of Professor Kelley's interpretation. J.C. stated that this was a testimony to the verisimilitude of Mayan art.

Lilli's mind raced with broader possibilities. "Maybe Professor Kelley is from the same family," she said brightly.

Dr. Rubenthal turned around and peered down the long slope of his nose at her. "Childish minds need not be heard!" he bellowed.

This time Lilli forgot her promises to her father. Her tongue itched to lash back and she did. "I think it very odd, Dr. Rubenthal, that all this time there are so many mysteries about Pacal and everyone has assumed that he had a club foot and then, coincidentally, Dr. Kelley comes here and he has the same defect! I never heard of a split toe, have you? I wouldn't even think to consider any other possibility but a club foot. *Only* because Dr. Kelley is here are we able to see Pacal and all the Mayan artists in a new light! Isn't it possible that you have clung to old assumptions for too long?"

"No one has ever accused me of narrow-mindedness," he said indignantly.

Lilli quickly realized she'd pushed Dr. Rubenthal too far. She thought it wise to back down and let the professor save face. She didn't want to jeopardize her father's position in any way. "Would you say that it's a strange coincidence?"

"Not strange at all," Dr. Rubenthal retorted.

"I agree with the child," Maria said as she stepped up behind Lilli.

"I think it's worth consideration," said Benny.

"Maybe it goes even further. Maybe Dr. Kelley is a reincarnated Pacal," Art said. Lilli noted the lack of conviction in his voice, however. She guessed that he was stating his views only to broaden Dr. Rubenthal's scope.

"Balderdash!" Dr. Rubenthal said. "Things are what they are, and that is what we're here for. Facts. And nothing else."

"Who knows what is, Doctor? We have already made this discovery that will help other interpreters for years to come. Maybe Art has something there. But we'll never know if we don't consider the possibilities. If it weren't for his kind of attitude, Professor, you would be out of a job," J.C. said firmly.

Dr. Rubenthal backed down at that and went about his excavating and uncovering the hieroglyphics. They worked all morning, broke for lunch, and continued until the day ended.

By evening, Lilli thought she'd never been so tired. She nearly had to crawl back to camp. Their dinner was a fine chicken stew, coffee, and a cake that had been soaked in rum. J.C. joined Professor Kelley and Dr. Rubenthal as they discussed their finds of the day. The others had gone off by themselves, and Lilli found herself with no one to talk to.

Lilli liked Maria for coming to her defense. Art's ideas fascinated her because she'd never heard them before. She was intrigued by this trio more so than by Dr. Rubenthal because these young people wanted to dig deeply into the psyches of the Maya and understand them as individuals and not only as a culture.

Lilli picked her way to the area behind the tents where Art, Benny, and Maria sat huddled in a circle around a small fire. She heard them talking about Professor Barrera, who with his staff of twelve had prepared a definitive dictionary of the Mayan language, which he had begun in 1974. Collating all existing dictionaries with all modern vocabulary sounded like a gargantuan project to Lilli, but one that would simplify the anthropologist's job. She knew that her father was waiting for this new dictionary. He had said it would help him verify legends and the maps he'd collected.

Lilli huddled behind a clump of banana trees, listening to Maria talking to Benny and Art. She didn't dare interrupt their discussion because she was afraid they might walk away from her. However, the more the trio talked, the more Lilli was intrigued. Eventually she left her hiding place and walked up to them. "How do they know they'll have everything when it's published?" she blurted out.

Maria looked up at her and smiled. "Come. Sit." She patted the ground next to her.

"They won't have everything, but it will be the best they can do at this time, Lilli," Benny said. "Twenty years from now, we will know so much more."

"Twenty?"

Benny laughed. "Sounds like an eternity to you, doesn't it?"

"Yes."

Maria smiled at Lilli. "You are not like other American children. You think for yourself."

"To a fault," Lilli joked back.

"Don't ever stop, Lilli Mitchell. There are very few of us who have the courage to do that." Art took a stick from the fire and lit a cigarette.

"Why does Dr. Rubenthal dislike me so much?" Lilli asked.

"He doesn't like us, either. But you are J.C. Mitchell's daughter."

Maria cut Art off. "Don't listen to him, Lilli." She glared at Art, who stared back at her for a long moment and then lifted his head to the starry sky and blew out the smoke.

"What's he trying to say, Maria?" Lilli demanded.

"In his enigmatic way," she said, shooting a damning look at Art, "he's saying that Dr. Rubenthal is a pompous ass."

They all burst out laughing.

Then Maria continued. "Dr. Rubenthal believes that as long as we come along on these digs and put a potsherd together here and a bone fragment with its mate there, everything is okay. He is *not* on the cutting edge of our field today. However, he *is* able to talk a lot of people into funding him. So the rest of us sign on for the experience. We all intend to write our own treatises . . . later."

"Much later." Benny guffawed.

"Much, *much* later," Art said seriously.

"Do you understand now?" Maria asked.

"Sure," Lilli lied. She didn't want them to think she couldn't keep up with them mentally because she was a kid. But the truth of it was that many things that had always seemed so straight in her mind were now confused. She could tell that these people did not admire her father any more than Dr. Rubenthal did. However, Lilli respected their opinions. It was odd that she would value an outsider as much as, maybe even more than, her own father. She felt guilty for doing so.

She stared at the glowing fire, not realizing that her shoulders had suddenly slumped and that her expression gave away her feelings.

Maria put her hand on Lilli's shoulder. "Something is troubling you. Maybe I could help?"

Lilli desperately wanted some answers, but how did she go about getting them without betraying J.C.'s confidence? "I wish I knew as much as you do. I wish I was older so I could really help my father out."

"We all wish that, Lilli," Art said.

"Really?"

Benny laughed softly. "Fifty years from now, we'll all still be doing the same thing and probably have even more questions than we do now."

Lilli stared at him. "Do you really think that we aren't getting any closer to some real answers?"

Benny's lightheartedness disappeared. "Frankly? Me? No. I think I'm getting real damn close. But then, my own hypotheses are considered outrageous."

As usual, Lilli's curiosity gave her courage. "I'll bet it's not as crazy as my hypothesis," she challenged him.

"I'll take that bet. You go first."

Lilli straightened up and assumed her most dignified stance. "I believe I'll be able to find enough clues on these digs to put me on the right track to find the city of gold."

There! I've said it, she thought with relief. Maybe now I can get even further than Pop. He'll be proud.

"The city of gold? One of the Seven Cities of Cibola?" Benny looked as if he were about to laugh.

"Yes."

"Lilli," he began sincerely, "the city or cities of gold were a marketing gimmick used by the Spanish in the fifteen hundreds to get other Spanish or French people to invest in and colonize the New World. There never was a city of gold. It's true that when Coronado saw the setting sun on some of the Indian cities, they appeared as if they were made of gold, but there really is no such thing. If anyone told you there was, they were just pulling your leg. I'm sorry."

Lilli wanted to cry, but stubbornly she wouldn't let herself. She didn't want to believe what Benny was telling her. Her father was a smart man. Why would he tell her something that was not true? Why would he lead her on a wild-goose chase? What was he doing down here if he wasn't looking for the city of gold? What was he really after? Did he think he could fool her forever?

What hurt the most was that her father thought she was this dumb. Maybe that was why he'd instructed her to keep her mouth shut. Her father was up to something, that was for sure. She just wished she knew what.

"Okay," Lilli said to Benny. "Now let's hear your hypothesis."

Benny cleared his throat. "I will tell you that my suppositions are *not* popular, Lilli."

"I understand that. Go on," she prodded. She glanced at Art and realized he was already snickering. At least no one had laughed at her outright.

"I believe that this planet was visited by aliens thousands of years ago and that we are the children of the sons of gods and the daughters of man. The sons of gods were the alien visitors and the daughters of man were the first homo sapiens who inhabited the earth then. I'm not alone in this theory. Jacques Valle, the French scientist, has expounded upon this phenomenon in several reports and books. I'm in a very small minority today, but I also believe that those same aliens still visit us."

Lilli snorted and then started laughing. "That's the craziest thing I ever heard!"

"You and about three-fourths of the academic world agree," Benny replied morosely.

Maria patted Lilli's shoulder again. "So you see? We are all entitled to our dreams and illusions. Maybe it would be better if we all thought a bit more like Dr. Rubenthal, eh?"

Lilli looked up into Maria's dark eyes. She knew Maria meant well, but she wasn't about to give up her quest without hard, factual evidence to the contrary. A few trips to the library in Houston would solve that. Lilli vowed that from this moment on she would conduct her own investigations and draw her own conclusions.

"Well, I guess I'd better get some rest," she said.

"Good idea. Tomorrow we set out for Yaxchilán. And hopefully, even more adventure."

"Good night," Lilli said, rising and brushing the dirt from the back of her shorts.

"Good night," the trio chimed together.

Lilli went back to her tent and noted that her father was still talking with Professor Kelley and Dr. Rubenthal. She lay down on the cot, crossed her arms behind her head, and stared up at the Coleman lantern hanging from the center pole.

Lilli's head was swimming with thoughts. Never had she believed her father to be capable of doing anything wrong. But here he was, pursuing a pipe dream. For some reason, Lilli did not doubt Benny or Maria; instead, she doubted her father. This was not like her. Or was it? She was seeing him in a new, garish light that was not as flattering as the one she'd used the previous year. Her mother had told her that growing up was going to make a big difference in her life, but Lilli didn't like the direction it was taking.

But I love Pop. How could he lie to me like this? Her eyes filled with tears. Why didn't he trust me?

Lilli wiped the tears away with her fists. The others tonight . . . they seemed not to trust her father. As she thought about it now, she realized that Maria had been quick to cut Art off. There had been several evasions and innuendos about either herself or her father on this trip. She wondered why her father was not respected as she felt he should be.

It had to be because he did not hold a professorship and was not published. She'd heard him talk about the publish-or-perish rule at Rice. She knew that he was constantly busy and stressed over keeping Antiquities alive. She knew that he had his own goals in mind when he went on digs. J.C. Mitchell didn't really care if Pacal had one split toe or two, but these men did. J.C. cared about finding the city of gold.

Lilli jammed her fist into the small pillow under her head. "City of gold!"

But there was no city of gold. Her father *must* know this. They were not going to find any clues in Yaxchilán. As far as she could see, all he was doing on this trip was some sucking up to Dr. Rubenthal. Why was Dr. Rubenthal so important to him all of a sudden? Had her father spun this story of the city of gold to appease her?

"Yes! That's got to be it!" she said aloud. "Pop is after something—and I'm not supposed to know about it. At least not yet. I hope he trusts me enough to tell me when the time is right."

Lilli smiled as she finally put her mind to rest and slipped into her dreams, hoping against all odds that someday her father would be lucky enough to find even one clue that would lead him to his dream.

Ten

Summer, 1977

Zane telephoned Lilli with the best news he'd had in a long time.

Lilli was sprawled across her bed on her stomach, her head hanging over the edge of the new yellow-and-apple-green chintz floral bedspread her mother had chosen when redecorating Lilli's bedroom—again. It reminded Lilli of the floor samples at the Needlework Nook in the Village, but as usual, she had had no say in the choice of colors for her very own bedroom. Rather than protest the process, which was therapeutic for Arlette and was loaded with the potential to thoroughly outrage her, Lilli chose to ignore the alterations altogether and focus her interests elsewhere. This attitude, of course, infuriated Arlette all the more, which served Lilli well in her battle for independence. The result of this ongoing battle of wits was that by the end of June, Lilli was ready to run when Zane called with his proposal.

"I got a job as a camp counselor at Canyon Lake for the month of August. It's a great place that just opened up. They've got horseback riding, scuba lessons—which I'll teach, of course—hiking, canoeing, tennis, basketball, and all the regular camp stuff. The kids are in the ten-to-thirteen age bracket, and I was told that most of their parents are loaded with dough. I was thinking maybe I could make some good contacts for my dad's business." Zane had graduated from high school a few weeks earlier, and because his father was so ill, he now had almost total responsibility for the business. He paused only to take a deep breath, not waiting for a comment from Lilli. "Anyway, Lilli, I want you to come with me.

117

I've already put in an application for you." Zane rushed on like a bullet train.

"Slow down, Zane." Lilli laughed, though she reveled in his enthusiasm. "I haven't even thought of going away this summer. I thought I'd just work with Pop like I always do."

"Aw, c'mon, Lilli," he pleaded, heartfelt disappointment evident in his voice. "You want to be with me, you know you do. I can pull some strings over there. You just call them today, now, and Mrs. Hancock will put you on staff. You've got all the credentials. You're certified to be a lifeguard, you got your CPR training even before I did, and what they really want is just some hard workers who are willing to work for peanuts."

"And that definitely qualifies me." She laughed. "But what about you and your dad's business?"

"My dad wants me to do this. He thinks it'll be good for *me,* but I think the contacts I make will be good for the business. Anyway, I'll still have a month to organize the business stuff before I go." His voice was pleading as he said, "Say you'll go, Lilli."

"I have to talk to Pop about it."

Zane tried not to let the edge in his voice show. He didn't want her to think that he was aware of the rivalry between J.C. and himself for Lilli's time and attention, but he failed. "Can't you make this decision for yourself? I thought you were grown up, Lilli Mitchell."

"I am!" Lilli replied defensively, in just the manner Zane was hoping she would.

"Glad to hear it! Now, you comin' or not?"

"Yes."

"Great! You call Mrs. Hancock. She'll give you all the information."

"Okay, but I still have to tell my pop. He'll be disappointed."

"Geez, Lilli, it's not for all summer. You can still work in the store in July. And that way, you'll have your birthday here, and we'll have the Fourth of July together . . . sort of like our anniversary, huh?"

"Yes," she said, softly, "our anniversary." But already her thoughts were on August and the romantic hill country and that big Western sky studded with zillions of stars. The vision of lying in Zane's arms, content and happy, filled her heart and solidified her decision.

It took less than an hour of begging and pleading with J.C. to gain his approval. Arlette sputtered a cacophony of moans and grunts that vacillated between approval and disapproval, which demonstrated her continual state of confusion as to how most effectively to control her daughter.

"She's going off with that bum!" Arlette stormed as she paced J.C.'s study shortly after Lilli went racing out the front door to Faith's house to tell her the news.

"She's not eloping, Arlette. She's taking a job at a camp, which I am sure thousands of teenagers do all over the country. Be glad she doesn't want to join the Peace Corps like my friends did—and I never *did* see them again."

Arlette chewed her bottom lip as she tapped her foot on the Persian rug. "You're too easy on her."

"You're too hard on her."

"I most certainly am not! I'm being realistic. You've got your eyes closed—no, glued shut! Lilli is going to be gone a month with that boy, and I know full well that if they haven't already been sleeping together, they will be by the month's end. Every time Zane comes over here, he can barely keep his erection down."

"Arlette!" J.C. exclaimed and then dropped his head and began shuffling his stacks of papers back and forth so as not to reveal the quivering in his hands at the thought of his daughter growing up this fast.

"Wake up, J.C. That boy lusts after Lilli like a panther in heat. If you let her go to that camp, she's going to come back pregnant."

J.C. was pensive for a long moment and then finally lifted his eyes to his wife. "I trust Lilli, and I'll back her up in any situation. I'll admit it—I don't like her growing up, but if I hold her back, then I'll really lose her. She's too important to me. If she wants to go, then I'll allow it. I stand by my decision."

Arlette's eyes narrowed as she tried to contain her anger. "You're making a big mistake. She'll get pregnant, you mark my words. There'll be a horrendous scandal, I'll be stuck raising the brat myself, and all my friends will ostracize me—and all because of her trampy ways."

J.C.'s eyes widened in shock. He spread his hands on his desk to steady the flow of boiling rage that surged through his body. Was this woman truly his wife? How could he despise her own flesh and blood with such intensity, and how could a mother, any mother, place her own concerns above that of her child? J.C. wondered often, now, what had ever possessed him to marry Arlette in the first place.

"My daughter is *not* a tramp," he growled with fierce conviction. "Lilli's decisions about herself and Zane are her own, and if she did make love to him, I'm certain with every ounce of my being that she would consider the matter with great care. She would do nothing that she didn't feel in her heart was right. And on that basis, I would still back her up. What concerns me more is your lack of concern for Lilli's feelings and your overemphasis on the social ramifications of her actions." J.C. stood up and started out of the room. "If you ever put your petty, narrow-minded socialite friends ahead of my daughter again, you'll be the one who has hell to pay." He left the room.

Arlette glanced around the study, where there was not a single touch of her influence to be seen. This was J.C.'s domain. Standing there alone and realizing that she had lost another battle against the unified forces of Lilli and J.C., Arlette vowed that it would not happen again. She would be patient with them both and with herself. Deep within her soul, Arlette believed that she would ultimately be the victor. Lilli was young and prone to mistakes; Arlette had wisdom and experience on her side. The day was coming when Lilli would be gone and she would have J.C. all to herself and she would finally win control over him, his business, and his money. Then and only then would she be able to relax. Then she would be happy.

Camp Wimberly was situated in the scenic hill country near Canyon Lake and Wimberly, Texas. The owners, Martha and Bob Hancock, had spent two years erecting log cabins with lake views, stables and corrals, a large recreation hall, and a gym and a cafeteria with the sole intent of catering to the overindulged, little-loved children of wealthy Dallasites and Houstonians. Both Martha and Bob had earned advanced degrees in psychology and both had over a decade of training in drug rehabilitation, which they made use of during the autumn and winter months of the year, when the camp was open only to recovering drug-addictive or alcohol-addictive preteens and teenagers.

Bob and Martha also realized that they, too, needed a vacation and therefore decided to keep the months of July and August for fun and recreation. The counselors they chose for the summer months, then, did not need to meet the high criteria that their winter counselors did, and, too, they believed that one of the best ways to keep high school and college students from experimenting with drugs was employment. Achievements built good characters. Achievements laid foundations for good self-esteem and confidence. Bob and Martha were committed to changing the world, if only in their own small way.

Zane arrived at camp three hours before J.C. drove through the wooden gates with Lilli in the front seat. The road to the main log cabin was dusty and dry, but Lilli had forgone the car air conditioner and rolled down the window to feel the hot, arid wind in her hair. From this vantage point, the lake below was crystal clear. Huge cypress trees scented the hot air and purple sage was blooming everywhere. In the distance where the scrub trees and bottle brush were thin, Lilli could see a doe and her two fawns scavenging for food.

J.C. braked in front of the registration cabin that doubled as Bob and Martha's living quarters. Lilli had just gotten out of the car when she heard Zane calling her name.

"Lilli!" Zane came racing across the wooded expanse between the main cabin and the row of smaller sleeping cabins. He was wearing hiking shorts, a yellow T-shirt, and black-and-white high-top basketball-court shoes. His wide, bright smile in his already tanned face brought a light to Lilli's eyes.

"Zane!" she exclaimed as she raced toward him and took his hands in her own and continued smiling happily up at him.

J.C. watched them and his heart fell.

Zane bent down to whisper to Lilli. "I'd love to throw my arms around you and kiss you, but I can't let Mrs. Hancock see us . . . propriety and all. They have very strict rules about the counselors dating each other. We'll have to be very careful."

"It's okay," she said. "It'll be great just being together and doing things together."

Lilli let go of Zane's hands and turned back to her father. "I guess we'd better unload my stuff, Pop."

"Sure thing," J.C. said and hit the trunk button from inside the glove box.

Martha Hancock assisted the five female counselors with the last of the paperwork, pointed out their cabins, and issued cot linens and towels to the girls. She then spoke to the parents about mail, telephone calls, the need for extra spending money, and final departure times for those staying two, and those staying four, weeks.

Once the orientation was over, J.C. felt assured that Lilli would be in good hands. He also liked the fact that she would be under the tutelage of not only trained professionals but also caring people. J.C. liked Bob and Martha Hancock a great deal.

It was nearly five o'clock when J.C. began his three-hour drive back to Houston down I-10. He was reluctant to let Lilli go, but this was a lesson in his own growth, and so he kept his spirits light for her sake as well as for his own.

That evening the counselors, Bob, Martha, and Katrina, the professional nurse hired to "cure mosquito bites, broken limbs, and homesickness," all met in the main recreation building. They sat in well-worn, upholstered chairs around a massively built stone fireplace, which Bob proudly announced he'd built himself. Here the young employees learned the rules they were to abide by during their summer stay. No alcohol, no drugs, no smoking—cigarettes or grass—no profanity, no fraternizing with one another; there would be only regulation Camp Wimberly T-shirts worn by all the staff; no cutoffs, no ripped jeans, modest swimwear only, and no swimming after ten o'clock; and in addition to the counseling duties, which entailed heading up activities, each employee would be assigned rotating duties in the mess hall, the stables, and the laundry rooms, and would distribute mail and packages to the guests.

Sunday night was the only night off for the counselors,

though in actuality the staff would merely be reduced, therefore giving each staff member every other Sunday night off. Lilli realized that she and Zane were on different schedules and would not have the same Sunday nights off. Her fantasies of endless nights on a hillside watching for shooting stars while Zane's arms were wrapped around her faded more quickly than a comet's tail.

On Friday morning at nine o'clock, Lilli received her first shock.

The line of cars delivering the young camp guests for the first two-week program began with a white Cadillac stretch limousine and ended at three o'clock in the afternoon with a silver Rolls-Royce. She saw so many Mercedeses, Jaguars, and Lincoln Town Cars, she wondered if there could possibly be one normal kid in the bunch. It took her less than a day to find out there were none.

Lilli's second shock was Zane's reaction to the wealthy boys. "I've never seen anything like this," he said to her after directing his foursome to their cabin. "Charles Gladstone the Third has alligator luggage and he's only eleven! And if that isn't enough, Barry Bassman brought his own Egyptian cotton sheets because his mother told him he might get head lice at a public place like this. What the hell did she send him here for if she thought it was unsanitary?"

"Zane, we knew they had money. You've known people with money before."

"Not *this* rich. Do you have any idea how rich the Bassmans are? One connection like this could make my father's business for the rest of his life. Bassman knows everybody who is anybody from Texas clear to California and back again to New York. He owns not only oil fields but gold mines, steel mills, a cereal company, and one of those new computer companies everyone is talking about."

"I take it you're pleased with this camp."

"Aren't you?"

"Yes, but I was here for the nature walks and to spend time with you," she said disappointedly and walked slowly away while Zane rushed up to the Corvette convertible carrying a ten-year-old heir to a billion-dollar investment banking firm.

Lilli's initiation to the world of the ultrarich Texas brats began with Evangeline Parker from Highland Park in Dallas. Evangeline's "daddy" was in oil, as were most of the high-rolling "daddies" who had sent their children to camp. These were the men who either owned the fields outright or speculated in oil futures, and in 1977 oil was flowing like a river of money into some very deep pockets.

Evangeline was twelve, with her thirteenth birthday only six weeks away. She had honey-blond hair that had been artificially sun-streaked by one of the best hair designers in Dallas. She wore two-hundred-dollar sunglasses, fifty-dollar blue jeans, and thickly padded bras. She wore more makeup than a *Cosmopolitan* cover model, and within fifteen minutes of her arrival at the camp, she had announced to her three bunkmates that she had already chosen Zane McAllister to be the man who would divest her of her virginity.

Sandy, Amy, and Kim were aghast, but egged her on despite the fact that their counselor was witness to the entire stunning conversation.

"How are you going to do that?" Kim asked the outrageous girl she'd met only an hour earlier.

"Simple. I've thought of a hundred ways. In the water, in the woods, in the mess hall. He'll do it. They all will, given half the chance. Men love young girls. My daddy told me that. Besides, even if he does think I'm too young, there is always the fact that I can slip him a little bonus for his efforts. A thousand ought to do the trick."

"You would *pay* a man to make love to you?" Sandy inquired, aghast.

"I'm screwing him, not making love. There's a difference. What's money for, anyway? Show me a man who can't be bribed and I'll show you a man with no integrity."

Lilli couldn't stand this line of thinking any longer and snorted her disapproval.

Evangeline turned her head toward Lilli. The others followed Evangeline's lead like sheep. "And what was that about?"

Lilli refused to let this obviously misled young girl get the better of her. "I think you're too young to know anything about love."

Evangeline whirled around and when she did so, her long

blond hair fell like a glorious sheet down her back. The sun through the screened window picked up the highlights and illuminated the air around the girl, making her look nearly angelic. Her words, however, dispelled the illusion. Evangeline's emerald eyes scanned the length of Lilli's body, and then she dismissed her with a quick lowering of her eyelids. "What are you?"

Lilli noted she did not say, "Who are you?"

"The maid?"

Lilli could not stop herself from smirking. "I'm your keeper. While you are here, you will follow the rules of this camp and its directors. You will not engage in improper conduct of any kind. That includes sleeping with the male personnel."

Evangeline was undaunted. She walked right up to Lilli and although she was not yet thirteen, she stood eye to eye with Lilli. "What's the matter? You already mark him for yourself? Too bad. I always get what I want. One way or the other."

Lilli didn't flinch. "I feel sorry for you. You're going to be very lonely someday if you use people like this."

"Who gives a shit?"

Lilli looked her straight in the eye with a rock-steady gaze meant to penetrate like a laser. "I do, Evangeline. I believe you're worthy of more in life than that . . . even if you don't."

Then, before Evangeline could say anything else, Lilli turned her back on the girl and walked out the door.

For the next two days Evangeline wielded her acerbic wit and angry sarcasm like snapping bullwhips. No one was immune to her attacks. Lilli said nothing to the girl, but she kept track of her actions and wrote down comments about each of her four charges every night in a journal. She finally went to Martha with her journal, her observations about Evangeline, and her conclusions.

"I think Evangeline is terribly unloved and a very lonely young woman," Lilli said to Martha over a cup of tea. "The other girls are a bit too materialistic for my taste, but they seem to be getting into the groove of the camp. Evangeline fights everything tooth and nail. It's as if she's got to be tough, and she needs an incredible amount of attention."

"Male attention?" Martha asked.

"Yes."

"I was afraid of that. I spoke with her father on the phone, which we do with all the parents when applications are being accepted. He offered to pay double just to get her in here. I got the feeling he just wanted her out of his hair for the summer."

"Isn't that true of most of these kids? They all seem so unhappy."

"Yes, it is. But he was more adamant than most. It amazes me that they aren't on drugs yet. I'm hoping to show them another way of life before they get into that trap."

"I think it's a great plan. I just hope it works."

"Me, too," Martha replied with a smile. "In the meantime, do the best you can with her. I'll contact her father and try to talk to her mother . . ."

"Her parents are divorced. She told me her mother ran off with another man. Evangeline has taken her father's side completely."

Martha shook her head. "Nobody leaves a happy home, Lilli. He had a part in it. Although I cannot imagine leaving my daughter, but we don't know the circumstances that drove that woman to run away. I'm going to find her."

Lilli couldn't help but think about her own parents and her mother's continual anger against her father. For the first time she wondered if there was something that her father was *not* doing for her mother that caused her to be vindictive. Her mother perpetually complained that J.C. did not pay enough attention to her. Was it true? Was she acting just like Evangeline? And why was it that Lilli could see the faults in Evangeline and sympathize when she couldn't give that empathy to her own mother? Had Lilli placed her father on a pedestal that was taller than he rightly deserved? She was amazed at how clear the mirror was that Evangeline had thrown up to her. It was the first time that Lilli realized that the summer's experiences might tell her more about her own life than she had learned any other way.

Zane had been at camp for only four days when he realized that he could no longer pretend that Lilli was just another camp counselor. Every day he would watch her leading a group of young girls on long nature walks. He was amazed at her enthusiasm for everything. She initiated a botanical trip for the girls, pointing out roots, herbs, trees, shrubs, and wild-flowers. She taught the girls how to erect deer stands and then got them up in the predawn hours to scout for deer. Instead of guns, the girls used Polaroids to capture the wildlife. Lilli taught swimming and diving. She could do a double back somersault dive better than anyone in camp. She inspired the girls and awed the boys. Zane had never been so proud of anyone in his life, and he fell more deeply in love with her than ever before.

It was after the Sunday night barbecue that Zane approached Lilli about his plan. It was her night off, but he was on duty.

"Can you meet me later tonight?" he whispered to her as the group was dispersing.

"But you're on duty."

"I've already got it arranged. I'll work until nine, and Tim said he'd cover for me at bed check. He's going to short out the light bulb in our cabin, and hopefully it won't get replaced until the morning, when Bob comes back around. Please, Lilli, I really need to see you alone."

She looked up into his blue eyes and saw the earnestness there. "I want to be with you, too." Her dashed romantic fantasies came back to her, pieced together and stronger than ever.

It was a long hike to the rocky water's edge in the moonlight, but Lilli already knew the way like the back of her hand. Zane was sitting on a huge boulder only a few feet from the lake, waiting for her.

"How long have you been here?" she asked as she rushed into his open arms.

"Too long," he said, kissing her ear and holding her tightly to his chest. Zane could no longer hear the flapping wings of night birds overhead or the wind as it fluttered small oak leaves. He could only hear the pounding of his heart and the sound of his blood as it rushed to his brain.

For months he'd wanted to know what Lilli's breasts felt like, and now the temptation overpowered him. He put his hands underneath her sweater and up her back to her bra. He fumbled for what seemed like forever with the hook.

"Here," Lilli said and unhooked it for him.

Her gesture shocked Zane, but he was glad to know she wanted him as badly as he wanted her. Her breasts were bigger than he'd guessed and they filled his hand completely with satinlike softness. He had never felt anything so exquisite in his life. The palm of his hand passed over her nipple, and suddenly he felt it become hard. He touched the bud and it tightened even more.

Then Lilli moaned.

He could see that her eyes were shut and her lips were parted. Zane realized he was making these changes in Lilli and she was allowing him to possess her body. Gently he lowered her to the ground.

Again, Lilli was different from any other girl he had known. She didn't deny her feelings. She was natural and giving. She trusted Zane and she loved him.

Zane had never been so filled with emotion in his life. This was the way sex was supposed to be, he thought as he pulled Lilli's sweater up and exposed both her breasts to his gaze. Moonbeams skimmed her white skin, making it glow like fine porcelain. He could see the blue veins just beneath the surface and thought fleetingly how delicate she must be, even though she always wanted him to think she was in control. Reverently, he placed his lips to her breasts, thinking that she even smelled like lilies. He heard her suck in a long breath when he let his tongue touch her nipple. He saw goose bumps spring up across her upper chest and rib cage. He was eliciting these responses in Lilli and the knowledge of it made him feel invincible.

He lay down beside her and unsnapped the waist of her jeans. Then he slid his hand across the flat plane of her stomach and down lower. Zane had never done anything like this before in his life, and he wondered if God would judge him wicked.

Just then Lilli said, "I love you," and washed away his sin.

Her pubic hair was sparse and soft like angel's hair. He was amazed at how hot her skin felt to him. He moved his hand down further and felt her wetness. He sank his fingers inside her.

Lilli moaned.

Zane felt his heart leap.

While his fingers strummed Lilli like a harp, his lips caressed her breasts. Lilli moaned and called his name over and over. It sounded like celestial music to him. Zane never thought about what he should be doing and how it should be done; he was moving along with an ancient rhythm inside him that gave him the confidence to do what he felt and to give to her what he believed she needed.

"I want to be inside you, Lilli," he said, thinking he would explode from his need.

She sank her hands into his hair and gently kissed the top of his head. "I want you, too," she whispered breathlessly.

Zane didn't want this moment to end, but he knew he had to stop. It was wrong, he heard his conscience say. They were too young. What if she got pregnant? And at the same time he felt the resonating of an even deeper, more ardent voice: what better way to show her that you love her?

Lilli did nothing to stop him. Her own body's passion and her heart's yearning for Zane filled her with an explosion of love and longing. Nothing had ever felt so right to her. She liked the feel of Zane's face against her breast. It was odd, but it felt as if she'd done this with him before . . . as if they'd known each other in another life.

She wanted Zane to be a part of her.

"I can't, Lilli," he said finally, then slowly, and with aching reluctance, withdrew his hand.

He kissed her breasts one last time, one by one, and then sat up. He gazed down at her. All the goddesses in mythology, all the angels in heaven combined, could never be as beautiful as Lilli, he thought.

He wanted always to remember her like this. He wanted always to think of this night when she gave herself to him out of unconditional love. He hoped that it would be like this for them every time.

"I love you, Lilli. I don't want to hurt you and I don't want your first time, *my* first time, to be ordinary . . . like in my truck or here at camp. I want it to be very special."

She smiled at him and brushed back a lock of golden hair off his forehead. "I know. And I love you even more for it."

"You do?"

"Yes," she said and sat up. She had to admit to herself that she was disappointed, though. To her, nothing could be more perfect, more spiritual, than to make love underneath a canopy of stars next to the water. She hoped he didn't think that she had to be made love to in a fancy hotel somewhere. She hoped that eventually he would allow the spontaneity of their love to guide them. "We have our whole lives, Zane," she said at last.

"Yes, Lilli. We have our whole lives." He smiled back, knowing deep in his heart that not only would he make their first time a night she would never forget, but that nothing and no one could really keep them apart. Not now, not ever.

Eleven

*B*y the time the first two weeks at Camp Wimberly were almost at an end, Evangeline Parker had made certain that everyone—owners, guests, and counselors—knew that she was not pleased with her accommodations. Evangeline had rightfully earned the moniker "rich bitch."

Lilli was demonstrating to Kim, Amy, and Sandy how to pack a knapsack for an extended trek into the wilderness when a bored Evangeline, lying on her top bunk, threw her copy of *Seventeen* onto the wooden plank floor. The sound was much like a loud slap, and it made Lilli jump. Evangeline burst into laughter. Lilli glared at the girl.

"Why don't you teach them something that's useful?" Evangeline asked. "We're all leaving tomorrow, and the last thing any of us will think about for a year, if ever, is surviving in the woods."

Lilli's frustration with Evangeline finally overcame her better judgment. "I think you ought to pay attention to this class. You're going to need it more than anyone," she said, her tone challenging.

Evangeline regarded Lilli haughtily. "And why is that?"

"Because your father is not coming for you tomorrow. You're staying here," Lilli said triumphantly.

Evangeline's demeanor did not change. Her face still looked as if it had been chiseled from stone. There was not a flicker of anger in her eyes, nor was there a trace of disappointment in her voice. "I knew that," she said flippantly as she tossed her long honey-colored hair to the side and gazed down at Lilli like an archangel from above. She threw herself into the lie. "I just didn't want the others to feel ashamed because their fathers could not afford to let them stay longer."

Lilli was astounded at the girl's ability to control her emotions. She'd never seen more perfect acting.

Kim rammed a flashlight into her knapsack and then looked up at Evangeline. "You're a shit, Evangeline, and I don't mind saying so in front of my counselor. Rules or no rules, you'll just have to dock me one, Miss Mitchell." Kim looked back at Evangeline. "You've spent the whole time lording it over all of us about how perfect your daddy is and the fact that you're his little princess. Well, you know what? I hope the two of you are happy, because I wouldn't trade you my dad for all the diamonds at Tiffany's. He may not be as rich as your dad, but he wants me back home with him and my mother and he sure isn't trying to pawn *me* off on strangers!" Kim tossed her knapsack aside and stormed out of the cabin, slamming the screen door behind her.

Sandy and Amy likewise abandoned their packing. "That goes for me, too," Sandy said and followed a silent, but obviously disgusted, Amy out the door.

Lilli continued to stare at Evangeline, who was watching the screen door. Lilli had never in her life seen such a picture of composure. If any of her friends had said such things to her, she would have been so angry she would have spouted a line of obscenities guaranteed to put her permanently out of the camp-counselor business.

It wasn't until Evangeline lifted her hand to push away a long lock of hair that Lilli noticed her hand was shaking. Suddenly Lilli's heart went out to this girl who hadn't the slightest idea whom to trust, whom to love, or how to go about making a friend. Lilli decided right then that she would be Evangeline's friend.

"How many, Evangeline?"

"How many what?" she snapped defensively.

"Camps. How many different camps over how many years has your father sent you to instead of spending time with you?"

"My daddy—"

"Cut the crap, Evangeline!" Lilli yelled at the top of her lungs. "Just answer the question."

Evangeline's eyes did not waver from Lilli's face. "Get out."

Lilli shook her head. "You forget. I'm paid to keep you

company, so you might as well get used to that fact. How many?"

Evangeline blinked, and when she did, Lilli detected the tiniest trace of a tear at the corner of Evangeline's left eye, but it dried quickly; a sheer act of willpower on Evangeline's part, Lilli surmised. "So many I've lost count." She paused for a moment. "Daddy can afford the best."

"I'm sure he can. How old were you when you first went to camp?"

"Three. Just after my mother ran away."

"Then you never really knew your mother."

Evangeline looked away. "I know enough. Daddy told me she was a whore. I hate her."

"I think you hate a lot of people, Evangeline. I think you hate your mother for abandoning you and your father for never spending any time with you. I know I would if I were treated like that. And you know what else? I think you hate yourself, and that I *wouldn't* do. You know why? Because you're all you've got, and if you learn nothing else while you're here at camp, it's that lesson. You have to learn to pack your own 'chute, Evangeline." Lilli pointed to the discarded knapsacks. "That's what I was teaching the other girls. Pack your own sack. It's *your* life you have to look out for, not your mother's and not your father's."

Lilli went to the door and opened it, but didn't look back when she said, "I'm here if you need me, Evangeline."

She closed the door softly behind her. She never heard Evangeline's muffled sobs.

Lilli's naked body was draped over Zane as he lay beneath her, taking one taut nipple between his lips, teasing it, and then relinquishing it to attend to the other. His hands clasped her rounded hips and he pulled her softness down onto his pelvis. He moved his hand up and clutched her hair and pulled her mouth to his.

"Lilli, you drive me crazy. I want you so badly," he groaned as he slid his tongue into her mouth and reveled in the smooth, sweet interior.

"I want you, too," she said breathlessly. "Please don't make me wait any longer." She reached down between them and jerked at the waist snap on his blue jeans. She unzipped his jeans and slid her hand inside. When she felt his hardness, she was momentarily startled. How could he suddenly be so much larger than she'd thought? Hundreds of times he'd held her close and she'd felt his erection against the flat of her abdomen, but she'd never touched him with her hand. She found the actual contact of his erection with the palm of her hand to be the most exciting and thrilling moment of lovemaking. She liked the way a deep animallike growl gurgled in his throat and the way he seemed to lose his senses as she slid her hand up and down his steel-hard shaft. She noticed that if she let the pads of her fingertips dance over the very end of his penis, his entire body seemed to jerk and convulse. Sweat broke out on his forehead. Lilli's own passion grew in direct relation to her realization of the power she held over Zane.

"Oh, God, Lilli," he moaned. "I didn't want it to be here."

"But this is the most natural place for us, Zane, here under the stars with only God watching us," she breathed. "Please, Zane, I want to know what it's like to have you inside me."

Zane rolled Lilli onto her back, her dark hair forming a rich pillow beneath her head. Quickly, he yanked off his jeans, which was the last bit of clothing that kept them both from losing their virginity.

He looked down into her violet eyes, wondering why he was not afraid to be kept their prisoner. He traced the edge of her heart-shaped face with the flat of his thumb. "I don't want to hurt you and I've always heard that it will."

"Is that what's held you back?"

"Yes," he said reverently. "I love you too much. I could never hurt you."

"I'm not afraid, Zane. I'm more afraid of *not* making love to you. I'm afraid of going through my whole life wondering what it would have been like, here, now, today."

"You talk like I'm going to lose you."

"Never, my love," she said, gazing deeply into his eyes. Never, my blue eyes." Then she took him in her hand and guided him to the softness between her legs. She opened herself to him. Slowly, he caressed her inner lips with his shaft.

Lilli closed her eyes as wave after pleasurable wave beat against her insides. She felt as if she were being lifted off the earth and yet she could feel the pinch of tiny rocks under her back. He lowered his head and teased her nipples until soft, high-pitched noises fluttered out of her mouth. Then slowly, gently, he pressed himself inside her.

Zane lost all control as he felt her wet walls pulse around his shaft. He pushed himself inside as far as he could and then slid back out. Push and pull. Push and pull. He found himself getting hotter and hotter. Lilli was sheathed with a slick film of perspiration as she clutched at his shoulders with her fingers and called out his name. She was not in pain as he'd thought she would be. She was experiencing the same ecstasy that drove him to the edge of reason.

Push and pull. He penetrated her again and again. Over and over. She raised her hips to bring him more deeply inside her until he thought he had passed into another dimension. They were floating through eternity, whirling in the abyss, their bodies, their minds united. Zane wanted this moment, this night, never to end. What a fool he'd been to deny himself and Lilli such exquisite pleasure.

Zane plunged himself into his Lilli again and again, until he noticed that she was panting like a wounded animal. Suddenly fearful, he stopped immediately and withdrew. "What's wrong? Did I hurt you?"

"Oh, no, my precious. Never. Never." She kissed his mouth and then took his hand and slid each finger into her mouth, one by one, and caressed the length of each finger with her tongue. "You make me feel wonderful."

Zane kissed her back and as he did he slid his hand between her legs. He was amazed at how wet and hot she felt and that parts of her were very swollen. He was delighted with all these physical changes that he had brought about in Lilli. He liked the feeling of his fingers against her swollen bud. He liked the way she moaned louder and louder as he stroked her again and again. He did not know if what he was doing was right; all he knew was that Lilli responded to his slightest touch and it was her reaction to him that made him hard again and made him want her even more than before.

Zane continued to stroke her with his fingers. Then, as he manipulated the bud with his thumb, he slid his forefinger inside her. Lilli held her breath for a short moment and exploded into an orgasm. Zane did not relent. He teased her with his fingers and forced the same reaction in her again.

Lilli took a dozen glorious assaults from Zane's hands and fingers before finally placing her hands around his engorged shaft and urging him to enter her.

Zane was shocked at how incredibly slick his stroking was this time. Lilli's passion for him had turned her into a warm, wet refuge, which he prayed he would never be forced to leave. Push and pull. Zane seemed to rise above the earth. He breathed Lilli's name and sank his lips into the base of her neck. Lilli clutched at his nape and tears of joy fell from her eyes. They exploded together in blissful harmony.

Lilli clung to Zane and wondered if it would always be like this for them, or was it that the first time was the only time sex was allowed to be nearly mystical?

"I love you, Lilli," Zane said. "You're mine. You belong to me and no one else."

"And you are mine," she said, looking up at him with love-filled eyes.

Zane rolled onto his side and pulled Lilli close to him. She rested her head against the cushion of his chest. They had eyes only for the moon, the stars, and each other. Neither of them noticed a pair of emerald-green eyes watching them from behind a huge purple sage bush.

Twelve

After the first set of Camp Wimberly kids left, Zane placed every one of their names, addresses, and phone numbers in a cheap address book he had bought at the gas station at Canyon Lake. He made little notations about each youngster in his book in much the same manner that Lilli kept her journal. Whereas Lilli wrote about personality traits and problems she could foresee, Zane wrote down anecdotes the children had told about their family life. Zane was specifically interested in which parents were potential clients for his father. On the side margins he indicated his personal estimation of the net worth of each of the families. He was amazed at how many of the youngsters were due to inherit large sums of money that went back several generations. It was a concept to which he had not been exposed during his rural upbringing. Zane, like his father, had always worked hard for a living, whether it was tending the small herd of cattle they raised each year or his father's and his own true interest, antique jewelry trading.

The second set of campers arrived with even more fanfare than the first. There were chauffeurs in full uniform, and several of the girls were assisted to their cabins by their nannies. The girls wore Gloria Vanderbilt jeans and carried Gucci handbags. The boys brought portable refrigerators, popcorn machines, and small-screen televisions with battery packs. The counselors rolled their eyes, for the camp literature clearly stated that televisions and radios were prohibited. No one liked the fact that once the parents left, all the appliances and "toys" would have to be confiscated and a great many protests would have to be endured.

Zane was assigned four thirteen-year-olds from out of state. Martin Johansen was from Minneapolis, Jason Caldwell was from New York, Andrew Bradley was from Boston, and William Malloy was from Long Island, New York. The four boys not only knew each other, they had chosen this camp as their annual reunion.

To Zane, they looked like the four preppy kids they were. They wore their hair short, but expertly cut and blown dry. They wore slacks, not jeans; cotton long-sleeved pin-striped shirts with their monograms on the sleeves, but not T-shirts. They all had white long-sleeved pullover sweaters tied around their necks, as if they were about to dash out onto a yacht. And not one of them was sweating in the hot Texas sun. They were cool as cucumbers, Zane thought. Too cool, and he didn't trust one of them.

"Yes, we've been together in the Poconos, in the Rockies, at Yosemite, and just about any other camp you can think of in the nation since we were seven years old. It's our only chance to see one another," Martin explained as he flung his leather hanging bag over the bunk. "We even paid extra to be put in this cabin together."

"I didn't know you could do that here," Zane observed appreciatively.

"Money buys everything a person needs," Martin said.

"Well, not everything," Zane said.

Andrew folded his thin arms across his thin chest and threw Zane a very smug look. "I suppose you're just enough of a hayseed to think that money can't buy love."

Zane did not hide his smirk. "I'm certain that in your world, Mr. Bradley, money most assuredly buys love. But this is Texas. Now, if you'll excuse me? I'll see you all at dinner tonight. Six o'clock."

He turned and left the cabin.

Jason went to the door and watched as Zane walked through the woods. "I don't like that guy." He turned back toward his friends. "What do you think, mates? Shall we educate Mr. McAllister?"

"I believe it's worth a try," Andrew replied, and the others nodded in approval.

Lilli's new girls, Karen, Blaine, and Sally, were younger than Evangeline and were far more interested in nature, ghost stories, and writing to their friends back home than they were in the boys at camp. They left Evangeline completely alone, which infuriated her.

Lilli was in her element with the new girls. She took them on hikes and told them every Indian tale she knew. She showed them how to listen to the sound of the wind in the trees and imagine how the land had been hundreds of years ago when the Indians practiced spiritual medicine to heal wounds and disease. "When the body is in dis-ease, many times, not all, illness can be cured by thinking about happy things, like beautiful flowers and skies. By concentrating on happy and positive things, many of us could avoid getting sick in the first place."

Karen was the group skeptic. "What about those plagues that wiped out whole tribes?"

"It's true that smallpox and diphtheria are tough enemies. Fortunately for us, we're learning to blend both antibiotics and vaccines with holistic medicine. But just think, many medicines are found right here in the ground in the form of roots and herbs."

"I think you're right, Lilli," Blaine said. "It feels good just breathing this clean air. It's so quiet and peaceful here. I get headaches from the noise in New York sometimes. I wish I could live here all the time. Don't you, Lilli?"

Lilli lifted her face to the sun and gazed out at the mesas and arid hills, then down to the crystal lake, still and calm in the distance. She wished that Evangeline had come along, although she didn't know if interaction with nature was the kind of therapy Evangeline needed at the moment. But she knew that she had to find a way to get through to the unhappy girl.

Now Lilli clasped her hands around her bent knees and smiled at the girls. "I have to admit I'm happier here than any place I've known."

"Do you think the Indians were smarter than we are?" Sally asked.

"Sometimes I think they were much wiser," Lilli said. "We can learn a lot from them." She noticed that the sun was beginning to drop below the western hills. "Time for us to head back, girls. It's our turn to prepare the campfire for tonight."

The girls rose and followed their leader back to camp.

* * *

Lilli met Zane behind the recreation room on Sunday night only long enough to steal a few kisses before lights-out. That Monday afternoon, between her shifts as lifeguard at the lake, she managed to hold Zane's hand for seven minutes and tell him that she loved him. By Tuesday Lilli became aware that Evangeline was following her nearly everywhere she went. She also discovered that Evangeline's vow to capture Zane had not been an idle one.

Lilli did not want anything to endanger his job, so she told him of her suspicions about Evangeline and suggested that they would have to be more careful about their meetings. Zane agreed.

On Wednesday Lilli came to get her girls for a canoe lesson. Everyone but Evangeline went racing happily out the door.

"You're not coming?" Lilli asked politely.

"No. I learned how to paddle last week. I have better things to do with my time," Evangeline replied with a threatening bite to her words.

Since Lilli had always believed in attacking a problem head-on, she walked right up to Evangeline and stared directly into her eyes. "Like spying? Too busy with spying on me?"

"That's right. And I've got enough evidence to get both of you fired."

"Really? Like what?"

Evangeline's eyes crackled with jealousy. Her voice was raspy with anger and hatred that had been born long ago, and although she was venting her emotions against Lilli now, Lilli knew that she was not the cause of this girl's misery. "I saw you with him down by the lake last week. I saw him screwing you. I saw you on top of him and him sticking it in you. I saw enough to ruin your reputation for the rest of your life. If Martha and her stupid Bob knew what the two of you were doing out there, they would kick you out in two seconds flat!"

Evangeline had worked herself into such a fury that by the time she finished, she was sputtering spittle into Lilli's face. But Lilli never flinched or blinked. She remained as cold as granite until Evangeline had finished.

"You saw it all."

"I did!" Evangeline folded her arms over her chest imperiously. Triumph rang in her voice.

Lilli remained silent and simply stared at Evangeline.

Evangeline had never been faced with this reaction. Why wasn't Lilli begging for mercy? Why wasn't she offering Evangeline anything, money, a favorite piece of jewelry, promises she could never keep to save her job and her reputation? Maybe Lilli was a tramp after all, Evangeline thought. Maybe she did this with all the boys. That didn't make sense, because Lilli was beautiful. She could have any boy she wanted and she had picked the best one in camp. She had picked the one Evangeline had wanted. Evangeline was incensed with Lilli's lack of reaction. She'd never met anyone so totally fearless.

"What are you, Lilli? Some kind of robot? Didn't you hear me? I said I was going to tell Martha and Bob the truth."

"I heard you."

"Well?"

Lilli stepped back a foot. "You'd better hurry up. They'll both be going to the lake for the canoe tryouts in a few minutes. You know how they loved that canoe race last week."

"You ... you don't care if I tell?"

"Frankly, no."

"Why not?"

Lilli moved closer again. "Because I don't think you will tell anybody anything, Evangeline."

"What makes you so sure?"

"Because if this was a matter of morals, we wouldn't be standing here talking about it. You'd already have informed Martha, and I would have been long gone. I think what you want, Evangeline, is to inflict pain. Sort of like a scorpion. You want to hurt the way you've been hurt. You thought I would go running away and leave Zane here for you to play with. Well, it's not going to work out that way."

"You think you're so smart," Evangeline said maliciously. "I *will* tell Martha. I *will!*"

"Go ahead. But if I leave, Zane leaves, too. You see, Evangeline, he loves me. I love him. We are best friends. You've never had a best friend, have you, Evangeline?"

"I—"

"No, you haven't. But you know what, Evangeline? I'd like to be your best friend."

"Why should you? You're just after my money like my daddy says all people are."

"I don't give a rat's ass about your money. I do sympathize with you. You had a mother who ran away and left you. My mother hates me, and sometimes I think she stays around just to make my life miserable."

"You don't mean that."

"I do. I think we have a lot to share with each other. We could be really good for each other if you gave us a chance."

Evangeline's hands were shaking from the anger she felt. She wanted to strike out at the world, which she believed had been so unfair to her. But she was unable to contain her rage for much longer, and her eyes welled with hot tears. "I-I'm not so sure."

"I can understand that. You must be saying to yourself, 'How can I trust her?' "

"Yeah." Evangeline wiped away her tears with the palm of her hand.

"We all have to start somewhere. Want to give it a try?"

For a long moment, Evangeline did not respond. Instead, she stared deeply into Lilli's eyes, as if trying to find reason to mistrust her. She could not.

"Okay," she agreed with the first genuinely happy smile she'd displayed since coming to camp.

"Let's shake on it," Lilli said, extending her hand, which Evangeline grasped hesitantly until she saw the smile on Lilli's face. Then she gave Lilli's hand a firm shake.

"Friends," Evangeline finally said, feeling a surprising warm glow of happiness.

Mishaps, small in nature at first, then escalating to danger-ous perils, befell Zane and his little troop at cabin number four. On Monday night the legs of Zane's cot collapsed and caused him a nasty bump on the back of his head. On Wednesday morning a small brushfire started not far from the recreation hall, and due to the strong winds and extremely dry terrain, it spread like a swarm of locusts, devouring all veg-etation in sight. If it had not been for Zane's quick action, rigging up the fire hose to the sump pump down at the lake's edge, the recreation hall would surely have caught fire. Zane was the hero of the week for his quick thinking, and neither Bob nor the other counselors could praise him enough.

Saturday night a tree limb broke off a tree and nearly missed crashing down on Zane as he exited the gym after his workout. It wasn't until Monday morning, when the wooden steps to the male counselors' cabin collapsed, that Zane suspected that foul play was to blame in each and every one of these instances.

Lilli went with Zane back to the place where the tree limb had narrowly missed him. She picked up the thicker end. "See that?"

"It's been cut off, probably by a hatchet."

"Like the one in Bob's cabin?"

"Exactly."

"Do you have any idea who would do this?"

"Yes. But I can't prove anything."

Lilli looked up at Zane. "You don't think Evangeline—that she was lying to me about being her friend, do you? She's been doing so well this past week."

"I guess it's just my male belief in double standards, but I'd hate to think a girl would be this devious."

Lilli looked away to the charred and burned knoll and knew that anyone, male or female, was capable of anything if pushed far enough. Evangeline was just beginning to understand her own emotional needs, few of which had ever been met. The young girl was learning about the deep anger and rage that occurs when inner truths are unearthed. Evangeline had finally understood that her father didn't love her after all and that she was simply a necessary convenience or inconvenience, depending upon the season or holiday of the year. At Christmas, she was needed to be his entertainment. By summer, she was shipped out of town while he spent his time with a new girlfriend. Evangeline was even coming to understand why her mother might have run away, and it frightened her to think that she had been wrong about her mother all these years. Evangeline's psyche was bruised and tender.

Lilli wondered if Evangeline had already gone over the edge. She had wanted to save her. Maybe she was already too late.

"I've got to see Evangeline," Lilli said, turning away from Zane.

"I'll be down at the lake when you're through. I have a scuba class I'm teaching," he shouted as she walked away. "Meet me there."

Lilli did not turn around but waved her arm over her head to signal that she understood him.

Zane followed the path to the gym and assembled the necessary gear he would need to teach his class. On a wooden homemade trolley he piled the regulators with their respective octopuses, air tanks, fins, snorkels, and masks. He rummaged around in a double-door locker and found a bottle of blue-colored liquid to smear on the insides of the face masks to keep them defogged. Since he wore his bathing suit under his walking shorts, he left his shorts in the locker along with his T-shirt.

By the time he got to the pier, most of his class was present. Barry, Martin, Jason, Andrew, and seven other boys were all assembled. Zane signaled to them to help him with the equipment. Barry was the first to oblige and took the tanks, since he was older and much stronger than the other boys.

One of the younger boys, Jimmy, pulled Zane aside and told him that he was asthmatic and was concerned about breathing the compressed air. Zane assured him that he would be fine, but to be doubly sure, Zane would let him be his diving buddy. "You did fine on land yesterday with our lesson. Just pretend you're still above water and don't panic. You're a good swimmer, Jimmy. Just keep close to me when we go down."

"Thanks, Zane." Jimmy's blue eyes were filled with hero worship.

Andrew attached the regulators to the tanks with quick, knowledgeable movements while Jason distributed the masks. Everyone fit his snorkel into the black rubber harness on the side of the mask and then doused the inside of his face mask with the defogging liquid. Barry paired up the fins by matching the sizes that were marked on the bottoms of the fins and then handed them out to each diver.

"I know you've all been over your rules and regulations several times," Zane said. "We aren't going very deep here because I just want you to get the feel of the water around you. What we will be experiencing here today is the same as a demonstration in a pool. This exercise today is not to be construed as a deep-water dive. We'll be taking that dive in a couple of days, at the end of camp, once you've all passed the written test. Today all I want you to do is become familiar with the feel of the regulator, the weight of the tank, and how to operate the octopus, which is used only in case of an emergency."

Zane fit his fins onto his feet, slipped his arms through the straps of the harness on the tank, and adjusted his face mask. He walked over to the end of the pier and jumped into the water. He stood in water up to his chest. "Everybody into the water and form a semicircle around me and remember, it is *not* deep here. Careful of the rocks on the bottom."

The boys entered the water one by one, careful not to crowd one another. They fiddled with their masks and regulators, since this was their first time with equipment. Zane could tell that they were all chomping at the bit to get under the water.

"Okay. Now, everybody pair off. Andrew, you go with Jimmy. Barry, you take John, and so on down the line. Now, everybody put your regulator in your mouth, and as you do so, blow out to clear the hose."

The boys followed Zane's instructions perfectly. "Remember that during your descent you will clear your ears by grabbing your nostrils, pinching them together, and blowing as hard as you can. This process is called clearing. Now, I'd like you all to adjust your face masks . . ."

"Would it be all right for us to move down a bit?" Barry asked. "The sun is right in my eyes here and I know the others don't want to say anything, but it would help a lot."

"Sure," Zane said as he followed Barry's lead by sidestepping his way to the left. "Check your regulators. Get used to the manner of breathing. I know it seems weird, Jimmy, not breathing through your nose, but you can do it," he said to the freckle-faced boy whose eyes were filled with alarm as they moved into deeper water. Zane knew he would have to keep an eye on Jimmy since he seemed close to panic. Zane wanted the boy to learn to overcome his fears, and once he did that, Zane had no doubt Jimmy would be a good diver.

"Okay. This is far enough. Come here, Jimmy. Take my hand. Okay, guys. Everybody listen up. Since Barry is the only one with any underwater experience, I want to take you each down individually. It's an incredible feeling to be suspended in the water. Granted there are no tropical fish here or corals, but this is just to get you certified and to help you feel comfortable with the breathing equipment."

The boys nodded to their leader.

"Jimmy." Zane turned to the younger boy. "Don't be afraid. You're going to love this. Just tell yourself that this is what it feels like to walk on the moon. Pretend you're in outer space."

Jimmy's flattened lips parted beneath the tight rubber edges of his face mask, making him look like smiling blowfish. Zane patted his back good-naturedly.

"Okay, we're going under for a look-see." Zane put his mask over his eyes and nose, gripped the mouthpiece between his teeth, took Jimmy's hand, ducked under the water, and swam out into the lake a few feet.

Zane knew that Jimmy was in no danger in this area, because the deepest that he'd found the water to be near the pier was only about seven feet. It was just enough to get the feeling of weightlessness that Zane wanted Jimmy to experience. The water was murky, though. Zane had hoped the water would be clearer. Also, the wind had picked up, stirring the surface even more, making visibility nonexistent past twenty feet. Still, Zane knew the boys would enjoy the experience.

Jimmy took to the dive like a champ. He worked his legs from his hips and was able to pick up a bit of speed. Zane watched the boy's bubbles and saw an even, steady stream rising to the surface, indicating that Jimmy was using the proper amount of air. Jimmy turned back toward Zane and waved enthusiastically.

Jimmy was obviously excited with his new skill as a diver, Zane thought. He zipped to the left and then to the right. He was young and energetic and did not seem to use up his air as most novices did. Zane was thrilled with the boy's success.

Zane signaled to Jimmy to return to the surface. The boy waved to the instructor, indicating he understood the directive.

Suddenly Jimmy stopped dead still. His muscles froze. His

legs and arms went limp. Zane didn't think. He acted. His feet shot out behind him and he whipped his fins through the water, making speed like a turbo. Incredible as it seemed, Jimmy seemed to keep sinking downward. Zane immediately surmised that somehow Jimmy had gone too far and found the drop-off. God only knew how deep this lake really was.

Just as Zane was zooming in above the descending Jimmy, he realized that straight ahead of him was an enormous gray boulder, common to the area. The gray of the boulder combined with the murky water to create a deadly illusion of space. Zane realized that Jimmy must have swum directly into the boulder and knocked himself unconscious. Zane had nearly done the same.

There were no air bubbles rising. Zane shot downward to retrieve the boy.

He blew out his air and took another breath and found that the air in his tank was completely gone. Stupid! Stupid! he chastised himself. He had been so concerned about the boys and their safety that he had failed to double-check his own tank. He held his breath.

One one thousand. Two one thousand. Zane counted to himself as he kicked violently toward Jimmy. Three one thousand. Four one thousand. Zane's arm shot out and he captured Jimmy around the shoulders and neck and began pulling him upward.

Five one thousand. Zane's muscles were screaming more from the lack of oxygen and his own panic than from fatigue.

Six one thousand. As Zane swam toward the surface he knew there was no reason to panic. He knew they would be fine. He reached around Jimmy's side, found his octopus, and exchanged mouthpieces. Zane took a deep pull on the air and found that Jimmy's tank was empty, too.

Seven one thousand. Zane kicked his legs faster. Eight one thousand. He had to get Jimmy to safety. If anything happened to this boy. . . . Zane knew he could control his breath long enough to get him to the surface, but Jimmy had asthma. Jimmy had been without air for long, precious seconds, longer than Zane.

Nine one thousand.

They broke the surface. Water spewed out of Zane's mouth when he spit out the regulator. He swam to the pier, pulling the unconscious Jimmy behind him. He shouted to the other boys to get onto the pier and help him. Zane held Jimmy up, and the boys pulled him out of the water. Jason took off Jimmy's face mask and snorkel, while Andrew helped Zane out of the harness that held his tank. Barry helped to yank off Jimmy's fins. The boys were too frightened to ask questions, but Zane could hear the mumbled prayers sprinkled with shocked remarks.

Zane laid Jimmy on his belly and began clearing his lungs of the lake water. It only took two deep pushes to release what seemed like several bucketfuls of water from the boy. Jimmy sputtered and choked, but the rest of the boys burst into a loud cheer as Zane turned Jimmy onto his back and pulled him into his strong arms for a big hug.

Zane had never been so close to tears. "Thank God, Jimmy. Thank God," was all he could say.

Jimmy seemed rather embarrassed by all the attention as the other boys slapped his back gleefully and tousled his red hair.

Zane rocked back on his heels and watched how the boys lavished Jimmy with their side of the adventure, even though none were directly involved. The sun glinted over the tops of the boys' heads, momentarily blinding Zane. He understood now what Barry had meant when he said the sun was a nuisance. At that moment Zane looked up and realized that Barry was not joining in the triumphant moment with the other boys. He was standing a few paces away from Jimmy. His face was blank and expressionless, and Zane felt chills race down his spine.

Zane stood up. He knew he had his culprit. Not just for this incident, but for all the "accidents" that had befallen the camp that week.

He walked up to Barry and pretended to put his arm around the boy. In fact, he had Barry in a headlock and had placed his thumb on Barry's jugular. "I think we need to talk," Zane said.

Barry's brown eyes held not a flicker of remorse, and Zane knew that for the rest of his life he'd never see anything as frightening as that cold, empty look.

"Take your hand off me," Barry said coolly.

"Not a chance," Zane said with a menacing grin. "You see,

I know who your daddy is out there in the East. He's a big shot in banking and in politics. He's got his eyes on the governor's mansion, and I'll bet my pair of snakeskin boots he wouldn't want any kind of scandal about his precious, perfect son to get out, now, would he?"

"I'll have you fired! I'll fix it so you never work at a camp again."

"I doubt that real seriously, you little shit. This is Texas, boy. We do things differently down here than they do out East. We don't take the time to make calls and consult our political friends. We just take care of business. Now, before I'd go telling your daddy about you fucking with the tanks and then maneuvering my class over there to where you knew we'd hit that drop-off, I'd simply take you down for a little dive of my own."

"You wouldn't dare." Barry riveted his challenging eyes on Zane.

Zane didn't blink. He returned the same empty, emotionless look Barry had given him. Barry shivered. Zane knew he had him.

"I'll do anything I goddamn please. I'm a Texan and I make the rules here. Besides, you forgot something."

"What's that?"

"You and I both know that your daddy doesn't give a shit about you. If he did, you'd be with him, not stuck out here in this godforsaken country with a pack of strangers."

Barry swallowed hard.

"I think we have an understanding now, don't we?"

"Yes," Barry replied weakly.

"Good. Now go over there and make a fuss over Jimmy before your fancy friends figure out what an asshole you really are."

Barry nodded tersely and did just as he was instructed.

When the diving class got back to camp, the boys couldn't wait to tell Bob and Martha about Jimmy's near demise and the exciting rescue. Bob took Zane aside and grilled him about the equipment. Zane told Bob that the equipment had not failed, but that he took full blame for the incident. He told Bob that he had been careless, and as a result he knew that Bob would be forced to fire him.

Bob knew Zane well, he believed, and he also knew a lie

when he heard one. There had been many odd accidents around camp that week, and most of them had happened to Zane. Bob believed that Zane was covering up for one of the boys, and although he wanted to expose the real culprit, he also believed in Zane's ability to handle these boys. Bob was not convinced, however, that Zane was handling the matter in the right way, but he had no choice but to go along with it.

"I believe you, Zane. However, for my records, I want you to put in writing tonight every detail you can remember about the incident. I don't want some outraged parent coming along and trying to sue me."

"Don't worry. I don't think you'll have that problem."

Barry watched Bob walk away before he went over to Zane. "You didn't have to do that. Cover up for me, I mean."

"I know I didn't. I probably shouldn't have."

Barry looked down at his dusty gym shoes and then back at Zane again. "Nobody's ever stuck up for me before."

"I know that."

"You do?"

"Yeah. But would you do *me* the same turn?"

"What's that?"

"After all those kids leave, you take Jimmy aside and tell him the truth. You tell him you owe him your stinking life, because you nearly stole his. Then you take your consequences like a man. If he chooses to tell his parents and they start crawling up your ass, you take it like a man. If you're going to play with real bullets, you better learn to carry the gun."

"Jesus! I can't do that!"

"You have no choice." Zane crossed his arms over his chest. "Maybe you could start liking people instead of hating everybody. Maybe you and Jimmy could be friends."

"He's just a kid. And a nerd."

Zane ground his teeth together to keep from shouting. "He's a human being, and that's a step up from your level."

Barry turned his head toward the group around Jimmy. He was amazed how everyone thought Jimmy was so cool now. They all wanted to be his friend. Maybe it wouldn't be so bad, Barry thought. Without another word, he left Zane alone, walked over to the group, and blended into the circle as if he'd been there all along.

* * *

Lilli snuggled against Zane's bare chest in the moonlight. They had made love for over an hour, experimenting with each other's bodies as if this, too, were a joyous adventure. They were leaving camp in the morning, their summer jobs having ended.

Zane stroked Lilli's bare back. "I wish it could have been better for you, Lilli," he whispered with a strain of melancholy to his words.

"Zane, it was perfect."

"No, Lilli. I mean I wanted your first time with me to be someplace really special, like the Plaza in New York. With room service and champagne and huge bouquets of white roses. I wanted to take you to the theater and see some really great show and then ride through Central Park in one of those fancy horse carriages. Lilli, I want to do so many things for you."

Lilli placed her finger against his lips. "Shhh. Don't be silly. I don't want all those things. I want you."

"But don't you see, Lilli? I want to give you those things. You deserve them. You're so beautiful and kind and giving. Just look what you did for Evangeline. She's turned out to be a pretty neat person after all."

"I think most people are, Zane, if they feel loved. I have so much happiness with you that I want everyone to be just as happy."

Zane propped himself up on his elbow. "Well, I'm going to New York someday, Lilli, and I'm going to become really rich and I'm going to buy you the best of everything. We'll travel the world. I want to buy you a real Paris gown and then I'll take you to the opera."

"Zane, you don't even like opera. And neither do I."

"Okay. You can wear it to a Willie Nelson concert."

"That's better." She laughed.

"Just dream along with me, Lilli."

"Is it so important . . . the money? New York?"

"Yeah. My dad could never get off that dusty old ranch that's not much of a ranch anymore. I want to make it to where he always wanted to go. It would really be something if a McAllister could conquer New York."

Lilli was pensive for a long moment. "Your father would let you go?"

"Sure, why not? I *won't* go while he's sick, but he wants me to go."

"My pop always says that families have to stick together—no matter what. He must have said that to me a hundred times. I think if you really loved your family, you'd want to stay in Texas."

"I love them, but I have to live my own life. And you wouldn't have to stay in Texas, Lilli. You could come to New York with me."

Lilli looked up into Zane's eyes. "I'd go anywhere with you, Zane." Then she smiled teasingly. "Are you sure you don't want to stay in Texas? Isn't Houston big enough for you?"

He touched the tip of her chin with his finger and then kissed her lovingly on the mouth. "It's New York, baby. All the way."

Then he pulled her into his arms and made love to her again. He was tender and caring as always, yet he'd learned by now to be just a bit lustful when he brought her to the edges of ecstasy. Lilli never dreamed that lovemaking could be so delicious and exciting. She gave back to him everything he gave to her and she cradled him in her arms in the afterglow. Just as Lilli was falling asleep, her mind filled with the events of the past month.

They had lived through a lot that summer. They had come to understand not only themselves but others and the odd and even dangerous ways that humans choose to relate to one another. The last two days in camp had found Barry and Jimmy becoming close friends. Martha's search for Evangeline's mother hit a roadblock after the first few phone calls. Before Evangeline left camp, Martha discussed her efforts with the young girl, and although the task appeared difficult, Evangeline seemed intent about discovering the truth about her mother. She thanked Lilli for opening her eyes to her problems.

"You're a good friend, Lilli. I wish I didn't have to say good-bye."

"Then don't. We'll keep in touch. I'm a good letter writer," Lilli said and hugged Evangeline tightly.

* * *

Lilli believed she had become a woman that summer, a maturation not solely due to her loss of virginity, but rather to the deeply felt emotional bond she'd formed with Zane. Lilli knew she held Zane not just with her body, but with her heart and soul. She knew there could never be anyone else for her. The thought of another man inside her was unbearable.

A bittersweet tune kept playing in her mind as she thought about leaving him. She would see him from time to time, as they did when he came to Houston, and there would be letters, of course, but none of that was the same as this month had been, when they saw each other every day and stole precious moments in the moonlight every night they could.

Lilli felt that if there was one period in her life when she could choose to stop time and live in a moment for eternity, she would choose this month, with this man. She felt at home with the moon, stars, and wind. Lilli didn't need luxurious suites and gourmet foods to know that Zane loved her. She wondered why he refused to accept this about her, but she released the idea because it cast doubt on her dreams of their future together. She told herself that everything would work out. She wanted to believe that they had their whole lives together, but some deep reverberating, sorrowful note haunted her mind and told her that *this* was bliss, and she should cherish it always.

Thirteen

Early June 1978
Bandera, Texas

The flu kept Zane at home that day. His mother had gone into town to run errands, buy groceries, and do some banking, which left Zane and his father alone.

At two o'clock, Zane experienced his first hour of being able to breathe freely. Finally, the over-the-counter drug was working. He went into the living room, sat in the brown tweed swivel rocker, and turned on the television set. Besides soap operas, game shows, and *Star Trek* reruns, there was not much worth watching. He started to watch *Star Trek,* one of his favorite shows, but he'd already seen this episode so many times he could recite the dialogue. He got up and turned off the set. It was then that he noticed the postman driving up to the mailbox.

Zane's face brightened. Out of habit, he realized, because today was bound to be like all the other days. There wouldn't be a letter from Lilli.

Just then his father walked into the room. Ted McAllister was unshaven, his hair was nearly gone from the chemotherapy treatments he'd been receiving, and he could barely shuffle across the multicolored shag carpeting. But Ted McAllister was a hero in Zane's book. The doctors had told Ted he only had three months to live, but that had been nearly two years ago. Ted was beating cancer the only way he knew how . . . one day at a time.

"You shouldn't be up, Dad," Zane said, sprinting to his father's side and helping him into the swivel rocker.

"Why not? The worst that can happen is that I'd die standing up. I'd rather go like that than in a hospital somewhere."

Zane sat on the flowered Early American couch. "You hungry? What can I get for you?"

"I'm fine, son. Just fine." He leaned his head back on the rocker. "I heard the mail truck. You'd think Lonnie would get a new muffler for that thing. Why don't you see if that girl of yours wrote to you?"

"She didn't."

"How can you be so sure?"

"She's with her father on another dig . . . She probably hasn't had time."

Ted frowned at his son. "Damn it, son, buck up. You can't go around all down in the mouth. Have you written to her?"

"Yes. But who knows if she got them or not? She gave me a place near one of their sites, but I've been sending most of them to her house, because she said her mother would have an updated itinerary."

Ted watched Zane's expression alternate from happiness to sadness as he talked about Lilli. There was no mistaking love, Ted thought. He was surprised that it had come so early to Zane when it had come so late to Ted. Ted had not met Hannah until they were in college. They married after he received his degree in business from A&M. Ted had not started out in life wanting to be a gemologist, but one failed business venture had led to another, and after ten successful years as a pawnbroker, he found there was a future in estate jewelry. Ted was a fast learner and realized he'd been blessed with a keen eye for jewels. It was the one attribute he'd passed on to his son.

Ted was proud of Zane and the way he conducted his life. He supposed Zane did plenty of the things the other boys did, but there was a maturity to Zane that even he had not possessed when he was young. Ted remembered the time when Zane and his basketball buddies had gotten drunk and had to be hauled out of the Guadalupe River three summers back. Ted had found a couple of *Playboy* magazines in Zane's room, although he never told Hannah, and he knew that Zane had smoked his share of cigarettes and even tried a joint or two. Ted knew that his wife would attribute Zane's good conduct to her Bible preaching, but he wanted to believe that Zane was just smarter than they were. He hoped that Zane could think for himself. This long-distance relationship Zane was building with Lilli showed him that his son did think for himself, because Ted knew that if Hannah could have her way, she would put an end to it.

"Go get the mail, son. I want to know if the Publishers Clearing House has sent my entry form yet."

Zane laughed and went to the mailbox and pulled out a stack of mail that was mostly junk. On the bottom was an air-mail letter from Lilli. "I don't believe it."

He rushed back into the house. "You were right, Dad!"

Ted smiled. "I must be getting psychic. They say that happens to you just before you die." Suddenly he turned away from Zane and looked out the window. He didn't want Zane to see the tears in his eyes.

Ted didn't like the fact that time was running out. He wanted to be around for Zane's first business triumphs in New York, as both of them had always dreamed about. Zane had the ambition and courage to succeed in the big city, qualities Ted knew he had never possessed. He'd wanted to be a hero to his son, but in his case, Zane had become a hero to his father. Ted knew he was guilty of living his life through his son, but he had so little life left. Zane was young and fearless and a hell of a lot more talented than Ted.

He could envision Zane in New York, living on Park Avenue, riding in limousines, and meeting famous and powerful people on a daily basis. Ted wanted Zane to have all the adventure in life that he'd missed by staying in West Texas. Although he had no real regrets, Ted still wanted Zane to eke out every last drop of excitement that life had to offer.

More than anything, Ted wanted his son to think that he wasn't afraid of dying, but the truth was that he was terrified.

Hanging on to the fringes of life, Ted McAllister had seen enough doctors and hospitals to last him into eternity. He didn't want to go back and wouldn't go back. In his estimation, chemotherapy and radiation had made him sicker than the cancer. Several times he'd just said to himself he was going to die and he'd gone to sleep with every intention of never waking up. But something inside him always made him wake up.

The problem was that the longer he stayed alive, the more questions he had. Ted had prayed to Jesus to be relieved of his pain, but the pain continued. He began to doubt; his faith dwindled. He wondered if there was a heaven. He knew now there was no hell like Hannah talked about. He was living in hell. It couldn't get much worse.

Ted finally learned that *he* kept himself alive. It wasn't a lot of prayers or doctors or radiation. His cancer had spread wildly at first; then the radiation and chemotherapy had stopped it. Then it came back again. Ted didn't like pain and so he willed it away. He decided he wanted to live, and the only reason he decided to live was because he was too damn scared to find out what awaited him after death.

Ted watched Zane's face as he read his letter. He was glad he'd adopted this new belief, if only for the simple reason that he'd stayed alive long enough to see his son fall in love.

"What does she say, son?"

"She's been going through some rough times. She's afraid her father is a dreamer . . ."

"Nothin' wrong with dreams, son."

"Yeah, but she thinks he's chasing after something that doesn't exist. It seems to me that her faith in her father has been shaken—again." He read a bit further in silence.

"She's worried about her year-end finals. She's never been gone this long. She's afraid they'll hold her back." Zane read further, and then he began laughing. "*Now* she says she intends to take a battery of tests when she gets home and thinks she'll test out of several subjects and skip a whole semester next year!" Zane finished the letter, where Lilli told him that she couldn't wait to see him and gave him her arrival date in Houston, which was only two days from now. "What a great girl."

"You really like her, don't you, Zane?"

"Yeah," he said, blushing, and then looked away from his father. "She's different. I mean really different. You know, before I met Lilli I thought all girls were like the girls I know here."

"How's that?"

"You know. They aren't even out of high school and all they want to do is get married. I know of only four girls who talk about careers . . . and they're ugly."

"Zane . . ."

"I know. It's not the Christian thing to say."

"I wasn't going to say that. What I was going to say is that it's only to be expected." Then Ted laughed. "Maybe the girls you know here just don't believe in themselves much."

"Maybe. But Lilli is beautiful, Dad. And smart and ambitious and funny."

"That last one? That's what will get you through life. Believe me."

"I can't wait to see her again."

Suddenly Ted was flooded with sentiment. He saw his son as a man. He would be nineteen on his next birthday, old enough to fight wars, to marry, to have his own life. And he could tell Zane was itching to get out there and go for it. Ted had taught his son everything he knew about the jewelry business. His son was the only legacy he was leaving the world. He hoped he'd done a good job. He thought he had. Ted guessed a parent could never be too sure. But in Ted's case, it was important he be sure.

"You gonna marry her, son?"

"I want to, eventually, but I know we have to wait. You know, Dad, she's younger than I am, but in some ways, she seems older. Lilli is so—"

"Different," Ted finished with a laugh.

"Yeah." Zane laughed with him.

Ted began coughing. It caused the pain to start again. Zane patted his father's back and rushed to the kitchen for a glass of cold water he poured from the container his mother kept in the refrigerator.

At just that moment Hannah came through the front door carrying two bags of groceries. One look at Ted told her he was in agony.

"Get his pills, Zane!" she said, dropping the bags by the open door and rushing to her husband's side. "Oh, this is all my fault for leaving you."

Ted was exhausted from the pain. "It isn't . . . it's nobody's fault. I'm sick, Hannah. It is what it is."

"This is a curse that has come down on our family. I just don't know why the Lord is doing this to us," she wailed.

"Hannah, the Lord has nothing to do with this, either."

Hannah wrung her hands as Zane came back to the room with his father's medication. Ted swallowed the pain pills and rested his head on the back of the rocker.

"I wish you wouldn't blaspheme the Lord," Hannah chided.

"Mom! Leave Dad alone. He did nothing of the kind."

Hannah turned righteous eyes on her son. "Don't you treat me with disrespect! That is a sin and you know it."

Zane would not buckle under to her. Not this time. "Do you think it is possible for you to make one statement to either Dad or me that is not connected with the Bible, Jesus, or sins? Just one, Mom." Zane stood, legs spread, in a defiant stance. He felt like David meeting Goliath. No, he felt even better than that. Like Zeus, that Greek god he had read about in mythology class. His father needed defending. He would save him.

Hannah rose up with equal defiance. Although she was a tall woman, she did not come anywhere near Zane's six-foot-two-inch height. She was formidable, though, for she believed she had Jesus Himself on her side and she wielded His wrath like a true Christian soldier. Her eyes flared with indignation. Her hands were balanced imperiously on her hips and she stood with her feet pressed heavily into the carpet. She shoved her face so close to Zane's he could feel her anger before she spoke a word.

"I am your mother. I will not be treated in this manner. I don't know where you get the idea that anything you have to say is of any account around here, but it's not. Your father is ill. I have nearly killed myself taking care of both you and him. The only reason he is alive is because I have prayed endlessly for his recovery. You get on your knees and thank God for your father's life. You beg Him for forgiveness for what you've done today." She placed one hand on his shoulder with a force Zane couldn't believe she possessed, and dug her nails into his clavicle.

He could fight her off, he knew. She was not stronger than he. But it was as if she were being aided by some invisible force. Her eyes bored into his. He felt his will cracking; then he succumbed to her power. His knees buckled. She dug her nails deeper and the pain shot down his arms and up the back of his neck. He began sinking to his knees against his will. He wondered if the Lord was standing at his mother's side.

Ted's eyes were bleary with the effects of the pain medication. "Hannah, leave the boy be," he croaked.

Hannah heard nothing but the sound of her own voice as she began quoting Scripture. Then she chastised Zane even more. "Beg Him!" she demanded.

"Please, God . . . forgive me," he finally said, knowing his mother's nails had punctured his cotton shirt and broken the skin on his shoulder.

Suddenly she pulled her hand away.

Zane hated her at that instant. Then he hated himself for harboring such intense feelings against his own mother. Guilt settled upon his shoulders like a lead mantle.

"Zane," Ted implored softly, "take me back to bed."

"Sure, Dad," Zane said. He took his anger, defiance, and feelings of injustice and let them infuse his muscles with strength. He bent over his father, put one arm under his legs and the other around his back, and hoisted him effortlessly into the air.

"Son, this isn't necessary . . . I can walk."

"Save your strength, Dad," he said and then turned to his mother. This time his eyes gleamed with a zealousness of their own. "I have enough strength for both of us," he said pointedly to his mother.

Hannah's chin jutted out and her lips were pursed, but she did not reply to her son's challenge. She simply watched Zane carry Ted out of the living room into the bedroom. Then she glanced down at the couch and saw that Zane had received a letter from Lilli.

Hannah frowned. Thus far, she had been successful in keeping most of Lilli's letters from Zane. She had read them all and kept them in a bundle in her dresser drawer. Lilli was not good for Zane. Her ideas were heretical at the least, and at the most, Hannah knew that Lilli was trying to take her son from her.

Hannah thought of the way Zane ministered to his father. She was afraid that today she had finally pushed Zane too far. From now on, she must be careful.

The next morning Zane awoke to find that his father was worse, much worse. But despite his pain, Ted was arguing with Hannah.

"I won't go, Hannah."

"It's not a hospital. No IVs. Not a single needle."

"It's a hoax."

"It's a Christian healer. He can save you. I just know he can."

"I told you three months ago I wouldn't go to this quack. He just wants our money and that's Zane's college fund. "I won't touch it. It's Zane's money."

"You're getting worse by the minute. We have to go. It's our only chance. This will work. I believe it will. You have to believe, Ted."

"I don't have to *do* anything, Hannah." Then the pain flooded him again. He moaned.

Zane eavesdropped on his parents' conversation. To him, every one of his father's groans was like a sharp dagger piercing in his own body. He couldn't take it; he wanted to run away.

"I have to go, Dad," Zane said, coming into the room. "I have an appointment with a client. But maybe I shouldn't leave."

"Go . . ." Ted's face was distorted with pain. "I'm going to live to see you make it in this business and get to New York. Remember?"

"Sure, Dad." Zane leaned down and kissed his father on the forehead.

He couldn't get out of the house fast enough.

When Zane returned that afternoon, he found two packed suitcases near the door. He darted into the kitchen.

"What's going on, Mom? What's with the suitcases?"

"We're going to Mexico City to see the faith healer. We leave in the morning."

"You can't! Dad doesn't want to go."

Hannah dropped the apple she was peeling and glared at her son. "Your father has had his worst day yet. Go ask him. We're going."

"But . . . Mom . . . Lilli comes home tomorrow."

"What?" She batted her eyelids rapidly as she cocked her head to the left. It was a mannerism she used every time she heard something she did not like or accept. Zane hated it.

"I wanted to see Lilli. I haven't seen her since March."

Hannah's eyes widened. "Really? You never told me about

that. How did you see her in March and I didn't know about it?"

I'm screwed, Zane thought. How could he have slipped up like that? He'd been able to keep nearly all his visits to Lilli a secret from his mother. He knew Hannah would have a conniption fit if she learned that he and Lilli had been together every time he went to Houston, which, if Zane had anything to do with it, would have been twice as often as he'd actually gone. "I guess I forgot to tell you."

"I guess. Or was it that you were lying to me, Zane?"

The hairs on the back of Zane's neck stood on end. She was getting ready to lambast him again. He had to deflect her. "No way. I've been busy, too, Mother, taking care of Dad's business. I've got my hands full. We're both trying to get through this the only way we know how. Gee, Mom," he said, using his charm, "you *do* like Lilli, don't you?"

Hannah knew she couldn't tell Zane the truth because that would only push him into Lilli's arms all the more. She had to play this game with her son or she would lose him for certain. Hannah believed that Lilli would trip herself up with Zane and that would be the end of it. Childhood crushes like this never really amounted to anything. Look at her own crush on Dick Brown when she was fifteen. He had left her and got Susan Malloy pregnant, and that was the end of that. She had been so infatuated with Dick that she'd nearly given her virginity to him. She had nearly sinned against the Lord. A sin such as that she would never forgive herself for. Dick hadn't been worth it. He hadn't loved her back. He was only out for what he could get. He was a bastard. No, Hannah thought. Lilli was a headstrong girl who would graduate from high school and go off with some Egyptologist or some university type. Once Lilli matured, she'd never want anyone like Zane.

"Lilli is a fine girl, Zane. I do wish she had some sort of religion, though. People who don't have such distorted views on things ..."

"Mother, must we get into that?" Zane turned around and left the kitchen.

He went into his father's bedroom. Ted's skin was as white as a sheet and he was covered in sweat. Zane could see his father's clenched jaw as he fought against the pain. He knelt beside the bed. "Pretty rough?"

Ted barely nodded his head. "Very."

"Mom says we're going to Mexico City. Are you sure about this?"

"It can't be any worse . . ." Ted groaned again.

"But it's a rough trip in the truck. I haven't cut the Esposito deal yet. I'm a week away from getting their money, but if I can set it up earlier, we'll have the money to fly down to Mexico."

Ted felt as if the pain would strangle him. Why couldn't he just die? He was afraid to live and he was afraid to die. It was limbo . . . no, it was hell and he wanted out. "Pills . . ."

"No amount of pain pills will help you through the trip."

How can I make him understand? Ted thought. I want you to get me Seconals. I want to die, Zane. Just let me die.

Ted just looked at his son. His eyes were bloodshot from the pain. He couldn't even talk anymore.

Zane couldn't watch his father's pain without feeling ripped in half himself. He stood, kissed his father's forehead as he always did, and went back to the kitchen.

"I'm not going to let you take Dad to Mexico City by truck, Mom."

"What?"

"You heard me. The trip alone will kill him. I'm going to get some money so that I can pay for plane tickets. Maybe your faith healer can give him a miracle."

"Of course he can, son. You just have to believe, is all."

Zane pulled his truck keys out of his pocket. "Yeah? Well, I believe I can do him more good in Houston than I can standing here. I'm going to talk to the Espositos." He started for the front door.

Hannah was instantly suspicious. "Zane! Come back here! You can't just go off. What if I need the truck? What if your father needs the truck?"

"He won't," he said firmly. He grabbed his mother's hand. "Look, Mom, if he's going to die, let him go. Don't call the ambulance. Just *let him go*. If he's still here when I get back, we'll know we're supposed to go see the faith healer."

Hannah still didn't trust him. "You're just trying to see Lilli, is all you're doing."

"I won't deny that, Mom. I intend to see her. But I'm also going to get Dad some money."

"Zane . . ."

He leaned over and kissed her quickly on the cheek and was out the door, across the porch, and in the truck before Hannah could protest. Zane revved the engine and put the truck in reverse. The back wheels churned up a cloud of dust that settled over the mesquite trees and scrub oaks in his wake. He couldn't wait to put the hill country behind him.

Fourteen

*O*nce he reached Houston, Zane telephoned the Espositos and set up a meeting for the next day. He told them they could meet at the Texas Commerce Bank where Zane kept the Spanish brooch in a safety deposit box. Mr. Howard "Buddy" Esposito was not adverse to making a deal with Zane a few days early once he understood Zane's need to finalize the sale.

According to Lilli's letter, she would be arriving at Intercontinental Airport at two-fifteen in the morning. He then telephoned Lilli's mother, Arlette.

"Hello, Mrs. Mitchell. This is Zane McAllister. I understand that Lilli will be arriving late tonight and I—"

"I don't know where you got that information, young man, but Lilli doesn't get in until late tomorrow. I'm sorry, but since she is so far behind in her schoolwork because her father decided to remain in Mexico a month longer than planned, she won't have time to see you when she gets in toni—tomorrow." She stopped herself immediately when she realized her blunder.

"I see," he said, suddenly suspicious of Mrs. Mitchell's motives. The undercurrents in her voice reminded him too much of his mother. "I must have misunderstood. So she won't be coming in until tomorrow, huh?"

"No. And she's going to be very busy. Maybe you could see her in a week or two."

A week or two? Zane couldn't wait that long. He was going to be in Mexico himself for an undetermined length of time. He didn't know when he'd be back. He had to try another tack. "I'll bet you really miss her, huh?"

"What? Oh, yes. Of course I do."

"So you'll be meeting them at the airport?"

"No. Mr. Mitchell always leaves his car out there. He has a friend who owns one of the Park and Go lots. He gets a big discount," she said proudly, liking to talk about their many connections.

"Wow! That's really something!" Zane said, pouring on the charm.

"Yes, it is," she replied.

"Well, I won't take any more of your time. I know how busy you are, Mrs. Mitchell. Please tell Lilli I called and that I hope she had a great trip."

Arlette paused, then asked, "You haven't heard that much from Lilli, have you?"

"Not really," he said truthfully.

Good. Arlette couldn't be more pleased. "I'll tell her you called. Good night, Zane."

"Good night, Mrs. Mitchell. It was a pleasure talking to you."

Zane hung up the phone. Then he jumped into his truck and headed toward I-45 North and the Intercontinental Airport.

He parked the car in a metered place that still had an hour of time on it. He raced into "B" terminal and checked all the monitors but saw no flights arriving at two-fifteen from any-where in Central America. He raced over to "A" terminal and checked all the flights there. Then he found an AeroMexico flight that landed at precisely two-fifteen. He made a note of the gate number and checked his watch.

It was ten-thirty. He had no place to sleep that night, and the airport was as good as any. He went down the concourse, passed through the metal detector, and found the gate. There were few people in the airport and already the concessions were closing down. Only the bars were staying open. He found a row of empty chairs that faced the window. He could see a plane docked at the next gate. It was being refueled. He had three hours and forty-five minutes to kill. He didn't know if he could wait that long to see Lilli.

Still half asleep, Lilli walked off the plane carrying a small duffel bag. J.C. was right behind her, checking his pockets for his baggage-claim tickets. They'd already gone through customs in Laredo.

Zane had fallen asleep in the chair, his head resting on his hand. He was unaware of the deplaning passengers until the man sitting next to him jumped up and cried "Margaret!" so loudly that Zane's hand slipped out from under his chin and his face fell on the armrest.

Immediately, Zane checked his mouth, afraid that he'd chipped a tooth. He looked up in time to see Lilli. At least he thought it was Lilli.

She was wearing a black turtleneck sweater, tight-fitting Western blue jeans, and her red Ropers. But the body that passed by him looked like the body of a fully grown woman. And she was taller. He would bet she was nearly five feet eight. This couldn't be his Lilli!

"Lilli?" he said faintly as he slowly rose to his feet. "Lilli, is that you?" he said louder.

The vision in blue jeans stopped in her tracks, tossed her shiny, long black hair over her shoulder as she turned her head, and stared at him with those violet eyes that had haunted his dreams for months.

"Zane!" She said his name and then looked at him as if he were the answer to her prayers.

Zane would never forget the look of love in her eyes that night. She dropped her bag on the spot and rushed into his arms. She flung her arms around his neck, not caring if her father or the whole world saw her.

She kissed him quickly on the mouth. Then on the cheek, then the mouth, then the other cheek, and back to his mouth again.

Lilli felt she had come back to life. This trip had been similar to the one to Guatemala the previous spring when she'd met with so many disappointments. Again J.C. talked about the city of gold to the dismay of the other dig members. Now he'd interjected a new theory about "rivers of gold." She was afraid that her father was a dreamer just as her mother had always said. She felt that she no longer understood her father or his motivations. She couldn't talk to him the way she had only months before. It wasn't all his fault, because she had changed, too. She spent her daydreams and desires on Zane, on wanting him the way a woman wants a man. It was the first time in her life she did not want to share her thoughts with her father. Something had been lost between them, and although she wanted to get it back, she knew she never would.

Then she saw Zane. Suddenly the world felt right again. He was half asleep, but he looked more handsome to her than ever. He held her so tightly she thought he would crush her ribs. She felt his hands press into her waist with a possessiveness and a longing she'd not felt from him before. When she looked up into his blue eyes, she realized that he was seeing her differently this time and it was more than the fact that he'd missed her. They had been apart for almost three months.

"You're not a little girl anymore, are you, Lilli Mitchell?" Zane said with appreciative awe.

"No," she answered, still gazing up at him, unwilling to take her arms from around his neck.

"Lilli," J.C. said, feeling awkward at interrupting their reunion, "I'll go get the bags and meet you downstairs."

She turned to look over at her father. "Thanks, Pop," she said casually, but suddenly there was a lump in her throat. When had her father sprouted those gray hairs at his temples? Had he always had those funny bags under his eyes, or was it just the long plane trip? It seemed to her that the furrows in his forehead were deeper than they had been only moments ago. He seemed thinner somehow and his gait lacked the spring she remembered. He was her pop. But that was all he could ever be to her. He couldn't be her Prince Charming.

J.C. left Zane and Lilli alone. He didn't see the tears in her eyes, nor did she see the ones in his.

"God! Lilli." Zane breathed the words into her ear as he nuzzled the side of her neck. "You're more beautiful than a dream." His hand slid to the back of her waist and pressed her body into his as she turned her face back to him.

His lips were soft yet insistent, coaxing her to melt into him. He ran his fingers through her hair, then pressed her face to his. She felt his tongue dart between his lips and then slowly touch the tip of her tongue. Shivers ran down her spine and around to her abdomen. She pulled him closer and pressed herself even tighter against him. She could feel his erection. The passion she remembered was still there between them. It had not disappeared; instead, it had intensified.

His lips became more insistent, and she wanted more of

him. When she kissed him back, using her tongue to taste the inside of his mouth, she felt him twitch and knew she'd created goose bumps for him, too.

They were lost in a place accessible only to lovers. There was no fear in this realm. This was where hearts were giving and joyful. This was what made life worth living.

When Zane pulled away from Lilli he was smiling. He rested his forehead against hers and kept his arms around her, enveloping her in a shield of love.

"I never thought I could miss anyone so much."

"Me, either."

Playfully, he slid his hand around her rib cage and indulged himself in a quick stroke against her breast.

"Watch out, you could get your hand slapped." She giggled as he kissed the end of her nose.

This time when they kissed, Zane was even more daring. His hands caressed her back, her ribs, her waist, and often brushed the sides of her breasts. He was lost in the kiss. His left hand fell to her hip and slid down the side. He grabbed her rounded derriere and leaned into her. Her pelvic bone was crushed against his erection.

Lilli felt all reason slip from her head. She felt fingers of liquid heat surge through her loins. She felt her nipples harden, and more than anything, she wanted to feel Zane's hand on her naked breast.

Zane's tongue danced with Lilli's, stoking the heat that coursed through her body. Her lips felt swollen, and to ease the pain she demanded more kisses.

Zane moaned low and finally broke away from Lilli. He was breathless.

She stared at his lips. They were wet and red from the pressure of her kisses. She wanted him again. "Oh, Zane," she breathed as her lips touched his again.

"I can't, Lilli," he pleaded.

"Why not?" she asked, crestfallen.

He smiled. "You don't know what you do to me."

"I think I have an idea."

"Okay." He grinned. "Then let's not do it in the airport. Besides, your dad is waiting for us."

"Huh? Oh, yeah."

Zane put his arm around her waist and they started walking

down the concourse toward the baggage-claim area. "I want to hear all about your trip. Do you think your father will let me drive you home? I doubt seriously that I could let you go."

"I think I could persuade him," she said confidently.

And Lilli did.

Zane pulled his truck to a stop around the corner from Lilli's house, away from the glaring streetlight. He turned off the engine, then put his arms around her and kissed her. It was a long and lingering kiss, the kind Lilli thought she would know only in her dreams. Zane had come to her in her dreams even before she met him. She wondered if it was true that some people did have precognitive dreams. She wondered if she was one of those people.

Zane kissed Lilli's lips, her cheeks, her eyelids, and her ears. He pulled her close to him and rested her head on his chest. "I've never felt like this before, Lilli."

"Me, either," she said with a sigh.

"I love you, Lilli," he said softly, then raised her chin up to his face with his forefinger. His blue eyes gleamed like dark, shimmering pools in the moonlight.

Lilli couldn't decide if Zane was more handsome in the sunlight or the moonlight. "I love you, too," she said.

"You don't think that what we feel is just a crush or something, do you, Lilli?" he asked sincerely.

"No. It's much stronger than that. I think we'll always be together . . ."

"In our hearts we always will be, Lilli," he said with a touch of sadness. "There's something I have to tell you. I have to go away."

"Where?"

"Mexico City."

"Mexico? I just got back here . . . Oh, Zane. Why? Why now?"

"My father. He's really bad off, Lilli. My mother thinks she's found some healer for him."

"Not that guy with the apricot pits or peach pits or whatever it is he says will cure cancer. He's in Mexico."

"No. This is a Christian faith healer."

Lilli let out a deep and very disgusted sigh. "You aren't serious?" She crossed her arms over her chest and moved away from him. "Why doesn't she go to Haiti? They have great witch doctors there."

"Lilli, why must you always make fun of my religion?"

"I'm not making fun. It's just not real, Zane. No one is going to lay his hands on your father and make his terminal cancer disappear."

"But it's happened before."

"Sure. There are miracles every day."

"Don't you believe in anything, Lilli?"

She looked him squarely in the eye. "I believe in love, Zane. I believe in you and me. I hope you go to Mexico City and prove me wrong. It's just that I've never seen it happen, that's all. My pop says . . ."

Zane turned away from Lilli. There were tears in his eyes. "I don't give a damn what your pop says," he retorted.

Lilli reached out and touched his hair. It was soft as corn silk. She had hurt him and now he wanted to hurt her back. Who was she to say there were no miracles? Who was she to take away Zane's hope? Maybe they would find their answers in Mexico.

"I'm sorry, Zane. I was just spouting off. You know me. I'm always saying the wrong thing at the wrong time. This has got to be a terrible time for you and your family."

"God, Lilli. You just don't know . . ." Zane dropped his head and started to cry. He clung to the steering wheel so tightly his knuckles were white. "My dad is going to die . . . I watch him every day and the pain is so terrible that sometimes I wish I had the guts to put him out of his pain the way we did with my horse Lightning a few years ago. But no! The law says that's wrong. The law . . . damn the law . . ." he sobbed.

Lilli put her arms around him and pulled him to her. He laid his head on her breasts as she slid beneath him and he stretched out alongside her. "Shhh. It's okay to cry. Let it all out." She stroked his hair and traced the edge of his ear with her fingertip. She caressed his back and shoulders and said nothing while Zane cried.

His nose was running and Lilli reached into the glove compartment and pulled out a travel pack of tissues. Zane blew his nose. Finally his tears diminished.

"I don't want him to die, and yet I do for his sake. I'm going to miss him. But keeping him alive is torture—it's wrong."

"I know," she said. "Sometimes I think ancient man knew a lot more than we do now. Before there were hospitals, before doctors kept people alive simply for the reason of inflating their egos so they could go around and tell their buddies they kept someone around for an extra fifty days, people died at home. Did you know that in some cultures, even in some areas and families in the South, it was the duty of the eldest to go into the sickroom and gently place the pillow over the dying parent's face? No one said a word. No one mentioned the law. They just said, 'He died in his sleep,' and it was accepted."

Zane sniffed as he assimilated Lilli's words. "Thanks," was all he said.

"You're welcome."

Zane sat up. "I'm going to miss you, Lilli."

"This isn't fair, Zane. I just got home and already I have to say good-bye. I'll write to you."

"Oh, sure," he said. "Like you did from Mexico."

"I did write! Nearly every day."

"Sure." He wasn't convinced. He had received a total of three letters.

"I'll admit that their postal system leaves a lot to be desired, but you must have gotten some of my letters. After all, you were here tonight, weren't you?"

He smiled. "Yeah. I guess I got the most important one." He pulled her over to him and kissed her.

Zane had meant it to be a good-night kiss, but he found he could not let her go. Suddenly he didn't give a damn about her parents, who were surely waiting for her. He didn't care about his problems at home with his mother, his dying father, or the Esposito meeting the next day. He cared about Lilli.

All night he'd wanted to feel Lilli's breasts in his hands again, and now the temptation overpowered him. It was too easy to slip his hand beneath her sweater and then around to the back. He unhooked her bra.

Her breasts overflowed in his hands. With his slightest touch her nipples became hard. Lilli pulled her sweater off and took off her bra. Then he lowered his head and traced the aureoles with his tongue. He felt the buds tighten even more. He teased her unmercifully with his tongue and fingers and felt her body heat rise. A gossamer-thin film of perspiration covered Lilli's chest and breasts. She sank her hands into his hair and pressed his mouth more tightly to her breast. With his lips he pulled at the tender flesh just enough to excite her. He smiled to himself when he felt her need quicken.

"Zane, I love you. I want you so much."

Lilli unzipped her jeans, took his hand, and placed it between her legs. "Please, Zane, make love to me like you did before. Like only you can do to me."

"God, Lilli. I think I could die from wanting you."

With her hand she could feel his erection through his jeans. She yanked at the buttons on his fly and pulled the denim apart. She couldn't rid him of his jeans and briefs quickly enough. Her hand grasped him tightly and stroked him firmly yet lovingly. Just the sensation of his smooth skin in her palm excited her. "Zane . . ." She breathed his name as her body's needs drowned out her thoughts.

Zane raised his head and took her lips in a ravenous kiss. His tongue rimmed the edges of them before entering the satin interior of her mouth. His heart seemed to slam against his chest with such a force that his breath could only escape in short, excited pants.

Zane could not hold himself back much longer. He pulled her jeans and panties down, and she kicked them onto the floor of the truck. Then with his fingers he probed the depth of her. "You're so wet, Lilli. My God, so very wet . . ." And as his tongue assailed her mouth once again, his fingers found that mystical hidden spot that made Lilli his. Back and forth he teased her, pressing ever so slightly and then releasing the pressure. He watched as she squirmed beneath him and her hips rose to meet his touch and then fell away like the ebb and flow of the sea.

Lilli's mouth ravaged his. Her hands grasped his shoulders and she was nearly breathless from the passionate torture he forced her to endure. Push and pull; he played upon the opening to her inner sweetness. He pushed his fingers inside her, and just when she was almost to the edge of the universe, he stopped, but only long enough to spread her legs and open her to his lips and tongue.

Lilli nearly screamed aloud from this new pleasure Zane was showing her. She felt at once deliciously wicked and yet tenderly loved. He flicked his tongue along the rim of her bud and then pushed his finger insider her. Lilli's hips moved up to meet his touch as her head pressed backward against the seat.

Lilli was no longer in this world. She climaxed over and over. Time after time she shot beyond the stars, beyond the planets, into a different dimension. She could feel Zane inside her now. She could feel the delicious stretching of her inner walls as he thrust himself fully inside her. She told him she loved him over and over again, though she never opened her mouth. She told him with her heart. She believed he heard her.

Zane collapsed in Lilli's arms, love-spent, happy, and yet sad that once again they were forced to say good-bye.

"I can't believe I have to leave you again, Lilli," he whispered. "I love you. It's so hard for me when we are apart."

"I love you, too." She kissed his lips tenderly. "I want you to go to Mexico City and find that healer person who will make your father well. He's going to be okay, Zane. And when he is, then you can come back to me."

His blue eyes were bright and all traces of sadness were gone. "I will, Lilli. I will."

Arlette had spent the day of J.C. and Lilli's return at Neiman-Marcus, shopping with her sister-in-law, Vicki. It was one of the most embarrassing days of her life. She had spent over an hour and a half choosing just the right dress to wear to the Heart Ball. Nothing pleased her.

Vicki was tired, Arlette could tell, but there was no way she was going home empty-handed.

"What's wrong with the black Scaasi? Or the gold Mary McFadden? They were both absolutely gorgeous on you," Vicki said.

Arlette cocked a perfectly arched brow at her sister-in-law and gave her that you-can't-be-serious glare. "The gold makes me look dumpy. All those pleats . . ."

"McFaddens all look like that!" Vicki threw her an equally disgusted look.

"I've gained three pounds—all in my stomach. I doubt I'll have time to lose it all before the ball."

"What if J.C. isn't even back in time? Then you'll have gone to all this trouble for nothing."

"He's coming back tonight. And if he doesn't, I'll go without him. Even he would tell you that these functions are imperative for his business. He finds half his clients at these balls. J.C. is no dummy, and without me, he wouldn't have as great a stranglehold on the River Oaks crowd as he does."

"You listen to me, Arlette Herbert." Vicki wagged her finger at Arlette. "My brother does quite well without your so-called help. In fact, he does well in spite of you. If you weren't so busy spending his money all over town, his business might be even more profitable than it is now. And he sure as hell wouldn't be taking the risks he takes trying to keep you in designer gowns and jewels!"

Arlette's jaw dropped and she gaped at her sister-in-law. "I can't believe you said that! You're just jealous, that's all." Arlette turned back to the black Scaasi and motioned for the salesperson. Suddenly it hit her. "What 'risks' are you talking about?"

"Nothing," Vicki hissed, trying to control her emotions.

"What aren't you telling me?"

Vicki glared at Arlette. "J.C. has been dealing in the black market for years, and I can't believe you don't know about it."

"He doesn't discuss his business with me."

Vicki's frustration caused her cheeks to flush crimson. "You should make it your business to know, Arlette. What if something happened to him? How would you handle his estate? He's been busting his ass for years trying to keep up with your overspending. These 'trinkets' you buy at the jewelry store add up. And it must be worse than ever lately, because I've never seen my brother so stressed out. I really worry about his health."

Arlette was indignant. "My husband is just fine. In fact, he wouldn't be so tired if he stayed home once in a whole instead of traipsing off to Mexico all the time." Arlette looked away from Vicki for a moment, but it was long enough for Vicki to see a flash of pain in her sister-in-law's eyes.

Vicki realized that she did not know her sister-in-law.

She'd never heard Arlette speak about her childhood or her parents; she never reminisced about the past. Arlette kept her emotions well hidden under a cool, sophisticated facade. If she had just once shown a trace of vulnerability, Vicki might have wanted to help her; but Arlette always managed to keep that tiny measure of distance between them. She would never be Vicki's friend.

"Those trips are J.C.'s lifeblood," Vicki said defensively.

"That's right. And it's the danger that J.C. loves. At least I understand that much about my husband," Arlette said, and with a flourish she pulled out her charge card.

The salesperson walked up and took Arlette's credit card. As the approval was being processed, she carefully stuffed tissue in the sleeves and bodice of the dress and then placed a beige Neiman's plastic dress bag over the garment. The phone rang at the checkout station and the young woman picked up the receiver.

"Yes, sir. She's right here." She handed the phone to Arlette. "The customer service manager wishes a word with you, Mrs. Mitchell."

"Thank you." Arlette removed a gold clip earring and put the receiver to her ear. "Yes?"

What ensued sent shock waves through Arlette. "There must be some mistake. I used that card just yesterday and everything was fine! Yes, I understand your position, but there's been a terrible mistake. I want to speak to your superior."

Arlette drummed her red lacquered nails on the counter while Vicki stood off to the side, listening.

"Hello. Yes . . . he did what? I don't believe it! I just don't believe it!" Arlette waved her diamond-ringed hand in the air as if she were defending herself against some invisible assault. "Never mind. Forget it. I'll use my American Express. It's not a problem." She slammed down the phone.

"A problem, dear?" Vicki taunted her sister-in-law.

"That son of a bitch. He canceled my Neiman's credit. I'll show him!" She handed the girl her American Express Gold Card.

The saleswoman took the card between her finger and thumb as if it were red-hot. She dialed the approval center and relayed the proper numbers to the operator. "I see. Thank you." She hung up the phone. "This card has been canceled. Perhaps you have something else?"

Arlette was in shock. Her fingers shook when she took the card from the woman and handed her a Visa.

The woman ran through the same process again. "He canceled this one, too. Would you like to write a check?"

Arlette was speechless. She didn't know where to turn. This had never happened to her before. Suddenly she was that dirty, cold child back in Bayou Teche. She was frightened and her head was filled with a buzzing noise. She felt faint. She was going to be sick. Where was her security? She looked to Vicki and realized that her sister-in-law was enjoying her pain. Vicki would never help her, Arlette realized. Not in a million years.

"I can't . . . write a check," Arlette replied in a voice so low the saleswoman asked her to repeat herself. She was poor again. Just like that. It was over. J.C. had betrayed her; he had humiliated her. He must be laughing to himself at this very minute. Arlette wanted to flee, but she didn't know who would save her. God! What could she do?

Vicki saw Arlette's shaking hands and then noticed that she had turned white as a ghost. Vicki put her arm around Arlette's shoulder. "Are you all right? Maybe you need something to eat? We can come back later for the dress. Okay?" Vicki said passionately and with a bit of guilt over treating Arlette so harshly.

Her head was filled with so much panic, Arlette barely understood what Vicki was saying. But when she did, her pride came swirling back to her. "Take your hands off me," she hissed under her breath. "I'm fine. There's been a little mix-up."

Vicki thought Arlette's anger was mightier than the heat from a blast furnace. She took a full step back. "Sorry."

Arelette turned to the saleswoman. "Put my name on that dress, you understand? I'll be back later with the money—in cash."

"Yes, ma'am," the woman replied with a polite smile.

By the time J.C. returned from Mexico, Arlette discovered that he'd closed all her charge accounts. She had overdrawn her checking account, and no deposits had been made into it.

Arlette was waiting up for J.C. when he walked through the door at three-thirty in the morning. She tapped her foot against the marble floor and waited while he dropped his bags in the study.

"Where's Lilli?" she asked.

"Coming right behind me," he said. "It was nice of you to wait up." He smiled and moved forward to kiss her. Arlette turned her face away from him.

"What? No welcome-home kiss?"

"You bastard! Do you think I would be civil to you after what you've done to me?"

"What I've done . . . ?" He looked genuinely confused.

"My credit cards . . ."

"Oh, that." He chuckled.

"*That!* That may not mean much to you, but I was publicly humiliated."

"Whoa! Wait a minute!" He shook his head as if to clear the angry fog from his vision. "Just where was this public humiliation?"

"At Neiman's—in front of your sister!" Just thinking about the incident rekindled Arlette's anger.

J.C. laughed. He looked at his wife and laughed again. "My wallet was stolen the day before yesterday. I called the credit card bureau, where I have our cards registered. I guess they canceled all our cards. I didn't think about your shopping sprees." He started laughing again.

Arlette watched him mocking her and she pulled back her hand to slap him, but J.C. was too quick. His hand shot into the air and intercepted her blow.

"Come with me," he said with equal anger. "I'm going to teach you some facts of life." He squeezed her wrist and dragged her into the living room. "Sit down!"

Arlette glared at him defiantly. She stood.

"Sit!" His teeth were clenched.

Arlette sat on the couch.

"It's true that I had my wallet stolen, but maybe it was a blessing in disguise."

"What are you talking about?"

"There is no more money."

"*What?*"

"There is money to maintain our home. You'll have a roof

over your head, food in your stomach, and if you truly need anything, come to me and we'll discuss it. But this freewheeling spending of yours has come to a halt. I can't keep up with it. I would have canceled the charge accounts eventually anyway. If you want to continue spending this wildly, I suggest you get a job."

"A job?" Panic flooded Arlette. What would her friends say? They would oust her in a minute if she couldn't keep up with them. How could she work on charity committees and go to lunches if she had to work? How could she explain to them that her husband was a failure? That she was a failure?

Arlette had never seen J.C. like this. Maybe something had happened to the store that she didn't know about. How bad could it be? "Are you going to lose Antiquities? Are we bankrupt?"

"No. It's not that serious, but it will be if you don't stop. I've been spinning my wheels for years trying to make you happy, but it's never enough. What is it about you that you must spend so recklessly?"

"I'm not reckless," she answered carefully. She had to play it cool; she couldn't blow it now. J.C. might get angry enough to divorce her, and then where would she be? No, she had to get a handle on her emotions. She'd come too far to lose it all now.

"Careless, then." He sat down next to her now that his own emotions had cooled.

"What is it, J.C.? You can tell me. Are we in financial trouble? What have you done?"

He took her hand. "I had a lot of time to think on this trip, Arlette. I'm getting older and I have to think about your future. Lilli's future. I've got college for Lilli to worry about and making certain that there is something left for her . . ."

Lilli, Arlette thought. Always Lilli. Precious Lilli.

"I'm making a lot of changes, Arlette. Things in my industry are changing. There are more regulations. More red tape. It isn't as easy to make that fast buck like I used to. These governments down in Mexico, Guatemala, and South America are getting real strict. I'm having a hard time buying choice pieces. The market is going up, and so people are hanging on to the good stuff and want higher prices. That costs me more money."

"I'm trying to understand," Arlette said.

He patted her hand. "I can't tell you everything about my business, but I *can* say that we'll be okay if we're all a bit more frugal. Let's try to help each other through this time. For Lilli's sake," he said pleadingly.

For Lilli's sake. Arlette let the words seep into her head. "I've been trying to help Lilli," Arlette said. "Honest I have. All these things I've done have been for you and Lilli." She swept her arm around the opulent and tastefully decorated room. "I've made a beautiful home. I've made wonderful business connections for you, and hopefully, the right kind of connections that will help her make a good marriage."

J.C. released his wife's hand and sat back on the sofa. "I'm afraid Lilli has already made that 'connection' for herself."

"Not Zane?"

"He met us at the airport and drove her home."

"Then where is she?"

"Probably a couple of blocks away, stealing some time alone with him. I know that's what I'd do if I were them."

"How can you be so permissive with her? This is a big mistake."

"You worry too much. They're young. She is, anyway. It'll pass."

"Do you really think so?"

"Yes, I do. Zane's working for his father now, and he's very good at what he does. I don't know if he'll go to college or not, but Lilli wants to accomplish so much with her life. I like Zane—I like him a lot. I just don't think they have the same goals. Before you know it, she'll be going away to college, and they'll forget all about each other."

Arlette smiled at her husband. This was not the time to press him about her accounts. She would get him to come around. In the meantime, she reveled in the fact that he was more on her side about Lilli and Zane than she'd thought. Her anger had completely vanished. "What makes you so smart, J.C.?"

He grinned playfully. "Just lucky, I guess."

Fifteen

The Reverend Michael Atherton was a short, balding man who said he was thirty-three, but he looked forty. He had a black mustache, thin frame, and blue eyes that could calm a hurricane. He spoke with a soothing, caring voice that instantly put Hannah, Ted, and Zane at ease. He told the McAllisters of healings he'd performed and made it clear that he was only a vessel through which God was working. They believed him.

Mr. Atherton was building a complex outside Mexico City where the sick could come to him for healing.

"We only have offices and a few bungalows now for the patients to stay in while they're here, but soon we'll have a care unit over there." He pointed westward toward a cleared area.

Zane shielded his eyes with his hand and gazed at the area. A concrete slab had been poured, obviously a minimum of a year ago, because there were two-foot-high weeds around the perimeter of the slab. Something must have slowed Reverend Atherton's plans, Zane thought.

"Why would you need a hospital if you can cure everyone?" Zane asked.

The reverend looked first into Hannah's adoring eyes and then back at Zane's critical face. "Hopefully, someday, son, the word will reach all the sick of the world and they will flock here. There are only so many patients I can see in a day."

"That's all it takes, then? A day?" Zane asked.

"Usually. Once in a while it may take a little longer. I do not question God, son. If it is God's will, then your father will be healed."

The reverend raised his voice on his last words, giving them great emphasis.

Zane didn't like the way the man was always touching his mother's arm or shoulder, turning her this way and that to see his complex. He thought the minister was a bit too chummy with his mother and he couldn't see what all this had to do with healing his father.

He wanted to know more from Mr. Atherton. He wanted to know why he didn't just line up patients and cure them one after another and do, say, a thousand healings in a day if he was so good. If he could heal everyone in the world, why wasn't he doing it? Why wasn't he famous? How come his mother only recently had heard of him, and then it was at her little church in Bandera? How could there still be an M.D. Anderson Hospital in existence if this man could cure all cancer victims?

"Mom, I think we should get back to Dad," Zane said. "It's for him that we came here, you know." He let his eyes rest upon Mr. Atherton's hand, which lay with too much familiarity on his mother's forearm.

"Yes, dear," she said a bit too giddily as she glanced away from the minister.

"Yes," the healer said, "by all means. See to your loving husband. Get some rest. You can purchase an evening meal in our cafeteria over there by the administration building. I'll see you at eight-thirty in the morning in the chapel."

"Oh, thank you, Reverend. Thank you," Hannah gushed.

Zane pretended it was the sun that hurt his eyes as he squinted at the minister. "Come on, Mom."

Hannah went down the concrete walkway with her son toward the wood-and-stucco bungalows.

Zane said nothing as they entered their bungalow. Ted was lying on a cheap bed covered with a scratchy serape. There was no air-conditioning, and there were two flies that bothered him even more than the cheap surroundings.

"How're you doing, Dad?" Zane asked.

"Not much better, son," he replied weakly.

Hannah went over to the bed and knelt beside her husband. She took his hand in her own. "The reverend will perform the healing tomorrow morning, my dear. Then you will see. Faith can move mountains. Faith is all you need to find paradise. Jesus said so."

Ted closed his eyes.

Zane looked at his mother. He could tell from one glance that his father was not getting better. He had no color at all and his voice was weaker than ever.

Hannah put her hand on Zane's knee. Her smile was euphoric when she looked up at him. "You'll see. Tomorrow you will see that I was right. Jesus will save him. I know He will."

The following morning, Ted was not strong enough to walk to the chapel, and so a nurse brought a wheelchair for him to use. Hannah was nearly giddy as they wheeled Ted toward the white stucco chapel. She told Zane she had barely slept the night before. She had spent most of the night on her knees praying for Ted. Hannah's excitement, anticipation, and heartfelt belief buoyed Zane up.

Zane pushed his father's wheelchair over the concrete, and each time they hit a crack or a lump of uneven paving, Ted groaned and Zane apologized. For Zane it was as if his father's pain were his own. He had brought all the pain medications with him, but they didn't seem to work anymore. His father had become immune to them.

Once inside the small chapel, Zane was astonished at the number of people filling the pews. There must have been nearly a hundred, he guessed. He and his mother sat in the fifth-from-the-last pew, letting Ted stay in his wheelchair in the aisle.

The Reverend Michael Atherton walked to his pulpit and began his sermon. Zane listened for ten minutes before his mind began to stray. He didn't know what he had expected, but it was more than this. They hadn't come here for preaching; they had come for healing. The fact that his father had to sit through a long-winded sermon made Zane angry. He fidgeted. He crossed and recrossed his arms. His mother was so in rapture of what the minister was saying that Zane felt the urge to pinch her, to bring her back down to earth. He turned to his father, who was watching him.

Zane smiled at his father, but it was a weak attempt.

Ted tried to smile back.

Zane was struck by the hopelessness he saw in his father's eyes. He felt as if he'd been gutted. Ted didn't believe the faith healer was going to cure him any more than Zane did, but Ted had agreed because he loved his wife. Zane's eyes shot to his mother. He felt contempt blur his vision. The way he saw it, Hannah didn't love her husband half as much as Ted loved *her*. She was so intent on proving she and her Bible were right that she had sacrificed her husband's last days to this torment.

Zane's hands curled into fists. He wanted to hit . . . something. He wanted to cry. He wanted to scream. He wanted to get his father out of this crazy place and back home, where the man could die in peace. Zane felt impotent. It was a feeling he hated.

Finally, Mr. Atherton asked those who needed to be healed to come forward, one at a time. An elderly black woman sitting in the first pew stood up. Seeing her white cane, Zane realized she was blind. He watched as the minister placed his hands on the woman's head, then gently lay his fingers over her eyes.

Suddenly she threw her hands up in the air. "I can see!" she shouted. "Lord, have mercy, I can see!" she wailed loudly. Several people crowded around her. Zane could see that her face was beaming, and she truly looked as if she could see. She threw down her cane and found her way back to her seat.

Another woman went up, and the minister placed his hand over her heart. He said a prayer and quoted James 1 and 5. The woman raised her lowered head and then flung her arms around him. "I'm cured! I'm cured! I'm cured!"

"What was wrong with her?" Zane asked his mother, but Hannah ignored him.

"All those in wheelchairs, come forward now. They are the most in need."

Hannah shot to her feet and pushed Zane ahead of her out of the pew. "I'll take your father."

Zane followed behind her. There were five people ahead of them. Zane watched each of the healings, but now he noticed that although the patients were smiling after the minister had laid his hands on them, he did not see any miracle cures. No one was getting out of his wheelchair and walking away totally cured, like the lame man had done in the Bible.

By the time it was Ted's turn, Zane's skepticism had grown considerably. He watched as the minister prayed over his father. "By placing my hands upon thy head in the same manner as did our Lord Jesus Christ, I invoke the power of the Lord Jesus to cure this diseased body of all its ills." And then he dismissed them.

Zane watched his mother push his father's wheelchair back up the aisle, but he did not move. He looked the minister straight in the eye. "Why isn't he walking?"

"Your father is very sick with his cancer. It will take an hour or so, but he will be cured."

Zane was not convinced.

Mr. Atherton glared at Zane. "Go back to your seat, son. Your father's illness has been cured. I promise you that in Jesus's name."

Reluctantly, Zane returned to his pew. He held his father's hand. The veins were more prominent than ever before. His father looked like a ghost. Tears filled Zane's eyes. He wished Lilli were there to give him strength.

The days passed, the healing rituals continued, and Zane's father was nowhere near a cure. But Hannah would not give up on the Reverend Michael Atherton. Zane did, however, the day he found out what his mother had been doing behind his back.

"How much, Mother?" Zane demanded as they stood outside the bungalow.

Hannah pressed her lips shut and wouldn't answer.

"How much of our money have you given that con man?" Zane was so angry he thought his pounding heart would blast out of his chest.

"Five hundred . . ."

"You gave him five hundred dollars? We can't even pay our bills at home and you do—this? Are you crazy?" Zane whirled away from her so as not to hit her. She was his mother, but she was so stupid. "Can't you see it? Can't you see this is a scam? This is not a man of God!"

"He is! I know he is!" She burst into tears.

"Mother, God is not going to cure Dad. God is going to take Dad away from us, if you'll just let Him."

"Noooo!" she wailed. "I won't let him die!"

"It's not your decision. You're the one who's playing God now, Mom. And it's wrong. Very wrong."

She sank her head into her hands and sobbed so heavily that her entire body heaved. Zane walked back to her and put his arms around her compassionately. "We have to go home, Mom. I don't want him to die in a foreign country. I want him to die in Texas. Let's go home."

Hannah could not answer; she was crying too hard. She let her son lead her back into the bungalow, where they packed their belongings. They left Reverend Atherton's complex that night.

It was nearly dawn when they arrived in Bandera, and Zane carried his father into the house and to his own room. He helped his mother to her own bed and tucked her in. She fell asleep instantly.

Zane went back to his father's room and knelt by his side.

"Thanks, son," Ted said and held his son's hand.

"I wanted you to be here, Dad."

"I . . . wanted . . . it, too."

Ted McAllister died in his sleep a few hours later.

Sixteen

*L*illi held Zane's hand all through the funeral, at the graveside ceremony, and then at the reception at the church hall. He was struggling not to show his grief, beating down his anger at the injustice of life that everyone feels when death visits their lives. Holding his hand, Lilli was sure she could feel his pulse increase at times when she knew he was battling back tears.

She watched as Zane doted over his mother, tending to her every need as if she were the child and he the parent. He took tea to her when she lay down in her room for a short nap before the guests arrived at their house. Although Zane's temper flared on occasion when he overheard her expounding on the faith healer in Mexico, Lilli noted that his attitude toward her was protective. When Hannah's religious zeal overpowered the conversations with her guests, Zane stepped in, changed the subject, and saved her from embarrassment.

Lilli knew full well that Zane did not approve of many of his mother's attitudes, but she loved him all the more for his ability to put his opinions aside and care for her in her hour of need.

Lilli fought her own tears throughout the day. It seemed that no matter what she did for Zane, it could never be enough. She wished that she could take this pain from him and bear it. It was on the day of Ted McAllister's funeral that Lilli knew she could never give her heart to anyone in her life but Zane.

When it was time to return to Houston, she could not leave.

"I need to stay here, Pop," she said to J.C. with huge tears in her eyes. "He needs me. And his mother said it was okay."

J.C. nodded and put his hands lovingly on Lilli's shoulders. "He does need you."

Arlette squinted her eyes against the brilliant sun. She rummaged through her purse, looking for her sunglasses. "Well, I think you ought to come back with us. Zane needs to spend time with his mother. I think you're being selfish, Lilli, to want to deny him this time with his family."

Lilli already felt as if her insides had been ripped to shreds, and she had little energy left to fight with her mother. She simply turned to her father. "Pop. Please."

"Stay here as long as you need to. If Zane can't get away to drive you back to Houston, I'll come get you." He kissed her forehead and smiled. "I love you, Lilli."

"I love you, too, Pop." She hugged her father tightly.

Arlette glared at the sight of her husband and daughter embracing each other. She turned and started for the Cadillac. "Good-bye, Lilli," she called over her shoulder.

" 'Bye, Mom," Lilli said with a heavy heart. She looked into her father's eyes. "Pop, why does she act like this? Doesn't she understand that Zane is grieving? That I'm grieving? Isn't there any compassion in her?"

J.C. sighed heavily. "Yes, there is. Your mother just has a hard time showing her real emotions. She'll come around in time as long as we stick by her."

"I know, Pop. I know. The family has to stick together to get through life. You've said that a thousand times."

"And I'll keep on saying it. No matter what, she *is* your mother."

"I know." Lilli kissed his cheek. " 'Bye, Pop."

"Good-bye, honey. Call me if you need anything."

"Okay," she said. She remained at the base of the steps to the house as her parents drove down the dusty drive to the paved road.

As they drove away, Arlette said, "You have no control over that girl anymore, J.C."

"If you want to know the truth, no one has had control over Lilli—ever."

"Yes, and that's your fault."

"I don't see it as a fault. Lilli is Lilli. I like her like that. She likes herself like that."

Arlette sighed heavily and crossed her arms over her chest.

She did not understand her daughter in the least. What on earth did Lilli see in this country boy, aside from his good looks? Zane was a nice boy, but what chance did he have to become wealthy? What was it about teenagers today that they did not plan their futures? They lived only in the present minute.

Well, Arlette thought, Lilli will find out the hard way. She'll make a disastrous marriage, and then when Zane leaves her or embarrasses her at some social function, she'll come home crying, and then it will be up to me to pick up the pieces.

Maybe it was a good thing for Lilli to see Zane in his element. Arlette could not imagine Lilli getting along with Hannah McAllister. In fact, she couldn't imagine anyone getting along with that woman. Arlette knew she had her own insecurities and problems, but at least her mind wasn't derailed like Hannah's. That woman she thought, smiling, was just the fly in the ointment who could break up Lilli and Zane.

The McAllister property covered twenty acres of rolling hills where deer, pheasant, and quail thrived. The nearest neighbor was two miles down the road to the east, Zane told Lilli as he held her hand on their way to his "secret place." They scrambled down a rocky hill, past scrub oaks, and finally settled in a clearing.

"I never guessed you would have a place like this," she said, looking up at the sky. "You always talk about the city so much."

Zane looked off into the distance. "I know," he said, "but even I need this kind of solace. Especially now. I'm glad you're here to share it with me."

Lilli smiled at him and squeezed his hand and let him have his moments of silence.

She thought the land was exotically beautiful and looked more like the travelogue pictures she'd seen of Africa than it did Texas. The wind was dry and arid and she could easily imagine the white pioneers who had crossed this country on their way farther west. She liked the scraggly, crooked mesquite trees and the fragrant cypress that dotted the landscape.

The mesas in the distance reminded her of Arizona and parts of Mexico. A hawk circled overhead and then flew away.

The sound of the hawk broke Zane's concentration and he put his arm around Lilli and pulled her close.

"In the spring a little creek runs through here, but it always dries up in the summer, and by winter, there's hardly a trace of its existence. But every spring it comes back without fail." He pointed to a spot about fifty feet away. "See that cluster of stones? I put every one of them there, but only in the spring when the creek is running."

"Are you a good stone skimmer?"

"Yep." He took a deep, painful breath. "My dad taught me. He was the best."

"Yes, he was, Zane. The best." She leaned down and plucked a piece of grass. "I wish I'd had a chance to meet him."

"Me, too. He liked you."

"He never met me."

"I read him your letters."

"Oh."

Zane's voice was infused with melancholy. Lilli wished there were something she could do for him, but sometimes it was best to let grief flow. She looked at the dry creek bed. She wondered if Zane would keep his grief till spring, or if he would let it run itself out now.

Zane did not cry. She knew it wasn't a matter of his being embarrassed to cry in front of her, because they'd already broken that barrier. He was still in shock, she thought. The real impact of his father's death hadn't hit him yet. She squeezed his hand.

"You love this land, don't you?"

"Yes. And no. Sometimes I hate it."

Lilli turned her head and lowered it so that she was looking directly into his downturned face. "I don't believe you."

He grinned mischievously. "It's too far away from you."

She kissed him sweetly. "Thank you for the flattery. But what's the real reason you don't like it?"

He touched her cheek and looked into her eyes. "How is it you know me so well?"

She shrugged.

He glanced up into the sky, searching for the hawk, which

was probably halfway to the Guadalupe by now. "I want a lot more out of life than my dad had. Maybe that's it. He was able to take care of Mom and me, but I want more."

"Like what?"

"Travel. I want to see Europe. I want to learn from the best diamond cutters in Amsterdam. I want to see real diamond mines in South Africa. I want to know everything I can about Brazilian emeralds and amethysts. I want to bid on incredibly old and fabulous designs that can only be found at Sotheby's or Christie's. I want to be the best I can be, Lilli, and I can't do any of those things stuck here in Bandera, Texas."

"Pop says you're very gifted. He said he's heard that you have some Old Spanish jewels hidden away. And he said that the insiders in the business told him it was you and not your father who cut the deal. Is that true?"

Zane laughed. "Yes, it is. I scored a coup there. But I couldn't have done it without my dad. The part that makes me sick is that now I'm stuck with all his doctor bills, over a hundred thousand dollars' worth, and I know—I know—that I could get five times the money if I could get to New York City."

"So go."

He looked at her and laughed at her naïveté. "Just like that. Just pack up my shit and go."

"Yeah. Who's holding you back?"

He was silent and just looked into her eyes. They both knew it was his love for her that kept him from his dream.

"Oh," she said sadly.

She kissed him. It was a longer kiss than she'd meant it to be. She hadn't intended to find herself wanting him, but it happened. This was not the right time, she told herself. She should wait and not push him during this emotional time.

He kissed her back. He breathed love into her and inhaled her love back into himself as if it were the only nourishment he'd had for months. He pulled her into his arms and held her close to him. He could feel her heart beating rapidly. His own heart matched her rhythms.

"I must be insane thinking I would ever want to leave you."

"Oh, Zane. I would miss you so terribly if you went away. It's bad enough as it is, living in two different places."

"And I thought you were so brave," he said and kissed her again.

"I'm here if you need me." I can't hold you back, she thought. It wouldn't be fair.

Suddenly Lilli was truly frightened for the first time in her life. She'd always thought their timing was off, but now she could see the future as clearly as if she'd taken a snapshot. Zane would eventually leave Texas and she would be left behind. She felt she could almost hear the wrenching of her heart. She wanted to drag him away with her to some place where he could never escape her, but she knew that wasn't right. If she truly loved him, she would have to let him go . . . and pray that he would still want her.

The sun was beginning to set, and the evening was growing cooler. Lilli shivered, not from the cold, but from the loneliness that engulfed her.

"Come on," Zane said. "We'd better get back. Mom will start to worry."

As they walked back, they saw Zane's mother standing on the front porch saying good-bye to the local minister, who had come to call.

"Here's Zane now," the Reverend Peter Schneider said, smiling at Zane and Lilli as they walked up the front steps and onto the porch.

Hannah's face revealed her irritation. "Where have you been?" she demanded.

"I was showing Lilli our property."

"It's a beautiful place, Mrs. McAllister," Lilli said politely. "Thank you for letting me stay overnight. I hope it's not an imposition . . ."

Hannah cut Lilli off with a curt wave of her hand and turned to the minister. "Thank you for your prayers and kind words, Reverend. As I said before, it was a shame that Zane could not benefit from your visit, but he was too busy entertaining his friend." Hannah stepped past Lilli as if she were invisible. "I'll walk you to your car," she said to the minister.

Zane shook the clergyman's hand. "Thank you," he said and motioned for Lilli to follow him into the living room.

Zane watched his mother from the picture window in the living room and wondered what his mother could be saying to the minister. Hannah's mannerisms were terse, and twice she jerked her head toward the house, indicating to Zane that he was the topic of their conversation and not her dead husband, the funeral, or her own sorrow. Finally the minister placed his hand on Hannah's shoulder to comfort her and then shook her hand. He got into his car and left.

When Hannah turned back toward the house, it was too dark to see her face, but Zane could tell from the purposefulness of her stride that she had plenty on her mind.

"I want to talk to you, Zane," she said tersely as soon as she came in.

"Sure, Mom."

"In your room." Her eyes shot to Lilli and then back to her son. "Where we can be alone."

When they left the room, Lilli felt like an alien visitor. Suddenly she wished she'd never agreed to stay overnight.

Lilli heard Zane's door being slammed shut and the faint sound of the lock being turned.

She couldn't believe it. What did this woman think she was going to do? Eavesdrop on their conversation? Lilli was used to being treated like this by her mother, that was different. Her mother was paranoid.

Lilli sat on the couch. She glanced around the room. It was such an odd jumble of cheap Early American furniture and handsome Old Spanish pieces. Cursed with too much curiosity, Lilli rose and circled the room. She discovered that the vases on the mantel were Sèvres. The ormolu clock was eighteenth-century. The bookends were Art Nouveau. The Impressionist paintings were fakes, but good ones. And on the bookshelves on either side of the flagstone fireplace were countless volumes on gems, stones, cutting, settings, and antique jewelry. The common pieces, those were Hannah's doing, Lilli knew. She had never met Ted McAllister, but already she was piecing together a picture of a man she would have wanted to know.

"He should have been the best in the business," she'd heard J.C. say about Ted. "Zane has his father's eye for quality."

Offspring living out the dreams of the parent, she thought. That's what Zane and I are.

I can't hold him back. I can't stand in Zane's way to have his chance at all the things his father wanted for him.

Maybe that was why Hannah disliked her so much. Zane hadn't told Lilli about his mother's misgivings; he didn't need to. Lilli had eyes. She could see the distrust and skepticism in Hannah's attitude. Hannah viewed Lilli as a force to be reckoned with, or worse, an obstacle to be overcome. Lilli was surprised that Hannah had allowed her to stay overnight; she had probably not even been aware of Zane's asking her permission.

Wending her way around the floor lamp with the colonial blue eagles on the shade, Lilli entered the hallway. She passed framed pictures of Zane when he was a baby. Zane at his christening. Zane in first grade, second, third. Zane in a group shot with his basketball team. Zane at some dance . . . Lilli stopped to peer closely at the washed-out blonde in the photograph. "Not his type." She passed the first bedroom and noted the perfectly made bed, the Spanish walnut semicircular desk in the corner that was filled to overflowing with papers, books, and bills. She guessed this was Zane's father's room.

The room on the opposite side of the hallway was furnished in Early American with a wedding-ring quilt on the bed. This was Hannah's room. Lilli thought it odd that Ted and Hannah did not sleep together. Perhaps it was because he was in so much pain toward the end that he did not want to disturb her sleep.

The bathroom was painted in colonial gold and green. Lilli frowned at the preponderance of the eagle motif. Eagles were on the shower curtain, the towels, the wallpaper; even the soaps were eagles. Lilli knew she shouldn't be judgmental, but it was going to be hard for her to get around those eagles.

Zane's room was at the end of the hall. Lilli stopped and hesitated. Zane's mother had been right; Lilli wasn't above eavesdropping. Feeling guilty but not guilty enough to stop what she was doing, Lilli put her ear against the wooden door. The voices were muffled, but she could hear them clearly enough.

"We weren't doing anything, Mom!"

"Don't raise your voice. She might hear you."

"It doesn't matter, because I'm going to tell her anyway. Lilli is my friend. I love her, Mom."

"Love? How can you know anything about love? You're too young."

"I am sick to death of you saying that. You weren't that much older than me when you met Dad."

"I was twenty-four. There's a big difference. She's not good for you, Zane."

"How is she not good? And don't give me this stuff about her religion."

"She's a jezebel. I see the way she looks at you. She will lead you down the road to evil."

"Oh, for God's sake! I'm not going to listen to this!"

Lilli heard Zane's footsteps growing louder. Then the door was unlocked.

Lilli sprinted down the hall, picking her feet up as high as she could so as not to be heard. Never in her life had she covered so much ground so fast. She nearly sailed onto the couch. Quickly she snatched up a magazine from the coffee table and pretended to read it. "Ugh!" she said aloud and put the copy of *Colonial Homes* back on top of the table.

Zane came storming into the living room. Lilli rose. Hannah was fast on Zane's heels.

"Zane, please stop." Hannah's voice had turned imploring. "Please." Her voice cracked. "I—I don't want you to go. I don't know what I'm saying. It's been such a hard . . . day," Hannah said as tears filled her eyes. "I need you, son."

Zane turned around and went to his mother. When he put his arms around her, she burst into tears.

Lilli felt awkward witnessing someone else's grief. She knew Hannah did not want her in the house, but she had nowhere to go, so she went to the kitchen and began preparing dinner plates for the three of them from all the food the neighbors had brought to the house that day.

As she sliced a honey-baked ham, she realized that perhaps Hannah wasn't all that bad. Perhaps Hannah's attack on her was simply her way, though an odd one, of venting her grief.

Lilli had never been to a funeral. She hadn't known anyone in her family who died. Her grandparents were all dead by the time she was born. Her Aunt Vicki was still alive and none of her friends had died. This was a new experience for her and she was just as unsure as Hannah and Zane about the proper manner in which to conduct herself. She wanted to be helpful, but she was afraid that she was contributing to Hannah's distress.

Nearly twenty minutes passed before Zane came into the kitchen. He was alone.

"I put her to bed. She's exhausted. She's not at all like herself."

"I don't expect her to be . . . normal. Not now." She handed Zane a plate with ham, potato salad, macaroni salad, and a dinner roll. "If it wasn't so late, I'd ask you to drive me back to Houston tonight. Staying here wasn't such a good idea."

He looked up at her with pleading eyes. "I want you here."

She sat down at the kitchen table. She moved her food around with her fork. She wasn't hungry. She noticed that Zane wasn't either.

He crumpled his paper napkin into a ball and threw it onto his plate. "I never knew I could be so angry at my dad."

"Angry?"

He nodded. "He left us. He got sick and left. It's not fair to Mom. She still needs him."

"She'll get over it, Zane. In time she'll come to terms with it."

"Yeah? Now there were tears in his eyes, but he wouldn't let them fall. "How do you know so much? What if she doesn't?"

Lilli turned away from the scathing look he gave her. It was as if he weren't seeing her at all. He was looking at her from a different perspective, one filtered through pain.

"I don't know anything of the sort. I guess I'm not much help at all."

"I don't think anyone can be," he said morosely.

Lilli nodded. She hoped she never had to endure what Zane was going through. Again Lilli found she was faced with more questions than answers. She wondered when life would start putting itself back together for him—and for her.

Seventeen

~~~

*T*he dream called to her and she followed it. It was her
father's voice, she thought at first, but then the sound
grew louder and more clear. It was Zane. He'd come for her.
He was urging her to leave the room. She stumbled out of the
bed, his bed, his bedroom.

He took her hand and led her down a dark passageway. She
rubbed her eyes, focused, and realized she and Zane were
walking down the hallway in his house. He pulled a suede
jacket out of the hall closet and placed it around her shoulders. He laughed at her for wearing one of his Western shirts
to sleep in.

He led her through the kitchen and outside into the night.

The cool air awakened her and Lilli realized she was definitely not dreaming. Zane bent down and slipped her Ropers
onto her feet.

"What are you doing? Where are we going?"

"To our place," he whispered and put his arm around her
as he guided her down the path that led to his most secret
hideaway.

The moon was full and the silver light frosted the limbs of
the trees. They hurried down the gulley and across the hills
and little valleys. Lilli nearly slipped on a jutting rock. She
could hear the sound of owls and a coyote in the distance.

Crossing difficult terrain was normal for Lilli, who'd spent
many a night, hot and cold, in the rain forests of
Mesoamerica. Easily she picked her way around fallen mesquite limbs. She saw a jackrabbit sprint for shelter.

By the time they reached the ring of mesquite trees, they
were both out of breath. Zane took her in his arms, pulled her
next to him, then wrapped his jacket around her slim body.

He was warm from the trek. She kissed his neck as she slipped her arms around his waist.

The muscles in his back were tight and hard. She put her head on his chest and could hear the steady, rhythmic beating of his heart. The heart of an athlete, she thought.

He placed his finger under her chin and lifted her face to him. "Your eyes are beautiful in the moonlight," he said and kissed her.

His lips were insistent as they begged hers to open to his tongue. She complied with his wish. She needed Zane at that moment, possibly more than he needed her.

Lilli had tried not to let Hannah's dislike of her intrude upon her feelings for Zane, but she'd not yet learned how to barricade her heart against malicious intruders. Lilli's feelings had been hurt. She needed Zane's love to make her feel better. She kissed him back, wanting him to know how much she loved him. She wondered if he could feel the tremendous power of her heart as its energy left her body and surrounded him.

His tongue darted against her own like a hummingbird seeking nectar. He unbuttoned the shirt she was wearing, exposing her breasts. She moaned when he continued to kiss her and ran one hand over one breast, then the other. She felt her nipples harden as his fingers passed over them again and again, forcing her to respond to him. She felt a wave of twinges deep, deep down in her abdomen and then those familiar shocks of heat and passion that careened through her loins. She felt her knees get weak; her thigh muscles seemed about to collapse.

"I love you, Lilli," he said simply.

Zane pulled off his jacket and placed it on the ground, and she sank down on it. Moonbeams pirouetted over Lilli's black hair. Despite the cool night air, she removed the suede jacket and the Western shirt, then looked up at him. Her eyes were filled with so much love, Zane was humbled by her gaze. He bent down and kissed her lips tenderly and whispered again that he loved her.

As she sat looking up at him, he removed his T-shirt, unzipped his jeans, and slid them to his ankles. Lilli saw that he was naked.

She shivered, and he placed his warm body over hers to

protect her from the night air. "You can touch me if you want," he said pleadingly.

Lilli was almost afraid of that incredible sensation she remembered now all too well.

"It's okay," he said, rolling off her and lying beside her. He placed his hand over hers and directed her hand. He guided her at first, which heightened the intensity of the moment for her. She felt as if every sexual nerve in her body had been electrically charged and she wondered if he was as sensitive as she.

A low, sensual groan escaped his lips and he buried his head between her breasts. He took his hand away from hers and allowed her the freedom to seek him out. He touched the angel hair between her legs and then slowly slipped his fingers inside her. She was warm and moist.

"Oh, Zane. I love you so."

He moved over her, again, spreading her legs farther apart with his knee. He entered her slowly, although he wanted to drown himself in her as quickly as possible. He pulled back, raised his head, and looked down at her.

"I don't want to hurt you, but God, Lilli, I've never wanted you as much as I do now. I can't get enough of you."

Lilli placed her hands on either side of his face. "My love, you are all I want. Now and always."

Zane's need for Lilli overcame his hesitation. With the end of his penis he stroked the hard bud of her passion. Again and again he teased her, and he could feel her moistness on him as he quickened the pace of his stroking. She moaned again, and then he thrust himself into her and entered paradise.

Lilli bit her lower lip, forcing herself to hold back the tumultuous sensations that were building to an explosion. As her hips tilted to take him in further, she knew only one thing: she wanted him to stay. Forever.

He continued moving in and out of her slowly, and as he did, she felt an inner pulsing. She felt as if she were drifting out of her body and yet deeper inside her own being. She was in the world but not of it.

Her hips arched up to him again and again, and he eased himself deeper into her. She kissed his ear and nuzzled her face in the crook of his neck. He smelled like pine and sandalwood . . . just like in the dream, she thought fleetingly, remembering that long-ago dream at Copán in which Zane had come to her.

Lilli was filled with Zane. Zane's head was filled with love for Lilli. He felt as if he would implode from within, but he knew he didn't dare indulge himself. He pulled himself up on his elbows and looked down at Lilli.

Tiny beads of perspiration encircled her neck like pearls. She opened her eyes. She smiled at him. Zane started to roll onto his side.

"Don't leave me, Zane," she whimpered. "Don't ever leave me." She clung to him for a long, glorious moment before he pressed himself into her.

He quickened his pace again. Closing his eyes, he felt nothing but the exquisite pleasure of being inside his Lilli. Pushing. Thrusting. Coming.

Zane brought Lilli to the edge of the universe. She felt her body careening over the edge of reality, and behind her eyelids she could see what looked like brilliant stars. If it were possible to see the divine world, making love was the only key, she thought as she began to plummet back to earth. Back to Zane.

Zane burst into his ejaculation with a groan of total abandon. His body quivered and shook as if the world had quaked. "Lilli, I love you. I love you. I love you," he breathed in her ear over and over. "There will never be anyone for me but you. Say you are mine. Now and always."

"Always, Zane," she whispered as he stroked her wet walls one more time.

Then he held her in his arms and rocked her like a baby. "My precious," he said and kissed her forehead, eyelids, and lips. She clung to him, encircling her arms around his neck. "We have to be careful, Lilli. I wouldn't forgive myself if you got pregnant."

"Don't worry, Zane," she said. "I realized how lucky I was not to get pregnant before. I haven't told anyone this, not even Faith, but I went to a doctor and he started me on the pill. I couldn't do that to you, my love. You have so many dreams to make real. A baby right now would ruin everything."

"God, Lilli, I wish you'd told me. I should have been there with you."

Lilli laughed lightly. "I wanted to do this by myself. I felt rather grown up."

He kissed her deeply. "You *are* grown up. Sometimes you act older than me."

As Lilli kissed him she thought that she didn't feel all that mature. There was only a three-year difference in their ages, but sometimes that difference seemed like a wide chasm. He talked of his future and of career goals when she was still wondering how she was going to pass high school exams. Her friends spent most of their time wondering what they would wear to the football games on Friday night and whether they should "go all the way," a decision she had already made. Lilli was stuck halfway between her teenage world at school and the very adult relationship she had with Zane.

Lilli believed that her love for Zane would never die. She believed they would be married someday and have children. She was frustrated by the fact that she was only in high school and that because society considered "young love" a matter of chemistry and hormones rather than intellect, she was doomed to wait for Zane "until the right time."

Zane sat up and helped Lilli into his shirt, then put the suede jacket over her shoulders. "We'd better get back to the house. Quickly he stood up and pulled on his clothes.

Lilli held Zane's hand as he led the way back up the path and away from their sanctuary. She decided she very much wanted to make love with him again, but not outside, not when, after lovemaking, they had to leave each other. They should be in a warm bed somewhere so they could hold each other close until dawn. She wanted to be able to wake up with him next to her and see his face before she saw anything else.

Again, Lilli thought, our timing is off.

Wrapped in her wedding-ring quilt, Hannah was standing sentry on the small back porch when Zane and Lilli returned.

Lilli gasped when she looked up at the older woman, her hair askew and snarled around her face. Backlit by the porch light, Hannah looked like a witch wearing a cape.

"Mom!" Zane was equally surprised.

"Get her out of here, Zane. That slut is not welcome in my house!"

Zane squeezed Lilli's hand. She squeezed his back.

"It's not Lilli's fault—" he began, but Hannah cut him off.

"Get her out of here! Do you hear me? Now!"

Zane clenched his teeth. "Fine." He started to pull Lilli inside to get her clothes.

"She stays out there." Hannah's voice sounded like the growl of a rabid dog. Her eyes spewed hatred and self-righteousness.

Zane had seen his mother like this once before. He remembered that she'd beaten him with his father's razor strap until he couldn't speak. Back then it was for nothing more than making fun of one of her prayers. She could control his life when he was five. He wouldn't allow her to control it any longer.

Employing massive self-restraint, Zane fought back his own indignation and anger. He slowly turned to Lilli. "Go get in my truck, Lilli. It's unlocked. You'll be okay." He jerked his head back to his mother. Then he said loudly enough for Hannah not to mistake his words: "And if my mother comes near you, lock the truck. The keys are under the mat. Drive into town and I'll meet you there. Do you understand?"

Lilli thought he commanded her with the same vehemence his mother had used. "Yes." She turned and raced toward the Ford truck. She jumped inside and locked both doors. She kept her eyes glued to Zane.

Zane walked up the porch steps. He put his arm out and moved his mother away from the door. She was so rigid he felt as if he were moving a stone statue.

"She'll ruin you. The Lord Jesus Christ will cast you both into hell."

Zane ignored her. He went straight to his room. He gathered Lilli's clothes together and put them in a small canvas bag. Quickly he scanned the room and eliminated the things he knew he would never need. He took his Rolodex, jeans, boots, a few T-shirts and sweaters, his jeans jacket, a black suit, four dress shirts, and toiletries. He grabbed his wallet, his keys, his bankbook, and the three hundred dollars he had saved. He took one Bruce Springsteen album and left the hard rock. He took his yearbook and then decided against it. He didn't ever want to remember the Zane McAllister he had been. After tonight he would be a new Zane. One he admired.

His belongings fit into one suitcase and one army-surplus duffel bag. "Not much to show for my life so far," he mused. "The rest of it will be better."

He was about to leave the room when he spied a picture of his father and him on a deer lease up by Canyon Lake. It had been taken before his father got sick. They were smiling and they had their arms around each other. He stuck the photograph under his arm and headed down the hall.

Zane passed his mother without a word.

Suddenly Hannah saw the duffel bag. "Zane? What are you doing?"

"I'm leaving."

"But you can't!"

"I can and I will."

She started running toward him, but her feet got tangled in the quilt. Throwing off the quilt, she followed him outside, wearing her slippers and a long flannel nightgown.

He tossed the bags into the bed of the truck. "I'll find a way to pay off Dad's medical debts, Mom. Don't worry about the money."

"But . . . why? You can't be leaving over this—this girl!"

He spun around. His eyes were flashing. "I am leaving for me. Not her. Like I said, she has nothing to do with this."

"Where are you going?"

"I don't know."

Suddenly Hannah felt frightened. "I won't let you go. I'll call the police! I'll pray that you be stopped. God will stop you from this foolishness, Zane. She is a jezebel! You remember I said that. You come back here!"

Lilli unlocked the truck door, and Zane hopped inside. He put the key in the ignition, and the engine roared to life. The truck wheels made a screeching sound as he raced down the drive and away from his home.

They were a quarter of a mile away and could no longer see the house or Hannah, but the sound of her voice seemed to carry through the West Texas hills like the shrill, screeching sound of a harpy.

Zane prayed for the first time that day. He prayed never to hear that sound again.

Lilli stood on the front steps of her house with her arms around Zane's neck. She had to force herself not to hold him too tightly. She'd heard a saying one time that said love was like a bird. Sometimes you had to let it go, and if it never came back to you, it wasn't yours in the first place.

Lilli felt a burning lump in her throat as she choked back her tears. She had come to think of Zane as part of her. She had made love to him. She was devoted to him. And yet she understood why he had to leave. It had more to do with Zane finding his own way than it did with paying off his father's debts.

She felt a bit foolish for not having anticipated this day from the beginning. Zane had never made any bones about the fact that he wanted to be in New York. She loved Texas, but he wanted to get away from it. If she had a choice, she would move to the country; Zane wanted only to live in the city. Lilli could do nothing but hope that he would come back to her. She didn't know when, and she didn't know how, and that was the part that frightened her the most.

Eighteen

*L*illi and Faith sat on Mrs. Barker's front porch drinking homemade lemonade. The oaks had sprouted their full summer's growth and laced their limbs together across University Boulevard, keeping the residents below a full ten degrees cooler.

Mrs. Barker's birthday had been the day before. From the time Lilli had been four years old, she had always made a practice of bringing Mrs. Barker flowers on May Day and on her birthday. It was a tradition for Lilli, and Mrs. Barker looked forward to her birthday because of the surprises Lilli always had in store for her.

This year, Lilli gave Mrs. Barker peach-scented soaps and shampoo, a chocolate mousse cake, and, of course, a bouquet of summer flowers. Lilli had made an extra-special big deal out of Mrs. Barker's birthday because for Lilli, there was little to celebrate in her life, now that Zane was gone.

"Do you have a boyfriend, Faith?" Mrs. Barker asked.

"Yes, ma'am," Faith answered dutifully. "I think maybe you know him. Paul Newsome. He lives just down the street."

Mrs. Barker smiled. "I know that. I was only teasing you." The elderly woman giggled. "I've seen the two of you walking home from school." She leaned forward in her antique green-lacquered wicker chair with the red-and-green English rose print cushion. "I've seen him stealing kisses from you, young lady." She playfully wagged an arthritic finger at her.

"Oh, Mrs. Barker . . ." Faith blushed.

"I can't believe it," Mrs. Barker said with surprise. "I didn't think you young girls knew how to blush anymore.

From the things I see on television, why, sometimes I just have to close my eyes!"

Lilli laughed along with Mrs. Barker and Faith.

"I feel sorry for you young people today," Mrs. Barker mused.

"Why is that?" Lilli wanted to know.

"No romance. Everything is sex, sex, sex. There's no mystery anymore."

Lilli's eyes were round with surprise as she looked at her cousin. Faith nearly burst out laughing.

"It sounds funny to hear you talking about ... sex, Mrs. Barker."

"Why's that?" She poured more lemonade and then took a very large bite of the chocolate mousse cake.

"Because ... well," Lilli began awkwardly, "because you're old."

"Precisely my point!" she said, holding her fork in the air authoritatively. "I should be a good judge of such things."

"Mrs. Barker, are you telling me that you've been a peeping tom watching Paul and me?"

Mrs. Barker chuckled. "Well, dear, when you keep choosing my old oak to kiss under, I could hardly miss you, now, could I?"

Faith blushed again.

"Is he going to marry you?"

Faith nodded. "Once he gets out of college. We have to wait a long time."

Lilli spun around to face her cousin. "You didn't tell me that! When did this happen?"

"At the senior prom. We decided then. But we're going to wait until he gets out of the University of Houston. I wouldn't want to stand in the way of his career," Faith said earnestly.

"What about your career?" Lilli asked pointedly.

Faith wrinkled her nose. "I haven't got one. At least I can't think of anything I want to do."

Mrs. Barker enjoyed listening to the girls' exchange. "But you have a career, don't you, Lilli?"

"Oh, yes, ma'am. I'm going to get my degree in anthropology. And I suppose I'll help Pop run Antiquities someday.

He's grooming me for it now, he says. I'm working there this summer," Lilli said.

"And you, Faith. What are you doing with your summer?"

"I'm a candy striper at the hospital. Then I have tennis lessons and I think maybe riding lessons. And I've decided to enroll at the University of Houston, too, but not until January. I wasn't sure until recently if I really wanted to go to college or not."

"You're going to college?" Lilli asked.

"Really?" Mrs. Barker chimed in. "And what course of study will you pursue?"

"Well, I guess liberal arts. Mother says that the freshman year isn't all that interesting anyway. If I don't like it, I could get a job."

"Doing what?" Lilli demanded.

Finally, Faith had just about all she could take of her cousin's superior attitude. "I don't know, Lilli. I can find something. Maybe I'll give you a run for your money and come to work for Uncle J.C. Hmm?"

"I'm sorry, Faith. It's just that you've never talked about doing anything but getting Paul to ask you to marry him, and now that he has, you've got all these other things in your head . . . college, job. I think that's great, is all."

"You do?"

"Sure." Lilli beamed at her sincerely.

Faith shrugged her shoulders. "I don't know. When we thought about how long it was going to be till we could get married, I thought, Gee! I'm going to get awfully bored waiting for my wedding day."

Lilli nodded. "Good point, Faith."

Mrs. Barker smiled at Lilli. "And what about you, Lilli? You're going to be what . . . sixteen?"

"Seventeen in a couple of weeks."

"Goodness me! Well, you should be having a young man come into your life pretty soon."

"She already has a boyfriend," Faith said too quickly and found herself a victim of one of Lilli's glares.

"Is that right, Lilli? Why haven't I heard about this young man?"

"I guess because he's a long way away." Lilli looked

through the porch screens at the oak tree arbor outside. "He's in New York City."

"How in the land of Goshen did you meet a boy so far away?"

"He used to live here." When he loved me. "His father died." And so do I every day he's gone. "His mother was kind of crazy after the funeral." I was the cause of his estrangement from his mother. "He left town and went to New York City." I haven't heard from him.

"Is he coming back to see you this summer?" Mrs. Barker was much intrigued.

"He hasn't said so. He's very busy." In fact, he's been gone two weeks, and I have no idea what he's doing. "He wants to learn about the antique jewelry business. And he hopes to work at Christie's someday."

"Why don't you go to New York and surprise him? Now *that* would be very romantic." Mrs. Barker clapped her gnarled hands together.

He hasn't asked me. Aloud, Lilli said, "I have to work this summer, Mrs. Barker. I have to save money for college so that I can become a world-famous anthropologist someday."

"Are you still going to make some great discovery, Lilli?" Faith asked.

Lilli looked at the red and white begonias in Mrs. Barker's garden. She could never figure out how her begonias were always twice the size of anyone else's. "Yes," Lilli said finally. "I'm going to make a discovery someday that will change everyone's perspective."

And perhaps, she thought, if she looked far enough and deep enough, she would be able to find love, too.

Nineteen

~

Z ane arrived in New York with little money and education but a lot of potential. His potential fit neatly inside
the palm of his hand in the form of a nineteenth-century platinum, jet, and aquamarine waterfall necklace from Seville. In
his other hand Zane carried the papers of its authenticity. This
piece, along with two pairs of diamond earrings and a Spanish comb from 1835 made of pearls and abalone shells, was
all that remained of his collection of Spanish jewels. Zane intended to sell the items in New York, get the highest price he
could for them, and drive straight back to Texas—and Lilli.

He wanted to make enough money to chomp a huge hole
in the mountain of debt left in the wake of his father's illness.
He'd meant it when he told his mother not to worry. He'd
also meant it when he said he couldn't take her manipulations
any longer. There was too much anger, too much pain and
grief in the McAllister house for him to stay in Bandera.

After getting a room at the YMCA, Zane went straight to
Melton's, a well-respected antique jewelry establishment. But
he couldn't get the receptionist, much less anyone else, to
talk to him. He didn't know at the time that Melton's was
readying itself for one of the largest private jewelry auctions
of the century. Hazzleton Winningham IV of the East
Hampton Winninghams had died childless and penniless. His
widow had been forced to sell the mansion, the art collection,
and the Bentley to pay off her husband's very, very private
gambling debts. She retained the condo in Boca Raton and
the London flat, both of which were paid for.

When eighteen-year-old Zane McAllister, country boy from
West Texas, clomped into the refined offices of Melton's on
Fifth Avenue, clad in a cheap polyester suit and a pair of

cowboy boots, the receptionist thought he was one of those singing telegrams. He was laughed out of the office.

Zane knew next to nothing about New York except that if one wanted to find money, one went to Wall Street. So he took the guided tour of the Stock Exchange. He had watched the frenzy of traders and the rain of papers for only thirty minutes when he realized it was nearly time for the market to close. At five minutes to three, he positioned himself outside the front doors of the Exchange and scanned the departing brokers and traders as they exited the building.

He watched the unlined faces of the young brokers who were eager to make their mark and pretended to themselves and their clients that they were in a position yet to be attained. These were not the kind of men Zane needed. These men would spend their money on gaudy status symbols meant to impress others, not on quality heirlooms to be cherished by future generations. He needed an older man, the kind who indulged himself to a fault. The man should be wearing expensive, classic clothing and have a car to match.

Zane found what he was looking for in Francis Kensington.

He walked up to the man dressed in a charcoal-gray pin-striped suit, white tailor-made shirt, and subdued gray-and-maroon paisley tie, who had just walked out of the Exchange building. Zane took note of the gold-and-pearl stickpin in his tie. The man would be difficult to impress. Zane knew he must sound sincere.

"Pardon me, sir," he began as the man neared the curb and raised his umbrella in the air to hail his driver, who awaited him a half block away.

"Yes?" the man replied without looking at Zane.

"My name is Zane McAllister and I have just traveled here from Bandera, Texas, to show you something."

Suspicion flitted across the man's round face. His heavy jowls dropped in a frown. "I don't know you."

"I know that, sir. But I think you should. I have a beautiful piece of heirloom jewelry that I need to sell. You see, my father had an operation—"

The man burst into laughter, and his cheeks turned red. "You'll have to do better than that, son. I'm from New York."

"I understand that, sir."

The limousine pulled up. The driver put the car in park, then got out. Zane knew his time was running out.

He reached into his jeans jacket pocket and pulled out the tissue-wrapped waterfall necklace. "I went to Melton's," he said, taking the necklace and holding it up in the man's line of vision. "They told me they were too busy to see me."

The driver opened the door for his employer.

Zane did not relent. He turned the necklace so that the sun glinted off the stones. "It's real, sir. Nineteenth century. I have papers to validate its authenticity. Perhaps you'd like to hear more about the history of the necklace. Its origin at Seville, perhaps, or its later sale to a Swedish princess."

Francis Kensington's heavy-lidded eyes could not conceal his curiosity.

The chauffeur stood to the side to allow his employer to enter the limousine.

Zane's eyes shot from the chauffeur back to the rotund man. "My dad just died. I need the money."

"Put the necklace away before someone on the street sees it and steals it."

Zane did as he was told.

Francis Kensington climbed awkwardly into the limousine. The chauffeur started to close the door. Francis held his umbrella out to stop the driver, then glanced up at Zane. "Well, get in. How can I read those papers of yours standing in the middle of traffic?"

Zane tried to remember that smiling at this juncture would seriously impair his negotiations. He forgot. He wanted to holler his joy right down the middle of Wall Street itself, but he didn't have time. He nearly dived into the limousine.

The driver closed the door. One hour later Zane closed the deal.

Francis Kensington owned residences in Paris, London, Manhattan, and Vail. He was unmarried, childless, and commanded an enormous empire of paper. Francis's company, Global Paper, was in the very new business of recycling used paper into new paper goods. Francis did not believe in buying anything new unless he had to. His homes were old; his furniture consisted of antiques or refurbished pieces. His limousine was five years old and previously had belonged to an

Arab sheikh. His clothes, however, were another matter. He bought them from the best tailor in London, and because of his two-hundred-and-sixty-five-pound physique, they cost him a lot of money. But Francis Kensington had a lot of money. He intended to make even more of it.

Four-star restaurants were high on his list of necessities. His homes were in the best neighborhoods: Grosvenor Square, Sutton Place, Rue du Faubourg St. Honoré, and a mountaintop overlooking Vail. His friends came from the elite corps of New York society, publishing, brokerage houses, and banking. They all liked Francis.

Because he donated a great deal of money to charities, he was the perfect escort for widows and divorcées who wanted to see their pictures in the society pages. Francis was a philanthropist extraordinaire. Since he had no children and at the age of fifty-five believed he was too old to father any, he decided to leave the world a better place upon his departure.

With three-quarters of a million dollars inherited from his mother, Francis had chosen to go into the recycling business. He believed that in ten years, perhaps less, Global Paper would truly live up to its name. Francis was a man ahead of his time: he espoused crusades that banned fluorocarbons, the destruction of the rain forests, the needless use of plastics, and the dumping of chemicals into the nation's waterways. Francis was a one-man branch of the EPA.

In order to reverse the course of human history and man's destruction of the planet, Francis realized he would have to make a great deal of money. Thus, he was looking for every deal he could find. He traded his stocks with a vengeance. He employed brokers in Tokyo at the Japanese stock exchange and watched the Japanese bond market like a hawk. He knew financial experts in Lugano, Switzerland, and in New York alone he had an entire floor of offices above the Global Paper offices where young, intelligent men managed Francis Kensington's money.

Francis knew everyone at Christie's, Sotheby's, and, of course, Melton's. When he saw Zane's antique necklace, he knew in an instant it was genuine. He was fascinated by this young man who had been turned down at Melton's. He was even more fascinated by the fact that Zane had picked him out of a crowd at the exchange. Zane might have been a country boy, Francis thought, but he was smart. Too smart. He was the kind of young man Francis wanted working for him.

"How much do you want for the necklace?"

"Thirty thousand." Zane started high to test his client.

"Twenty."

"Twenty-seven."

"Twenty-five."

"Done."

Francis unlocked his briefcase, took out his checkbook, and wrote a check for twenty-five thousand dollars.

Zane pulled the necklace out of his jacket pocket and handed it to Francis. "It was a pleasure doing business with you." He folded the papers of authenticity and held them out to Francis, and Francis handed him the check.

"What are you going to do with all that money, son?" Francis smiled and looked down at Zane's scuffed and dirty cowboy boots.

"I told you. My father was very sick. When he died, he left a mountain of bills. I'm going back home and try to get them paid off."

Francis's curiosity was aroused. "Twenty-five thousand is a lot of money . . . just how much money *do* you need?"

"Nearly four times that. He had cancer. He fought it for nearly two years. My mom is alone—"

"Do you miss her?" Francis interrupted.

"Not really. To be very honest, I'm glad to be away from that part of my life. She and I . . . well, we don't get along the way we should, I guess."

A pensive look settled on Francis's face. "That happens sometimes. Even in the best of families. Sometimes our parents don't want to let us go."

"Yeah."

"Tell me, Zane, why is it that you couldn't sell this piece to Melton's?"

Zane shrugged his shoulders. "They were too busy to see me, and I was in a hurry."

"Ah, I see. You're the impatient sort."

Zane chuckled. "I guess that's true."

"That can be an attribute. At times. Like now, for instance. You need a lot of money to help your mother. I'm only supposing here, but what happens if you go back to Texas and can't find any buyers for your pieces? I'm assuming you have more . . . uh, inventory?"

"I do. Not much of this quality." Zane liked talking with Francis. He seemed to know more than most people he'd met. "I have a good eye for antiques. My dad was the best in Texas. He taught me all he knew, but—"

"It's okay. You can tell me."

"It may sound disrespectful of the dead, but I believe there's a lot more to learn. And I want to know it all. And I can't learn it in Texas. I've always believed I needed to be in New York. This is where it's going to happen for me."

It was the cue Francis needed. "Then why go back?"

Zane stopped for an instant as a picture of Lilli flashed across his brain. It was the first time he'd thought of her today. "There's a girl."

"Does she love you?"

"Yes."

"Then she'll wait. Besides, no girl—woman—wants a man who can't provide for her."

Zane laughed. "You don't know Lilli. She's going to do just fine on her own."

"Maybe so. However, I have a proposition for you."

"Sir?" Zane sat at attention.

"If I get you into Melton's and they agree to hire you, which they will, of course, once they see you in action, then you in turn will keep me informed of prizes like this one when they become available."

"Is that against the law?"

"Not at this time, no. I'm not asking for a discount or even to be chosen over someone else's bid. I simply want to know, in your opinion, when you find the best of the best."

"The best of the best."

"Nothing less."

"Yes, sir."

"I can have one of my staff find you suitable and affordable quarters here in the city. I can introduce you to the kinds of people you need to know in your business."

Zane was speechless. He'd never been offered assistance like this from anyone before, and especially not from a total stranger. Maybe his mother had been right when she told him always to look for the good in people. "I don't know what to say."

" 'Yes' would be fine."

"Yes."

They shook hands just as the limousine rolled up to the curb in front of The Four Seasons restaurant.

"My driver will take you back to wherever you are staying. Here is my card." Francis handed Zane an engraved cream-colored business card. "Be at my office first thing in the morning and we'll get this Melton's thing wrapped up. Then we'll talk."

"Yes, sir!" Zane said with a grin as wide as Texas.

Francis got out of the limousine. Then he turned back to Zane. "Oh, by the way, Zane . . ."

"Sir?"

"The necklace was worth the thirty thousand. You're good, but not that good—yet." Francis closed the door and walked away.

Zane couldn't wait to call Lilli.

"Hi! Lilli! God! It's great to hear your voice!"

"Zane! Where are you?"

"In a phone booth. I wanted to wait to call you until I had some good news. And—guess what? I got a job and a place of my own! I'll have a phone in a couple of weeks. The phone company here isn't quite like it is back home. Gosh, Lilli, I'm so excited about everything that's happened."

"Tell me!"

"I met this man, Francis Kensington, and he's really helped me a lot. I sublet a one-bedroom apartment from one of his employees who had to go to London."

"Zane, that's great . . . I miss you."

"I miss you! God! You have no idea. I want you to come see me. Come to New York."

"You what?"

"You heard me. If I pay half your plane ticket, could you swing the other half? I have to see you, Lilli. I need to hold you."

"I don't know. I'll have to talk to my parents."

After a long pause, Zane's voice dropped to a sorrowful octave. "Your mom will never let you come here."

Lilli wished she could be enthusiastic, but it was impossible. "She can be very stubborn."

"Among other things."

"Have you talked to *your* mother? How is she?"

"Very depressed. I told her to see her minister. She needs somebody to talk to about ... Dad. I don't seem to say the right things to her. I start to tell her about what I'm doing here or that I've sent money to the doctor, and she starts quoting from the Bible. If I didn't know better, I'd say her mind has snapped."

"Oh, Zane, how awful!"

"She'll be okay in time."

"Yeah."

"See what you can do about arranging a trip to see me. I love you, Lilli. I want to hold you so bad."

"Me, too, Zane. Me, too. 'Bye."

Zane received a long letter from Lilli every week. She told him she had to work for the rest of the summer, but that she'd talked both her parents into letting her come to New York the week between Christmas and New Year's. It seemed like an eternity to wait, but Zane was busy and he told Lilli he'd wait forever if he had to.

In September, Zane enrolled for two classes at Columbia University's School of Continuing Education. One of the classes he signed up for was anthropology, because he thought it would keep him closer to Lilli. Once she got to New York, he would impress her with his new knowledge.

From time to time, Zane thought he might steal away for a weekend and fly back home, but work, school, business trips, seminars, and estate auctions all kept him from going back to Texas. He felt as if he'd been sucked into a whirlpool. One business deal led to another. Francis always had another party for him to attend, another luncheon with wealthy foreign dignitaries or a wealthy dowager.

"It's important to meet with her," Francis would say. "Women like your Texas accent," he would joke.

Zane felt obliged to acquiesce to Francis's requests.

Francis had taken Zane to a moderately priced tailor on Seventh Avenue who performed exquisite work for a reason-

ble price, using less expensive fabrics than Francis demanded for his own clothes.

In those first months when Zane missed Lilli, the way she
looked, talked, tasted, he took up jogging to sweat off his
erections. He joined William Guidry, one of the art appraisers
at Melton's, at his racquetball club, where even his workouts
ed Zane to meetings with potential clients. That fall Zane
played a lot of racquetball, lifted weights, sat in hot saunas,
and took cold showers.

As the months passed and he clocked off the time, his
body's proportions altered drastically, due to his weight-
lifting routine. He alternated weight lifting with an aerobic
workout of jogging, swimming, and biking.

Now when Zane McAllister put on his jeans and T-shirt on
a Saturday afternoon for a walk around Manhattan, he was re-
ponsible for dozens of cases of female whiplash.

Thoughts of Lilli receded as he became completely absorbed in his new life. Life in New York. Life with the rich
and famous. Life in the fast lane.

"Hi, Zane. It's Lilli."

"Hi."

"I—I was doing my homework and I hadn't talked to you
for a while. Two weeks and two days, to be exact. I was . . .
wondering if you were all right."

"Yeah, I'm fine," he said, sipping a cup of cold coffee he'd
made two hours earlier when he started working on a lengthy
proposal for a buying trip to Vienna. "I'm sorry I haven't
called. I've been really busy. Work has got me running nonstop. I can't tell you the name of my client, Lilli, but I just
got back from Chicago, where I cut a great deal on a fifteen-
carat emerald that has not been out of that family's vault in
over fifty years. Nobody in New York could believe I pried
it out of the old man's hands."

Lilli noticed that as soon as he started talking about his
job, his excitement level rose several notches. He couldn't
talk fast enough. This was the Zane she remembered, and yet
he was different. He was so focused on his work. It was as
if there was nothing else in life but jewels and deals. She still
held out the hope that there was room in his heart, in his life,
for her.

"So. What have you been up to?" he asked.

"Oh, the usual. I got an A on my English lit paper, but I didn't do so well on my advanced geometry test. I got a low B."

"Gee, sorry to hear that."

Lilli wished with all her heart that she could make her life sound as exciting as Zane's, but the truth of the matter was that she was still in high school and he was out in the world making a life for himself. She didn't even have an expedition with her father she could use to sound as worldly as he. Nervously, Lilli twirled a piece of hair around her finger. "I—I can't wait to see you at Christmas, Zane."

"Me, too," he replied with so little emotion that Lilli felt her stomach churn.

"I know you're busy. I guess I should let you go." Please, she thought, don't hang up. I need to hear the sound of your voice even though you seem so preoccupied. What's happening to us, Zane?

"Yeah. I really should go. I love you, Lilli."

"I love you, Zane. I hope you never forget."

"I won't," he assured her and hung up.

December 26, 1978

Lilli arrived at La Guardia Airport at two-thirty in the afternoon. For months she had waited for this moment. She had dreamed about it at night and fantasized about it during the day. She just knew that Zane would meet her with open arms and surprise her with a bouquet of roses. When she walked off the plane she scanned the waiting crowd three times before the realization hit her: Zane had not come to the airport.

"He's late. Maybe he got stuck in traffic," she mumbled.

Lilli's heart felt like lead. She forced back her tears and walked toward the baggage-claim area. With every step she anticipated the joy of seeing him running down the corridor, but as she followed the passengers from her plane to the luggage area, Zane was nowhere to be seen.

She hauled her hanging bag and suitcase off the conveyor belt and was about to go back up to ticketing and book a re-urn flight to Houston when she noticed a man dressed in a chauffeur's uniform holding a sign that said "Mitchell."

Lilli walked over to the man. "I'm Lilli Mitchell."

"Your ride is waiting. Let me get these bags for you," he said politely and ushered her toward a gray Cadillac limousine.

"Did Mr. McAllister arrange for this?"

"My account reads 'The Melton Company.' "

"Yes! That's him!" Lilli's heart lightened.

As they drove into Manhattan, the driver explained to Lilli that he was taking her to the Russian Tea Room on West Fifty-seventh Street, where she was to meet her "party."

Lilli had no idea whether the Russian Tea Room was truly a simple tearoom or an expensive restaurant. But she knew that her violet silk dress and black heels would be appropriate in either place. She was glad that she had decided to dress as sophisticatedly as possible for Zane.

The driver arranged for Lilli's bags to be placed in the cloakroom at the elegant restaurant. Lilli tipped him and then followed the maître d' to Zane's table.

Zane was sitting in a booth against the wall with two impeccably dressed middle-aged men. He was listening intently to their every word. As she approached the table, the tall, thin, gray-haired man noticed Lilli first. He smiled at her and nodded as if he knew her. Then he nodded to Zane, who turned his head and saw her.

Zane rose and stretched out his arm to her. "Lilli! You're here!"

"Yes," she said, not hiding her reservations, "I am here."

Zane's smile was genuine, at least, Lilli thought. He put his arm around her shoulder.

"Gentlemen, I would like you to meet Lilli Mitchell from Houston. Lilli, this is Ross Weinberg and Gilbert Hays."

"Pleased to meet you, Lilli," Ross said, extending his hand.

"A pleasure," Lilli said, shaking his hand.

"You are absolutely lovely," Gilbert said as he half rose from his seat.

Zane signaled the waiter to bring another chair.

Gilbert turned to Zane. "I can tell by the look on this young lady's face that she would be most appreciative of our

departure. I'll call you in a few days with my answer, Zane."
He stood and shook Zane's hand.

Ross followed suit. "I like what you've proposed, Zane.
You can tell them at Melton's that I'll do business only with
you and no one else."

"Yes, sir, Mr. Weinberg. I'll tell them. I can't thank you
enough for giving me this opportunity."

"I've always prided myself on finding new talent, Zane. As
long as you remain as determined as you seem to be now,
you'll make it in this business. Remember, I've got my eye
on you."

"Yes, sir!"

Zane said his good-byes, and after the two men left, he
took Lilli's hands in his own and squeezed them. "Gosh! You
look more beautiful than I remember, Lilli."

Lilli tried not to feel sad at this moment, but she couldn't
help it. "I think you forgot a lot of things, Zane," she said.

He kissed her hand. "No, I didn't." He stared into her eyes
but was unable to read her thoughts. "Did you like the limo?"

"It was fine."

"I would have picked you up myself, but I was really busy
and this lunch was too important. Do you realize those two
men could single-handedly make my career? What a coup
that would be! I'd be the youngest manager Melton's has ever
had. I'm on my way, Lilli."

"I can see that, Zane." But to where, my love?

"I can't get over how wonderful you look. Tell me about
you. Tell me what's going on."

"There's not much to tell. I aced all my exams. I should
make the dean's list again . . . despite advanced geometry."

Zane stared at Lilli, his expression blank.

"What's wrong?"

"I was just thinking. . . . It seems like high school was a
thousand years ago. I mean . . . well, what I meant was, so
much has happened to me since I came to New York. It's
been six months already. Half a year."

Half a lifetime, she thought morosely.

Zane noticed the sad shadows in Lilli's violet eyes, and
with a pang he realized he'd put them there. It was up to him
to banish them. "I have so many things planned for us, Lilli."

"Really?"

"I thought tonight we'd see a play. If you'd like, we could go to the Met tomorrow. Do you like opera?"

"I don't know. I've never been."

"My favorite is *La Traviata.*"

"You like opera?"

"It grows on you." He smiled broadly. "I found I like a lot of things I hadn't tried before. Even sushi." He laughed heartily. "Well, c'mon. I cleaned up the apartment just for you. I can't wait to show it to you. I even bought a new couch for the place. My very first piece of furniture. I ordered it just after I got back from Paris."

"When did you go to Paris?"

"Last month. I thought I told you."

"No, you didn't." Never had the chasm between them seemed so wide. Zane's world was more removed from Lilli than she'd feared. She felt stupid for flying to New York to see him. She was a seventeen-year-old high school kid, and he was now a businessman, respected by men older than her father. They were light-years apart, and she hadn't the slightest clue how she could bring him back to her. Lilli had always believed herself to be strong and independent. She'd been so cocksure of herself and her ability to whack away at life and its challenges, much like she chopped up the jungle with her machete, but this time she was being taught humility. Lilli felt as if she'd just lost a part of herself, and for the first time, she didn't know what to do.

Lilli loved Zane's apartment, possibly too much. Lush ferns in macramé hangers filled the corners. There was a new leather camelback sofa against the window, which looked out over the city. A stack of expensive books on jewelry, antique jewelry, and gemstones sat on a glass-topped coffee table. A pair of battered fauteuil chairs flanked a small fireplace. The kitchen was no more than an alcove, but it was equipped with the latest appliances, gadgets, and gourmet utensils. "Who's the cook?"

"I am," Zane said as he placed Lilli's suitcases in the bedroom. Then he joined her in the kitchen. "I get tired of eating out."

Lilli picked up a French cuisine cookbook that was lying

on the butcher block. "A far cry from Texas barbecue, isn't it?"

"I'm sure I can still smoke the hell out of a brisket," he said and walked over to her and put his arms around her. "I missed you, Lilli," he said and kissed her.

After waiting half a year to kiss him, Lilli didn't think she would be surprised by the touch of his lips, but she was. He was kissing her hello and she was already kissing him goodbye.

In the days that followed, Zane pretended there were no long silences between them. He pretended that Lilli was as interested in his work as he was. He chose not to see the distance that yawned between them. He feigned interest in her tales about the French club, classes, the school election, and her work in her father's store. Even though they could commiserate about the mutual problems with their mothers, their bond was not as strong as it had once been. Zane's life was so very different now, and the part that hurt him so deeply was that it was no one's fault. Zane still loved Lilli, but they weren't the same people anymore. He wasn't the same.

Watching Lilli, Zane could see that she felt the same things in her heart. He thought he would never see a sadder sight.

Lilli's trip to New York lasted until New Year's day morning, when she had to fly back to Houston in order to be ready for school to start the next day. As she boarded the plane, she felt like a five-year-old being put on the bus, and Zane was her father. They were only two years apart in age, but at this juncture in her life, it might as well have been thirty.

Zane had made love to her nearly every day, shown her Manhattan, his office, and introduced her to his older and very sophisticated friends, all of whom made pointed remarks about her being a high school student.

"Why, Lilli, I can't believe you're still in high school. Were you held back? You look so much older, dear," one chic twenty-something brunette had said at the New Year's Eve cocktail party at Francis Kensington's home.

A woman from Long Island had remarked on Lilli's black velvet cocktail dress. "Don't do the bow in back, sweets. Too cutesy," she said as she stuck a cigarette holder in her mouth and lit the cigarette with a solid gold lighter.

One of Zane's business associates kept insisting that Lilli was "really" Zane's sister and that she should go off with him to see the bedrooms. "Francis has the best taste, dahling. You simply must see these rooms."

"No, thanks," Lilli said.

At four minutes past midnight, after a long and ardent New Year's kiss from Zane, she begged him to take her back to his apartment. Zane misunderstood the reason for her request, but the result was what Lilli had desired. Zane immediately whisked her down to a taxi and they were back at his apartment, in his bed, in less than thirty minutes.

When Zane made love to Lilli, his passion was more intense, more giving, and more exciting than ever, but each time he kissed her, touched her breast, and whispered to her that he loved her, Lilli wondered if this wasn't the way the music sounded when a swan's song was played.

After Lilli left, Zane still wrote to her, although even less frequently than before. He never told her that he didn't love her, because that was not true. He did love her, but in the way that first loves should be: half myth and half reality. He had come to realize that if he stopped to fit Lilli into his life, he might not make it to the top. And Zane wanted to be at the top.

As time passed, New York girls threw themselves at Zane. He also met Chelsea girls in London pubs and Parisian girls at art auctions; all in the name of business. The only problem Zane had was that he never met anyone as beautiful or as giving and loving as Lilli. He had chosen to let her go, but he hated himself for doing it.

Twenty

August 1980

*L*illi walked down the stairs wearing her red Ropers and nothing else but her bathrobe. The electric rollers in her hair flopped up and down, since she took few pains to insert them correctly as her cousin, Faith, had instructed. "Primping," as Lilli called it, was a waste of time. Fortunately for Lilli, her beauty was natural and heartstopping. She could have done without the rollers, but she intended to work at her father's antique gallery that day.

"Mom! I can't find my blue jeans skirt. Did Maria try to wash it again?" Lilli started toward the kitchen when she noticed that the door to her father's study was ajar.

She saw him lying with his head on his desk. Lilli smiled. Poor thing, he must have worked all night, she thought. She pressed her hand against the door and pushed it all the way open.

J.C. was slumped across his desk, his right cheek flattened against an open book. The desk was in total disarray, with ancient maps taped onto current road maps. Topographical maps of Mexico, Central America, and South America hung over the edges of the huge desk. There were Xeroxes of letters from both famous and not-so-famous archaeologists.

His reading glasses were still perched on top of his head, and Lilli recalled the many times he thought he'd mislaid them when all the time they were on his head. He looked so tired, she thought, so vulnerable. She wondered what it was that had driven him so intensely these past months. Day after day Lilli had inquired about his work, but J.C. was curiously silent about it.

For the first time, J.C. had begun to lock his study, telling

Lilli that he wanted Arlette and her "damn maid" to keep their hands off his work. His clutter was an organized clutter, and only he knew where he was going with it all.

"At least tell me what it is you're after," she remembered asking only the week before.

"No," he had answered tersely.

Lilli had wondered how she could wrangle more information out of him. "That a map of Peru, Pop?"

"So what if it is?" He hadn't looked up at her, but kept checking the map and then went back to a letter that had arrived that day from Columbia University with obviously another piece of the puzzle.

"You've talked about going to South America for a long time. Think we might go any time soon?" she probed.

"Might."

"Aw, come on, Pop. Have a heart! You've been working on this stuff for over half a year . . ."

"More than three years now," he said wearily. "I'm not going anywhere until I'm sure. Very sure."

"Okay, Pop," she'd said and then given him a quick kiss.

Now Lilli looked down at him, asleep atop his desk, wondering if the previous night's foray had unearthed any new clues. Lately she worried about his relentlessness and his near-obsessional pursuit of some phantom treasure. He pushed himself to the extreme, working at the gallery all day and then in his study all night. He no longer laughed and smiled as much as he used to. His face had become deeply lined of late and he always looked serious. Lilli wished she could lighten his load for him. She was working at the gallery nearly as much as he, but perhaps she could do more. If only he would open up to her the way he'd done in the past and tell her what was driving him so hard.

Lilli placed her hand on his back and nudged him slightly. "Pop, it's time to rise and shine," she said, smiling. She glanced out the French doors onto the garden. "It's a gorgeous day. Not a cloud in the sky." She nudged him again, this time a bit more forcefully.

He was warm to the touch, but as her hand rested upon his back, she noticed that he was not snoring as he usually did when he was this soundly asleep. "Pop?"

She shook his shoulder. His arm slid off the desk and dangled at his side.

"POP!!"

Lilli's cry screamed through the house. "No! No! Not Pop!"

Lilli started to shake violently. She touched her father's head, cheek, neck, and back, looking for signs of life and finding none. "No! No! No!" she wailed over and over. Tears blinded her, and she felt that at any moment her legs would no longer support her.

"Someone help!" she screamed. "It's Pop, it's Pop!"

Dishes crashed in the kitchen, and a few moments later Maria appeared at the door of the study. Lilli could hear her prayers in whispered Spanish as she sank onto the leather sofa and fell into hysterics.

"Lilli?" Arlette Mitchell called out as she came down the stairs. "Lilli, what *are* you screaming about! It's not ladylike to—" Arlette stopped abruptly in the doorway to the study. Shock turned her face to granite. Her eyes were wide but emotionless. Lilli noticed that her mother had to clutch the doorjamb for support. "Is . . . he . . . sick, Lilli?"

How like Arlette to expect the answers to come from her, Lilli thought. How many times had she played the parent to her mother's child?

Lilli was sobbing so hard she was having trouble breathing. She felt as if someone had punched her in the chest. "My pop is dead!" she screamed. "Dead! Dead!"

Lilli fell across his body, her arms engulfing his lifeless form, and cried. She knew her life would never be the same again.

In the beginning, the gossip and rumors around J.C. Mitchell's death were rampant. It was a natural death, to be sure, with no mention of foul play. However, there were those men and women, the finest in Houston's society, who exchanged raised eyebrows over lunch at Grotto's or dinner at Cafe Annie, wondering who in town would show up at the funeral. It was a double-edged sword, they said. Arlette Mitchell was not a favorite, but she had been around for decades. She was a large donor to the arts, and they needed her money.

On the other hand, there was not one among them who

could deny that it would be just like Arlette to have pushed J.C. over the edge with her demands. It was her insatiable need to always "make the columns" that no doubt had given J.C. a bad heart.

J.C. Mitchell, owner of Antiquities, one of Houston's finer art and antiques galleries, had always been the topic of speculation in town; he'd been a man who was at once revered by his clients and some members of the Houston community and, on the other hand, was castigated by authorities and experts in the archaeological field, to which he'd always aspired.

J.C. Mitchell had thought of himself as an adventurer, a seeker of truth and knowledge. Lilli, too, believed no differently about him. Others, however, had long wanted to put a stop to J.C. Mitchell's archaeological digs. Over the years valuable, perhaps history-altering, artifacts had been discovered by J.C. Mitchell and his well-meaning daughter, and all had been sold on the black market.

None of the prominent Houstonians who owned these pre-Columbian treasures would admit to their association with J.C. Mitchell and, in fact, were perhaps his most vocal detractors. When he was alive, they supported his digs and paid handsomely for bits of pottery, flints, pieces of jade, gold, and emerald. With his death, they were caught on a tightrope, fighting over one another to run back to safety.

They felt sorry for Lilli. Although only nineteen, she had won their hearts in a way that Arlette's parties and J.C.'s secret discoveries never would. Lilli adored her father, plain and simple. Many a wealthy Houston father wished his daughters and sons would love him in the way that Lilli loved J.C. Mitchell. She was J.C.'s soul mate, they said. It would have been no less than a sin if anyone else had found him that morning.

Zane's hands were shaking when he read the cablegram. It was from Lilli.

Zane McAllister. Melton's Antique Jewelry and Auction House. New York. New York. Stop. J.C. dead this noon. Stop. Come back. Stop. Love. Lilli.

He dropped the cable on the desk as if it had burned his hands. He could not believe the great J.C. Mitchell was dead. J.C. was life itself—he was bigger than life. J.C. had been the only other man besides his own father who had seen his potential. Most important, he'd taken the time to tell Zane how impressed he was.

Zane had admired J.C. He wasn't afraid to pit himself against the elements, against bureaucracies, or against ghosts from past eons. And he was a man who followed his dreams. Yet if he were truthful with himself, Zane would have to admit that J.C. had intimidated him. Flat out, J.C. had been a hard act to follow, although Zane hadn't wanted Lilli to think that.

Now J.C. was gone, and Zane was learning to be his own man. He'd tried . . . damn, how he'd tried to forget Lilli! But he saw her face in other women, heard her voice in his dreams, and sometimes, on very lonely nights, he remembered all too well the feel of her body next to his.

Now she was calling him back.

Zane looked around his very small office. It wasn't actually an office, it was a "place." They had made a "place" for him at Melton's. A "place" had been made for him at one of the oldest antique jewelry houses in the world.

He would go back for the funeral because Lilli needed him and because he still loved her. But Texas was no longer home to him; New York was. And he would not give it up.

Twenty-one

Z ane arrived in time for the funeral that Tuesday morning. Lilli stood next to her mother in the front pew at St. Anne's Catholic Church. Zane slipped quietly into a back pew as the priest began the requiem mass.

For two years he'd—successfully, he thought—suppressed his emotions about his own father's death and believed he was over it. Now he realized that he had been wrong.

Zane remembered little of the happenings of his own father's funeral. But as he sat there watching the unfamiliar ceremony, he remembered every intimate moment with his father . . . happy childhood times, holidays, the winning basketball game his sophomore year, learning the antique jewelry trade at his father's side . . . and mostly he remembered the dark days of cancer. He remembered that horrid trip to Mexico, and he remembered his father's last day and night.

Zane had never been in a Catholic church before. To dispel the painful thoughts of his father, he forced himself to concentrate on the ceremony. He was intrigued by the rituals performed for the dead. The priest said some prayers, and then he shook a silver instrument that looked like a microphone and spewed holy water over the casket. Then he swung an incense burner around the base of the casket, filling the church with a pungent scent, and said more prayers. To Zane, the purple drape over the casket, the deep purple-and-black vestments the priest wore, and the acrid incense made death seem very real.

He had been surprised to learn that the funeral was being held in a Catholic church. Lilli hadn't been raised in any religion; she had told him that. Perhaps her father had been raised Catholic and wanted to be buried in a Catholic ceremony. Somehow, these old traditions and rituals fit him.

From this far back in the church, Zane could barely see Lilli. However, at one point during the Mass she went to the lectern and gave a reading. Then, as she returned to the pew, she lifted her head and scanned the faces of the mourners. Was she looking for him?

He stepped into the aisle so that she could see he was with her. A faint smile curved her mouth, and in that moment he thought the Mona Lisa was never as beautiful as Lilli.

Zane's stomach was in knots throughout the long and, to him, tedious Mass. He thought the priest would never dismiss them, but finally the front doors of the church were opened. He watched Lilli as she held her mother's arm while they walked down the aisle. As she came closer, he could see that she had been crying. Her eyes were red-rimmed, but even still, they shone with happiness when she saw him.

Lilli did not take her eyes off Zane. She had been afraid he would not come. Then the day before, the maid had informed her that he'd called to inquire about the time of the funeral and the location of the church. There had been no other message.

When she saw him, she barely recognized him. He looked so old—all the boyishness in his face was gone. His shoulders were so wide he looked as if he could pick up the church. But his eyes, she would know his eyes anywhere. As she drew near, she reached out impulsively to touch his hand. He'd changed in many ways, but the touch of his hand was the same. She felt the connection between them, the electricity, the rightness of them. She could hear her father's voice echo in her heart: "There will be a connectedness, Lilli. You'll just know."

Lilli had not been wrong about Zane. She still loved him; she could never love anyone else. They had both changed a great deal in the past two years, but the place she had in her heart for Zane had not changed.

Their eyes met. Liquid violet and sun-flecked blue.

"Lilli, I'm so sorry," he said over the lump in his throat.

"Me, too," she whispered, knowing he was not talking about her father. Neither was she.

Arlette tugged on Lilli's arm like an impatient child. Lilli didn't want to leave, but this day was for her father, not for Zane.

People filed out of the church, pew by pew, and by the time Zane's pew left the church, Lilli and her mother were already in the limousine at the head of the procession. Since Zane had taken a cab to the church from the airport, he asked the woman who had sat next to him in the church if he could ride with her.

It took over half an hour to reach the cemetery, and another fifteen minutes for everyone to assemble in the stifling summer heat.

Fortunately, the long Catholic ceremony in the church left little to be said at the cemetery.

Zane again remained in the background while the final prayers were said, the casket lowered, and Lilli received condolences from her friends. The priest had announced that a catered dinner would be held at the Mitchell home and all were invited to attend.

Zane was surprised when Faith walked up to him and invited him to ride in her family's car. He accepted and started to walk away with Faith and her fiancé, Paul Newsome, when he heard Lilli call his name.

She came toward him. His mind was filled with a thousand things to say, but his mind and tongue did not connect. He said nothing.

"How long will you stay?" she asked simply.

"I have to leave Thursday. I'm closing a deal in Boston."

"Two days," she said with a voice so mournful that Zane winced. Then she smiled at him and took away his pain. "We'll make the most of it."

Just then Arlette came up behind them. "We have to go, Lilli. There's so much to do at the house." She grabbed Lilli's hand and nearly yanked her away from Zane. Before they were out of earshot, Zane heard Arlette say, "Who was that man?"

"Zane McAllister, Mom," Lilli replied.

"Impossible." Arlette stole a glance at Zane over her shoulder. Contempt glinted in her eyes.

It was nearly seven o'clock before the crowd at the Mitchell home dwindled to Arlette's sister-in-law, her attorney, her doctor, and the secretary from Antiquities. Zane was afraid he'd never have a moment alone with Lilli.

"I have to get more liquor. Want to go with me to Spec's?" Lilli asked him.

"Sure."

They left through the French doors in the kitchen, which was overflowing with dirty rented plates and glasses. Maria was filling the dishwasher, the caterer having long since left.

They rode in Lilli's new vintage Mercedes-Benz. It had all new tan leather upholstery and gold pinstriping. The radio needed work and it had a hundred and twelve thousand miles on the odometer, but Lilli loved it. Arlette, of course, hated it, partly because it was so very individualistic and partly because J.C. had given it to Lilli, displaying, once again, his mental and emotional bond with his daughter.

Zane whistled appreciatively. "When did you get this?"

"For graduation. Pop gave it to me. Mom threw a fit. She said it was too extravagant, although Pop told me he got a great deal on it. Like always, she was just mad because he wasn't spending the money on her. I guess he thought my graduation was a good enough excuse to get around her protests."

Zane shook his head. "It's funny, but I've met a lot of women like her in New York. Spoiled by their rich daddies. They can't wait to spend *my* money, too."

Jealousy made Lilli's breath catch in her throat. She hoped Zane hadn't noticed. "I'm sure selfishness is not strictly a Texas attribute," she said, trying to keep her tone casual.

"Definitely not," he said and looked out the windshield as they passed the familiar old oaks along University Boulevard. His mind was filled with the pain of letting Lilli go and an aching need to get her back, but he didn't know where to start. He didn't want to foist himself on her at this time. He remembered the grieving he had gone through after his father died. She needed time for herself now. She and J.C. had been so close, and Zane wanted her to heal.

Lilli was silent, not knowing what to say to Zane. She'd tried not to think of him with another woman, although common sense told her he must have dated someone. He was handsome and talented and she knew that plenty of women found him attractive. When she had visited him in New York, she'd noticed the appreciative female looks he'd received. It was torturous for her to imagine him making love to anyone but her. She had kept that part of her life exclusive to him. She still dreamed of Zane at night, and she wanted desperately to ask if he dreamed of her at all.

"What are you going to do, Lilli, now that J.C. is gone? Are you going to college?"

She turned the corner onto Kirby. "I have to wait until the will is read. I'll know more then."

Zane did a double take. "Is this the same Lilli Mitchell I knew? The one who had plans for every decade of her life? You're going to let a will dictate your next course of action?" Then he stopped himself abruptly. He had no right to criticize her; he didn't even know who she was anymore. Yet, seeing her again, he knew that his feelings for her hadn't changed, and he felt a great ache at having let her go. He wanted her back, but realized that she might not want him anymore. How could he tell her that the one thing he wanted to do was take her in his arms and make her promise that she would come away with him? And what right did he have to ask that when he wasn't willing to move to Texas for her?

Zane decided to be wise. He would keep his desires and emotions to himself.

"Yes, I am," she said defensively. "In case you couldn't tell, I've changed, Zane." She swallowed a tear. "I'm not a kid anymore."

Lilli watched how coolly Zane acted toward her and she believed that she'd made a mistake inviting him. He seemed to have changed a great deal. In fact, she felt as if he'd chucked his heart away. This man of muscle and steel and money was nothing like the boy she loved. She didn't like this new, cool, and sophisticated Zane. She wondered what he'd thought was wrong with the old Zane that had made him want to reinvent himself.

Zane knew that Lilli was assessing him as she drove, and he watched as disapproval filled her eyes. It's better this way, he thought. She's in shock and grief right now. It would be wrong of me to make demands on her heart when she can't possibly know what she's feeling. She probably wouldn't even want to hear what I need to tell her. And why should she even believe me? I already let her down once.

As she was saying something else about the fact that she'd grown up, Zane couldn't help the way his eyes fell to her luscious figure. He'd never seen anyone in movies or on a magazine cover who was more incredibly beautiful. "You certainly are not." He reached over and touched her hand. "You've turned into a very beautiful woman."

"Thank you." Lilli did not trust herself to say anything more. She wished he hadn't touched her hand; it stirred up memories better left forgotten.

Neither of them spoke for several minutes. Then Zane broke the silence. "I'm so sorry about your father, Lilli."

"It's not your fault Pop is dead." She sniffed back a second wave of tears. She felt abandoned by her father and rejected by Zane. The world as she'd always known it and trusted it had vanished like the morning fog. Reality cast glaring shadows on her future, and she was afraid.

"Lilli, pull over for a minute. I want to talk to you, and I can't do it while you're driving."

She nodded and pulled the Mercedes over to the curb and turned off the ignition. She turned and looked at him, her eyes filled with tears.

Zane had never seen Lilli like this. She was always the take-charge person. She always knew what to do. He'd thought her invincible. He discovered she was not. She was vulnerable. She was hurting, and it was his guess he had more to do with her tears right now than her father. "I'm sorry I got so caught up in myself, my world, my problems, that I forgot about you. I hurt you, Lilli, and I'm truly sorry."

The wound in Lilli's heart from the past months of not hearing from Zane reopened. "I loved you, Zane," she finally found the courage to say. "After I left New York, it was never the same for us. It's not your fault, it's just the way things are, and I hate that part about life. I didn't do anything wrong and I feel like I'm being punished anyway." She looked at him through a wall of tears that made him appear like a wavering mirage.

"That's just how I feel, Lilli," he said.

"You do?"

"Yes," he said with a heavy sigh. "God help me, Lilli, but I don't know what to say to you now. What to do. I'm afraid if I even touch you, I'll be opening a can of worms . . ."

Lilli placed her hand on the nape of Zane's neck and drew his face toward hers. Before he knew what he was doing,

Zane's mouth was on hers in a hungry, passionate kiss. He touched her hair and let a long strand wind around his fingers and down across the palm of his hand. It felt like silk. It smelled like lilies. Behind his closed eyelids he felt the burn of acrid tears.

Lilli pulled away first and looked at him. "Maybe I should have fought for you."

"Maybe it was best that I had that time to myself. To learn about myself."

"And what did you learn, Zane McAllister?" She lifted his face to the level of her eyes. She peered deeply into his blue eyes, searching for a flicker of dishonesty, but she found none.

"That I still love you."

He kissed her again. His lips molded to hers as he slipped his arms around her and pulled her close to his massive chest.

Lilli felt such a burst of love and passion that she nearly started to cry. The months of waiting had come to an end. She felt as if she'd been rescued by the angels and swept into paradise. The memory of all those times when she had needed him so desperately, ached just to hear the sound of his voice on the other end of the phone, screamed through her mind like wailing banshees. They tried to warn her to protect her heart.

Lilli did not listen.

She kissed him back with a heart filled with love. She welcomed his tongue with eagerness. She touched his cheek with her hand and then let it slip around to his nape, where she clutched a long lock of blond hair. She could feel him trembling. She could feel his heart hammering inside his chest and she knew that he was as frightened as she. They had given each other tremendous love and terrible pain. He had been her first love, her only love, and he still was.

Her mind and heart were at war. Within the circle of his arms, Lilli experienced anew all the love and joy she'd known with Zane years ago. She wanted him to make love to her. Her body craved the feel of him inside her, but she knew now not to trust her own flesh. Her body would betray her.

He touched her breast and Lilli began to melt. Zane unbuttoned the two top buttons of her suit jacket and gently slid his hand down to her breast.

"Oh, God, Lilli . . ." He groaned as he fought his erection.

Suddenly Lilli broke away from him. "I can't. Not here. Not now."

Zane sucked in lungfuls of air. "I'm sorry . . . I got carried away."

Lilli quickly rebuttoned her jacket. She turned away from him and put her hands on the steering wheel. She let her mind dictate her next move. "I'm the one who got carried away." She turned the key in the ignition. "We'd better get to Spec's and then head back home."

Zane's hand clamped down on Lilli's forearm like a vise. "We're not leaving here until I know that you don't still hate me."

She looked at him, raised her hand to touch his cheek again. "I don't hate you, Zane. I never did."

There was a lump of gratefulness in Zane's throat. He could only nod his head.

Lilli pulled the car away from the curb and headed for the liquor store.

J. C. Mitchell's last will and testament was read in the legal offices of Frank Dunhill, of Dunhill, Majors and Wasserman. Lilli, Arlette, Vicki, and Faith were all present, since Frank had informed them that they were the principal heirs to J.C.'s estate.

Frank Dunhill was one of Houston's top attorneys. Although he did not command the publicity or the fees of "Racehorse" Haynes or Joe Jamail, Frank had garnered a lion's share of important estates, divorces, and large civil suits. Lilli remembered her father stating that Frank was wily like a fox, but he was honest and he was a genius when it came to estate planning.

Frank was a tall, handsome, prematurely gray man of forty-two who wore Italian loafers, English suits, designer ties, and a year-round tan. He was well built and kept his physique slender with killer tennis matches and noontime jogs down Allen Parkway. Frank was divorced and liked to claim that his was the costliest divorce in Houston. Everyone knew it was true, because he'd had his friend Earl Lilly handle his case. Frank's divorce was a long time coming, according to the society gossip. His affairs were legendary, and everyone in town knew that the only reason he'd remained married for fourteen years was because his wife was naive. Once she learned the truth, she cleaned out the house down to the solid brass switch plates and the designer drapes, went to Mexico, and racked up his charge plates to the limit, then returned to town and told him what she wanted. Frank gave it to her. All seventeen million of it. She moved to Austin and never told a soul that she had known for fourteen years that Frank was a homosexual.

Lilli watched her mother as she played the grieving widow to the hilt. Lilli wondered if J. C. had ever told Arlette the truth about Frank.

Arlette crossed her legs very slowly. Frank watched her short skirt ride up on her thigh.

You're wasting your time, Mom, Lilli wanted to say, but didn't. It would serve her right to be jilted by Frank.

It made Lilli sick the way her mother was carrying on. She knew that during times of grief, people reacted in very strange ways. Zane had argued with his mother and left Texas for two years. If that wasn't out of character, she didn't know what was. All her life Lilli had hoped that her mother loved her father, but she could see now that she hadn't. Lilli believed that J. C. had loved Arlette, although she couldn't see why. He had not had affairs. Yet, in a way, Lilli could see now that his trips, his digs, even his relationship with her, were his outlets. He had reached for adventure instead of love. He'd heaped his affection on Lilli, who needed it desperately.

God! The world sure is a screwed-up place, Lilli thought as Frank rearranged the papers in front of him.

He smiled charmingly at Arlette. Then he gave perfunctory smiles to Lilli, Vicki, and Faith.

"Ladies, I'm glad that you could all make it today," Frank began. "I want you to know that I worked with J. C. on this will several years ago. J. C. knew then that his heart was failing him."

Lilli gasped. "What?" Her eyes shot to her aunt, who shook her head.

"I had no idea!" Vicki said.

"I didn't either," Arlette said indignantly. "He never said a word. Why? I could have gotten him to the doctor! I could have saved him!" She held her handkerchief to her eyes.

Lilli had the distinct impression that her mother had been taking acting lessons.

Even Frank threw Arlette a condemning look before he began again. "He was afraid that if he told you, any of you, he would be forced to live the life of a semi-invalid. J. C. intended to live every day to the fullest. He lived as he died, pursuing his dreams."

Arlette scowled.

Lilli nodded.

"It is with that thought in mind that I will continue and read his, er, rather unusual will."

Lilli braced herself.

"To my wife, Arlette Herbert Mitchell, I leave our home and all its current furnishings and art, except for the entire contents of my study, which upon the reading of this will shall be locked away from anyone's view. That is to include my daughter, Lilli; my sister, Vicki; and her daughter, Faith. If Frank has borne out my instructions to the letter, the movers should be in the house at this moment removing my letters, diaries, books, and files.

"I am disposing of my personal possessions as I see fit. I do not trust my wife with any of them, as I believe she would either destroy important notes, thinking they were valueless because she could not pawn them somewhere, or sell my treasure to one of my competitors for a handsome sum. I do not trust my daughter with these articles because she might keep something for sentimental value that I have earmarked for another end.

"Too, all of the items in Lilli's room, including the furniture, antiques, and art, shall remain in her possession. At this reading I have arranged for all those items to be removed from the house and brought to a town house that I have purchased for my daughter in which she may continue to live, or sell if she decides these accommodations are not satisfactory to her. For the past six months this town house has been sublet by a gentleman who was aware of my condition and who knew that once I died, he would have to vacate the premises immediately.

"Lilli, I am bequeathing to you my business known as Antiquities. It is your future. I hope it will become your world and I am hoping you will make it more profitable than I did in these last years. I am afraid I neglected it badly. I believe that you have learned well under my tutelage. It will be necessary for you to resurrect the business in order to provide a living for yourself and your mother."

"What? What did that just say?" Arlette interrupted Frank.

Frank lifted his head from the will. "It says, Mrs. Mitchell, that you are dependent for your income upon Lilli's ability to make Antiquities profitable. J. C. is very specific about this point. He is—was—in hopes that you would help your daughter at the store. He wanted you to learn about the business also. In fact, that was one of his greatest concerns."

Arlette's finely tweezed eyebrows arched in suspicion. "Continue."

"Very well." Frank read on. "Until Lilli reaches the age of thirty, I am appointing Arlette as the trustee to Antiquities. It is my wish that without me around, my wife and my daughter will come to know each other better and that they will learn to work together and to depend on each other. I want there never to be animosity between them. Life is precious, my dear ones, and I am only now beginning to realize just how short these days are.

"To continue, during the fiscal year Lilli will have complete control of the cash flow, and Arlette must request from Lilli money for her taxes on the house, which no longer carries a mortgage upon my death, and for whatever living expenses she incurs. Lilli may also draw her current salary, with a cost-of-living increase each year. However, at the end of the fiscal year, the profits of the company are to be placed in a trust, and Arlette will hold the purse strings. Any additional money Lilli needs to run the business is to come from this trust, at Arlette's discretion.

"It is my desire that both of you become good businesswomen. The provisions of this will should put my desire to the test.

"To my sister, Vicki, I leave twenty thousand dollars with the provision that it be invested by Bart Jenson, my stockbroker at Dean Stanley Reynolds, who tells me that in ten years you will profit handsomely.

"To my niece, Faith, I leave five thousand dollars with the same provision.

"On Lilli's thirtieth birthday, I request that all four of you

be assembled again, when I will grant my final bequests upon
you all."

"You mean there's more?" Lilli asked in surprise.

Frank nodded. "A great deal more. But I'm not at liberty
to say what."

Arlette was furious. "He's trying to run my life from the
grave! He can't do that!"

"He most certainly can," Vicki said with a triumphant grin.
"And if I know my brother, he intends to do a damn good job
of it."

Faith stood up and went over to Lilli. "Are you all right?
You look a little pale."

"It's so weird, Faith. It's like he's still alive, but I can't see
him . . . Just hearing his words like that. I expected a bunch
of legal mumbo jumbo, but that was Pop talking. It really
scared me." Lilli began to cry. "I miss him so much!"

Faith put her arms around Lilli, and Lilli let her head fall
onto Faith's shoulder. Lilli had the oddest feeling that J. C.
was in the room with them. She had known that his will
would be different, but she hadn't realized it would entail this
responsibility to her mother. Lilli didn't even like her mother,
much less want to work with her. This was not only going to
be difficult; it would be impossible.

Mother is going to screw me up, Lilli thought. She knows
nothing about this business, any business, and now she's
trustee. What was her father thinking of? He would want her
to live her life to the limit. Give the world a jolt. Make people rethink their comfortable assumptions. That was what he
would have her do. But this relationship with her mother?
Why, Pop? Why?

And, too, what was this thing about them all meeting again
when she turned thirty? What was he going to spring on her
then? And why couldn't she look at his old files and maps?
What had he been doing these past years late at night when
she'd catch him poring over books, ancient papers, and crumbling maps?

J. C. had changed in these past years.

Lilli was more confused than ever. Her life had taken a
drastic and uncertain turn, and the thing that frightened her
the most was that she didn't know what to expect or whom
to trust.

Twenty-two

R iveted by shock, Arlette sat in the chair. This couldn't be happening. How could J.C. do this to her! After all she'd done for him . . . been a faithful wife, kept up the social connections that were so important to his work, raised the daughter she hadn't even wanted!

Living under Lilli's critical eye would be like wearing a straitjacket twenty-four hours a day. The day when J.C. had canceled Arlette's credit cards, she'd gone into an anxiety attack. It had lasted for over a month. She felt like that again; her heart was racing at double speed. She hated this feeling. She had lost power, lost control, over her own body.

Arlette put her hand over her heart and pressed as hard as she could, hoping she could slow it down. Instead, she felt dizzy and out of breath, even though she had not moved from her seat. For a split second she thought she was going to die.

I won't die, she said to herself. She forced herself to look out the window at the bright sky and tropical clouds. Below them was the Galleria, then the tree-lined streets of Post Oak, San Felipe, and Woodway. She could see the cars streaming down the 610 Loop and veering off to Highway 59 South. People moving. Going. Buying things to enhance their lifestyles. Making their worlds prettier, brighter, better. Just like I need to do, she thought.

"Frank, I need to talk to you," she finally said. "Alone." She cast her eyes in Lilli's direction.

"Fine," he answered. He stood, went around his desk, and whispered to Lilli, Faith, and Vicki that he wanted to see them in the conference room to sign papers and for a private conference. They all nodded and agreed.

When Arlette and Frank were alone again, he sat next to her in the chair previously occupied by Lilli.

"I want to contest the will," Arlette said firmly. Once she had spoken the words aloud, her heart instantly began to slow. She had made the right decision.

"I thought you might."

"You did?"

Frank leaned slightly back in the chair and folded his hands in his lap. His gaze was steady and wise. "It seems to be the thing to do these days. Sometimes such moves are warranted. But it would cost you nearly all the cash in your savings. The other attorney and I would make some money. The money you could have made through Antiquities would be held up. The time it takes to go through the probate court would drive you nuts . . . all that waiting. And frankly, in your case, I'm not so sure you'd win."

"What?" Arlette's eyes grew wide with incredulity. "This is the craziest will I've ever heard. No judge is going to let J.C. rule my life from the grave! He wants all the money to go to the hands of a teenager."

"Lilli is of legal age in Texas. But there is more to this than that. Actually, if Lilli contested the will, she would be the one to win."

"You can't be serious."

"I am. After she spends all year working for the profits, she is forced by the conditions of this will to turn every penny over to you. Frankly, this office has a ten-year history of your spending habits. It was part of the background I demanded when J.C. made out this will. I thought it was a very unusual will myself, but that was J.C. As far as the court is concerned, Lilli is doing all the work for very little reward. She has far more constraints placed on her than you do. J.C. is banking on her loyalty to him and to you to keep her here in Texas. Think about this, Arlette. She doesn't *have* to stay here and support you. She could just wash her hands of the whole thing, walk away, let you have Antiquities, and go do any damn thing she wants. You have no experience, no expertise in this business. Lilli knows damn near as much as J.C. did. For the past several years, he paid little attention to Antiquities; he was too involved in his wild-goose chases after buried treasure. But Lilli could very well make that business into something bigger than J.C. ever dreamed of.

"Anyone can contest a will these days, Arlette, but I think

you should know what you'd be facing. In the majority of cases where a will is overturned, it is because there are glaring discrepancies. A key family figure was left out completely, or there were serious inequities. In your savings account there is only twenty-five thousand dollars. You have enough money in your checking account to get you through the next three months if, and I mean *if*, you learn to manage your spending. You have no major bills, other than food and utilities. Things like extravagant clothes, trips, hundred-dollar haircuts are a thing of the past for you."

"This is crazy, Frank. I can't live like that."

"You're going to have to."

"I don't want to!" She pouted angrily.

Frank's exasperation was hidden beneath his professional demeanor, but as he continued talking to Arlette, he realized that she was the child and Lilli was the adult, just as J.C. had always said. He marveled at J.C.'s fortitude over the years in staying married to this woman. He folded his arms over his chest and let Arlette finish her tantrum.

She was sniveling. "You don't understand. J.C. didn't understand. I *have* to keep up . . . They'll all think I'm poor if I don't keep up. They'll turn their backs on me. Soon the lunches will stop . . . then the invitations to dinner parties. Lord knows it's bad enough that J.C. left me unescorted. How could he do this to me!"

Frank had been through many a will reading. He was accustomed to odd behavior and he expected personal revelations, but they made him uncomfortable. He liked giving out the bottom line, getting his fee, and going on to the next case. He'd always believed he was a good lawyer because he didn't get involved; he had no time for human foibles. Frank could only pretend to be patient during encounters like this one. In his opinion, he'd never met anyone as shallow and insecure as Arlette.

"It's not going to be that bad," he said. "You and Lilli can work together. You are her mother, after all. Frankly, Arlette, you've got the better part of the bargain. There is no stipulation in the will that you have to work at all for the income you'll receive."

"No," she said, routing through her Louis Vuitton purse for a handkerchief.

"I would advise you to think about helping Lilli. A job would give you something to do and give you that extra money you want to spend."

Arlette wiped away her angry tears and slammed her fist down in her lap. "A job? Now I know you've lost your marbles, Frank. I have a job taking care of my home and daughter."

"Lilli won't need you anymore, Arlette. She has her own town house now."

"Forget it, Frank. I wouldn't lower myself." Arlette thought of those days before she'd met J.C. No, she told herself. I will never go back to that life. That life doesn't exist for me. Never again.

"Try to help Lilli with the business. From what I can see, she's got a mess on her hands. She needs new inventory to stock the store. It's going to be tough on her."

"Lilli's smart," Arlette said. Smarter than I am. Prettier than I am, too. And young. She's got it all. And now J.C. is trying to make sure I have nothing. I won't stand for this. I'll find a way out. I'll show him!

"Lilli is very smart, Arlette. And loyal to her father. If I know her, she'll die trying to make his dreams a reality."

Arlette lifted her chin as she restored her composure. "Yes. She is that." She looked away from Frank. "She adored him . . . to a fault." Arlette's spirits brightened. That's right! Lilli's Achilles' heel was her adoration of J.C.! How could she have not seen it?

She turned back to Frank, stood, and put out her hand to shake his. "Thank you, Frank. I appreciate the time you've spent with me. I guess I just need a chance to think about all this. Maybe I'm still in shock over J.C.'s death. I just don't know what I'm thinking right now."

Frank rose and ushered Arlette to the door. "Good-bye, Arlette. I'll keep in touch."

"Do that, Frank," she said sweetly.

Too sweet, Frank thought as he closed the door. He walked back to his desk and punched the intercom to his secretary. "Buzz the conference room for me and tell Lilli I'm on my way to extend my farewells."

"Yes, sir," the secretary answered.

Frank started for the door, retracing Arlette's steps. As he did, he noticed that the air seemed colder than in the rest of the room. He didn't trust Arlette one iota. He hoped Lilli didn't either.

Twenty-three

~

Zane postponed his trip to Boston and rented a car for his drive to Bandera to see his mother. He'd thought a great deal about his father over the past two days, and those memories led to concerns about his mother. Since his move to New York, he'd kept in touch with her by telephone, and he had sent her money every month. But he had been too angry at her, at her treatment of Lilli, to return to visit her. Now, as he drove through the switchback of Devil's Backbone and saw the craggy hills and flat mesas of the hill country, Zane felt a tug on his heartstrings, not for his mother but for this country. He missed the land. He missed his father and he realized that grieving was not a matter of time, it was a matter of heart.

He drove to Canyon Lake from the east, and from his vantage point the afternoon sun reflected off the lake and gilded the dry hills with golden light. The mass of homes around the lake were perfectly coifed for the weekend tourist trade with newly mowed lawns, American flags mounted in the yards, geraniums in huge Mexican pots on the piers, and lakeside gardens. Zane drove north, away from the lake and into the hills, where the McAllister property was set apart from its neighbors. He drove up the rocky drive to the old house. He had telephoned his mother earlier that morning and told her to expect him. He was surprised that she was not standing on the front steps waiting.

"Mom?" he called as he went to the front door and tapped on it. He tried the door, but it was locked. "Mom?" he called louder as he knocked on the door. He could hear no sounds coming from inside the house. He pounded on the door with the flat of his fist. He peered in the small window set high in the door and realized that all the draperies were closed, a habit Hannah had acquired during his father's last years when he napped during the afternoon.

Just then he heard the closing of an interior door and soon he could see a dark form moving slowly toward the front door. The bolt in the door was pulled back. The door opened.

"Mom?" Zane stared at the old woman who opened the door and gazed blankly at him.

Hannah said nothing. She didn't have to say a word, Zane thought. Her appearance said it all.

Hannah looked as if she'd died herself. Her hair was completely white now and looked as if she hadn't washed it in weeks. Her face was pasty, the skin slack and wrinkled beyond her years, and she stood humped over as if the problems of the world rested on her shoulders. Her movements were slow and almost mechanical, but the thing that frightened him the most was that there was no light in her eyes, no joy in her voice, no emotion in her soul.

"Zane," she said and put her arms around him and hugged him.

As he held her, he realized that she was nothing more than skin and bones. "Mom, it's good to see you. Good to be back home," he said.

"Come in," she said and stepped back so that he could enter the house. Then she shut the door behind him. "I'm making some tea for us in the kitchen. Won't that be nice?"

"Yeah, Mom, nice," he said, looking around the living room. There were newspapers stacked against the wall that must be two years' accumulation, he thought. The plants had died in their pots and Hannah had not bothered to throw them out. She had not had the screen in the large front window repaired, although he remembered sending her money the previous year for the repair and for a new air-conditioning unit. Something was terribly wrong.

Zane followed her into the kitchen. "When you called this morning," she said, "I realized that I probably should have baked your favorite pie for you. Apple, wasn't it?"

"No, Mom, I hate pie. Dad liked apple pie."

"What?" She slowly turned her head and looked at him quizzically for a long moment. Then she shrugged and went to the gas stove and lit the burner under the old scorched teapot.

Zane looked around the kitchen. Although this room was clean, he realized it had been put in order only recently. The sink was cleared of dishes and newly scrubbed, but he noticed that the cabinets were greasy and the floor had not been mopped in a very long time. There were no fresh flowers on the table, which had always been a habit of his mother's, even if they were only wildflowers from the hillside. When his father was alive, Hannah had always been a perfectionist about house-keeping. In fact, Zane had believed her meticulousness an obsession. Now she'd taken a one-hundred-and-eighty-degree turn.

Zane pulled out a wooden chair from the table and sat down. Hannah placed a tea bag in each of the two mugs and poured the hot water over the tea bag. To anyone else, this simple ritual would not say much, but to Zane it caused alarm bells to clang in his head. Hannah had never used a tea bag in her life. She had always bought the best teas available, placed the treasured tea in a silver-plated tea caddy, and then used her mother's pink-flowered china teapot. Once the hot water was added, a quilted tea cozy was placed over the pot until the tea was perfectly steeped.

Zane watched as his mother placed her hands on the table and then lowered herself slowly into her chair. She did not smile at him as she sipped her tea. She did not comment on the taste of the tea as she used to. Zane realized with a wrench that his mother had died the day they buried his father. Grief wore many faces, he knew, but this was the saddest of all.

"Mom, are you all right?"

"Yes," she said dully.

"You miss Dad?"

"Sometimes."

"Are you eating, Mom? You look thin."

"I'm fine."

"You get out often? See your friends?"

"Haven't got any friends."

Zane's eyebrows shot up. "Of course you have friends. Don't you see the reverend anymore? And your church group. What about them?"

"I don't go there anymore," she said, taking another sip of tea. She wiped her mouth with the back of her hand, not with the cloth napkin underneath her elbow.

Zane had never seen his mother like this. It was almost as if someone else possessed her body. He was suddenly very frightened. "Tell me why you don't go there, Mom."

"They lost their way."

He shook his head. "I don't understand."

"They aren't listening to the Lord in the way they should."

"And how is that?"

"They refused to listen to me when I told them what the Lord said to me."

Although Hannah's voice rose and revealed the first bit of emotion Zane had seen so far, a curious vacancy still occupied her eyes. Still wary, Zane was careful not to push her over the edge.

"When did the Lord talk to you, Mom?"

"Day your father died."

"You never told me."

"I know."

"What revelations did you receive?"

Hannah's head cocked to the right ever so slightly, a familiar habit of hers when she let her guard down. Thank God, Zane thought. Some things are still the same. He knew now that he'd maneuvered her correctly.

"It was magnificent, Zane, the sight I saw. All light and sound and music. I didn't really see Him, you know, but I could feel Him. It was wonderful, Zane. I felt peaceful and happy. And warm. And then He went away. I fell asleep for a while and then later I heard a voice and it told me that your father should have believed and he would still be alive." Suddenly Hannah's face contorted into a grimace. "He told me that your father failed. He failed in life, Zane. He didn't believe. He should have kept his faith when we went to Mexico. I told you it was good for Ted to go there. But you wouldn't believe me. No! You were the one, you were the one who made us come back. Ted never had a chance! It's your fault he's dead! And the Lord will come and visit misery upon your head, Zane. You are doomed!"

Hannah's voice had risen to a high pitch. As she spoke, spittle rained from her mouth. Her eyes flamed and her jaw muscles tensed. She looked like a madwoman.

My mother is insane, Zane thought. My mother is insane.

He felt tears well in his eyes. How could this have happened? Had it happened the day his father died? Was this some reaction to grief he didn't understand, or had this insanity always been there, sneaking up over the years?

"I'm not doomed, Mom."

"Yes, you are. You live in that evil city. Murder, drugs,

rape . . . the devil's playground, New York is. Only evil people live there."

"Who told you that? The Lord?"

"No. The Reverend Michael Atherton."

Anger raced through Zane's body. "That con man from Mexico? You still talk to him?"

"Yes," she said indignantly. "He calls me every Sunday."

"Every Sunday. And that's why you don't see your church friends anymore. You are talking to Michael Atherton."

"Yes. He's a true man of the Lord. He has the power."

"What power?"

"The power to heal. To save lives. To save souls."

Zane's stomach felt tied into knots. "Mom, that screen in the living room isn't fixed. I sent you some money for that. And for a new air conditioner. And you told me the roof needed repairing last month. The money I send you every month for food, the taxes on the property, stuff like that. What do you do with it?"

Hannah's lower lip thinned as she smiled at him with a malicious self-satisfaction. "I send it to Michael."

"Jesus!"

"Don't curse."

Zane slammed his fist on the table. His tea mug jumped. "Jesus knows *exactly* whom I am cursing. Michael Atherton is a con and a crook. He's no man of the Lord. He's shit, Mom. He should be in jail. Don't you see it? Tell me you haven't lost all your mind! This man preys on lonely, grieving people like you. He's not your friend. In fact, I'll bet my last buck that he told you to 'forsake' all your real friends. He told you that even I wasn't a friend, didn't he?"

Hannah's eyes had narrowed suspiciously. "How do you know what he said?"

"Because these kind of people are all like that, Mom. They get vulnerable people like you were when Dad was sick to distance themselves from their friends, who could truly help them. They'll say that your family is the real enemy and that *they* are the ones with the truth. They ask for your money and say it's for the Lord. They brainwash you. They trick you into giving them power over your life. What Michael Atherton is, Mom, is a cult leader."

"He is not! And I won't hear any more of this blasphemy!"

"I'm trying to talk to you, Mom."

"I won't listen."

Zane didn't know a great deal about cults, but he did know the basics. What he needed help with now was keeping his communication open with his mother. If he walked out of here now, he might lose her forever, and although they'd had their differences over the years, she was still his mother. And, as angry as he had been at her, he still loved her. On the verge of despair, Zane grasped at his last hope.

"Mom, pray with me," he said, reaching across the table for her hand.

"What?" Her eyes softened for the first time that day.

"Hold my hand. Pray with me."

Slowly, Hannah uncurled her arthritic fingers and reached over and took her son's hand.

"Mom, I love you. I don't want us to argue."

"I don't either. But you must see the light."

"Okay. Let's try that. Remember when you said the Lord came to you when Dad died?"

"Yes."

"I want you to know I believe you."

"You do?" Hannah's eyes were filled with surprise. "No one at the church believed me. They thought I was crazy."

Zane shook his head. "Well, I don't. I don't really know why, but I think that really happened. At least the first part of it when you felt happy and warm. The rest of your story is wrong, Mom. I think those were your thoughts, your anger at Dad's passing. I think you need to learn to distinguish between the two . . . the Lord and your own thoughts."

"Your father failed!" she said adamantly.

"No, Mom. You're mad because he left you alone. And loneliness is not good for anyone. That's why I want you to see your friends."

"They don't care about me," she whispered and dropped her head.

Zane realized right then that he was breaking through. "Yes, they do. So do I. I love you, Mom." He squeezed her hand. "Now, I want you to think about that one moment when you were with the Lord and you felt warm. Now, say the Lord's Prayer with me."

They prayed aloud. Zane reached across the table and took

Hannah's other hand. Instinct told him that if he could touch her, connect with her physically and mentally, he might have a chance to save her. He knew that it would be impossible for him to change the course of the insanity in one day, but he could start her back on the right road. He could no longer avoid the pain of his past by shutting doors. As they prayed, he promised himself that he would see his mother more often. Somehow he had to get her out of Bandera once in a while so that she did not become prey to Michael Atherton again. Perhaps he could get her to New York. There, when she saw where he lived and worked, she wouldn't condemn him so quickly. And when he went to Europe, he could use his frequent-flyer miles to buy her a ticket. He wasn't sure if she'd do it, but he'd cross that bridge later. His mother needed to see more of the world, he thought, more of life, and when she did, he knew she would open her mind rather than close it. There was a great deal of life they could share together, and Zane was determined to make her see that they needed each other.

After they finished praying, Zane was witness to a small miracle: a rosy glow came to Hannah's cheeks. He knew she was back among the living.

Zane spent the rest of the day restoring his mother's world to normal. He hired a handyman to fix the screen and repair the roof. He coerced his mother into driving with him to New Braunfels, where they went to the supermarket, and he bought enough food to feed half of Bandera for two months. Then they went to the hardware store for fresh paint for the outside of the house, and then to the nursery for houseplants. He bought a flat of geraniums, a purple sage, and six flowering cacti to plant around the front of the house. He took his mother to a beauty shop, where she had her hair cut and a silver rinse shampooed in. He bought her a new dress for her to wear on Sunday, and for dinner they shared the best Texas barbecue he'd had in two years.

When they went back to the house, Zane worked until past midnight scrubbing the kitchen, planting the flowers, and packing up the last of his father's clothes. They decided together to donate them to the homeless in San Antonio. Before Hannah finally went to bed that night, she walked up to her son and put her arms around him. "The Lord sent you to me today."

Zane kissed her forehead. "Yes, He did, Mom. He truly did."

Twenty-four

In 1980, the Houston nightclub scene was dominated by the "Urban Cowboy" theme. Mickey Gilley's Bar in Pasadena lost the local fist-slinging cowboys and cowgirls and gained an unprecedented tourist trade. The mechanical bull bucked nonstop all night and long-necked beers were guzzled by the case. In central Houston, country/Western bars lit up the thoroughfares of Westheimer, Richmond, and Woodway. But nowhere was this urban cowboy more urban than at Elan, the club where the movie *Urban Cowboy* had been filmed.

Young and rich Houston girls in skintight leather jeans, fringed suede jackets, ostrich boots, and white Western hats rubbed shoulders with rugged-looking young men wearing tight T-shirts and even tighter Levi's. They danced the two-step and seductive country waltzes to the strains of Boz Scaggs and Alabama. Would-be stockbrokers, real-estate developers, oil managers, and entry-level computer wizards downshifted from long hours in their Brooks Brothers suits to nights spent in Western costumes. Houston was putting on a party, and the world had come to see it.

Zane elbowed his way to the bar, thinking that even in Manhattan he'd not seen a place this crowded. He ordered a beer and, sipping it, glanced around him. There was a young woman standing next to him. Her clothes were so tight he thought he could see the outline of her every mole. Like the others around her, she wore her long hair piled in a haystack, and long earrings made of Indian beads, feathers, and swatches of gold leather.

Zane was aware that these young women were watching him, too. They canvassed his body the way a man assessed a woman. Their stares were bold, meant to intimidate all but the most adventurous of men. These women knew what they wanted and believed they would get it.

Nowhere did he find an old-guard Houston girl, the kind who wore her great-grandmother's platinum-and-diamond brooch at the throat of her Western shirt. He saw no antique Rolexes, no heirloom jet or aquamarine earrings such as the Cullen, the Davis, or the Moody family would own. This place reminded him too much of New York and the loneliness he'd come to know there. There was nothing enduring here. There was no one here like Lilli.

Zane looked up at that moment and saw Lilli walking toward him.

Necks turned, craned, and stretched to see the beautiful brunette dressed in a narrowly cut Old Spanish riding habit of dark magenta, a white long-sleeved blouse, and a Spanish lace ascot tied at the throat. The jacket molded around the curves of her tiny waist, full breasts, and round hips. She wore enormous gold bangle earrings, which Zane recognized were early-nineteenth century. Beneath the long gaucho pants she wore black riding boots. Her dark hair fell in a shiny curtain down her back. She looked like a Spanish princess from another century. The men stood aside and let her pass, an unusual gesture in a place like this where the men liked to remain rooted to the spot, forcing women to brush their breasts against them to get through. These were men who used a woman until they were tired of her and then found another. These were men with small souls and big wallets. These were the men who knew they could buy any woman they wanted. But they could never have a woman like Lilli.

Zane knew how they felt. Just to have Lilli smile at him was a triumph. To believe that Lilli still truly loved him was almost too much to hope for. But Zane did hope.

Lilli paid no attention to the charming smiles as she passed the men, but they didn't mind, because Lilli not only commanded attention, she commanded respect.

She looked up at him and smiled. She inhaled the scents of sandalwood and pine. She remembered the dream she'd had so long ago of him. She wanted to hold him, but something within her told her that this was not the time. She knew she and Zane were bonded somehow, in some way; she just wasn't sure how.

"I asked you to meet me here because I was across the street at a client's condo. This place is too noisy. Could we go someplace else to talk?"

"Sure. Where?"

"Well, we could go to the Remington. I'm staying there, and it's close."

"It's perfect."

Lilli's car was brought to the front of the club and Zane tipped the valet. Lilli drove them to the Remington, less than a ten-minute drive from the club. She pulled up in the circular drive at the luxurious hotel, stopped the car, and handed the keys to the valet.

Zane escorted her inside. The marble, glass, and mirrored lobby was dazzling. Huge floral arrangements in three-foot-tall vases sat on round tables in the middle of the foyer and on tables in the reception area, looking like exotic sentries.

"Let's go over there," he suggested, pointing to an over-stuffed couch in the corner of the sitting area near the window.

"Fine."

Zane sat next to her on the sofa. "Lilli, I'd like for us to start all over. Now, like we are . . . as adults."

"I'm not sure."

"About what? Me? You?"

"You," she answered quietly.

"What about me?"

She looked him straight in the eye when she replied. She didn't want there to be any misunderstandings this time. "Your ambition is overwhelming, Zane. I'm not sure there's any room in your life for me."

He looked down at her hands. They were shaking and he knew he was the reason for it. He lifted her hands to his lips and kissed them tenderly. For the rest of his life, he never wanted to see Lilli's hands shake again. He wanted to think of her as strong and feisty, opinionated and determined, but never afraid. Never afraid of him. "I've had my priorities all screwed up, Lilli. I'll admit to that. I've learned a lot since I've been back here. The funeral . . . seeing you . . . seeing my mother. I pushed myself too hard when I went to New York. I was obsessed with succeeding. I had to prove to my father that I could do it. I wanted him to be proud of me . . .

even though he wasn't around to see it." A sob choked off his words.

Lilli lifted her hand and touched his temple. She smoothed his hair back around his ear. "Go on."

"I kept busy so I wouldn't have time to think about how much I missed him ... or you. I can remember days when I didn't eat and worked until dawn. I turned the fast lane into the Autobahn."

"And what do you think now?"

There was still a softness in her eyes, a hope and caring that he hadn't seen for a long time. His heart ached over how much he'd hurt her.

Zane had used work to push Lilli out of his life. When she'd come to New York, he saw her as a little kid—which, in truth, she had been. Now, although she was only nineteen, she seemed more mature than anyone he knew.

He took her hand and pressed it to his cheek. "I was wrong, Lilli. You're right about that. I guess I was trying to be proud of myself, too."

"Like paying your dad's debts?"

"Yeah. But now when I look in your eyes ... I know what I lost. I don't want to lose it again."

"Oh, Zane, do you really mean that?"

"I do, honey. I do."

"I'm scared. I don't want to be left behind again."

"I'm not going to do that. I promise. I could never let you go again."

Suddenly Lilli leaned over and kissed him tentatively. It was a frightening step she was taking. She'd been shut out of his life once, by fate, by bad timing, perhaps by Zane himself. She could get hurt. She could also win the brass ring, she told herself.

His kiss was like the Fourth of July and a ticker-tape parade all at the same time. She wanted to smile and laugh and kiss him again. He kissed her on the cheeks, the eyes, the ears. He kissed her mouth happily, then hungrily. She reveled in the touch of his tongue against her lips as he coaxed them apart to gain entry. Lilli had never been able to fight the surge of passion that his kisses elicited in her.

Zane groaned and put his hands around her waist. He pulled her closer to him. His heart hammered in his chest.

The sound filled his ears and he was afraid that the other patrons would hear his heart and know how much he wanted Lilli.

"Lilli," he breathed between her kisses. "I think we should go upstairs."

She drew slowly away from him. She looked into his blue eyes and saw the flecks of gold there just as she'd remembered. If she stayed here, she could run away from him and keep her heart safe. If she went with him, she would have to risk her love again. It was unwise to go with him, her brain told her, but seldom had Lilli been wise. She'd been foolhardy, adventurous, outspoken, and curious. She'd been wary and suspicious. But seldom had she been truly wise.

She felt as if she would lose herself in his eyes. She could already tell that the sound of his voice was once again becoming too familiar to her. He had invaded all her waking thoughts since the moment she'd seen him at the church. She wanted Zane in her life. She had since the day she'd met him when she was only fourteen. God help her, now she both wanted and needed him.

He held his hand to her cheek and she kissed his palm. Zane held her face in his hands. "God, I love you, Lilli."

"I love you, too." She whispered it like a prayer.

They stood and walked to the elevators.

If he'd been a king and they'd been in a medieval castle, he would have picked her up and carried his true love up the stone stairs to his tower rooms. He would have ordered his servants to pamper her and care for her. He would have commissioned a jewel-encrusted gold tiara for her head and a diamond waterfall necklace for her throat.

The elevator doors opened on the sixth floor. They walked down the hall. They stopped at number 614 and Zane unlocked the door.

He looked at his beautiful Lilli. He could wish all he wanted to be her king, but wishing wouldn't make it so. He was just a man.

He slid his arm around her back, bent down, put his other arm under her knees, and hoisted her into the air.

"Zane?" She gave a bright, merry laugh. "What are you doing? We aren't married or anything. It's not like it's our wedding night."

He gazed deeply into her love-filled violet eyes. "To me it is."

He carried her into the room and kicked the door shut with his foot. He walked to the king-sized bed and gently laid her down. He leaned over her and kissed her. "I meant it, Lilli. I love you."

She reached up and put her arms around his neck. "And I love you, Zane."

He lay down next to her and began to untie the delicate Spanish lace at her throat. "You wore this outfit for me, didn't you?"

"Yes," she said, feeling the heat from his hand as his fingers brushed her chin, and then her throat as he untied the knot.

"Thank you," he breathed into her ear as he used his tongue to trace the outer shell. He closed his eyes and lost himself in the scent of her. Her silken hair against his cheek felt like an angel's caress. Deftly, his fingers unbuttoned the jacket and then her blouse. Lilli was not wearing a bra. Zane's breath caught in his throat as he touched her skin. His hand moved from the flat of her stomach up to her soft, full breasts.

Lilli sank her hands into his thick hair and watched as it curled around her fingers like golden rings. She had forgotten the sense of abandonment she'd felt before when Zane touched her breasts. She'd forgotten how fast her heart could beat. She'd forgotten how hot her blood could boil when he touched her nipples. Now she remembered and she lost herself to the ecstasy.

With his lips pressed to the base of her throat, Lilli knew she could keep no secrets from him. Now he knew that she was his. She was the prisoner of her own desires. She wanted all of him, but her mind told her to be wary.

He lowered his head and captured her nipple between his teeth. She gasped. Memories came rushing back to her like bittersweet strains of a love song. He teased her other nipple between his thumb and forefinger. A groan escaped from his throat. She remembered that sound. That sound had haunted her night after night for nearly a year after he left. It had faded reluctantly, and now she hated him for bringing it back to her. She tried to force herself away from him. She shouldn't be there. She should hide from him.

She lifted her head from the pillow and looked down at his golden head. She remembered the boy who had been crushed by his father's death, and she could feel her heart opening to him. Instinctively her arms went around him and drew him closer to her. God help her, she wanted to protect him from pain. But who, she thought, will protect me?

At her touch, Zane's breathing grew quieter. He pressed his erection against Lilli's hip; his hands could not touch enough of her quickly enough. He wanted her, all of her. Now.

Zane unzipped the gaucho pants and slipped them off as Lilli pried her boots from her feet. He whipped off his Western shirt, jeans, and boots with lightning speed. Suddenly he was eager to have her, and yet when he pressed the button next to the bed and extinguished the light, the darkness reminded him of their first time together beneath the stars and he stopped himself.

He wanted always to remember this night; he wanted it to be just as special as that first night, for he knew now, deep in his soul, that Lilli was his for eternity. She had written to him once that she believed they were bonded to each other, "two lost souls in an angry world." He hadn't believed her at the time, since his mind had been filled with ego and New York, but now he did. He felt as if he'd come back home, home to a place he'd always dreamed about. She was his everything. He wanted to be everything to her.

He stretched out next to her and tenderly gathered her into his arms.

"Just hold me," he said.

He wanted to feel the length of her against him, somehow thinking absurdly that he could press all of her, from head to toe, inside him, making her part of him physically in the same way she was part of his soul. He rolled her over and buried his face between the mounds of her breasts. He tasted her breasts and nipples before running his tongue ever so slowly down to her abdomen. Then he moved down to the triangle between her legs.

"Spread your legs for me," he said in a soft, yet demanding, tone.

The ravishing began.

Lilli felt as if her mind had left her body. Sensations of rapture shot through her and exploded in bursts of light behind her closed eyes. Fireballs ignited and spun into a frenzy deep inside her loins. She felt his tongue flick against her skin with the lightest caress. Her body turned to liquid heat. She felt herself melting. She could stand the wait no longer.

"Take me . . . now . . ."

He moved on top of her and pushed her legs farther apart with his knee. She felt the crush of his body atop hers and reveled in the delicious feel of his weight on her. She felt the pressure of his hips as he poised himself to enter her. The torture of the wait was excruciating.

"Now!" she demanded.

Then he filled her with himself, stretching her and forcing her to take all of him deep within her. Her arms encircled him and pulled him closer.

He nestled his face in the crook of her neck.

"I love you, Lilli," he whispered, his voice so filled with emotion that it threatened to crack.

She wanted to respond but could not. Lilli was spinning among the stars. She could see galaxies of twinkling planets behind her eyelids. They exploded and then came back into view, one by one, beckoning her to travel the distance . . . to fly to heaven. Lilli obeyed.

"Zane," she cried out when she climaxed.

He covered her mouth with his own and swallowed her cry. Then he lifted his head and lost himself in the depths of her eyes as he continued to stroke her with himself. He kissed her swollen lower lip, pulling it gently between his teeth as he plunged into her again. He raised himself on one elbow and watched himself enter her again and again.

Lilli shut her eyes and felt herself floating away into another orgasm. "Oh, God," she gasped and arched her hips to take him deeper inside.

"Lilli . . ." He groaned and thrust himself deeply into her. His fingers dug into her flesh as he pulled her hips to him one last time. "Lie very still." He exploded inside her.

Lilli could feel his ejaculations as they shot from him, one after another. She held him tightly, wanting this closeness never to end.

Zane lay atop her, damp with perspiration. Finally, he

rolled off but kept his arms around her so that when he rolled on to his side, she moved with him. He looked into her eyes and saw that her pupils were dilated. That was a good sign, he knew, because he'd read somewhere that when a person saw something pleasurable, his pupils dilated. This was the look of love, Zane thought.

Lilli lifted her head and gently touched his temple. "I love you, Zane. I want to be with you always."

"Forever," he said and touched her cheek. "You are the most beautiful of all God's creations," he whispered and let his hand roam down the sleek column of her throat and onto her breast.

Zane was filled with so much happiness he thought his heart would burst. He saw a vision of their future. He saw himself and Lilli working together. He saw them laughing, talking, and sharing meals. He saw Sundays in New York, walking through Central Park. He saw Christmas with shopping, parties, and decorating a tree. He imagined Lilli carrying his child. He'd always thought he would be afraid of being a father, but with Lilli, it would be wonderful. She had the ability to take away his fears. He needed her natural curiosity about life to help him enjoy his days to the fullest. She would never let him get bored, nor would she ever hold him back. He could be everything his father had wanted for him and more. Zane could be all that he wanted for himself.

Lilli placed her hand over Zane's, then lifted his hand and held it to her lips. She kissed each finger, one by one. "You've shown me paradise, Zane McAllister. Now what do you intend to do for an encore?"

Zane chuckled and kissed her forehead. He tasted salty pearls of sweat. "I want to marry you, Lilli."

Lilli's face broke into a smile. Suddenly the world had been put right. She was amazed at the capacity she had to love Zane. Just when she thought she could love him no more, she found she could.

"Are you sure?"

"Very sure. Now say yes."

"Yes, Zane. I want to be your wife."

Zane's happiness nearly lit the dark room. Exuberantly, he hugged Lilli to him. "Thank God." He slid his hand down to her belly. "I was afraid if you said no, I would be forced to ravish you again and get you pregnant. Then you would have to marry me."

"You wouldn't!"

"I would," he replied triumphantly.

Lilli's eyes were horror-stricken. "I didn't even think . . . you don't . . . think I could be, do you?"

"There's always that possibility."

"Zane McAllister, you take that smirk off your face. You look as if you would be pleased if I did get pregnant."

"It wouldn't be so bad . . ."

"Only disastrous, that's all!"

"Why?"

"Because, I—I—"

He smiled roguishly. "You what? Would be an unwed mother? That's nuts. I'm going to marry you. I would be thrilled to have a baby with you—especially if she looked like you." He kissed the tip of her nose.

Lilli was not prepared for such lightheartedness, but then, with Zane she didn't have anything to fear. He loved her. She loved him. So why did she suddenly feel afraid?

Zane sat up and pulled the edge of the bedspread over them to ward off the slight chill from the air-conditioning. "Since when did you become a worrywart, Lilli?"

Lilli felt the prick of tears at the corners of her eyes. "Since Pop died . . ."

Zane put his arms around her again. "I'm sorry. I nearly forgot. But think of it this way, Lilli. Maybe fate brought me back so that you wouldn't have to be lonely."

She looked into his eyes. "I think that's exactly what happened. And you know what else?"

"What?"

"I think you were lonely, too."

He nodded. "I just didn't know how much until I saw you." He buried his face in her hair. "God, I love you, Lilli. I can't wait until you move to New York. I want you to meet my friends. See where I work. I swear to God, you'll be fascinated by all the things there are to see and do. I just can't believe my good fortune . . ."

Zane did not notice that Lilli's jaw had dropped open.

"Zane?" she interrupted.

"Yeah?"

"I don't remember saying I was going to New York."

He kissed her forehead again. "That's right, you didn't, and it was presumptuous of me. I'm sorry. But, Lilli, it's where I work, and I think this time you'll like it. You're older now. I've got a better handle on my career. I'm not so scared now, and I'm sure you'll come to love it. And if you didn't, well then, I'd make sure we made a lot of trips back here." He hurried on, caught up in his need to convince her to live with him. "I have to come back to Texas to take care of my mother. I saw her yesterday, and I realized how much she needs me. Oh, Lilli, we can work it out. I know we can."

Lilli's face moved an imperceptible measure away from his. She dropped her hand away from him. "But I just inherited Antiquities."

"Tell me."

"According to the will, I have to take over the business."

"Can't you sell it?"

"No chance. Pop left it on the verge of bankruptcy. It scares me to death. I don't have enough knowledge about business. I mean, they didn't teach this in high school!"

"Honey, I had no idea. Maybe I could help. First, you need a good accountant."

She nodded. "Frank, my attorney, has found one, and Frank's willing to help out all he can, but he can't do it all. I've got so much to learn so fast. I feel like a five-year-old who's been sent to college instead of kindergarten."

"I wish I could help."

"Me, too."

Zane's mood was dour. But I'm not helping, he thought. I'm only making your life more difficult by putting demands on you. Even if they are because of my love for you . . . my dreams for us.

"Pop is counting on me to make it successful."

"Lilli"—Zane ignored the warning chills on the back of his neck—"your father is dead. You can do anything you want."

"No, I can't."

Suddenly Zane felt his blood turn to ice. "What are you saying, Lilli?"

She swallowed. Something was wrong. What was it? They loved each other. Was she losing him or throwing him away?

She felt as if she were standing on the edge of a ravine and he was on the other side.

Zane jumped out of bed. The city lights spilled through the opening in the nearly drawn draperies and illuminated his strong body. "Do you love me?"

"Yes. With all my heart." Tears filled her eyes and there was a searing pain in her throat.

"Then come to New York."

"I c-can't!"

"You *could* . . ." If you wanted to badly enough, he thought. How could he be losing her? He had just found her again. Why was she doing this?

"I promised Pop."

"Do you love him more than you love me?" He snarled the challenge.

"I have to do this!"

"No, you don't!" He was shouting, and he forced himself to calm down. "Oh, Lilli, don't you see? You're making the same mistake I did."

"I don't see it that way. This is different!" She bounded from the bed and began putting on her blouse.

"Lilli," Zane pleaded, "stop this nonsense. Your father is dead. We have a future together . . ."

"Sure," she retorted. "*Your* future. I go to New York and have your baby and wait on you hand and foot. Inch by inch I lose myself and my respect for you. I won't do it, Zane. I'm not going to be some kind of possession. There are a lot of things I want to do, too. And I can't do them in New York. And I can't give them up. Not for you, not for anybody!"

He watched her put on her boots and gaucho pants. He was still naked. He was vulnerable. "Lilli, I don't want you to do that. I want you to be all that you can be. Go on your digs. Study. Learn. Work. Jesus Christ!" Frantically he ran his hand through his hair as she grabbed her jacket. Suddenly, he reached out and pulled her to him. "Look at me and tell me that you don't love me."

Lilli's heart felt as if it had been split in two. "I do love you. It's not about that."

"Okay! Okay," he said as panic rushed through him. "Let me think. I could move to Houston," he suggested. But as he looked into Lilli's eyes, he realized he'd be throwing away all that he'd worked for. Realistically, he couldn't do it.

How could fate be so cruel? he thought. They were right for each other, and they loved each other. But they were young and had so much to accomplish—separately. Their lives did not blend right now, and it was hell.

Lilli wished she could pack up and leave her father's death-bed wish in Houston and never look back, but she was plagued with a sense of responsibility. She was not only going to break Zane's heart and lose him forever, but she was also going to cause her own downfall. She gazed at him with eyes filled with love and pain and knew she had no choice.

"We both know you can't be in Houston, Zane. Your business is in New York. You've always belonged there, and I'd never ask you to give that up. But I can't leave Houston. I owe Pop, Zane. I'm his only child."

"I know."

She could not tear her eyes from him. Lilli knew she would never love anyone but Zane. She was his soul mate, always. She lifted her hand to touch his hair. Just once more, she thought.

He grabbed her hand in mid-motion and gently stopped it. "I'm not good at good-byes, Lilli."

She couldn't look at him any longer. She would always bear the guilt that she had done this to him, but she had to go. J.C. had loved her, too. Slowly, she walked toward the door, still tasting Zane's lips on hers, still feeling the pressure of him inside her. She must be crazy to leave him, she thought, but she had a duty to J.C. that she could not abnegate. She felt morally responsible to carry out her father's wishes. Never would she have believed that loyalty could carry such a heavy price tag. She felt as if the harpies from hell had come and ripped her soul from her.

She looked back at him one last time. The city's lights outside the window illuminated his face and she could see tears glistening on his cheeks.

"I'll always love you," she said softly and left.

Zane didn't know then that he would hear the quiet closing of the door in his dreams for a decade to come.

Part
Two

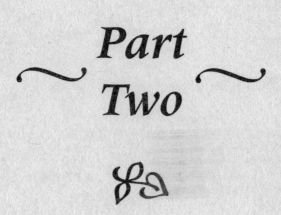

Twenty-five

*I*n the throes of yet another "new look" for her store, Lilli
riffled through her desk in search of a lost invoice for the
tasseled hatboxes she intended to stack in the front-window
display. In the back of the middle desk drawer she found a
photograph of her and Zane taken during J.C.'s wake at her
mother's home. In the picture Lilli was encircled by three of
her mother's friends while Zane stood an arm's length away
to her left, looking at her with compassionate eyes. Just off
to the right, at the edge of the photograph, was her mother,
with no one at her side. Lilli stared at her mother's face and
realized that even then, ten years ago now, her mouth was
stretched into a thin, tight line and her eyes were focused on
Zane. For years Faith had tried to tell Lilli that Arlette was
jealous of her, her talent, her relationships with J.C. and
Zane, and her youth. Lilli hadn't wanted to believe it, but she
could almost feel her mother's animosity in the photograph.

She dropped it onto the desktop as if it burned her fingers.

It made sense. Too much sense.

Lilli's battle with her mother had escalated over the years
until now it was open warfare. In the first months after J.C.'s
funeral, Arlette had kept her attacks to malicious verbal digs
during conversations in which she would purposely undercut
J.C.'s affection for Lilli.

For the most part, Lilli ignored her mother, telling herself
that her mother would never change and she herself could do
little about it. Lilli remembered all too well her father's tenet
that "the family must stick together." Arlette was her mother
and Lilli intended to honor her.

Also, those were their first months of learning to work together—or not work together, as it turned out to be. During the course of her marriage to J.C., Arlette's one contribution to the business had been her effort to climb the Houston social ladder. Arlette gave dinners and parties at their home for potential clients. She organized open houses at the store for old clients, friends, and always, hopefully, the media. She worked incessantly on one charity board after another. She volunteered for positions as the Ballet Ball chairman, the Junior League luncheon committee co-chair, and publicity head for the Zoo Ball. J.C. always gave Arlette her due and praised her profusely, especially in front of his clients.

After J.C.'s death, Arlette dropped out of all the major charity work.

"Why are you dropping out of the Zoo Ball committee, Mother? They're depending on you."

"You know very well why I have to do this."

"Explain it to me—again."

Arlette's shoulders were rigid as she walked over to the fauteuil chair and lowered herself elegantly onto the down seat. "Since you have been unable to bring in the kind of money your father did . . ."

Lilli rolled her eyes and threw up her arms. "Do you have any idea how deeply in debt we are? Over fifty grand, Mother. Fifty."

"Precisely. We're practically destitute because your father didn't have any better sense than to leave his business to a child."

Lilli clenched her teeth together and swallowed her anger. "I'll figure it all out. But if you aren't going to come in to work every day, the least you can do is hang in with the Zoo Ball people. I went back over Pop's records, and every year the week before the ball, we had a run on odds-and-ends pieces like the fake zebra-skin rugs and the synthetic leopard-upholstered wing chairs."

"I can't possibly wear the gown I wore last year. I've been pinching pennies these past few years, too, Lilli. I've worn everything several times over. I need a new ball gown."

"How much?"

"Five thousand."

Lilli turned her back on her mother. "That's insane. We can't afford that much. Look for a less expensive dress."

"I need to look good this year, Lilli."

"What's so special about this year?"

"I'm a widow now."

Lilli turned a quizzical eye on her mother. At first she couldn't understand what Arlette was trying to say, but when she did, Lilli felt sick to her stomach. Arlette was already looking for another husband. "I can't help you out, Mother."

Arlette glared haughtily at her daughter. "I should have known better than to come to you." She stood and was about to leave. Then she turned back to Lilli. "Don't expect me to come down here and sweep floors like you asked me to last week. I'm not a maid."

Lilli hurled her own barb. "Honest work never hurt anybody."

Arlette left that day and didn't set foot in the store for over a year. That was the beginning of the cold war between mother and daughter.

Four months after J.C.'s death, Vicki asked Lilli what had been done about J.C.'s clothes and personal items.

"Nothing as far as I know. I asked my mother about the gold cuff links Pop bought in Mexico City a few years ago and she said she still had them. I've been so busy here that I haven't had time to go through his things and pick out what I want."

Vicki nodded. "Since Frank has sealed up the things from J.C.'s study, I know there isn't much I could get, but I would like one of his wool cardigans. Just to have. You know?" Vicki bit her lower lip, which was trembling.

"C'mon. We'll go over to the house right now and look through his closet."

"Are you sure?"

Lilli put her arm around her aunt. "Of course. I'll call and see if Mother is home."

When Lilli telephoned, there was no answer, but since she still had a key to the house, she didn't think there would be a problem. Arlette had never liked J.C.'s bulky Irish wool cardigans because she thought they were too scratchy.

When they arrived at the house and tried the door, Lilli's key did not work.

"That's strange. Arlette must have changed the locks," Vicki said.

"I-I can't believe she'd do that. This is my home . . ."

"Was your home. It's Arlette's house now," Vicki warned.

Just then Arlette came up the driveway in her Cadillac. She bounded out of the car and raced up the walk, brandishing her umbrella at Lilli and Vicki as if they were burglars. "What are you doing here?"

"Calm down, Arlette," Vicki said.

Lilli could not stanch her anger. "What do you mean by changing these locks? How am I supposed to get in?"

Arlette glared at her daughter as she elbowed her way between her and Vicki. She retrieved her key from her handbag. "You come over here when you're invited. You have your own home now."

Vicki winked at Lilli. "I told you."

Arlette's head jerked upward. "Told her what?"

Lilli broke into the conversation before Vicki could answer. "That I don't have a home here anymore."

Arlette unlocked the door and pushed it open, then turned in the doorway and stood with her feet planted firmly apart. "I asked you what you want here."

Vicki heaved a deep sigh. "All I wanted was one of J.C.'s Irish wool cardigans. I know how you hate them—"

"They aren't here," Arlette snapped.

"Did you give them to charity?" Lilli asked.

"They're in storage," Arlette said, crossing her arms over her chest. "You can't have those or anything else of my husband's."

"Mother, it's just a memento. Vicki wanted—"

Arlette's eyes glistened maliciously. "I don't give a damn what Vicki wants. Or you, for that matter."

Just as Lilli was about to protest, Vicki held up her hand to stop her niece. "I've heard of some pretty rotten tricks, Arlette, but this is about the meanest. You put my brother's clothes and things in storage, not because you wanted to keep them safe, but only because you knew we'd want them. You did this just to spite your own daughter. Didn't you?"

Arlette did not reply.

"There's not a sentimental bone in your body, so our pleading with you is a waste of time. But let me tell you this,

Arlette Mitchell. If you ever, *ever* need me for anything, it will be a cold day in hell before I lift a finger for you. You got that?"

"I think so," Arlette replied coldly.

Vicki grabbed her niece's arm and headed to the car. Lilli thought she would never forget the sight of her mother standing nearly spread-eagled across the threshold of her home as if she were guarding it against a hostile attack. Arlette had thrown down the gauntlet. It took years for Lilli to pick it up.

The first time she did was in June of 1983. Arlette was seated with four society women at the center "power" table at Tony's for lunch when Lilli and Faith were seated two tables away.

"Should I go over there?" Lilli asked.

"No. It's my celebration today and I don't want Aunt Arlette to ruin it. After all, how many times are Paul and I going to sign the papers on a first house?"

"Oh, shit," Lilli swore under her breath. "She's coming over here. And who is the woman in the red straw hat and red linen who's coming with her?"

"My God. That's June Farrington, the oil magnate's wife. They have a home at St.-Jean-Cap-Ferrat that I've heard is incredible. I've got to hand it to Aunt Arlette, she *does* get around . . . as it were."

"Lilli!" Arlette came over to her daughter and gave her an "air kiss," then kissed the air by Faith's cheek as well. "Girls, I want you to meet June Farrington. June, this is Lilli, my daughter. And Faith, my niece."

"Lilli," June said with a perfect smile. "Please excuse me for the interruption, Lilli, but I wanted to tell you how impressed I am with your store. You were unavailable when I was in last week, and I thought the Carlos the Fourth dining chairs were exquisite. I just know that someone is going to snap those up before I get a chance to talk to you about them."

"As a matter of fact, they arrived only ten days ago and we have had a great deal of interest in them."

"When can we talk about them?" She quickly reached into her handbag and took out an engraved card, which she handed to Lilli.

"I'll call you later this afternoon," Lilli promised, putting the card in her own bag.

"Wonderful, dear."

Lilli's smile disappeared when she looked at her mother, who was scouring her face as if she'd just broken out in hives. "Something the matter, Mother?"

"I was just wondering if you'd decided what to do about your nose."

"My nose?"

"About having the bulb taken off the end and thinning the bridge." She cocked her head toward June. "Lilli hasn't had a date in so long, we've quit counting, and we thought perhaps it was because her nose is so terribly out of balance with the rest of her face." She regarded Lilli with an icy glare. "June knows the best plastic surgeon in New York. Don't you, June?"

"Uh, yes," June mumbled, suddenly embarrassed. "I'd be happy to recommend him to you, Lilli."

Obviously, Arlette was no longer satisfied with her private jabs and hurtful comments. She now wanted an audience, the same audience Lilli needed for her business. Arlette was letting Lilli know, albeit subtly, that she still had power and would still wield her control. Lilli couldn't let her mother get away with these petty cruelties.

"Thank you, Mother. After you get your face-lift and liposuction done, I'll be right behind you." Lilli smiled boldly and lifted her ice water in a mock toast to her mother. "I'll call you, June."

Arlette returned to her table in an indignant huff.

Lilli and Faith laughed throughout the entree and on into the dessert course.

Over the years, Arlette fine-tuned her skill of pushing Lilli's emotional buttons to coerce her daughter into writing her checks whenever she needed extra money, which was often. Arlette would meet Lilli for lunch on the pretext of doing Lilli the favor of giving her the latest mailing lists from one of her charities. Lilli needed these lists, and she knew to bring her checkbook.

"How much this time?"

"Lilli, don't be so crass. You know what your father always told us. No matter what, we had to stick together. In the end, Lilli, I'm the only family you've got."

"I have Aunt Vicki and Faith."

"That's not the same thing."

"No, it's better."

"I hope your father didn't hear you say that."

Lilli felt forced to acquiesce. "How much?"

"I'm going to Las Hadas with Bill Harleson. I need some new clothes. Three thousand."

"Do you have the list?"

"You may have it as soon as I get the check."

Lilli felt like a member of the CIA paying for top-secret information, but she wrote the check.

The bribery lasted until Lilli put a stop to it and refused to pay. Arlette went into a rage, although she did not reveal the depth of her bitterness to her daughter. She simply vowed to herself that she would get even.

Lilli would never be quite certain when her mother's jealousy of her and anger toward her father crossed the line and became hatred, but by 1990, Arlette was on a path of vengeance.

Arlette was dressed in a chic new cream-colored wool suit when she sat next to June Farrington at the Rivoli for dinner on a Monday night in November. She had practiced the lines she would say to June in front of a mirror, making certain she did not appear insincere.

"I just don't know who I can turn to, June," Arlette said, casting her most bewildering look at her friend. She wrung her hands in her lap.

June was truly sympathetic, as Arlette knew she would be. "Arlette, dear, I've never seen you so perplexed. What is it?"

"My . . . daughter."

"What about Lilli?"

"I-I suppose in matters like this I shouldn't say anything to anyone, but I just found out myself and I don't know what to do."

June fought her own exasperation at Arlette's habit of perpetually beating around the bush. However, June adored gossip, and if there was anything she could spot, it was the essential ingredients of a good story. Lilli Mitchell was one of

Houston's most beautiful up-and-coming members of the chi-chi crowd. June simply *had* to know. "If it's too serious, perhaps you should talk to a professional."

"Oh, dear. I don't think I could tell this to a stranger. It doesn't seem proper." Arlette realized June was losing patience with her. "I went to dinner last night with Ralph Knots, the astronaut, and he told me that he'd heard a rumor about Lilli and he wanted to know if it was true. He said that . . . oh, God, June! This is just so awful. I mean . . . I can't believe it, but when I look at the facts, I can see how it could be true . . ." Arlette had lowered her head in shame. She paused for a moment and peered up at June.

"Is it drugs? So many people are on them these days. It's not so bad. I know the names of all the rehab centers."

Arlette shook her head. "He commented on the fact that Lilli is nearly thirty and isn't married."

"So?"

"Lilli hasn't been engaged. She claims she's too busy for men. I've tried to introduce her to nice young men, but she puts me off. She turns them down as if they have the plague or something. I mean . . ."

Suddenly June's face lit with shock. Her hand flew to her mouth. "My God, Arlette. Is she a lesbian?"

Arlette simply nodded her head. "That's what Ralph heard. It can't be. Can it?"

June grabbed her water glass and took a large swallow. "I know she's your daughter, but honestly, Arlette, people have been wondering what's the matter with her. She went to the opening of the new Pappas Restaurant solo. She went to the Zoo Ball solo. She's been going on more of those . . . archaeological trips lately—by herself." June placed her hand over Arlette's. "I'm so sorry, dear. I really do think you need to get her a shrink."

Arlette had to work at it, but she finally managed a single tear. "You won't tell anyone about this, will you, June?"

June shook her head, and with her eyes filled with sincerity and compassion, she said, "I won't breathe a word, dear."

In less than twenty-four hours the gossip was all over Houston.

Lilli never discovered where the story had started, because she didn't pay any attention to the rumor mills whether they were about her or not. Faith, on the other hand, kept bringing Lilli back to the matter at hand.

"You've got to do something about this, Lil."

"What? Go out and marry somebody to stop their wagging tongues? I haven't got the time. Besides, in a week or two it will all die down."

"Don't you even want to know who started this crap?"

"Who cares?"

"You should. It could affect business."

Lilli turned off the calculator and closed the checkbook she was reconciling. "Okay. Who do you think is the mastermind?"

Faith raised an eyebrow and leaned over to Lilli conspiratorially. "I traced it back. Seems your mother had a little something to do with spreading it to June Farrington."

"She wouldn't dare," Lilli said reflexively and then she contemplated the information. Tears filled her eyes. "God, Faith. To think my own mother hates me so much. Why? What did I ever do to her?"

"You were born and you came between her and J.C. She wasn't the top banana anymore."

"So what do you suggest?"

"Get out and meet some guys. Go places. Be seen like she is. Don't sit here in your little cave. Beat her at her own game."

"I haven't got time for that!"

"If you don't, you could lose the business. And then where would this empire be that you're trying to build?"

"You really think I should?"

Faith smiled broadly. "Trust me."

Lilli did as her cousin suggested and made the rounds to all the "in" places with friends of Paul's and Paul's friends of friends. Faith had been right. In a few weeks another rumor came along and dispelled the one Arlette had begun. The gossip mill forgot about Lilli Mitchell and her supposed gay lifestyle. But Lilli didn't forget. She went back to work with the haunting fear that Arlette's malevolence would rise again when she least expected it.

1990
New York

That first year after Lilli left him, Zane continued to write
to her and call her when he couldn't stand the emptiness any
longer. At first they were desperate calls pleading with her to
come to New York, but Lilli always declined, telling him that
it was too painful for her. She told him she had to move forward with her life. She told him she was incredibly busy
making sense of the bills that hadn't been paid for months
and the accounts receivable that hadn't been billed for over
eighteen months. She told him about the storewide sale she'd
had and how she'd sent notices out to previous customers.
But it rained that weekend and very few customers showed
up. Realizing that she needed to reach a broader group, she
planned another sale and tried to take out a large ad in the
Houston Chronicle. However, because J.C. had not paid
the advertising bill to the *Chronicle,* the paper would not run
her ad. Next she went to the *Houston Post,* where they'd
never advertised, and placed a large ad at half the price. The
customers flocked to the store, and she sold nearly half the
inventory. She could pay her bills, but then Lilli was faced
with the dilemma of having to restock her inventory with no
cash. She began taking antiques and family heirlooms of any
style and period on consignment. Her sales increased sixty
percent the same month.

Lilli changed the store hours to include Friday nights and
Sunday afternoons, despite the blue laws in Texas against
Sunday sales. She never advertised her Sunday hours, and she
made no final sales on Sunday. On Monday, however, she
telephoned every customer and closed her deals. Her profits
inched upward.

Talking to Lilli and sharing in her frustrations and triumphs
was almost as exciting to Zane as being with her. He came to
count on his phone conversations with her. He always told
her that he loved her. She told him that she missed him terribly.

For years Zane tried to convince his mother that what she
needed was a visit to New York for the Christmas holidays.
Finally, Hannah agreed. Then at the last minute she changed
her mind. Zane was determined that his mother not be alone

that Christmas of 1984, so he went to Bandera to visit her. He also went to Houston to surprise Lilli, only to be told by her secretary at Antiquities that Lilli had gone to Cozumel with her mother, Vicki, and Faith for a much-needed rest. According to the secretary, Lilli had been very near collapse from overwork. Zane felt shut out of her life because she hadn't told him about the trip. However, he was forced to forgive her because he'd never told her he was coming back to Texas for the holidays.

Easter came and went, and by the summer Zane realized that Lilli seldom returned his calls anymore. Her letters had dwindled to a trickle, and then finally he received a letter in which she told him that she needed to put the past behind her. Her emotional turmoil was not good for her health.

Zane didn't know she could break his heart again. But she did.

After that, Zane threw himself, with even greater fervor, into his career. He was amazed at how well he did. Because he'd already spent five years building a base, the extra effort he now expended resulted in one incredible deal after another.

Zane did not socialize or live in the world of the ultrarich, but he needed them for his business. He was charming, and his good-heartedness and loyalty showed in the way he dealt with his clients. The word that Zane McAllister gave a good price for a great piece of jewelry spread from New York to Paris to Vienna to Geneva. In Amsterdam when a spectacular piece came up for sale, it was Zane's phone that rang, and he was always ready and willing to catch the next flight out, no matter what time of the day or night. Zane had learned how to make a lot of money for his employer. As the years passed, he realized he needed to make his deals for himself. He wanted to run his own business. To do this he needed Francis Kensington.

"Consultants in New York used to be a dime a dozen. Now they're a penny a pound," Francis Kensington said to Zane as they rode down Fifth Avenue in Francis's newest acquisition, a 1932 Bentley. "The stock market crash of '87, the S and L debacle, the flagging computer industry, and the last dying breaths of the industrial age have all compounded to put half of the white, male New Yorkers out of work and into the business of pounding pavement."

"I understand that, Francis, but I think I'm ready."

"You know so much."

"I do," Zane said confidently, although he was becoming impatient with his friend, whose favorite pastime, Zane believed, was holding him back. He was thirty-one years old. Hardly a kid anymore, but to Francis, Zane would always be a country boy.

"You've got the best of all possible worlds. You're well paid. You travel at the company's expense. You're respected and you have none of the hassles of running your own business. Your tax burden alone—"

Zane held up his hand. "I know, Francis. I've heard this speech a hundred times. More. I want more."

"More what? Money?"

"That. But no. More than that."

"Security? There's no security in owning your own business. You'll report to every customer, supplier, and employee. Now they will be your bosses."

Zane turned away from the older man, who was getting red in the face as he always did when he was agitated or upset. Zane knew Francis had a heart condition. His overeating and lack of exercise were killing him. Zane liked Francis. He respected him. He didn't want to lose his friend. So he refrained from pushing the issue.

"Talk to me," Francis pressed.

Zane watched the noontime sidewalks fill as secretaries, bankers, shop assistants, and young managers all left their buildings for lunch. Two young women with Dolly Parton look-alike bodies dressed in vivid-colored Spandex mini-dresses stood at the stoplight and bent over to peer into the Bentley. Their deep cleavages were impossible to ignore.

Francis clucked his tongue. "Women have no mystery anymore. No wonder the country is going into a decline."

The light changed and the driver whisked through the intersection.

"Mystery," Zane mused. "Maybe that's what I'm after."

"Maybe." Francis eyed his friend. "Maybe you're just bored."

"I am that," Zane said a bit sadly. "I thought there would be more . . . somehow."

Francis placed both his hands on his silver-topped walking stick. "There is more. And you're right. You should go out and find all that you can. Squeeze the life out of life. Go ahead. Maybe it's time you left retail jewelry. The paychecks are steady and the promotions are assured, but that's not what you're looking for, is it, Zane?"

"You always said I was too young. That no one would take me seriously."

"I was right. But I've also been protective. Business can be so difficult sometimes. I'm tired of the whole thing myself. I've been thinking of selling out."

"What? Francis, you never told me."

"Yes. Well, I like to keep things like that under my hat until I'm sure. Seems there's this big conglomerate out of Maine that wants to merge. I told them no. So they merged with United Pacific Paper. Now they both want to buy me out. I think I'm going to do it. I get to teach them my tricks with recycling. They promise to stop tearing down the forests. I keep telling myself I've done some good for humanity before I leave."

"This is incredible, Francis. I'm really happy for you."

Francis turned his enormous head and looked at Zane. "I believe you."

Zane couldn't miss the emotion in Francis's voice. They were not friends in the way Zane was with Mike and Joe, with whom he played tennis and lifted weights. He didn't spend hours on Friday nights hanging out at the pub on Eighty-eighth and Third with Francis, but with Bob and Ken. Francis was more like Zane's father or a wise uncle he wished were family so that he could see him more often.

Francis was his Sunday afternoon friend. Francis took Zane for rides in his newest car and they talked about all manner of things—the books they'd read, the plays they'd seen, the local gossip, and, of course, Zane's future. Francis seldom spoke of his own business or his investments. He never shared his home or made plans for even a dinner engagement with Zane. Francis was a private person, but he was always interested in Zane and his problems.

To Zane, Francis was the dispenser of wisdom. Francis

shared with Zane the names of a few friends who he believed would be interested in the kind of jewelry that Zane's latest employer, Swithington Jewelers, sold. These were always understated pieces in simple settings with rare, exquisite, and costly stones. Francis's friends were not monied exhibitionists who wore their bank accounts on their fingers, but neither were they wealthy enough to purchase the kind of antique jewelry that Zane knew he could procure if he had a bankroll to get him started. He'd tried to save a bit of each of his paychecks, but they never seemed to stretch far enough. And with the passing of each year, Zane's dream stretched out in front of him like an abandoned road.

For a long time, Zane's pride was the barrier between him and his dream. He felt he was less of a man to ask for help, but finally one day he appealed to Francis for a loan. Francis told him he'd been waiting almost a decade for Zane to ask.

Francis didn't give Zane money, but rather a lovely piece of jewelry from his collection to test Zane's acumen. When Zane brought back four times its worth, he gave Zane half the profits as his commission. Zane parlayed this sale into another and another, until now he had the bankroll he needed to go out on his own.

Over the years on their Sunday rides, Zane had made a mental note every time Francis spoke of one of his friends. Zane had gone home and written down the name and any other pertinent information he could remember about the person. Ten years later, Zane believed he had the king of Rolodexes. This was the clientele upon which he would build his business.

Because of an offhanded remark Francis had made, Zane found, in a Connecticut farmhouse, a Renaissance pearl headdress and the documentation to prove its origin in France in 1493. The piece was priceless and had been in the owner's family for two hundred years. However, a series of calamities had befallen the family, from exorbitant medical bills to a severe loss in the stock market and foreclosures on all the properties save the last house in Connecticut. The sale of this headdress would keep the family secure for years.

Zane did not take the first offer he received; it took him four months to find the proper buyer. In San Francisco, a fantastically successful female writer offered two million dollars for the piece, stating that her first historical novel had been placed in Chantilly, France, and she had once described this same kind of headdress on her heroine. She pursued Zane until the sale was concluded.

Francis told Zane he'd known all along what Zane was up to. Francis prided himself on being sly. He had wanted Zane to have this gift of his very private contacts, but Zane had not known why. If not for Francis's contacts and that long list of hidden treasures, Zane would not be thinking seriously of hanging out his own shingle as an antique jewelry dealer and gemologist.

"Be careful, Zane. Not all your clients will be on the square like my friends."

"I will. If need be, I can open a small retail shop. Engagement rings and what not."

"God! How crass!" Francis moaned. "You're better than that." He shook his head. "You are a dreamer, Zane McAllister. You'd be sick of the ordinariness of it in less than a month and you know it."

"That's true. It was just a thought."

"I like to think of you as an adventurer, and if I were truly honest with myself, I would have to admit that I like to tell myself that I was a key contributor to your success."

"You've been my ally from the beginning. I owe you a great deal."

"Forget it." Then Francis smiled. "Go after that adventure. When it was my turn, I certainly did." Suddenly Francis was a million miles away, thinking of another time. "Remember when you took your vacation and went to Burma and you saw the five-hundred-carat ruby? You say you need mystery? Ha! You didn't find enough of that at Mogok? Why, the most spectacular rubies in the world come from there."

"I came back with that pigeon blood ruby I nearly stole from that Thai trader."

"He was a fool."

"They all believe that looking at a pigeon blood ruby is like looking into the face of God. He was myopic with a case of cataracts and he believed he couldn't see anything. He said it was a fake."

"Like I said, he was a fool."

"I got lucky."

"I've been well aware, as are all traders, that a great deal of bribery and collusion goes on daily with the Thais. I even read about it in *National Geographic,* for God's sake. Wasn't that enough mystery for you? Not enough excitement? What, do you want to start smuggling stones into the country now?"

"Of course not. I've scooped up enough Australian sapphires, seen the Luc Yen mine in Vietnam, and gone to Tanzania for some not-so-great sapphires. As far as gemstones are concerned, I thought I'd hit Bogotá."

"For emeralds?"

"Yes. I think they're becoming even more rare than ever before."

"I agree. But all the synthetics . . ."

"You and I both know that the markets only want the real thing. Nothing but the best."

Francis studied Zane for a long moment. Then he began to chuckle.

"I'm pleased that I'm a source of amusement for you."

"Forgive me. It's just that you young people go off to the far reaches of the earth to stake your claim with no thought of what you're going to do with your treasure once you've found it."

Zane smiled. "I've already covered that. I have a buyer. He's prepared to purchase everything I can find."

"Everything?" Francis was curious about this buyer. All of Zane's really heavily monied clients had come through him, or so Francis thought.

"Yes."

"And if you stumble onto a truckload of emeralds?"

"He'll buy them all."

"I don't believe it." Francis shook his head in disbelief. "Very few people have that kind of money—at least none you know."

"I know this one."

"Really? Who is it?"

"He's a rap singer."

"Shit," Francis said appreciatively under his breath.

It was the first time Zane had ever heard Francis swear.

* * *

It took Zane only fifteen minutes to inform his employer of the past ten years, Robert Swithington III, the grandson of the original owner, that he was quitting his job as general manager.

"You have found something better, have you?" asked Robert.

"Yes."

"And that is ... ?" Robert tugged at his Ralph Lauren suspenders, a darkly woven tapestry of hunting scenes. Zane knew that Robert was scared to death of horses or anything on four legs, for that matter, and it amused him that he made such a show of wearing equestrian-inspired accessories.

"I'd rather not say at this time."

Robert curled his full lower lip down until it looked as if it would touch the bottom of his chin. Zane always had to hold back his laughter at times like this. "Keeping secrets, are we?" Robert said condescendingly.

Robert had never liked Zane, but found him a necessary evil because Zane was the one thing that Robert was not—a great salesman.

Zane charmed the ladies, whereas Robert's haughtiness turned them cold. Zane kept his eyes and ears open to his clients and led them into the close like a hunter trapping a fox. Zane's uncanny ability to keep his finger on the pulse of the trends in the jewelry business had impressed both Robert Swithington, Sr., and Jr., but not the Third.

Robert the Third was incredibly jealous of Zane, his talent, and his ease with people. He hated his smooth Texas drawl and the hayseed compliments he paid sophisticated New York women, who returned again and again to buy from him. Robert would not admit to himself that Swithington's business owed much of its huge profit margins to Zane.

Robert believed that many of Zane's contacts came to him by virtue of the family's good connections and the quarter of a million dollars they budgeted annually for advertising. Many of Zane's customers came to him from the glossy ads they ran in *Vanity Fair, Metropolitan Home,* and *European Travel and Leisure.*

Robert didn't like Zane's overconfidence. Whenever Zane closed a particularly profitable deal, Robert was the first to point out the good name of the company and the yearly advertising budget. Robert made it a practice never to give Zane his due.

The Swithingtons had not counted on Zane's departure.

Since the first of January, 1990, Robert the Third had been put in charge of the store. He knew that his father and grandfather would not be pleased to hear that while under his tenure, Zane was suddenly leaving.

"Is it something I've done?"

Zane's eyes showed surprise. "Of course not. You've all been very good to me. I've enjoyed the work. It's just that it's time for me to move on. Make my own way."

Robert stood and gently placed his hands in the pockets of his wool slacks, where he could discreetly wipe his perspiring palms. He couldn't let Zane know how important he was to the business, or that he was in large measure responsible for Robert's own promotion to vice president. "And what would that be?"

"I'd rather not say."

"Come, come, Zane. We're practically family here. You've been with us quite a number of years now. Isn't that so?"

"Yes." Zane was suspicious as he watched Robert circle his huge mahogany desk. In all his years at Swithington, Robert had paid little attention to Zane, so why was he acting so chummy now?

"I think it only right that you at least give us a forwarding address."

"I can be reached at my apartment, for the time being. I'll let you know of any changes."

Robert's face flushed red. "You want a raise, is that it?"

"No."

"More vacation time?"

"No."

"More time to go on those crazy jaunts of yours to Sri Lanka, hmm?" Robert kept walking toward Zane until they were standing nearly nose to nose.

Zane had had no idea Robert would react so vehemently over his leaving. It was a shock—and it was also a pleasant revelation. Suddenly Zane realized just how good he was.

He smiled. "No."

"Ha!" Robert raised a finger in the air. "I finally have it!" His eyes blazed as he turned away from Zane. He marched back to his desk, then faced Zane again. "You're going into business for yourself!" he accused.

"Yes," Zane replied calmly.

Robert stared at him. Zane thought he could hear a low growl in the other man's throat, but then dismissed the notion. Robert prided himself on being too genteel to stoop to primitive emotions.

"Tell Mary to cut you a two-week severance paycheck, clear out your desk immediately, and leave your display-case keys on the tray in the outer office."

"Of course," Zane replied and turned toward the door.

"McAllister!" Robert commanded.

Without turning around, Zane put his hand on the doorknob. "Yes?"

"Don't come back."

"I won't."

Zane closed the door quietly behind him.

Twenty-six

Z ane met Marci at the deli around the corner from where she was shooting a fashion layout for *Glamour.* Marci Lange was not a beautiful girl, but she had dazzle and, most important, the camera loved her. Often, Zane could not believe that the Marci he lived with was the same girl on the covers of *Mademoiselle* and *Harper's Bazaar.* Marci was only twenty, with gangly legs and arms and perfectly shaped breasts. She had wheat-colored hair that fell halfway to her waist, green eyes that rivaled the finest beryls Zane had ever seen, and a voluptuous mouth that other women would kill for. Marci was fun, sweet, and a bit brighter than most actresses and models.

He had thought they would "work out." Zane had explained the rules to Marci—that he was not interested in getting married right now and that they were not to discuss it. Zane didn't tell Marci that he was still in love with a woman back home in Texas, because he had worked diligently at eradicating Lilli from his life.

Zane chose Marci because she looked nothing like Lilli. He knew he had to start a life for himself. He couldn't go on forever loving a memory. He told himself he was growing up and putting his childish dreams behind him. He tried very hard to love Marci the way he'd loved Lilli, but he couldn't.

Marci told Zane that she wasn't interested in marriage or kids yet, either. She was a model. She had a career to build. She had dreams of acting in the movies. Marci said she understood his position and agreed they would not hassle each other about the "M" word.

That was over a year ago. Things change in a year.

Marci picked at her cole slaw, the fork dangling from her

thumb and forefinger. She propped her elbow on the table and rested her head in her hand.

Zane sank his teeth into a thick corned beef sandwich, and as he munched away he noticed a tiny tear trickle down the side of Marci's nose. She seemed to be unaware of it, as if this happened often. Zane knew something was wrong.

He wiped his hands on a paper napkin. "What's wrong, Marci?"

She jerked her head up and stared at him, her green eyes swimming in pools of tears. "I'm moving out. I mean I moved out. This morning, after you left for work. It didn't take long."

"When were you going to tell me?"

"Now. I'm telling you . . . now," she choked.

"Can't we talk about this?"

"What's there to say?" She slammed her fork down on the table with more force than she'd intended. She glanced to the right at the customers at the next table as embarrassment flushed her cheeks. "You don't love me and my wishing it so won't make it happen."

"Marci." He reached for her hand, but she snatched it back as if she'd been bitten by a snake. "It's not your fault . . ."

Marci's face contorted into a mask of controlled rage as she glared at him. "I know it's not my fault. It's *your* fault. You've got the problem, man. Not me!"

Zane gaped at her. She looked as if she could kill him. He'd never realized that Marci, barely out of her teens, was so emotionally attached to him. He'd never thought about it before. They had fun, great sex; she liked football and working out. She was the perfect companion. He hadn't realized until he looked into her pain-filled eyes what he had done to her. He was responsible for Marci's unhappiness today. True, he'd never lied to her, but he hadn't been truthful either.

Zane hadn't been truthful to himself.

Ever since the day Lilli had walked out on him, Zane had shut down his emotions, although he hadn't realized that until now. Looking at Marci, he wondered if he was doomed to a life alone because of his inability to love somebody other than Lilli.

Marci struggled with her anger, but it was more powerful than her self-control. "You think you're so wonderful?"

Marci spat. "You're not. Making love with you is like doing it in a goddamn TV commercial. Lots of bumping and grinding, but no soul. I need some soul, Zane."

Zane knew better than to interrupt her. He wanted her to vent her frustrations on him. He didn't want her to know that her accusations hit him in the solar plexus. Maybe it was the way she salted her sentences with profanity that reminded him of Lilli. Maybe it was the fact that she told it like it was, never whining or pleading. Maybe it was because he was not a kid anymore. Zane was rethinking his entire life, and everything from his career to his love life seemed to be in chaos.

"You deserve better, Marci," he said sincerely.

"You bet your ass I do! And Sam is just the guy to give me what I want."

"Sam?" Zane's eyes widened.

Marci's beautiful lips curled into a victorious smile. Her eyes softened at the sound of Sam's name. "Yeah. Sam."

"Your photographer?"

"What's the matter, Zane? Hasn't a girl ever tossed you over for another guy? You get what you give, Zane, and for a very long time, you haven't been giving. With you, I never felt so insignificant in my entire life. It's a rotten feeling." Marci stood and grabbed her Nike bag and slung it over her shoulder. "Next time you find a girl you like, Zane, don't neglect her like you did me. I have to go. I'll leave a message on your recorder with my new phone number when it's installed next week, in case I left any of my stuff behind."

"Okay." Zane nodded and swallowed hard.

"See ya," Marci said.

"See ya," Zane replied.

Marci did not kiss him good-bye, or shake his hand, or even look back at him as she walked away. They parted as they'd come together, as strangers. And Zane was alone again.

Zane did not sleep that night. He lay facing the ceiling, counting the moon shadows that slipped between the vertical blinds in his apartment. He had wanted to share his good news with Marci about quitting his job, starting his own business, and his conversation with Francis. Then he remembered that Marci wasn't all that interested in antiques or jewelry.

She liked contemporary things, such as the black-and-teal-speckled wallpaper she'd bought and put up in the bathroom, the vertical blinds, and the chrome-and-black ceiling fan.

When he thought about it, he was amazed that he and Marci had been together at all. She seldom asked him about his goals, his dreams, or his background. She didn't probe his thoughts or provide profound observations. She never asked him about his new client who Zane believed would make him wealthy. It wasn't that Marci didn't care, he realized. It was simply that she had learned early on in their relationship not to ram her head against the steel walls he'd put between them.

Zane had protected himself well from emotional pain. He'd cut off the world and buried himself in his work. He was leaving Swithington's with a roster of their finest clients. Already he had been commissioned to attend an auction at Sotheby's in London to buy a certain diamond bracelet for a former Swithington client. But Marci didn't care to hear about his coup, because Zane had seen to it that Marci would never get close to him.

"You got what you wanted," he said aloud. The emptiness seemed to suck him in and pull him down into a black tunnel. At the very end of the blackness he thought he could see two sparkling pools of purple light. Lilli's eyes. His breath caught in his throat at the thought of her.

"Jesus! Am I never going to forget?"

Zane threw his forearm over his eyes, blocking the vision. He struggled to focus his thoughts on something else . . . his meeting the next day; anything but Lilli.

It was no use. Whether or not there was a Marci in his life, there would always be Lilli to haunt him.

Cold Tap was the Rap King of 1990. He'd beaten out Ice-T, Boo-Yaa T.R.I.B.E., and Kool G Rap for the most controversial album of the year with his hit single, "Shoot 'Em on Sight."

At only twenty-two, he was a multi-multi-millionaire. At the end of the year, he signed a sixty-five-million-dollar deal with MCA Records, beating out Prince's sixty million, and was way over the top of ZZ Top's forty-million-dollar contract.

Cold Tap was a black ghetto kid from Manhattan who was an only child and raised by a single mother who put herself through law school and sent her son, Morton Edgerton, to a Catholic high school on the Upper West Side and then kicked him out of the house for smoking pot. At seventeen, Morton was on his own.

He danced, sang, and acted anywhere and everywhere he could in New York. He lied and cheated his way into auditions, making up tall tales about an imaginary agent who hadn't gotten around to typing his résumé or duplicating his head shots. What he had was talent.

In 1989 the music world didn't give a flip about talent. It wanted cute kids who could beat out rap. Morton hitchhiked his way to Los Angeles and got an audition at Warner Records as a backup singer.

He changed his name to Cold Tap and hung out at the studio all day and all night writing rap, chanting out rhythms, and generally bugging the hell out of anyone who came near him. Finally, an overworked and overwrought woman producer turned to Cold Tap and screamed, "Shut up!"

"Not until you *really* hear me sing."

"If I let you cut a demo, then will you shut up?"

His grin beamed as bright as the sun. "You won't say that after you hear me."

"Prove it," she challenged.

And he did.

Cold Tap celebrated the New Year in Aspen with some of the biggest names in Hollywood. He learned to ski, drink champagne till dawn, and listen. Cold Tap listened to everyone, especially the stars who had once been big, invested their money wisely, and now had no need to work the grueling, killing schedules that entertainers must to stay on top. Cold Tap decided, there on the Colorado mountain slopes, that what he really wanted to be was retired.

Cold Tap went to New York to consult with a stockbroker whom his agent at ICM had recommended. To test the broker he invested ten thousand dollars in the suggested stocks and lost his money in two months. Cold Tap figured his odds were better in Las Vegas. He fired the broker and decided that when he invested his money, he wanted something he could put his hands on. Cold Tap had always liked jewels and land. He wanted them both.

Cold Tap made it his business to be well informed about jewelry. As his fame increased, so did his invitations to charity events and personal, private appearances at the homes of some of New York's wealthiest citizens. Cold Tap often commented on an unusual brooch or an expensive necklace. He made it a practice to inquire of the owner where the piece had been purchased. Over and again, the name Zane McAllister was mentioned in conjunction with the rare gems Cold Tap coveted.

Cold Tap's Manhattan offices on Fifty-seventh Street were sleek, futuristic open rooms with floor-to-ceiling walls of glass overlooking the city. Plexiglas workstations were crammed with computers, phones, fax machines, and laser printers. Next to his beveled-glass-topped desk stood a NordicTrack, a Stairstepper, a Soloflex, and a slanted bench and full set of weights. Black leather sling chairs made of brass and chrome were grouped around a huge marble slab that served as the coffee table. Floor lamps of twisted iron and shades of overlapping cowskins illuminated the corner area.

In the opposite corner was a Yamaha keyboard and synthesizer, stereo equipment, amplifiers, and tiny Bose speakers that rested on what looked like huge boulders, but were obviously tables.

When Zane walked into the room, he felt like Barney Rubble meeting the Jetsons. No wonder this guy wanted to buy an emerald mine, Zane thought; he's looney tunes. Zane saw his dream of riches shatter around him.

Cold Tap's latest single blasted from the stereo speakers as he bopped his way around his desk toward Zane.

Cold Tap was wearing a purple muscle shirt, a Yankees baseball cap turned around backward, sweatpants that were eight inches too short, gym socks, and Nike Air high-tops. He was young and good-looking with a glistening, dark body pumped to the max, and he was cocky as hell.

With all that money and more rolling in, I would be, too, Zane thought as he smiled and shook Cold Tap's hand.

"Zane McAllister."

"Cold Tap." He gestured toward the arrangement of sling chairs. "Have a seat, man."

"Thanks."

Cold Tap sat opposite Zane in a chair, picked up a remote control, and turned off the stereo. Then he pushed another button on the control, and the office door opened. A beautiful girl, who looked to be Iman's double, walked into the room wearing a very tight black miniskirt, high black suede boots, and jet-black hose. She wore a gold sequined scarf tied around her ample breasts and a long black silk jacket over the entire ensemble.

Cold Tap turned to Zane. "This is my secretary, Cecily. Would you like some herb tea? I have Earl Grey if you'd rather . . ."

"Herb is fine," Zane replied dumbfoundedly. He turned appreciative eyes back to Cold Tap as the girl left the room.

Cold Tap hit the remote again, and a section of the wall behind them began to move.

"What the hell?" Zane nearly jumped out of his chair.

A panel in the wall to the right of Zane moved to the corner and revealed a ten-foot-high library. There were books on gems, jewels, mining, and cutting. Scores of magazines, some dating back thirty years, filled the bottom three rows. "I've been reading up on emeralds," Cold Tap said with a mischievous grin.

"I can see that." Zane whistled as he rose and went to the racks of books. He ran his finger across the spines.

"Now that rubies are not being mined any longer, I figure the world is going to be bidding those babies up pretty high. I don't have that kind of money, but the way I figure it is that the guys in Sri Lanka who own the mines, now those are the ones with the real bucks. They decide when they'll let a stone loose. I figure I can do the same thing with emeralds. They aren't all that plentiful, either." Cold Tap nodded to the books. "That's where I got my idea."

Zane followed his eyes. "I've read them all." Then he walked over to a rather odd grouping of history books. Most were about the conquistadores and the fall of the Aztec and Incan empires to the Spanish. Zane pulled a volume off the shelf and turned it over.

"Interesting that you should choose that book," Cold Tap said.

"Why?"

"That's the one that talks of the legend."

"What legend?"

"When the conquistadores conquered the Incan people, they found emeralds everywhere. The Incas had used them to barter and placed them in their temples. When the Spaniards demanded to know where the emeralds came from, the Incas died rather than reveal the secret. The Incas gave them all the emeralds that had already been mined, but it has been said since then that the biggest emerald mine has yet to be found."

Zane closed the book and placed it back on the shelf. "You impress me as being not only successful, Cold Tap, but also intelligent. Surely you don't really believe that myth, do you?"

Cold Tap grinned. "Why should you give a shit whether I believe it or not? I'm giving you a healthy commission to go to South America and buy some emeralds for me. Check things out. See what the locals have to say about the 'source mine.' "

"That's what they call it?"

"Yeah. 'The source.' "

"It's your money," Zane replied, shrugging his shoulders.

"That's right." Cold Tap grinned again. "And don't you fuckin' forget it."

"I won't," Zane said. "I don't know much about this legend and you do, so I'm at a disadvantage."

"I'll give you my books and a couple of maps. You won't be going into the jungle blind."

"Jungle?" Zane's eyes widened.

Cold Tap's wide grin grew even wider. "Yeah. After you visit Cuzco and the dealer in Bogotá, you'll be going to the jungle. It's all arranged. Cecily will give you the itinerary. It'll be a piece of cake. Sort of like following the yellow brick road."

Yeah, all the way to Oz, Zane thought as he swallowed deeply. He shook Cold Tap's hand as they parted. This guy truly was looney tunes. Pure one hundred percent looney tunes. And so was he, for agreeing to work for him.

Twenty-seven

*L*illi adjusted her face mask and checked her regulator.
Both tanks had been refilled and she was ready for the
second dive of the day. The dive master, Martine, was just as
eager as she was to investigate the odd-looking protrusion
Lilli had discovered on the ocean floor. However, Jack
Conway was tired, grumpy, and still hungover from the half-
dozen margaritas he'd downed the night before. He was content to stay on the boat and work on his suntan; and as usual,
he complained about Lilli's indefatigable curiosity about possible sunken treasures.

"You know goddamn well there's nothing down there but
some coral, shells, and a bunch of hideous fish. Besides, it's
dangerous to go down more than ninety feet."

Lilli rolled her eyes and lifted her mask to her forehead so
that Jack could feel the full brunt of her exasperation with
him. "For sport divers, yes, that's true, Jack. But Martine and
I have been diving for ten years together. I know the ropes
around here. I've been much deeper and haven't had problems. You don't have to go with us. It won't reflect badly on
your manhood if you don't."

Jack's dark brown eyes spat fire and he placed his hands
on his bare hips. "Cut the crap, Lilli. My manhood is just
dandy and I'm not hearing any complaints from anybody but
you."

Lilli shook her head. Jack Conway was Arlette's idea of a
"wonderful catch," although Lilli could barely tolerate a conversation with the man. She had agreed to this date with Jack
to get her mother off her back. These days the two of them
constantly sparred over Lilli's lack of wedded status. Lilli
was too busy with work to worry about men. It was her
mother, not Lilli, who fretted over the fact that she was al-

most thirty and still single. Lilli rather liked her unconventional single status. She had long ago closed her heart to love, and she intended to keep it that way.

It wasn't that she didn't like men. She did. Sometimes she truly relished their company and conversation. The problem with her was that she could not even kiss a man without thinking of Zane. Lilli was still in love with Zane McAllister and she knew it. She was a hopeless flop at love and she tried not to dwell on the subject any more than was necessary. Zane was a man she could never have.

Lilli should have known not to bring Jack on this trip, but he'd insisted. He'd never been to Belize. He thought they were going to party and make love all weekend. Lilli thought otherwise.

She had wanted to get away from the rat race in Houston. She wanted to forget business, the store, her mother, and everything else that was wrong with her life in Houston. She wanted to vanish into another world, another realm, and the only way she knew to escape reality these days was diving.

"Come on, Martine." Lilli pulled her mask over her nose and eyes. She placed the mouthpiece in her mouth and blew out the tubes. She picked up her finned feet and flopped to the boat's edge.

Lilli jumped feet-first into the water and sank swiftly. She cleared, breathed in, and let her air out slowly as she kept sinking.

The water was crystal clear, a glorious turquoise blue and then green. As the light dimmed, she flipped on her underwater light. Fantastic lemon-yellow and silver tropical fish darted around her in schools. Beautiful navy blue fish followed her downward and then they, too, swam upward toward the light. Martine flicked on his underwater light and raced downward past Lilli, following the rope on the marker they had left on their first dive when they had run low on air and were forced to return to the surface.

Lilli knew that Martine was as excited about their discovery as she was. For years he'd dreamed of finding lost treasure, but he'd never come close. Martine Allesandra knew as many of the legends and tales as Lilli did, but luck had never been on his side. They both knew the stories of explorers who had come to this area in the twenties and thirties and actually found treasure chests of buried pirate gold and jewels.

This cove and the surrounding beach area had proved to be favorite burial sites for the pirates Morgan and Bluebeard. In the 1920s and 1930s, divers had found jeweled daggers, doubloons, swords, knives, pearl necklaces, and tiaras, all from the sixteenth-century legendary raids on Spanish galleons. Morgan's men had remained in this western part of the Caribbean, married, and fathered children. Their children and their children's children had been privy to the stories, kept the family maps and directions secret, and even uncovered and reburied family treasures. As the centuries passed, the children moved away or families died off. The treasures were forgotten by all but a few.

Martine's father had been a dive master on an expedition in 1932, when two Americans had dug around in the sands and found an old trunk filled with jeweled daggers and jewelry. To escape the authorities, the Americans had hidden the treasure inside spare tires and then rowed the treasure out of the cove to a waiting yacht. Some of the pieces found their way to the Smithsonian. Others were sold privately, and still others were kept by the explorers themselves.

Lilli was mindful of these facts as she continued her descent. Over the years, she had heard the stories about the discovery of conquistador armor and gold hidden in caves in New Mexico and Arizona. Archaeologists and anthropologists had told her about finding incredible treasures by following aged maps, intuition, and curiosity. As a child, Lilli had learned from her father that the seemingly illogical in life harvested more treasure than the logical. She knew that Jack thought she was being illogical and she didn't care. She wanted to find her own treasure.

Suspended in the water, Lilli felt as if she were an alien on a distant planet. She had no weight, no concept of time or space. The darkness engulfed her, and it was difficult for her to see the ocean floor except for the beams of light that focused on the marker.

Martine zoomed quickly in front of her, anxious to begin digging. He pulled on the suction hose he'd brought down with him from the surface to vacuum the sand away.

As they swept the area with the hose, their hands, and a

broom that she had brought with her, Lilli could see that they had uncovered the prow of a small boat, a dinghy, perhaps.

Martine was overly anxious and had a difficult time keeping himself focused on one area. Lilli motioned for him to stay with her on the front of the prow. He reluctantly obliged. Lilli moved her light in closer and inspected the rotted wood. The prow was too small to be part of a ship or a galleon. It was definitely a dinghy. It would have been too good to be true, Lilli thought, to have found treasure so easily. This dinghy might not even be more than fifty years old.

As Martine uncovered more of the dinghy, Lilli noted that there were no nails holding the wood together, but rather, the boards were attached to the frame with wooden dowels. That meant the dinghy could be quite old. Suddenly she began to feel excited, the way she had on digs when she and her father uncovered unusual artifacts.

She nodded vigorously to Martine. Sensing her excitement, he began scraping more sand and silt away from the boat. Lilli's heart was beating like a metronome. In her mind she was already concocting a story around the sinking of this dinghy. It was old; perhaps it had been used by one of the pirates as he transported his treasure from the main ship to shore. Perhaps he ran aground on one of the sharp coral reefs. Perhaps there had been a storm that tossed him overboard or capsized his little boat . . .

Martine had managed to clean away an entire side of the boat, and walls of silt fell away. Then the interior of the dinghy was uncovered. There in the middle of the boat was a chest. A real chest. It was locked and rusted. Martine tried to lift it, but even with the buoyancy of the water to aid him, it was still too heavy. He motioned excitedly for Lilli to help.

Lilli grabbed one of the iron rings on the side of the chest and yanked as hard as she could. The chest moved. She yanked again, and with Martine's help, they moved it out of the dinghy. They attached the rope from the marker to one of the rings.

Suddenly Lilli remembered to look at her gauge. She'd used up her air faster than she'd anticipated. She motioned to Martine that it was time to surface. With the marker attached to the trunk, they could pull it up with the crank on board the dive boat. Martine nodded his agreement and picked up his underwater light.

Just as they were about to ascend, Lilli stopped and remembered her underwater camera dangling from her weight belt. She quickly snapped a half-dozen shots of the dinghy and the chest. The flash went off like a strobe. Lilli gave Martine a thumbs-up sign as they headed for the surface.

Jack was covered with coconut-scented tanning oil and was half asleep when Lilli and Martine broke through the water and shouted to him.

"Jack!" Lilli screamed excitedly as she swam toward the dive boat. "Jack! You won't believe it." She was breathless with enthusiasm as she took off her fins and tossed them aboard the boat.

Jack slowly returned to consciousness. He turned onto his side and shut off the reggae music that wafted from the speakers on the portable radio. "Don't tell me. You found a treasure chest."

"I did! We did! Martine and I!" She hoisted herself onto the deck and then offered Martine her hand.

"Yeah? I'll believe it when I see it," Jack said and passed his hand through his wavy black hair. He turned his face once again to the sun. "You can't tell me that you come down here for a little sport diving and hit the jackpot. What do you take me for? A fool?"

The hairs on Lilli's neck bristled. She clenched her teeth tightly together to keep from exploding in anger. As she looked at Jack, she frowned, thinking he looked more like a Las Vegas mafioso type in his Speedo bikini than a Houston stockbroker. Never again would she give in to her mother, Lilli thought. She should be there with someone who understood her, who shared her enthusiasm, and who knew that she needed this kind of excitement to stay alive.

Martine was beside himself. "It is true, *señor!* We found it! I will be a rich man forever!"

Jack yawned.

Suddenly Lilli grabbed Martine's hand and motioned for him to keep quiet. He obliged, although she could tell he didn't know what she was up to.

She glanced toward the water. The buoy was still attached to the rope. Instinct told her not to let Jack know what they had found beneath the water. She didn't trust him, especially with this information.

Lilli laughed loudly and heartily. Martine cast her a quizzical glance. "You're right, Jack. It was a joke. Martine and I thought we could fool you."

Martine gaped, but Lilli shot him a quelling look.

Jack did not look up. "I thought so. You should know I'm too smart for you."

"Yeah, I know that, Jack. You're just too smart for me."

"Well, now maybe you'll take me up on my idea to catch that flight to Grand Cayman tomorrow so we can really live it up."

"You know, that's a great idea, Jack. In fact, maybe you should catch the flight out tonight, go on to Grand Cayman and get us a room, and sort of check out the place. I can stay here tonight and help Martine pack up all his gear and whatnot. Then I could join you tomorrow. What do you think?"

Jack gave Lilli a suspicious look. "Don't kid a kidder, Lilli. You want to make another dive and I know it."

Lilli pursed her lips together but said nothing.

Jack smiled. "That's okay, too. You want to have fun. I want to have fun. This roughing-it stuff just isn't my style. So I think I'll take you up on that. Yep. That's a good plan."

Lilli smiled winningly at Jack. "You're a great sport, Jack."

"Thanks," he said. He lowered his head, closed his eyes, and concentrated on his suntan.

Lilli spoke to Martine in Spanish, instructing him to put Jack ashore and get him on the night plane out of Belize. She and Martine would then return to the cove, bring up the treasure, and split it. Martine nodded and then went to the helm and started the engine.

As the dive boat raced back to shore, Lilli knew Jack would be angry at first when he realized she would not be joining him in Grand Cayman. Five minutes, she thought; he'll be mad for five minutes. Then he'll go to the bar and in less than another five minutes he'll have found a new girl.

Lilli sighed with relief as she dismissed the matter of Jack. She had more important things to think about.

Lilli wasted no time in registering her discovery of the sea chest containing a jeweled dagger, eighteenth-century Spanish combs, strings of pearls, and jewels with the government officials of Belize, and in arranging for their transport to Houston. She notified a friend of hers at the National Geographic Society and arranged for a story and photographs to be taken of the treasure. She called an archaeologist friend, Nancy Sutton, at the University of Houston, and together they cataloged the items and began testing and dating the contents. Lilli told no one of Martine's half of the plunder, in deference to her friendship with him.

The Houston *Chronicle* ran a story about Lilli in the Lifestyle section, as did the business section of the Dallas *Morning News*. Several other area newspapers ran similar articles and due to all the local media attention, Lilli's telephone at the store rang constantly. Since her mother, in ten years, had never worked a day in the store, Lilli found it necessary to hire her cousin, Faith, on a part-time basis, just to help with the extra calls. Faith had stayed on, and Lilli was finding her a great help in the office.

Lilli brought her red Infiniti G-40 to a halt in front of New Antiquities in Highland Village, two doors down from Grotto's Restaurant. Faith pulled up and parked right behind her. Lilli had moved the business to this location four years ago when she was faced with making a total change in marketing or bankruptcy. J.C. had dreamed of becoming the foremost pre-Colombian art dealer in the country, but after the oil crash of 1986, Lilli could see there was little chance of that ever happening. In fact, through the seventies and into the eighties, Texans as a whole grew less interested in quality and timelessness and spent their money on expensive, flashy new items. These changes forced Lilli to change her vision for Antiquities. She decided to give Texans what they wanted.

Thus, New Antiquities still carried some fine Old Spanish antiques, but mixed with them were expensive custom-made sofas and chairs, exquisite reproduction tables, lamps, mirrors, area rugs, and unusual china, crystal, and silver. After four years of painstakingly choosing every piece that went into her store, Lilli almost felt successful. Her clientele included not only the "ladies who lunch" who spent their mornings at Tootsie's dress store across the street, but also customers from Sugar Land, Clear Lake, Katy, and the Woodlands. She carried a crossover array of items from ten dollars to ten thousand. She hired young college girls as her sales staff and taught them that service was what would make the difference with New Antiquities. Every girl had to know how to properly box and wrap every item, down to a single Christmas ornament.

Lilli took design classes at the University of Houston. She honed her skills and let her creative talents emerge. If she couldn't find the proper items she needed for her store, she asked her sales reps, friends, and customers. She was amazed at the help she received. Her sales increased slowly but steadily.

Holidays were a bonanza for New Antiquities. The previous year Lilli had turned the store into a fairyland for Christmas and bought eight twelve-foot artificial trees and decorated each one herself in eight different color themes, using the finest glass ornaments from Germany and Austria, silk flowers, twisted grapevine garlands, and bolts of gold brocade, burgundy velvet, and silver metallic ribbon. Lilli intended to do the same this year.

As she took her briefcase out of her car and locked the door, Lilli turned to her cousin, who was just getting out of her own car.

"Good morning, Faith." Lilli said cheerfully.

" 'Mornin'," Faith replied.

The two women walked to the front door of the store. As Lilli unlocked it, she said, "You look tired, Faith. Anything wrong?"

"Oh, Mindy has that flu that's starting to go around and I was up most of the night with her."

"I hope she gets better soon. You take good care of yourself. I can't risk losing my number-one employee at the busiest time of year."

"Don't worry, I've got the whole family on extra vitamins. Jason told me he'd take the vitamins if we'd get him Nintendo for his birthday. Six-year-old boys have a way of wrapping their fathers around their fingers. Paul gives in to Jason so easily because he feels he missed having a lot of things when he was a child. I think someone should hold firm on these things, but that 'someone' always turns out to be me. By the time my kids are teenagers, they'll think I'm the

Wicked Witch of the West." Faith put her purse under the checkout counter and followed Lilli to the back offices and hung her coat on the rack there.

Lilli switched on the coffeepot and checked the recorder for after-hours calls, but there were none.

Faith tore off the top of a Sweet 'N Low packet and dumped it into her Styrofoam cup while she waited for the coffee to brew. "You're so lucky, Lilli."

Lilli's head jerked up. "Me? Lucky?"

"Yeah. You don't have all these problems with kids and colds and . . . errgghh! Husbands! You can come and go as you please. Do what you want when you want. Look at all this attention you're getting because of that treasure. How exciting! I wish I could have been there."

Lilli poured coffee into her cup, then into Faith's cup. She kept her head lowered so that Faith could not see the pain in her eyes. It always amazed her that Faith felt this way about her, especially when *she* wanted what Faith had. "I wish you could have been there, too. It was exciting, Faith."

Lilli went to her desk and sat in the brocade-covered office chair that she had specially ordered. "But it's not a life, Faith. Do you know what I mean?"

"No." Faith leaned on the cherry wood credenza and turned an intense gaze on her cousin.

"You and Paul have your differences, but you do love each other. You'll figure out a way to make compromises and do what's best for the kids. I have no doubt about that. Paul is a fair man and a good father, although you have a point about his tendency to give them too much materially." She paused for a long moment, then said softly, "I'd give anything in this world to have those kinds of problems. I wish I had a husband and children."

"I wondered when you would finally say it."

Surprise widened Lilli's eyes. "You knew I felt like this?"

"Yes."

"How could you? I didn't even know I felt like this."

Faith gave Lilli a comforting smile. "It's been a long time coming, but you've given Paul and me a million signals over the years. I think you did know, but just didn't want to admit it. Maybe because it would be too painful."

"It is," Lilli said sadly. "I never thought it would turn out this way."

"I know. I thought he would come back for you."

Suddenly Lilli started fidgeting with the papers on the desk. She opened her date book, closed it, and opened it again. "I'm afraid I don't know what you're talking about."

"You most certainly *do* know what I'm talking about," Faith said. "Maybe you can pull this Miss Successful Businesswoman shit on your mother and the employees who don't know you, but this is Faith here. I know what makes you tick, Lilli, even if you don't."

"Oh, you do, huh?"

"Yes. Since the day J.C. died, you've been trying to prove he was some kind of god or something. You thought he knew everything about business and the antiques trade and you've found out now that he was good, but you're even better. The fact that you can keep that mother of yours in enough dough and off on trips when she gets in your hair too much is a miracle, if you ask me. Even *that* was more than J.C. could manage. On top of that, you've made a name for yourself here in town. People really like you and don't hold it against you that your mother is a shallow social climber . . ."

Lilli started to giggle. Then she broke into laughter. "Jesus! And I thought *I* was hard on my mother."

"Arlette is Arlette. Nothing and no one is going to change her. Especially you. So don't beat yourself up over her."

"I'm not doing that. I try to ignore her as best I can."

"Really? Then how come when she comes waltzing in here demanding to know what you've done with her business, you practically get the hives? Sure, you give her some pocket change and send her on her way, but you've never pressed the issue with her—had it out, as it were."

"I see what you mean. But I have my reasons."

"Which are?"

"I want to get along with her. It's just that she *is* a shallow social climber!" Lilli burst into laughter.

"Very funny. But I don't think that's what your father had in mind when he wanted you two to work together. Arlette hasn't matured an inch since J.C. died. All that's happened is that you've taken his place and you're dedicating your life to your mother!"

Lilli's face turned to stone. "I wouldn't go that far, Faith. I'm doing what I want to do."

"Oh, yeah, sure. Prove it."

"What are you talking about?"

"Call him."

"Who?"

"Zane. Pick up the phone and make contact. See what's going on with him. Is he married? Got kids? If so, maybe then you can put away the past, once and for all."

Lilli turned away from her cousin. "I did that a long time ago. Besides, he has a life of his own now. I can't do something like that. I'd look like a fool."

Faith rolled her eyes. "God forbid you do that! Better to spend your life wondering. Better to waste the rest of your life loving somebody you can't have. Better to never plan your own future. You have a life ahead of you, Lilli. Why not go grab some of it? You're supposed to be the adventurer. Let's see how adventurous you really are."

Faith walked over to the desk, lifted the receiver, and stuck it in Lilli's face. "The area code for New York is two-one-two."

Lilli glared at the receiver. She put her hands in her lap underneath the desk so that Faith could not see that she was trembling. "Oh, shut up, Faith. Go turn the lights on for me, it's nearly opening time."

As if in slow motion, Faith replaced the receiver. "Sure, Lil. Whatever you want," she said and quietly left the office.

Lilli swallowed hard to keep from crying, but still the tears welled in her eyes. The telephone seemed to swim in front of her as she stared at it through a veil of tears. Zane. Zane. Zane. His name flashed across her mind like rockets. Then she heard the sound of his name as she whispered it aloud. "Zane." Her mind wandered through the heavy mists of her memory to a place deep within her heart, a place she seldom visited. There she heard the sound of his voice, could feel the touch of his hand, could smell the scent of sandalwood and forests all around her. There she was with him again. There she found joy.

"I can't . . . ! I can't . . ." she wailed to herself and dropped her face into her hands, then put her head down on the desk.

Twenty-eight

~

1991
New York

Zane answered the telephone on the first ring. "McAllister here."

"Cold Tap here. I've got a little side deal I want you to take care of for me."

"What kind of deal?"

"Have you heard about the sunken treasure they found down in Belize?"

Zane slapped his forehead with his hand and let his splayed fingers slide down to his cheek. "No. No, I haven't, Cold Tap." This is all I need, Zane thought. "Why don't you tell me all about it?" he replied, struggling not to reveal his condescension.

"I can tell you don't believe me, but it's true. I'm readin' about it here in the *National Geographic*. Hot off the press this story is. They got a jeweled dagger, some doubloons, and a bunch of other stuff. I want the dagger. Make some calls. Find out how much they want. I'll go twenty-five thousand."

"What if it's worth only five thousand?"

"See?" Cold Tap laughed heartily. "That's what I have you for, to tell me these things." He rustled through the magazine pages. "You need to call Houston. Some gal by the name of—Mitchell . . ."

"Lilli . . ." Zane breathed the name.

"Yeah. That's it. How'd you know that?"

"I'm psychic," Zane said sardonically.

"No, you ain't, but I wish you were."

"I'll take care of it," Zane said.

307

"See that you do. Then we'll get back to that other matter of the mine. How's that coming anyway?"

"Slow. But it's coming. I'll have more information after I talk to Gunwalther on Friday."

"Okay. Talk to you then."

When Zane hung up the phone his mouth was dry. Lilli. She seemed to be everywhere around him lately ... in his dreams and thoughts. Too much in his thoughts. "Lilli." He spoke her name aloud as if it were a foreign word. He repeated it. "Lilli." An odd ache began in the center of his chest.

Zane wished he couldn't remember what she looked like or the touch of her skin against his or the feel of her lips, but he did. Too much so. His mind was transported back in time as if he'd been with Lilli only yesterday. He could remember the soft timbre of her voice when she told him that she loved him, and the rise in tone when she could not suppress her fiery nature and she spoke exactly what was on her mind. Zane chuckled as he remembered the way she always seemed to take over any situation, forever needing to leave the mark of her red Ropers on the world.

"She was some kind of girl ... she was my girl ..." he murmured. "But that was a long time ago."

Zane could feel the weight of the past descend on him like a shroud. What had Lilli been up to lately? He'd heard she'd abandoned the pre-Columbian art market during the oil crash. It had been a wise move. Contemplating that move now, he realized it had taken a great deal of courage and commitment to her own future, rather than the memory of her father, to change the course of the business and open New Antiquities. Maybe Lilli had changed in other ways. Maybe she wasn't so goddamn stubborn about things—about him—anymore. Maybe ...

"Oh, hell!" Zane cursed aloud. "Lilli will always be Lilli and that's all there is to that."

He called directory assistance for Houston and asked the operator for the number of New Antiquities. After he received it, he depressed the receiver button, then placed his call. It was answered on the second ring.

"New Antiquities. Faith speaking. How may I help you?"

"Faith? Is that you?"

"Sir?"

"It's Zane McAllister, Faith," he said as he passed the receiver into his other hand. He was unaware of the wide grin he wore and the fact that his hands were sweating.

"Zane?" she replied anxiously, yet with surprised pleasure. "Are you in New York? What are you doing? Why are you calling? Lilli isn't here."

Zane's heart was beating like a trip-hammer at the sound of Lilli's name. *My God, I've got to get a grip here. I'm acting like a kid. This is business. Strictly business,* he told himself. "She isn't?"

"She's still at home. It's been so hectic she decided to take the morning off. Do you have the number?"

"No, I—"

Faith excitedly rattled off the phone number. "Did she call you?"

"Huh? Uh, no. Not that I know of. Was she supposed to?"

Faith instantly realized she'd blundered. She had assumed that Zane was answering Lilli's call to him. But this was better, wasn't it? Zane was calling Lilli at the same time she had been trying to persuade Lilli to phone him. This was wonderful! It was fate! Kismet! "She was thinking about it, yes. Give her a call. I'm sure she'd love to hear from you."

"Thanks, Faith," Zane replied, still a bit astonished at the reception he was receiving. "It was good talking to you. I hope to see you real soon. Good-bye."

"Good-bye, Zane," Faith replied politely and hung up the phone. "And hello once again. Life, I love ya!" Faith clapped her hands together.

The dream swept Lilli under its power again. She saw the Mayan rain god whirling around her as bright flashes of light mesmerized her. It was the same rain god she'd seen in her dreams long ago when she'd gone on digs with J.C. The rain god swooped over her prostrate body, chanting words that she did not understand. From the distance she heard someone call her name. As the sound rolled across the vapors to her, Lilli knew it was Zane who was calling to her. She felt the force of his call pulling her, as if she were steel and his voice the magnet. She could not stop herself from hurtling toward it, no matter how hard she tried. In the dream, Lilli did not protest, but rather, she allowed herself to move toward him. His voice was everywhere around her and inside her. She had thought that the sound had come from outside her, but as it grew louder she realized that Zane's voice was within her—inside her heart. He was a part of her and she was a part of him.

"Are you here again?" she asked.

"I never left," he said and kissed her.

Lilli leaned into the kiss, feeling his warm lips against hers. She felt herself fusing to him, melting into him. She felt safe, warm, and protected, and she wanted the feeling to last forever.

The telephone on the nightstand next to Lilli's bed rang four times before she reluctantly abandoned her dream, rolled onto her side, and picked up the receiver.

"Hello?"

"Lilli." Zane spoke her name.

Lilli felt the dream begin all over again. He was with her, inside her and around her. She knew she had to rid herself of these ridiculous fantasies before she crossed the line into psychosis. "Shit . . ." she said sleepily and started to hang up the phone on the phantom caller.

"Lilli? Are you there? Lilli! It's Zane," he said, a tinge of desperation in his voice.

Lilli's eyes flew open with shock. Zane? Zane!

Her hands became palsied and she reacted as if she'd picked up a red-hot poker. She dropped the receiver. "Zane?" she yelled into the receiver, which had fallen to the floor. She bent over to pick it up and tumbled out of bed. "Zane?" She righted herself and pressed her back up against the side of the bed and pulled her knees to her chest. She cradled the receiver next to her cheek. "Hi," she said, caressing the earpiece.

"Hi."

Lilli was smiling from ear to ear. "I can't believe you're calling me." Hope. I must hope.

"I—I was wondering how you were doing. How are you, Lilli? Really?" She sounds like she did when we were kids, Zane thought. She sounds like she's happy to hear from me.

"Fine. I'm fine. I've been fighting this flu everyone has."

"Yeah. It's pretty bad here, too."

His voice was deeper, more cautious, less emotional than

she remembered. That was to be expected. He was older now. "Why are you calling me?" she asked. I wanted desperately to call you so many times. I wanted to tell you that I had made a mistake. I should never have walked out of that hotel room that night. I was wrong. Dead wrong, and I've been sorry for it ever since.

"I have a client who told me about the sunken treasure you found. I guess you're pretty famous now."

Why aren't you telling me you miss me? Why do I wish so much that you would? "Who is your client?" Lilli asked, trying to sound businesslike.

"That's not important. However, he is very interested in buying a jeweled dagger you found—"

"It's not for sale," Lilli said tersely.

"He's prepared to spend quite a bit, Lilli."

"Forget it," she found herself saying angrily. What was the matter with her? Why was she acting like this? Why did she want to hurt him when she had been the one who left him?

"Lilli, I'm coming to Houston to see that dagger," Zane replied emphatically.

"I'm . . . going to donate it to the Smithsonian."

"No, you're not. I checked you out, Lilli. You've got a reputation for donating damn near everything you uncover to museums and the Heye Foundation. Do you think it's good business to give away these artifacts? You sure aren't following in your father's footsteps when it comes to selling, are you? He sold everything he could find."

"I don't need you insulting my father. Just knock it off, Zane. I thought you wanted to buy this piece. You're not making this easy for yourself."

"Sorry. Old habit."

"One you need to break."

"I apologize for the crack about J.C. This piece is different, isn't it, Lilli? I know for a fact you've contacted several collectors about this dagger. I intend to put in a bid for my client."

"Fine. Do what you want," she grumbled, crossing her left arm over her chest.

"I'm coming to see you, Lilli," he said finally and hung up the phone.

Lilli sat on the floor listening to the sound of the dial tone, still not believing what had happened. Zane had called. He was flying to Houston. She would be seeing him about a business matter. But that was all. And that was the part that was killing her.

Lilli wanted to see Zane so badly she thought she would split right out of her skin. Zane, on the other hand, had been cool and professional. His research was accurate. He would come here and make his observations, submit his bid, and conclude his transaction; then he would go back to New York and forget about her all over again.

Unless . . .

"Unless I *do* something about it," Lilli said aloud. "But what?"

She drummed her fingers against her cheek and then glumly looked out the window at the billowing subtropical clouds. She was being a fool—again. Her world was poles apart from Zane's now. He'd been gone from Texas for a long, long time. They had both matured and had new, and undoubtedly different, experiences. Why, Zane could be married for all she knew. Thank God she hadn't brought that up! He would think she still cared for him.

No. Under no circumstances would she let Zane know that she'd spent even a single moment thinking about him. She had more pride to let that happen.

Zane ran down the concourse, glancing at his Piaget watch and then at his American Airlines ticket, which would take him from La Guardia Airport to Houston Intercontinental Airport. He was late and he hated being late, but he hated being early and being forced to waste time in an airport. His silk tie flew to the side as he sprinted down the concourse carrying his briefcase and overnight carry-on. He was unaware of the lustful glances he received from stewardesses and young, sleekly coiffed New York women as he dashed by, still not breaking a sweat. It had been a long time since Zane had ever looked at one of his admirers. He was looking forward to his future.

He dashed up to the desk, checked in, and immediately walked onto the plane. He found the aisle seat he'd requested so that he could get up and walk around easily during the flight, a necessity for Zane since his legs were long and had a tendency to stiffen up on him if he sat too long in one position. He stashed his carry-on bag under the seat in front of him, then hoisted his briefcase to his lap and pulled out his notes on both the emerald mine and the jeweled dagger that Cold Tap requested he purchase. He buckled his seat belt and began reading over his reports.

During the Spanish conquest of South America, enormous quantities of emeralds were taken from the Incas, but the exact origin of the stones was never discovered. Incan legends told of the source mines, yet at no time had archaeologists or geologists been able to define and locate the meaning of the "source."

Zane's study of the Colombian Andes Mountains revealed that the Cordillera Central showed ancient crystalline rock, from the Cambrian to the Carboniferous ages, that possessed an intrusion of heat-altered rock. But it was on the Colombian western branch where beds from the Cretaceous period were located.

He knew he would start on the western side.

Most of the mines were located around Chivon and Muzo, and also at Coscuez and Somondoco. The most commercial mines were at Bogotá, and although he would fly there, he would avoid bartering with any of the merchants.

Zane was looking for a bargain, and to find that, he would be forced to look for emeralds in remote places.

Over the years, he had traveled to some of the world's most remote places in search of gemstones, and the more he read about Cold Tap's project, the more fascinated he became. Finding the source mine, which had eluded the Spaniards five hundred years previously, would be like looking for a needle in a haystack. It could take a lifetime to piece together legends, fact, and these odd-looking photocopied maps that Cold Tap had found in museums and in private collections, Zane thought, but his curiosity had been piqued. Not since those first days in New York had he felt this kind of excitement. Life had become dull and routine for him lately. He'd been across the country buying and selling private jewelry collections a thousand times. European buying trips had become old hat. He saw few challenges in his business, other than simply making the next deal happen again. Zane hated to admit it, but his life had gone stale.

And yet here he was, hired on the whim of a rap singer, of all people, to embark upon possibly the most exciting phase of his life. Due to his client's outrageous tastes and desires, Zane would soon be face-to-face with Lilli and that part of his life he'd wanted to forget but never could. Zane wasn't sure what was going on in his life, but it was obvious to him that he was not driving this car, and all he could do was put on the brakes or hit the accelerator.

Zane chose to hit the gas.

Twenty-nine

Arlette Mitchell tapped her black-and-white Chanel pump against the Berber carpet in the attorney's office. Frank had kept her waiting for over fifteen minutes, and Arlette thought him rude. She liked being attended to promptly and at her convenience. After all, she thought, who did he think was paying him?

Finally the office door opened and Frank walked in. He had not aged a day since he'd read J.C.'s will, Arlette thought to herself, amazed. She wished she could say the same. Although she'd been able to squeak out enough money from Lilli's tight fist to have her eyes done two years ago, she was in desperate need of a full face-lift. But even that was not enough anymore to ward off Father Time. Her body was sagging like a pair of stretched-out pantyhose, and Arlette hated it.

"Arlette," Frank said and faked his best courtroom smile for her. "You're looking well. I saw the item in Maxine's column about you and Armando Scatelli. When's the wedding?"

"We haven't set a date." She smiled thinly.

"I see. What can I do for you today?" he asked, sitting down behind his desk.

"I want to know precisely why you've put off the second reading of J.C.'s will."

"I haven't put it off. I've simply been swamped with a long court trial. Didn't my secretary call you and tell you that I've set a date?"

"No, she didn't."

Frank flipped the pages on his calendar. "Yes. Here it is. On Tuesday."

"And Lilli knows this?"

"I'm certain of it. I have a note here that Lilli confirmed her schedule with the secretary. Anyway"—he smiled at Arlette's peevish face—"everything should be in order."

"What's in the will, Frank?" Arlette demanded as she approached his desk and leaned commandingly forward.

"I can't tell you that."

"Yes, you can."

Frank fought an acute desire to grab this creature by the elbow and usher her out of his office. Nothing would please him more. "I'm not interested in anything except J.C.'s wishes, Arlette. He was a good friend to me, besides being my client."

"Lilli's going to get it all, isn't she?"

"I can't say. However, she has done an admirable job of not only looking after the business but actually making it grow through some very tough times, times that J.C. could never have foreseen."

"And I, on the other hand, haven't done much to help."

"You said it, I didn't," he replied. There was something about this woman that brought out the worst in him.

"Frank . . ." Arlette glared at him.

"Sorry," he said flatly and then returned to his normal professional demeanor. "He wanted you to work together. It can be said you haven't stood in Lilli's way—exactly. However, I know that he wanted you to learn about business."

"I hate that kind of thing. And you and I both know I would have been a nuisance to Lilli. She did better without me around. Therefore, in my own way, I *was* helping her."

Frank nodded. "It's convoluted, but that could be said," he replied.

"So give me a hint about this addendum, if you can call it that."

"I'm not at liberty, Arlette, and you know that. Just be patient. I'm sure it will all work out to be the right thing for everyone concerned."

Arlette straightened up as she realized that Frank was not going to help her out. "What time on Tuesday?"

"One o'clock."

"Fine. I'll be here." She turned and started walking toward

the door. Without turning back toward him, she asked, "It's ironclad, Frank?"

"Ironclad, Arlette."

"There's no way I could assure myself of winning it all?"

Frank should not have been surprised. He was used to greedy relatives, but it always sickened him when he witnessed a mother pitted against her own child. For some reason, he was never shocked when children were grabbing for some old slob's dough, but surely the sanctity of motherhood should have played a role in this family matter. Sadly, there was nothing sacred to Arlette except money.

Frank shook his head. "The only thing that could throw a monkey wrench into this thing would be if Lilli weren't your daughter," he replied, wishing for Lilli's sake it were true.

Arlette walked to the door. "I'll see you Tuesday, Frank."

"Of course," he said, and she was gone.

Lilli saw the green-and-white cab pull up in front of New Antiquities and knew instantly that the passenger was Zane.

As she turned back to Kathryn Kimmons, her client, panic gripped her. She knew she should go to the door and greet Zane professionally, take him to the office, show him the goddamn dagger, and send him on his way. But she didn't.

She stood riveted to the spot, staring blankly into Kathryn's blue eyes.

"Are you all right, Lilli?" Kathryn asked.

Lilli's mind was swimming with the sound of the door opening, Zane's measured, careful steps across the wood floor. She could smell him as he approached . . . sandalwood, as always. She could feel his shadow engulf her as if it had physical properties of its own.

"Lilli." He breathed her name rather than spoke it. "I—I'd forgotten how beautiful you are," he said earnestly as he surveyed her gleaming, long black hair, her alabaster skin, and her eyes, those deep, sensual violet pools she turned on him.

Zane's heart skipped two beats.

Lilli could hardly breathe. Suddenly she wanted to run to him as she had when they were teenagers and throw her arms around him and tell him everything that was in her mind and heart. But she remained standing, staring at him.

Kathryn watched the intense exchange between the two.

"I'll talk to you later, Lilli," she said and left. Lilli hardly noticed.

She remembered her meeting with Zane in San Diego back in 1986. Outwardly, he'd seemed to have done well for himself, and she remembered the suit he'd worn then, similar to the one he now wore. But there was something else about this Zane. He seemed more peaceful. His eyes did not hold that heightened anxiety and insatiable anticipation she'd seen before. There was an inner serenity to him that she found comforting. He'd obviously come to grips with his life, found satisfaction in his career. Perhaps, like her, he'd discovered self-satisfaction in his achievements. She certainly had. She liked the extra time she now had for her adventures. And she took great pride in all she had accomplished.

They had both grown up and it was good.

He'd been gone from her life for over a decade. She had loved him unconditionally. She thought of him often, but she had to wonder, Did she still love him the way she once had?

Lilli dropped her eyes. "Thank you," she said simply. Then she raised her head and looked at him. "You are more handsome than ever. New York has been good to you."

"Yes, it has," he said with a tinge of trepidation. But not as good as it could have been if you'd been there with me along the way.

Zane tore his eyes from Lilli's heart-stoppingly beautiful face. She was a treasure he'd not understood how to own. He could admire her like an old master's painting in a museum, but could he have her? Could he touch her? Touch her soul? His fears caused him to panic. He glanced at his watch. "I—I'm really pressed for time. The dagger . . . ?"

Lilli was so lost in thought that she nearly didn't hear him. "Huh?" Then her head snapped to attention. "The dagger. Of course. It's in the vault in my office. Right this way," she said with the professionalism that had kept the best clients in Houston coming back again and again.

Zane bristled at her crisp, cold tones. He felt the door to his heart closing against his will. He followed her past old-world chairs upholstered in deep, rich burgundy brocades and gold-fringed cream damask footstools and reproduction Flemish end tables and gilded wall sconces. He was pleased at the keen eye Lilli had developed for blending expensive antiques with new china, silver, picture frames, and accessories. Everywhere he looked he saw a steely eye for profit and an incredible sense of marketing. Every silk flower, every bookend and lamp was displayed to its full potential. These vignettes were designed by a master artist and it amazed him to realize that Lilli had done all this herself. She had far surpassed J.C.'s accomplishments at the store, and to top it all, she had stumbled onto an incredible treasure in the Caribbean, again eclipsing her father's success. She was an amazing woman, his Lilli.

No, he corrected himself. Just Lilli. She wasn't his anymore.

Lilli liked the feeling of Zane's presence. She remembered too sweetly the delicious sense of warmth she felt in the past whenever she was with him. She remembered thinking that when she was with Zane, somehow dreams would come true. She wanted to dream those dreams again, but her adult mind told her that she'd been wise to put away childish things. However, there was an aching void in her life, and for years she had ignored its presence. Without Zane, without his love, life was off kilter for Lilli. In those few breathless, awkward moments, Lilli had been suspended above herself where she could view her life as the angels did, and she found that she had been so very, very blind the day she'd left Zane.

How complicated life was, she thought.

In youth, choices seemed so obvious. To love or not was simple. Maturity had taught her that often love was not enough. Her fierce loyalty to her father had forced choices upon her at a very young age. She might never know if she'd been wise or foolish to remain in Houston and build New Antiquities. Her accomplishments had given her self-esteem she might never have gained had she chosen to marry Zane and simply be his wife. Although she had once criticized him for his overriding ambition, she realized that her ambition matched his. She was not the kind of woman who was content to live her life through a man. She had always wanted to slice off life in big portions and savor them. Zane was the same, and perhaps now it was that quality in him that could be their bond.

Lilli walked around her desk and crouched in front of the safe. She twisted the combination lock and then placed her hand on the lever and opened the door. She wanted to prolong this transaction, but she couldn't think how. She wanted to talk to Zane and get to know him as the man he was now. Even if he didn't want her, she wanted to spend time with him.

Carefully, she took out the cloth bag that held the Spanish dagger. She took her time as she placed the bag on the desk, opened it, and removed the treasure. Then she stood back and let Zane make his examination.

He reached in his pocket and withdrew his jeweler's loupe. He inspected every stone, their facets and color. He examined the gold, the still razor-sharpness of the edges of the dagger, and its balance.

Lilli had seen many dealers and experts over the years. She knew all the tricks they used to wrangle a lower price. Lilli had bargained with the best of them. She was ready for Zane when he turned to face her.

"It's an exquisite piece," he said appreciatively.

"It's the best of the lot."

"Are there others?"

"There were. I've sold nearly everything, but there is nothing else of this quality."

"I see," he mused, looking down at the dagger.

"You can see that the jewels are authentic. The rubies are Indian . . ."

"Without a doubt," he said. "I've not seen any better, even in Sri Lanka."

"Nor I," she replied and noted an almost imperceptible twitch of his right eyebrow. She remembered that indicator—it meant that Zane was impressed with her knowledge. She hadn't known he'd been to Sri Lanka. Where else had he been? Whom had he met? How much had he changed since he'd left Texas? Was there any of the old Zane left? She wanted to know. She had to know. She couldn't go through the rest of her life wondering . . . always wondering.

"I'll give you ten thousand."

Lilli shook her head. "I'm sure you would. Thirty."

"Fifteen."

"Twenty-five."

"Eighteen and not a penny more."

Lilli smiled. She had him. "How about nineteen, and drinks tonight are on me."

Zane's eyebrows rose in surprise. "Deal."

Lilli's smile was dazzling as she looked at him. "I'll draw up the paperwork immediately."

The Post Oak Ranch on the east side of the 610 Loop near the Galleria was the glitziest country/Western bar in Houston since Elan in the late seventies. Even on a Tuesday night, white stretch limousines wound through the maze of oak trees spun with crystal lights and deposited celebrities, wealthy post-Yuppie investment bankers, computer wizards, and aging jet-setters at the front door. The crowd was upscale and bore no resemblance to the cowboys and rodeo crowds that frequented the ice houses and honky-tonks around town. The women were dressed in chic leather dresses and fringed suede jackets that were sold in Galleria shops. The men wore custom, one-of-a-kind Western shirts and Western suits designed for city dwellers who liked to pretend they were cowboys. The Post Oak Ranch was for grown-ups in costume.

Lilli did not change clothes before meeting Zane at the bar. She had the shop to close, paperwork to finalize, and two faxes that needed attention. The early-evening crowd was still dressed in business attire, and she felt at ease in her surroundings. She was smiling when she walked up to him.

He took her hand and led her to a high table at the side of the bar. "I'm really pleased with my purchase today and so is my client. I just got off the phone with him. He is so anxious to see the dagger he said he would meet me at JFK."

"He thought you got it at a good price, then?" she asked, sitting on a high bar chair.

"Yes, he did," Zane said, sitting on a chair beside her. He was surprised at this queer feeling of triumph over Lilli, as if he'd needed some reassurance as to his prowess in the marketplace. Or perhaps it was his own need to prove himself to her. God knew that he was attracted to her more than he'd ever been to any woman. Even now, dressed as she was in her business suit, he was aware of her long slender legs and the fact that she had unbuttoned the top two buttons of her blouse and replaced her gold button earrings with a pair of antique silver shoulder dusters.

God help me, he thought. I want her. Badly.

Nervous, Zane ran his tongue over his lips.

Lilli's eyes followed the movement of his tongue. She remembered all too well the times, the thousand and one times, he'd kissed her. She knew the taste of his tongue, and the way he could drive her out of her mind with his teeth, tongue, and lips. She uncrossed her legs and then recrossed them.

"How do you like this place?" she asked finally, tearing her mind from the seductive fantasy she'd begun to weave. They were friends now and that was all.

"It's okay."

"That's all? I've only been here once. It reminded me of what a country/Western bar would be like in New York. That's why I chose it. I thought it would remind you of home."

"You remind me of home," he said. *You are my home. Texas is my home, and I never thought so much about it as I have since the minute I saw you today.*

"Tell me about your life in New York, Zane. I haven't seen you since San Diego. Are you still happy there?"

A waitress came to the table to take their order.

"I'll have a Corona in the bottle, with two limes," Lilli said, not waiting for Zane to place his order first.

"The same," Zane said.

After the waitress left, Lilli turned her eyes back to Zane. "Well?"

"It's exciting. There's no place like New York. I like the adventure. I like pitting myself against experts who are twice my age and have ten times the knowledge and experience. I can learn from them."

"And you couldn't learn from anyone here?" Lilli blurted out and then quickly bit her tongue.

His eyes mellowed. "I learned a great deal from your father. And from you."

"I learned . . . from you."

You learned how to love just like I did, he thought. "Thank you for that," he said softly as the music began. It was one of those lovesick country ballads that always sounded sappy to someone who'd never lost his heart, but to those who knew the experience firsthand, it was unbearably sad.

"I used to hope—I mean, this was a long time ago—that maybe you might need to call me ... about business, I mean," she said.

The Coronas arrived.

Lilli grabbed the long-necked bottle and took two swallows of ice-cold beer. Her mouth had suddenly gone very dry. She jammed the lime slices into the neck of the bottle with a vengeance. *Jesus! I'm so stupid! Why can't I say what I feel? What's wrong with me? Why did I ever come here?*

Zane watched Lilli wrap her lips around the beer bottle and remembered how he'd teased her when they were young that he would teach her to do that to him. She'd laughed at him, punched him in the arm, and they'd tussled and tossed and made love.

Made love.

Sadness and remorse flooded Zane as he looked at the woman he would always love.

"What's the matter?" Lilli asked.

"Nothing," he said quickly and took a long swallow of his beer.

"You look as if you lost your best friend."

His eyes were smoldering when he looked at her. "I did lose my best friend. A long time ago."

Lilli felt her heart hammering and her ears buzzing. *He was here, sitting right next to her, and she was acting as if he were no more than one of her regular customers. She had spent so many sleepless nights dreaming about Zane, she'd probably lost three years off her life span. She had stubbornly refused to commit herself to any other relationship because Zane had cast such a great shadow over her life that no other man could measure up. She should be telling him what was in her heart, but instead, she was pushing him away. She was shocked at the impersonal tones she used with him. She wanted him to take her in his arms and kiss her, and yet she kept presenting him with her ice-maiden mask. What was the matter with her?*

Zane wanted to reach out and touch her hand. He hadn't so much as placed a hand on her back or touched her sleeve. And yet that was all he could think about. *Maybe he should take a chance. And maybe he should tell her how he felt ... once and for all.*

"Lilli." He sighed with trepidation. He swallowed hard and pressed on. It was now or never, he told himself. "God, Lilli, how I've missed you."

Tears pricked Lilli's eyes. I can't let him see me cry. Her only defense was to bring the subject back to business. "You never told me the name of your client. I think I have a right to know who bought my dagger."

Zane's eyes were focused on Lilli's mouth. Jesus! He wanted her. He wanted to pound some sense into his stubborn Lilli. He wanted to kiss her, to crush her mouth to his with such a force that she would be permanently attached to him.

"I'm not allowed to reveal his name."

Emotions long put away overwhelmed Zane, and he could no longer think. He could only feel.

He reached across the table, placed his hand around Lilli's nape, and forcefully drew her face toward his. Like an eagle swooping down from the sky, Zane's mouth captured Lilli's lips and carried her away. His lips were insistent as they forced her to respond to him. He pushed her to the limit of her emotions and pried open her heart just as he willed her to open her mouth to him. His tongue darted into her mouth, seeking refuge.

His kiss was a thousand times more intense, more emotional, and more stirring than anything Lilli had remembered from their childhood together. This was a man's need for a woman. He licked the sides of her mouth and sent rolling waves of chills across her abdomen. She felt her insides grow hot and moist. For the first time in eleven years, she wanted to love again. She wanted to be filled with him, to feel the exquisite sensation of being stretched with the full length of him. She wanted to know that wherever she looked, all she could see was Zane.

Her blood raced, her body temperature soared, and suddenly the room was too small, the air too cloying, the people too curious. "Zane, please don't . . ."

"Why not? There . . . isn't someone else, is there?"

"No. No one."

"Not for me, either."

Lilli was breathless after the kiss. "There's never been anyone but you . . . for me."

"Then why can't we—?"

"Oh, Zane. It was so long ago," she interrupted. "We were children." She was trying to remain calm, but she felt that every nerve ending in her body had been awakened.

"Was it too long ago, Lilli?" He had to know. Suddenly he could see the rest of his days stretching out before him like a long, dark tunnel. Perhaps he should get up, walk away, and leave the pain behind. But he didn't. He remained rooted to his chair. He was making a great many changes in his life, especially with his new business. It was a building time, a time of new beginnings. For so long he'd lacked the courage to step out on a limb concerning many aspects of his life. Not until now had he felt enough self-confidence to start his own business. How odd that his feelings about Lilli coincided with the other changes he was making. Maybe it was time he let go of his fears and really moved forward with his life.

Her eyes were filled with anticipation when she looked at him. "Not to me it wasn't. Sometimes it seems like only yesterday."

Zane's heart lifted. "It's like that for me, too. It's just that I thought you were out of my life for good."

"So did I. But somehow you keep coming back."

"I know we can't start over. But we could start again."

"Do you want that?"

"Yes, I do."

Lilli's smile was as tentative as her trust. "So much has happened to us, individually, I mean. We're like strangers."

"In some ways we are. In other ways we could never be strangers," he said. "Ask me anything, Lilli. I'll tell you everything you want to know."

Lilli laughed lightly. "Maybe I'd better not know everything."

He laughed with her. "Maybe not."

"You've told me about your career, but what about you, Zane? What all do you want from life at this point?"

He glanced down at the beer bottle and began peeling away the label. "It's funny you should ask that," he said at last. "I have been making changes. I guess you could say I've rethought just about every facet of my life. For the longest time I thought I could only make it big in my business as long as I was in New York. But you know, things are changing. Between computers, faxes, and the fact that my clients are all over the world, I realized not long ago, that I don't actually spend that much time in New York."

"Where do you spend your time?"

"On American Airlines." He laughed and sipped his beer. "And you know what, Lilli? I'm getting tired of the rat race."

"I thought it was the fast lane."

He shook his head. "That, too. Five years ago I accepted every Christmas invitation I could for skiing in Vail or St. Moritz. I went to Barbados for Easter and Vermont for Thanksgiving. But the past year, year and a half, I've spent my holidays in Bandera with Mom."

Lilli's heart skipped a beat at the thought that he had been in Texas, that he seemed to be getting back to his roots.

"How's she doing?" Lilli asked, still trying to keep their conversation casual.

"Much better. They've made some tremendous strides in bipolar disease, which is what they call manic depression, and with the new medications she's on, she's happier than she's ever been. They also found that her thyroid was out of whack, and she's on Thyroxin."

"Zane, you must feel wonderful about this. To know that all those horrible outbursts of hers when we were kids were not our fault. She was sick, that's all."

His smile was compassionate. "I never knew you felt guilty about those times, too."

"I did."

"I'm sorry I put you through that," he said, thinking of the night his mother had gone into a rage finding him and Lilli together. The night he'd decided to leave Texas.

"It's okay. It wasn't your fault. It wasn't anybody's fault. It was the way things happened. It was painful for us both, but maybe it was the way things were supposed to be."

"Did you ever think, Lilli, that our timing was off?"

"Yes, I did. I have—many times."

Lilli looked at this handsome man. At times, from a certain angle, she could see the boy in the man. They weren't strangers after all, she thought. Part of him was still the boy she had known, and part of her was still the girl he had known.

As Zane talked about his mother and the things he'd done around his mother's house to fix it up for her, Lilli felt her hope being renewed. Maybe they could come back together somehow. Maybe they were meant to be together after all. Maybe their timing was finally right.

He was smiling when he asked her, "Could I take you to lunch tomorrow, Lilli?"

"I have an appointment at my attorney's tomorrow."

"For what?"

"My father's will."

Zane felt fear slice through his heart. She had chosen her father and his dreams over him once before. To be fair, he'd chosen his own self-serving ways. The adult Zane knew that he would have to eradicate his own fears before he could even hope to have a life with Lilli. There was no time like the present.

"The meeting can't take all day," he said.

"When it comes to a confrontation with my mother, it could take all month. When do you fly out?"

"I have a reservation on the five o'clock flight."

"Damn." Lilli looked away and then quickly looked back at him. "Do you really want to see me again?"

"Yes, I do. We have a lot to talk about. It's just that I've got to get this dagger back to New York. My client—"

Lilli held up her hand, a good-natured smile on her face. "Hey, don't worry about it. We're both professionals. You've got a full calendar. So do I."

"I'll call you, Lilli. I think we need to talk."

"So do I, Zane."

"C'mon. I'll walk you to your car."

Zane paid the tab and walked Lilli to her car. He wanted desperately to kiss her and fulfill the sexual fantasies he'd been playing in his mind all night. Instead, he brushed his lips against her cheek, inhaling the scent of lilies. "Good night, Lilli, and good luck tomorrow."

"Thanks," she replied and clung overly long to his hand. She wanted to remember the touch of his skin and the golden flecks in his blue eyes.

"I'll call you," he said as she got into her car.

"I hope so," she answered and closed the door. As she drove away, she glanced in her rearview mirror and noticed that he was still watching her as she entered the traffic.

* * *

Lilli awoke from a deep sleep to the ringing telephone.

"Lilli?"

"Zane?"

"Were you asleep?"

"Yes. What time is it?"

"Three in the morning."

"My God." She sat up in bed. "Weren't you asleep?"

"No."

"Is something the matter?"

"Yes."

"What?"

"Lilli, I still love you. I've been afraid to tell you that for a long time. I just wanted you to know."

"I've always loved you, Zane. But I'm scared that we'll hurt each other again."

"Me, too."

"So now what?"

"I've got to think about this. But I just had to ask you how you felt exactly."

"Zane, my mind is freewheeling. We do need to talk. But you're leaving for New York tomorrow."

"So? I can be back in Texas within a week."

"You're serious?"

"Yes. I always believed we had something special. Something bigger than ourselves. I think I've tried to fight it all these years, but fate or something keeps bringing me back to you. We need to spend more time together."

"I agree."

"Great. I'll call you tomorrow night from New York to make arrangements. And, Lilli . . ."

"Yes, Zane?"

"I do love you."

Happiness curved the edges of Lilli's mouth upward. "I love you."

It was six in the morning when the telephone rang, awakening Lilli for the second time that night. She thought it was the alarm clock and slapped the snooze button on the radio alarm. The telephone rang again.

"Hello?"

"Lilli? It's me, Zane."

"I thought you were going to call me from New York."

"I couldn't wait. Look, I've got to drive out to Bandera and see my mom before I fly out. I won't get another chance to call you today. I just wanted you to know that I feel really good about this. I feel like we're off to a good start."

"I hope so," she said tentatively.

"You don't sound so sure anymore."

"I'm afraid. Aren't you afraid?"

"Yes. But you know, I've been thinking about it. All night, actually, and the way I figure it is this. We've only got so much allotted time on this earth and I've wasted quite a bit of it living without you. So, with the time remaining, however long that is, I've decided I should spend it with you. Now, I've been living with fears and doubts for a long time and it hasn't paid off all that well. My options are to stay with the status quo or to change. I think I like the adventure of the change."

"Adventure? You?"

"Yeah. I've been to a lot of places in the past decade, don't you remember me telling you?"

Of course Lilli remembered their conversation in the Post Oak Ranch! "Yes."

"I have to run, Lilli. Just remember that I love you."

"I'll remember," Lilli answered, hoping that this time her dreams would come true.

Thirty

*O*ver the years, deceit had become an ally of Arlette's. She had lied to all of Houston and her family about her background for so long that her lies had become her truth. Today Arlette was about to embark upon her most elaborate and important lie of all. Her plans had been carefully laid, and because they were based partly on the truth, her plan could not fail.

Lilli arrived at Frank's office twenty minutes ahead of schedule, but used the time to make necessary business calls. The truth of the matter was that since Zane's departure that morning, she hadn't been able to keep a single constant thought in her head. Even the scribbles in her Daytimer, rather than her normal precise listing of daily duties, bore testimony to her confusion.

I want him more than anything, and yet I always manage to screw things up. God! Life used to be so simple—I think. Maybe it was always this complicated and I was just too dumb to know any better. I've got to get my life straightened out or otherwise I won't have any life.

Lilli had just hung up Frank's phone when the door to the office opened. It was her aunt Vicki and Faith, and Lilli walked over to them and greeted them with warm hugs. "I'm so glad you're here."

"We're always with you," Faith said lovingly. "That's what families are for."

Just then Arlette entered the room dressed in a new black-and-white-houndstooth Chanel suit. Lilli knew this was her fourth new suit in less than a year. Where was she getting the money for this stuff? The black Chanel handbag retailed at Neiman's for over seven hundred dollars. The shoes were over two hundred. Lilli chastised herself for not going over her mother's charge accounts in the past four months or so. She knew better than to let anything to do with money slide when it came to Arlette.

"Great suit, Mom. You get that on sale? I hope."

"I was lucky to get it the day it came in," Arlette replied triumphantly as she sat in one of the chairs facing the desk.

Lilli groaned as she sat in another chair. "I was afraid of that." Two grand, she thought. Easy.

"Don't fret, dear. Armando bought it for me."

"He's not coming here, is he?" Lilli would not put it past her mother to have the bad taste of trotting her newest beau in front of the family.

"Of course not. He's waiting for me in the reception room." Arlette raised her chin haughtily.

"Good thinking," Lilli said.

"Don't you act high-and-mighty with me. I'm still your mother."

Lilli turned hard eyes on Arlette. "A fact of life I'd like to forget. You fail to realize that I'm the one who has worked like a dog for the past eleven years putting those designer clothes on your back while you haven't lifted a finger to help me."

"The hell I haven't. Everything I've done has been for you."

Lilli put her fists on her hips. "When I had to move Antiquities and I needed your help wrapping furniture and paintings, you declined. You could have helped me clean, paint the walls, and restock, but you were always too busy. You never showed up except to point out to me what you felt should have been done. If I ever made a mistake, I heard about it."

"It's just like you, Lilli, to bring up something that happened years ago. You've never learned to live in the present. The day you moved I had a luncheon. My meetings are important for our social connections. Your father always told me that. I thought we were sticking together."

As she stared at her mother and heard the same words that Arlette had used for eleven years, Lilli was suddenly painfully aware of how her mother had manipulated her over the years and how she had allowed herself to be manipulated. Her loyalty to and love for her father's memory had enslaved her to her mother's greed and selfishness. Lilli had wanted a loving mother, just like everyone else, but she now realized that Arlette had never provided that kind of nurturing for her, and never would. Lilli felt she was more closely bonded with her aunt than she would ever be with her mother. For years Lilli had wanted to change her mother, to hide her faults and deny her malicious behavior. Everyone else saw the devilishness inside Arlette. Now Lilli was fully conscious of it, was finally able to admit it to herself, and it sickened her.

"For a long time I thought that nothing I have ever done has pleased you. But now I realized that nothing you've done has pleased me." Lilli could hardly believe she was saying these words to her mother.

Arlette's expression was brittle: "You call that little shop a success? It's nothing. You're nothing but a shopkeeper, Lilli. You've hovered on the edge of bankruptcy for years. One wrong move and poof! You're out of business. You haven't got what it takes."

Vicki, who was sitting on the other side of Lilli, put her hand on her niece in a protective gesture.

Lilli squeezed her aunt's hand but kept her eyes riveted on her mother. "I have exactly what I need, Mother. I have a family . . . only you're not it."

Lilli was disgusted with herself for having always run from her confrontations with her mother, just as she'd run from Zane. How was it that she was fearless when it came to business and risk-taking with her store, not to mention braving Guatemalan jungles, Mayan ruins, and even ghostly Aztec burial grounds, where it was said that evil spirits lurked behind every rock and tree, and yet in her personal relationships she had been the original gutless wonder? She liked this newfound feeling of strength and she was quietly elated to see Arlette back off.

Frank had entered the office during the heated exchange. Although he didn't say a word, Lilli couldn't miss the admiration in his eyes as he sat down behind his desk and looked at her.

He began opening various folders and as he did so, Lilli noticed that among the legal papers were photographs, topographical maps, road maps, and directions drawn in J.C.'s hand. All thoughts of her problems with Zane and her mother fled. Her natural curiosity urged her to sit more erect in her chair. This was not going to be a normal will reading. Something very unusual was going on here, and knowing her father the way she had, she expected it would be just like J.C. to make this, his final message, interesting as hell.

"Ladies." Frank nodded solemnly. "Let me assure you all from the very outset that J.C.'s wishes have been carried out to the letter insofar as this office is concerned. Everything I am about to discuss with you may sound strange, but it is all perfectly legal. Let me inform you, Lilli and Arlette, that you always have the right to contest this will. However, J.C. not only sought my advice on this matter, but he also had one of the state supreme court justices give him an opinion. J.C. knew for two years that he was dying. His plans were carefully laid and he sought expert advice in many areas. I have a notarized affidavit here." He paused and handed them the document for their perusal. "And as you can see, everything is according to the letter of the law."

Arlette frowned. "Just how bizarre is this going to be, Frank?"

Frank smiled wryly. "Very."

"That's my pop!" Lilli said proudly.

Arlette groaned, then moved to the edge of her chair. "I understand how tidy J.C. could be about details, especially when it came to something he wanted. But he didn't know everything," she said bitterly and pointedly to her daughter.

The force of her mother's hatred nearly knocked Lilli off her seat. She would never understand her. For some reason, Arlette believed that J.C. had "owed" her more than she had ever received. Her mother had been bristling under the confines of J.C.'s first will for eleven years, and it was killing her.

Arlette must have been hurt terribly by someone or something in her childhood, Lilli thought, and that trauma had done much to create the unhappy person she was today. But lots of people suffered just as much in their lives and they did not allow misfortune to twist their minds and close off their hearts. No, her mother had chosen her path of vindictiveness and selfishness. It was hard for Lilli to realize that her own mother was jealous of her, but that was the truth of it. She had known it for a long time and she had trusted in time to heal her mother, but the opposite had happened. All Lilli's efforts to make her mother happy had been in vain.

Arlette sat next to Lilli with vengeance on her mind, and Lilli could feel it. It sickened her.

Lilli flinched reflexively. An atomic explosion was tame compared with her mother when she didn't get her way. They were all in for a long and volatile afternoon.

"First, I must ask Vicki something."

"Yes, Frank?" Vicki replied, rather surprised that he would address her first.

"The twenty thousand that J.C. left you. What did you do with it?"

Vicki shrugged her shoulders. "I did what J.C. requested. I let Bart Jensen invest it for me."

"So did I," Faith chimed in. "According to my statements, my five thousand is now worth over sixty thousand dollars. Of course, since it was doing so well, I added some to my original investment."

Arlette's eyes widened, and she whirled around in her chair to face her niece and sister-in-law. "I don't believe it."

"Well, it's true." Vicki backed up Faith's statement. "I'm not going to tell you what my account is up to, but I did the same as Faith and added to the account." Vicki's eyes narrowed. "I don't know why you're interested in our savings, Arlette. You'd only have spent the money if J.C. had left it to you."

Arlette's cheeks flamed with anger. "Why, you—"

Frank didn't waste a second jumping into the middle of the fracas. "Arlette, you'll be glad to know that J.C. *did* leave you money, which was also invested by Bart Jensen. J.C. made a very wise choice. Because of Mr. Jensen's astute investments, there is now over one million dollars in that account."

"One million!" Arlette's face radiated pure joy.

"A million?" Lilli was breathless, thinking how that kind of money would keep her mother off her back for a long, long time. It was an answer to a prayer. "Why didn't we know about this before?"

"At the time, I'm sure J.C. had no idea it would do that well, since his investment was under two hundred thousand. I want to point out that the capital gains distribution and the dividends were always reinvested. This was part of J.C.'s plan. He had his reasons for doing so, which I will go into shortly."

"A million dollars! What I could do with that money . . ." Arlette's mouth was watering, and Lilli was shocked when she saw her mother literally lick her lips.

She turned her head away from her mother and back to Frank. "Why do I get the idea that there's a catch to all of this?"

Frank's smile was wry as he looked from Arlette to Lilli. "Because there is a catch. In fact, there are several." He shrugged his shoulders. "J.C. was always the adventurer."

"Shit," Arlette grumbled under her breath.

Vicki was quick on the uptake. "What did you say, dear?" She directed her question to Arlette.

Arlette clamped her mouth shut and slumped back in her chair like a petulant child.

Frank kept his tone professional as he went back to the papers in front of him. "Even though J.C. could not know the performance of the fund, he did believe that a tidy sum of money would materialize over the years. That money is to be awarded to Lilli—"

"To Lilli!? What about me?!" Arlette nearly screamed.

"Please let me finish, Mrs. Mitchell," Frank said politely. It is to be awarded to her upon completing a mission for him."

"Mission? What kind of mission?" Arlette demanded.

Frank scowled at Arlette this time. "Lilli, if you accept this challenge—it's up to you, remember—all the money is yours. If you decide not to go, the money will be awarded to your mother. You will then keep the store and all its profits and not have to share any of the fruits of your hard work with Arlette. She will be well taken care of with this money. It will be dispensed by this office on a monthly basis so that Arlette will never again be a problem to you."

Arlette was incensed. "Now see here, Frank! I am a grown woman and I know very well how to handle money."

"Sure!" Vicki couldn't help retorting. "You use a sieve with a large hole in the middle."

"Shut up!" Arlette hissed. Her face was flushed and her hands were shaking. She wanted that money, every penny of it, and she was damned if she'd let Lilli get hold of it. She was sick and tired of people running her life and telling her what to do. She was sick of her daughter dispensing tiny sums of money during the year, like some miser, and then waiting until the end of the year before dispensing any real money. It came to her like manna from heaven, those year-end profits. Arlette lived for the year-end audits when the accountants would expound upon Lilli's success and then beg her to leave enough money for Lilli to keep the business going and place her orders for the New Year. Arlette hated giving back part of the money to that stupid store. She hated knowing that Lilli had so much power over her. It wasn't right, damn it. It just wasn't the way things were supposed to have turned out.

Arlette had been angry at J.C. all her life. He'd never made the kind of money she thought he should have made. He always spent too much on those damn digs of his. He'd left her at home while he romped all over Central America with his precious daughter. And now Lilli had won out again, and it infuriated Arlette.

It was time for Arlette to get even with J.C. and Lilli. It was time, all right. After she brought Lilli down a peg or two and showed J.C. he couldn't remain immortal by running her life from the grave, she would prove to them who had the real power in this family. Yes, she thought, it was about time to settle a few scores.

Arlette nearly opened her mouth and then thought better of it. Let them play their hand first. J.C. thought he'd been so clever working out the details of his will. Well, not clear enough, she thought.

"What I would like to know, Frank," Lilli asked, "was why my father took away all his books and files and had them sealed up. This has bothered me for years. It doesn't make sense. I wouldn't have thrown his things away."

"I'm sure you wouldn't have, Lilli, but the truth of the matter was, he was guarding many things by locking away those files."

"Such as?"

Frank took a long swallow. "This is going to be difficult for you, Lilli, as attached to him as you were, but your father ... I'm afraid that many of his colleagues considered him to be an opportunist. He took artifacts and sold them on the black market. Some people might call him a thief, although I wouldn't. The laws about that kind of thing were more lax back then. Times are changing."

"My brother was no thief!" Vicki shot to her feet.

"This is such bullshit!" Lilli exclaimed.

Arlette remained silent. This was perfect. Just too utterly perfect. She'd waited a long time to give Lilli a jolt. Now she didn't have to do anything. J.C. had done it himself. Ah, revenge! It truly was sweet.

"When you were young," Frank explained, "your father took you on many illegal digs. Back then, it wasn't exactly kosher, but he wasn't the only one doing it. These days it's nearly impossible to molest those sites. The Mayan treasures are now considered to be some of the world's most important artifacts. Back then, most of the world hadn't even heard about the Maya. In any event, your father's reputation became tarnished because of his earlier exploits. In the two years before his death, he formally presented his theories and findings to the foremost experts in anthropology and archaeology. He struggled to create a good name for himself, but few people in the academic world would give him a second look, and they certainly didn't want him on a dig."

Lilli remembered their trip to Guatemala and the archaeologists she'd met. She remembered their hushed voices around the campfire when she or J.C. would approach. She remembered how she and her father were treated with disdain and skepticism for a long while, at least until they got to know her. But she was the one they warmed up to, not her father. Now Lilli knew why.

It broke Lilli's heart to know that her father had not enjoyed the respect and admiration of his peers. She had made him into a god when he was nothing of the kind. He wasn't a bad man, she knew. But the things he'd done were wrong. Whether in the name of adventure, commercialism, or even exploration, J.C. Mitchell might have been responsible for removing some extremely valuable pieces of history that could possibly help the world.

"I wish I could make it all up," Lilli said mournfully, looking down at her clenched hands.

"You can," Frank replied.

Lilli's head sprang up and her eyes were wide. "How?"

"That's where I was leading with all this. J.C.'s maps that he had me lock away should lead to the greatest treasure of all. He spent every living minute of his last two years in pursuit of this treasure."

Arlette's greed seemed to settle in every tight corner of her face. "What . . . treasure could be so great?"

"Many times J.C. spoke to me about the city of gold . . ."

"Oh, God," Lilli moaned and passed her hand over her face. "Not that fairy tale again. Everybody knows there is no such thing. The Spaniards made up that story so that more Spaniards would buy land in the New World and come to colonize it. It was a real-estate scam, for God's sake!"

"Let me finish," Frank replied. "That particular story is a fake. However, here is a translation from an Incan text in stone, found in the Andes in Colombia, that tells of rivers of gold high in the mountains."

He handed Lilli a typed sheet with the University of Pennsylvania's letterhead at the top. The translation was there and it sounded accurate and quite feasible. She handed it back to Frank. "That makes sense to me. Gold was found in mountain streams near San Francisco over a hundred years ago. Panning for gold is common. If the natives found gold in the streams, then they might call it rivers of gold."

"J.C. thought it was more than that."

"Like what?"

"I don't know. That's what he wants you to find out. Here, let me read this last section of the will, which is nearly like a letter to you, Lilli." Frank paused and found his place. "If I know my daughter, by this time you will have made a name for yourself in Houston with our store. In fact, it's my bet you've got lots of respect, kiddo. Maybe more respect than I could ever hope to have. Because of that, it is important to me that you go to Colombia, and using the map I've drawn by piecing together legend and facts, maybe you can find those rivers of gold for me. If you do, the academic world, even old Dr. Rubenthal, will sanction your discovery. You'll be famous, Lilli. You'll have helped the world in a way you never dreamed possible. I believe in you, Lilli. I know you can do this. It's just one last dig—for me. I hope that you will vindicate my name for me. I could not do it on my own."

Lilli's eyes were filled with tears. Her mind spun her back to Guatemala. She remembered confronting J.C. about his fascination over South America. He'd talked about going there many times, but he would never say why he was drawn there. She'd felt he was onto something ... something big, but he'd always denied it. Her intuition had been right.

Lilli wasn't sure about rivers of gold or what she would find, but she knew her father would never ask her to do something that he didn't believe in. His heart had known what he wanted. And for Lilli, that was good enough.

"So"—Frank looked at Lilli with expectation—"will you do it?"

"For Pop? Sure."

Frank beamed. "Good. I knew you'd say yes."

Arlette squirmed in her chair. "Let me get this straight. If Lilli goes to South America and finds this cockamamy city of gold—"

"Rivers of gold, Mother," Lilli interjected.

"Whatever. Then she gets not only the gold she finds but the million besides?"

Frank started to answer, but Lilli held up her hand to stop him. "No, Mother. The government of Colombia keeps the gold. Maybe I could bring you a nugget or something. I'll bring back something more precious than gold, though. I'll be bringing back Pop's dignity. That's worth millions to me."

Arlette ground her teeth. It's time. It's time. "Well, I'm not so sure about all that. His dignity. His reputation. Ha!"

Vicki and Faith bristled simultaneously and glared at Arlette.

Arlette turned a pair of cold and calculating eyes on Frank. "Are you finished, Frank?"

Taken aback, he replied, "Yes, except for the dispensing of the materials Lilli will need for her expedition."

"She won't need any of that."

"What?" Lilli turned incredulous eyes on her mother. As she looked into Arlette's granite eyes and hardened face, she shuddered to think that this was the woman who had given birth to her. She wondered sadly if Arlette had ever, even for a second, had any feelings for her daughter.

Arlette reached into her purse and pulled out a stack of letters, bound neatly with a yellow ribbon. "I want you to take a look at these, Frank." She handed the bundle to the attorney. "It distressed me to bring this out into the open now after so many years of keeping the secret. I've spent many a sleepless night before coming to this conclusion. I know the truth will hurt not only Lilli but Vicki, too. I didn't want to hurt them . . . the shame and all."

Arlette hung her head in an overly dramatic gesture as the shocked group watched her every movement. "I want you all to know I would never do anything to malign J.C.'s good name. After all, he was my husband. His name is mine. And, too, I didn't want any of you to think badly of me. But after you know the truth, you will." She paused and took a tissue from her purse and dabbed at dry eyes. "I know Lilli hates me. She always has. So has Vicki. But I wanted us to be a family. However, after Frank reads these, he'll realize, as will you, that we were never really a family."

Frank pulled letter after letter out of one envelope after another.

"What are they?" Lilli demanded impatiently.

"Love letters." Frank continued reading.

Lilli was genuinely confused. "What the hell do they have to do with rivers of gold and trips to Colombia?"

Frank checked the canceled dates on each of the envelopes and the signatures on the bottom of the pages. "Who is Jack?"

"Jack Rabineaux from Louisiana."

"I never heard of him."

"He was my sweetheart from Bayou Teche, where I grew up. It takes a lot of courage for me to show these to you. For years I've kept my past a secret. I didn't want anyone to know how very humble my beginnings were." She turned to Lilli and for the first time that day, Lilli saw sincerity in her mother's eyes. "We were dirt-poor, Lilli. That's something you've never had to experience. You've always had everything you needed, growing up. I can remember times when there wasn't enough food to go around for all of us kids."

Lilli was confused but pressed Arlette. "I have aunts and uncles I don't know about?"

"Yes. I had two sisters and three brothers. My mother died several years ago."

Lilli was still reverberating from the news that she had grandparents she'd never met . . . aunts, uncles, cousins, all of whom had been kept hidden from her. Lilli felt doubly betrayed. "And you never told me? How could you do that, Mother? How could you keep me from my own family?"

"They aren't your family. They're mine!" Arlette's eyes narrowed. "The world doesn't revolve around you, Lilli, even though J.C. wanted you to think that it did. I was ashamed of my family. I still am. My father was a cruel, vicious man. He was a drunk and beat us every chance he got. My mother stood back and watched him do it. She didn't lift a finger to save any one of us. I hated her for that. I still do." Arlette seemed to be in a trance as she spoke. It was as if she had been catapulted back in time and were reliving every sordid moment. "My only ally was my sister Angelique, but she betrayed me in the end. She ran away, leaving me to care for the rest of the family like I was supposed to be their mother or something. I was too young to have to work so hard. We never had any fun. We had to wear each other's clothes until they turned into rags. Whenever we went into town people would gawk at us and laugh. 'There go the Herberts . . . white trash . . . their daddy's in prison,' they'd say."

Arlette's cheeks flamed crimson as she returned to the present. "Families cause pain, Lilli. I never had it soft like you. You never had to eat snakes and rabbits and squirrels to keep from crying out in hunger in the middle of the night. You have no concept of how cruel life can be, but I do."

"And you think you can protect yourself by inflicting cruelty on me before I hurt you?"

"You're my daughter . . ."

"But does that protect me from you?" Lilli demanded.

"I—I—" Arlette stumbled over the truth.

Lilli pointed to the letters in Frank's hands. "What do these love letters and Jack Rabineaux have to do with me?" she asked warily.

Arlette's eyes darted to the shocked faces around her and she realized she'd revealed too much about herself. Instantly, she assured her familiar mask as she plunged into her attack. "In the interest of justice, I believe I have to tell the whole truth now." Her back stiffened as she felt her own power race down her spine. "I have tried to protect you, Lilli . . ."

Vicki could contain herself no longer. "You're only interested in yourself, Arlette. Lilli may not realize what a vile creature you are, but I sure as hell do. I believe your story about your family. I knew there had to be something back there in the past to make you so mercenary. But I believe you'd risk anything, even this exposure, to get that money from Lilli."

Lilli turned her attention back to Arlette. "You knew this Jack Rabineaux after you were married to Pop?"

"I was dating him when I met J.C. and he was a very persistent man. He wouldn't give up on me. Tried to get me to leave J.C. and marry him. Our affair was rather hot—to say the least."

"What are you saying, Mother?" Lilli felt the foundation of her life crumbling, but she didn't fully comprehend why this was happening.

"What is she saying, Frank?" Lilli's eyes were filled with terror when she looked into Frank's compassionate face.

"She's saying that this man"—he looked down at the signature—"Jack was her lover at or about the time she got pregnant with you." He glanced over at Arlette and when he spoke, his words hissed through his teeth. "Isn't that about the size of it, Arlette?"

Vicki lunged to her feet. "You bitch!" She reached out as if to strangle Arlette, but Faith grabbed her mother's arm and pulled her back.

"Yes, Frank." Arlette sniffled. "That's the truth of it."

She turned wet eyes on her daughter and Lilli realized it was the first time she'd ever seen her mother cry. How odd that she should feel pity for her mother at a time when the woman was trying to destroy her. Or perhaps it was the fact that her mother was such a lost and desperate soul . . .

"I don't believe it," Lilli said defiantly. "Pop would have known. I would have known."

"I knew! I know! J.C. was sterile. Why do you think there were no other children, Lilli? Surely you know more about the birds and the bees than that!"

Lilli's hands were shaking. "You're lying to get the money."

"It's more than just the money. It's time the truth was known. I can't carry my sin anymore. I can't stand you thinking that I hate you all the time. I don't hate you, Lilli, you're my daughter. It was just that I was always afraid you would find out, and then what would I do? I didn't know if I would lose you or if we would become close once you learned J.C., the god of all men, was not your father. I didn't know how you would react. I just couldn't stand it anymore. I had to do something." Arlette sobbed and covered her face with her hands.

"So you chose today to do it. When you found out there was a million dollars riding on the line if you could discredit me—prove I was not the rightful heir. Is that about the size of it? MOTHER!" Lilli had never been angrier in her life, and this time she welcomed the confrontation. "How convenient."

"The will is a consideration, of course. Actually, I look at it as a catalyst to bring out the truth. This should have been done a long time ago and it's all my fault." Arlette made a show of sobbing into another tissue.

"I don't want to believe you, but knowing you, Mother, my common sense tells me you're telling the truth. Maybe those people in Bayou Teche were right. You were and still are white trash.

"What I *do* believe is that my father loved me. He loved me unconditionally with all his heart and he was the best father a girl could ever want. If it *is* true that he's not my biological father and that he knew about it . . . that in itself tells me he was damn near the god you accuse him of being. Think how much love he must have had for me. All those years to let everyone, including his sister, believe that he was my father and never to have breathed a word of it. My God! I love him all the more right now because he was a better parent to me than you ever were. And you know what? I think that is what you've always been jealous of. It tears you up that he loved me, and there wasn't room in your heart for both me and Pop. You wanted him body, soul, and pocketbook."

Lilli grabbed the stack of letters and shoved them back at Arlette. "This is your garbage. It makes me wonder if Jack Rabineaux was your only lover. You and Armando deserve each other. You were always out to get whatever you could.

I feel sorry for you, Mother, because in the end we all get exactly what we sow, and your harvest is going to be nothing but trash." Lilli let the letters drop into Arlette's hands.

"Another thing you should know, Mother ... everyone is talking about your engagement, and what they're saying isn't pretty. Armando has a reputation for bilking wealthy widows and divorcées out of their money. He did it to Macy Evanston and Trudi Dalton. His pattern is just the same with you as it was with them. He makes a pretense of having money, buying you gifts and jewelry because he believes you have money. But I promise you, if it's the last thing I do, I'll make dead certain you never get another dime from me, my store, or Pop's estate. Are we clear about that?"

Arlette kept her hands clenched tightly together in her lap so that no one could see her shaking. She pressed her lips together. She knew she had been bested, although she still couldn't believe it. She'd always been able to manipulate Lilli, but her daughter had changed. She wanted to believe that she could retaliate at some future date, but from the determined look in Lilli's eyes, she knew that Lilli was too strong for her.

Arlette rose without another word. Lilli noticed that her mother's eyes were dry as a bone.

Before Arlette could reply, Frank said to her, "These letters don't prove anything. If you want to contest this will by using the question of Lilli's paternity as grounds, I want you to know that you'll have to find another attorney. I'm on Lilli's side here. And another thing. Think long and hard about this, Arlette. You'd have to exhume the body to prove DNA, which is a costly venture. Or you'd have to find this Jack character, and he'd have to agree to the tests. You'd better be damn sure you've got a case."

Arlette did not respond. Instead, she nodded to her sister-in-law and niece and quickly left the room.

Once Arlette was gone, Lilli's self-control collapsed and she started to shake. She couldn't—wouldn't—believe that J.C. was not her real father. He was her pop. He was her life. God in heaven! How could this be happening? But she did believe the things she'd told her mother. Never before had his love been so precious to her.

And what kind of vile, hateful creature was her mother? If

Arlette had told her she had another mother, *that* she could have believed. But to think for one single, solitary moment that J.C. had been duped all his life as she'd been . . . It made her want to kill her mother.

The emotional volcano within Lilli erupted and she burst into tears. Still stunned from Arlette's performance, Vicki and Faith put their arms around Lilli to comfort her.

Frank immediately took charge. "Lilli, calm yourself. This ploy of Arlette's isn't going to work."

Lilli wiped her tears away with the palm of her hand. "Ploy?"

"You know good and well that she was bluffing and you did a great job of calling her on it."

"I'm not going to let her poison my life any longer," Lilli said defiantly. "Whether it's true or not, Pop loved me and that's all that counts to me. Frank, I'll do everything I can to make sure she doesn't get a penny of Pop's money. I'll go on this hunt and I'll find what Pop wants me to find. I want to clear his name. I want everybody to know that I'm J.C. Mitchell's daughter and I'm proud of him. I remember how intensely he studied these maps and charts. I don't think he'd send me down to South America on a wild-goose chase. He put a great deal of thought and planning into this will and the particular way he set it up. He knows something—a lot more than I do—and I want to know what it is.

"Frank, you do everything the law allows to get that woman cut out of my life . . . financially. Not one more cent of my income or profit is going to her. If she needs anything, she can go to work like everybody else. Her days of entitlement are over. She's going to rue this day till the end of her life. If she thinks it was hard for her before, she hasn't seen anything yet."

Frank smiled. "Consider her off the payroll. This is one job that will truly be my pleasure."

Thirty-one

Cold Tap, dressed in camouflage overalls and a wind-breaker, met Zane at Kennedy Airport. Zane's client wore a boyish grin that made Zane feel a bit like Santa Claus as he wended his way through the deplaning crowd. Cold Tap engulfed Zane in one of the biggest and strongest bear hugs he'd ever received.

"Gee, you missed me that much?" Zane teased.

"You're aces with me for getting that dagger. I just heard through my grapevine that a second dagger from that same hunt sold in Mexico City for twice what I paid. You're one hell of a negotiator."

"I do my best," Zane said, grinning.

Cold Tap's own smile grew larger as Zane withdrew a black felt drawstring bag from his briefcase. "I just want to hold that dagger. Know it's mine."

"No problem." Zane handed him the bag. "I'll get my loupe out once we get to the limo and you can inspect it properly then—"

"We're not going to the limo," Cold Tap interrupted.

"We're not?"

"Nope. In fact, we've only got twenty minutes to board our next plane." Cold Tap took Zane's elbow and ushered him around a slow-moving couple. "Everything is all set for our trip. I took care of all the details while you were gone."

"What trip? What details?"

Cold Tap kept rattling on as they darted around children being dragged along by their parents and elderly couples deplaning from Miami. "I had a blast, man. A true, energized blast. I got to thinking. Why should you have all the fun, huh? So I ordered all the gear, found the best guides, got the tickets ..."

346

Zane's expression went through several changes as the truth hit him. "We're flying to Colombia today. Is that right?"

"Right on!" Cold Tap slammed his wide palm against Zane's back. "I bought everything you'll need. I even got your passport from your apartment, which took some doing and you can change into something more appropriate on the plane if you like. I got a great deal on some stuff at Banana Republic."

Zane shook his head and rolled his eyes as they raced to the Avianca International gate. Their plane was already boarding. "Great timing," he said appreciatively to Cold Tap. They received their boarding passes and walked directly into the plane.

It was hard for Zane to realize that only the night before he had been with Lilli. Lilli! He had promised to call her as soon as he got back, and now, here he was on a plane to South America. Well, he would call her as soon as he landed. He knew she would understand. After all, she had said they were both professionals. Her reentrys into his life never failed to illuminate his shortcomings and yet simultaneously make him see life as he'd never seen it before. Everything seemed possible when he was with Lilli. Colors were brighter, songs more melodic and the very air around them was charged with electricity. Lilli brought the sun with her and showed him how placid and narrow his life was without her. He both loved and hated her for it.

Thinking of Lilli, Zane smiled as he sat down next to Cold Tap in the first-class seats marked 2A and 2B. The stewardess pulled the hatch door closed as Zane was buckling his seat belt. The plane backed away from the jetway.

I'm going to South America, Zane thought. I was in Texas this morning, and now I'm on my way to South America. "This isn't happening," he said under his breath.

Cold Tap's grin was wider than ever. "The hell it ain't!" he guffawed and jabbed a playful fist into Zane's bicep. "We're going to South America and we're gonna make history!"

"I hope so," Zane replied. He hoped that changing history would be a good enough excuse to get Lilli back.

In *Elegías de Varones Ilustres de Indias* was the first chronicle of the legend of El Dorado and the first reports of the gold and emeralds that Zane and Cold Tap sought. According to this telling of the legend by an Indian from Colombia, El Dorado was the Incan king whose kingdom was so rich in gold that each day he was covered with oil on which gold dust was sprinkled so that he became a golden man. The king disrobed at dawn each day, got onto a raft, and was rowed to the middle of a lake where he made his sacrifices to the gods. "His regal form was overspread with fragrant oil, on which was laid a coat of powdered gold, from sole of foot unto his highest brow, making him resplendent as the beaming of the sun." Many of the followers came to view this ritual and made "rich votive offerings of golden trinkets and emeralds rare, and diversed others of their ornaments" by throwing them into the lake.

The Spaniards in 1530 believed in another version of the legend, which placed the lake in northern Colombia and told of the king taking large quantities of emeralds and gold into the lake and casting them into the waters while his followers stood around playing musical instruments.

Many Spanish went to Lake Guatavita in northern Colombia and found golden trinkets and treasures, but for over four hundred years no one had found all the emeralds or the "source" of the mine itself.

Other explorers believed the story that the golden king and his riches were located in the land of Biru, or Peru. When the Spanish conquered Cuzco, they found a temple and palace filled with gold. The pottery, plates, and cups were embellished with emeralds. There were three chambers filled with gold furnishings and these were studded with emeralds. There were five rooms with silver objects. One hundred thousand gold ingots weighing five pounds each were waiting to be made into art objects. The chapels and burial chambers of the ancestors were filled with statues and images of birds, fish, and small animals, breastplates and ear spoons, all made of gold. In the great Temple of the Sun the walls were covered with heavy gold plates attached to the wall with bronze bolts. The royal garden consisted of trees, shrubs, and flowers, all made of gold. Even the field of maize outside the courtyard was not real, but of silver cornstalks and golden ears of corn. In all, there was one hundred eighty thousand square feet of golden corn.

The Incas never used gold as money or for exchange. They had been told by the gods that gold was the property of the gods and could be used only as a gift.

In their ever-increasing greed, the Spaniards never accepted that Cuzco was the home of El Dorado, no matter how much gold and silver had been found, and certainly the emeralds had never been discovered.

Cold Tap's studies had covered a wide canvas of sources, from T.A. Joyce's 1912 edition of *South American Archaeology* and his second book, *The Weeping God*, published in 1913; H.D. Disselhoff's *El Imperio de los Incas;* J.H. Del Mazo's *Machu Picchu*, published in 1975; to the 1874 edition of Raimondi's *Minerales de Peru.* The bibliography of periodicals was five pages long and included *American Journal of Anthropology, Academia Colombiana de Historia: Biblioteca de Antropología,* and *University of California: Publications in American Archaeology and Ethnology.* Cold Tap held the belief that the correct reading of Indian clues and enigmatic maps would someday lead a lucky fellow to the true "source." He intended to be that lucky fellow.

Zane broke his promise, Lilli thought when he didn't call her that first night upon his return to New York. She kept her spirits up for another twenty-four hours, but they were dashed when the phone still did nothing. On the third night she telephoned him, and since he was not home, she left a message on his recorder.

"Zane, this is Lilli. I thought I would hear from you once you got back. Or have we crossed signals again? I hope you're all right. It was great to see you, Zane. Talk to you soon." She hung up, knowing that all she could do was wait . . . and hope.

In that first week after her meeting at Frank's office, Lilli's mind was filled with her plans for her trip to South America. She studied her father's notes, journals, and maps. She cross-referenced his findings with published articles and books she found in J.C.'s library collection and at the University of Houston Library and the Houston Public Library. When she couldn't find the proper references, she contacted out-of-state libraries and the Heye Foundation in New York. Lilli became obsessed with her project, as if her life depended upon its success. In a way, it did.

Try as she might, she was still haunted by the fact that her mother had turned on her, tried to destroy her emotionally and taint her father's legacy. Every time she thought of it, her blood boiled. At this point, Lilli didn't care if it took her the rest of her life; she was determined to find those rivers of gold even if she had to tromp through Siberia. Now not only did she feel pressed to clear her father's reputation, but she also had to put an end to her mother's manipulations once and for all.

Lilli pulled out a magnifying glass and carefully went over the crumbling map she held. In J.C.'s notes she'd read that this particular map was the oldest one in his possession. It was a copy of an original drawn by an Incan Indian guide in the early 1800s, which was itself a translation of an ancient legend going back to pre-conquistador days.

Because J.C. had been convinced that the rivers of gold were to be found in Colombia, Lilli assumed that the old map was of that country. Painstakingly, she cross-checked the similarities of the topography and that of the Colombia Andes south of Bogotá. J.C.'s notes indicated that the rivers of gold would be found in the northern Andes in Colombia, near the border of Equador. But each time Lilli checked the old map against the newest maps and photographs she'd obtained at the Houston Public Library, something didn't jibe. For one thing, there was a small lake on the old map that didn't exist in the newest photos. She telephoned a client of hers whose brother, Barry Whiteman, a would-be explorer and mountain climber, had gone to Colombia numerous times when working for a Venezuelan oil company. She took the maps to Barry and he agreed with her that something about J.C.'s calculations was dreadfully askew.

Barry lived in a small, two-bedroom bungalow in the Montrose section of Houston. He was in his early thirties and had thinning brown hair, sparkling blue eyes, and a warm and sensitive smile. His house was decorated in a collage of South American artifacts, early-college-era sofas, makeshift tables, and cheap lamps. Though he worked as an engineer for one of the oil companies, his job was not his life. He lived for his vacations, which he spent in the most remote places on earth. He had been to Tibet, the northern Ukraine, Japan, and Java, and had spent six years exploring South America.

When Lilli shook his hand and walked into his living room, she felt as if she'd met a kindred spirit.

They exchanged pleasantries and quickly got down to the matter at hand.

"This can't be Colombia," Barry told Lilli. "This lake to the south of the peak throws everything off. Of course, the lake could be dried up today, which is why the photos don't show it. I suppose J.C. would have thought of that, too. I know how hard your father worked to develop his theory, but I think he was wrong, Lilli."

Sadly, Lilli nodded. "I have to agree with you. He's guilty of supporting his hypothesis with facts, rather than letting the facts lead him to his theory." She rubbed her chin thoughtfully with her index finger. "I want to find the truth. And I'm not going to find anything in Colombia, am I?"

"No. But, I don't think J.C. was that far off, Lilli. I think he just wasn't looking at this map the way the ancient chroniclers drew it," Barry said and jumped to his feet. "Here." He pulled his chair in front of Lilli and grabbed her hand. "Stand on top of the chair."

"What?"

"Just do as I say!" Barry said excitedly and pushed her to the chair.

Lilli stepped up onto the chair seat. "Now what?"

Barry's eyes were sparkling with excitement. "When I first started going to South America, I did the same thing J.C. did. I was so busy looking at the ground, I damn near missed the whole thing."

"What whole thing?"

He sighed heavily as if frustrated with Lilli's shortsightedness. "Many of these old maps weren't drawn by exacting cartographers. They didn't have the proper instruments or the same need to be precise. A lot of J.C.'s notes mention the Indians who had gone to Machu Picchu to hide from the Spaniards. What if this map was drawn by one of them? They were far removed from the valley, which they could draw from memory, but nobody was out there with measuring equipment. From the top of a mountain, the world looks like a different place. Will you buy that?"

"Sure."

"Well, look!" he said and dropped the antique map onto the floor. It fluttered slowly and landed at Lilli's feet. She gazed down on the map as if she were an angel in heaven looking down on earth. Then Barry quickly went to the stack of maps they'd been using for their cross-check and pulled one out and carefully placed it on the floor.

Lilli glanced from left to right. From the old to the new. Back and forth her eyes flicked. Time seemed to stand still as a sense of wonder overcame her. She had found what J.C. had missed all these years. "The old map looks like an aerial view of Peru."

"The Incas used to call it the land of Biru."

Lilli clamped her hands to either side of her face as her eyes popped wide in wonder. "Peru." She breathed the word reverently. She stared at the map. "And that is Lake Titicaca, there is Cuzco, and that's Machu Picchu."

"Precisely," he said confidently.

"Pop was just too sure it was Colombia to see it."

Barry was still smiling broadly as he looked up at Lilli's astounded expression. "What do you say?"

Lilli didn't hesitate for a moment. "I say we're going to Peru, and the sooner the better."

"Atta girl!" Barry said and put his hand in the air for a high-five to seal the deal.

Thirty-two

*I*t was hard for Zane to believe that it had been over a week since he and Cold Tap had landed in Bogotá and met with the government officials who regulated emerald mining in Colombia. They visited the mines at Muzo and Somondoco, both of which were controlled and run by the government. Cold Tap was fascinated by the factories where the gems were cut and polished. In a tiny shop not far from Bolivar's Garden in Bogotá, Cold Tap told a gemologist that he was going into the mountains to find the "source" mine. The man broke out into peals of laughter.

Zane noticed a local Indian man seemingly inspecting the jewels in one of the glass cases nearest the door. Zane could tell that the man was more intent upon eavesdropping on Cold Tap's conversation than on looking at the jewels.

"It will do you no good," the gemologist told Cold Tap. "It is a fool's journey. Even if you find it, you must only carry out what you can put in your pockets, and then you will have to smuggle them out of the country. The government will not let you own the mines. It is against the law."

Cold Tap was silent for a long moment. "And do all those in Colombia follow the law?"

The man laughed again. "Few." Then he shook Cold Tap's hand. "Good luck. You will need it."

Zane watched as the Indian slipped out the door. As Zane left the building with Cold Tap, he saw the Indian waiting.

"Señor." The man signaled to Zane with a wink. "The old man in there, he is not so wise. The 'source' exists. May the gods lead you." He smiled at Zane and then shoved his hands into the pockets of his baggy trousers and walked away.

Zane couldn't help but wonder if the land would prove to be as mysterious as the people.

* * *

Zane and Cold Tap met with their three guides, Topa, Silva, and Carlos, who had arranged for the Jeeps that would take them into the mountains as far as they could travel by road or rutted paths. From that point they would transfer their gear and supplies to three oxen and travel by foot into the upper Andes.

The terrain was perilously steep, and because of heavy rainfalls, there was tremendous erosion and the possibility of mudslides, all of which made their climb quite precarious once they were forced to leave the Jeep behind. Nevertheless, the little band trudged upward, following the map Cold Tap had commissioned Dr. Robert Angleton of the University of New Mexico to draw for him.

This map was the culmination of years of Dr. Angleton's intensive study of the Incas and their legends and the information Cold Tap had acquired in his short, though concentrated, interest in emerald mines. Dr. Angleton had formulated this map from bits and pieces of legends and Incan lore that described the "source" mine. To that he added information that had been gleaned by archaeolgists known for their adept transcriptions of Incan hieroglyphics found throughout the Andes. He matched information from the Academia Colombiana de Historia in Bogotá with Zane's findings he'd compiled from the Biblioteca Boliviana and Arqueologica in Lima, Peru. Earlier, Dr. Angleton had consulted with Zane by telephone on several occasions regarding everything from the equipment, food, and pack animals, in this case oxen, to the type of clothing they would need and the best guides to hire as they prepared for this exploration. It was Dr. Angleton's enthusiasm over what he believed would be a positive outcome of the journey that convinced Zane that Cold Tap's trip to the Andes was more than just a lark. Zane also remembered that Dr. Angleton's only regret was that he could not accompany Zane and Cold Tap, because the terrain was too treacherous for a man of eighty-two; otherwise, he would have liked to join them.

They made camp that first night in a small jungle clearing. The ground was moist, and therefore very little dried firewood was to be found. Cold Tap, in his Westernized wisdom, had thought of this dilemma before embarking on the trip and brought along several cases of Mountain Logs, those instantly ignited fake fuel logs sold in the supermarkets in New York. Cold Tap relished his role as group leader and carefully arranged a smaller fire of Kingston charcoal briquettes over which he placed a wire rack. He withdrew four filets mignons from the Styrofoam cooler he'd packed with dry ice. However, at nightfall this high in the mountains, keeping warm was more of a dilemma than cooling the food.

Cold Tap reminded Zane of those British explorers to Africa a century ago who traveled with their own valets, gourmet cooks, and servants. He liked to be comfortable.

Cold Tap stirred a small pot of beans over the charcoal fire while Topa, Carlos, and the pack boy, Silva, sat off to the side near the cliff wall, waiting patiently for their dinner.

Zane was staring at the glowing briquettes, thinking of Lilli . . . as usual. He had tried to call her from the airport in Bogotá when they landed, but there had been no answer. Her machine hadn't picked up, either. Now he had no idea how long it would be before he would be near a phone again. And he had promised to call . . .

Cold Tap seemed well aware of Zane's solemn mood. "I've seen some dudes with a long lip, but you beat all, man. What's eatin' at you?"

Zane gave Cold Tap a half smile. "It's that obvious?"

"Damn straight. My bet is the Incas over there are talking about you and not me." Cold Tap looked down and carefully skimmed the sides of his pot to keep the beans from burning. "What's her name?"

Zane's face showed his surprise. He needed to talk about Lilli. Cold Tap was no Ann Landers, but they were on a mountaintop in the middle of the Andes, and at least he could console himself with the fact that Cold Tap was concerned. "Lilli."

Cold Tap's black eyes widened. "The dealer in Houston with my dagger."

"The same," Zane admitted.

"Shit. You got it pretty bad, man, for only being with her for a day."

Zane took a deep breath. "It's more than that. She's more than that. I fell in love with her when I was seventeen."

Cold Tap whistled. "I see."

Suddenly Zane noticed that Topa and Silva had stopped laughing and were now whispering quietly.

Zane shook his head. "She loved me. I loved her, with all my heart. Then I left her. I went to New York and, well . . ."

Cold Tap rolled his eyes heavenward. "And you got on the fast track and never looked back."

"How did you know?"

Cold Tap grinned mischievously. "I'll bet you thought I was just another dumb black singer."

"I—"

"Don't answer that. It's okay. Goes with the territory. I know a lot. I've been around and I know a lot more than you, pretty boy. Now, don't take offense, but that's how most of us see a guy like you. You got the big head in the big city and thought you were Joe Cool. We all do that. Then life takes us down a peg or two. We get older. Maybe a bit wiser. Then we realize even if we had all the money in the world, if there isn't somebody special to share it with, it's just not so much fun anymore, is it? I mean, what's the point?"

Zane was astounded. He realized that Cold Tap was talking about himself just as much as he was dispensing advice to Zane. "You think about the same things, huh?"

"More than I used to. I got enough fame for the next sixty guys I know. Yet I still worry. Not just about a woman. I'm still worried about makin' it, always wonderin' if the next song will go gold, then platinum. Will they pick up my next album? Will the tickets sell? Will the concert bust? Will the fans desert me?"

"I never thought of that."

Cold Tap's expression was deadly serious when he looked over at Zane. He pointed his stirring spoon at him for further emphasis as he spoke. "Your problems are so easy to solve, it's pathetic."

"They are?"

"Shit, yeah!"

"How?"

"You love her?"

"Yeah."

"Does she love you?"

"Deep down? Yeah, she does."

"Then for God's sake, just marry her and screw her every

morning and every night and you'll both be happy. Jesus! Sometimes I don't know about you whiteys."

"But it's not that simple."

Cold Tap threw his spoon to the ground and it bounced off a rock. "Sure it is. You just got too much pride and ego. And you're not even a rap singer."

Suddenly Cold Tap sniffed the air. He could tell something was burning. He whirled around to check his steaks. "Aw, man! I burned the goddamn filets!"

Zane burst into laughter as Cold Tap frantically removed the charred steaks from the grill. Fortunately, they were burned only on one side, and as the group pounced upon the dinner Cold Tap had prepared for them, they all proclaimed it was the best steak they'd ever eaten . . . ten thousand feet up.

The terrain continued to be treacherous but the group made steady progress. That night as they sat around the warm, glowing campfire, the group listened to legends from Topa, their guide. Topa was a small man with a face so filled with weathered lines he looked to be nearly one hundred years old, although he claimed he was but fifty. Topa had a keen sense of humor, which he was able to impart to them through his broken English and great and frequent use of hand gestures. With wit and charm, he kept his two employers disarmed. Each of Topa's stories led to another and another, and their endings only fed a natural curiosity within Zane he'd never known before. Surprisingly, he found his desire for information insatiable. He wanted to know everything about these people who lived so high in the mountains so long ago and how it was they knew so much about astronomy and the charting of the planets. In a way, Zane thought, it was as if they were still there, still guiding the human race toward the truths it sought.

He had not thought much about spirituality, or his own spiritual life, since his father's death. Now he realized he wanted to find that part of himself.

The next morning Zane consulted Dr. Angleton's map. "Let's proceed to the north."

Topa's ancient face was solemn. "North is good. One must

always travel the right path. It's not the destination that is so important, it is the destiny."

"Fine, whatever," Zane said to appease him as he rolled up his bedroll and tied it to the ox. "Let's do it."

The tiny exploring party proceeded around the north face, where they noticed that the vegetation was sparse due to the lack of sunlight and even lower temperature. Because the terrain was extremely rocky, their progress was slow.

At one point Zane saw a white-tailed mouse skitter past them, which told him they were still below seventeen thousand feet, since these mice did not live above that altitude. Bogotá itself was at eight thousand feet and they'd already crossed the thirteen-thousand-foot level. Zane did not believe that emeralds could be found this high up, although the Incan legend said that the "source" was high in the mountains.

They were moving nearly straight up at times and the only vegetation they were seeing now was steppe vegetation. Gone were the pines and even tropical plants and orchids of the lower regions. They saw an increasing number of condors, which were said to fly as high as twenty-six thousand feet. Only the highest altitudinal animals were seen or heard now, like the puma, viscacha, chinchilla, and an occasional guemal.

Zane stumbled on another rock. There was little bright sunshine on this side of the mountain face, but Zane thought he saw a glittering rock. He pulled out a small chisel and hammer from his backpack and chipped away at the stone. He held it up.

"Whatcha got?" Cold Tap asked.

Zane tossed the stone away. "Nothing."

Topa, Silva, and Carlos shook their heads and laughed at Zane and Cold Tap as they moved farther up the mountain. They stopped numerous times to investigate glittering rocks. Day turned to night and they camped again, sleeping upright with their backs against the mountainside.

The next morning Zane was cold, stiff, and hungry. They ate cold biscuits and drank bottled water, then set out. They scoured the area, hacking off pieces of rock, hoping to find a real emerald, but they found nothing.

On the fourth day, Zane fell into the routine with too much ease and he was surprised at how the desire to find these green stones had overcome him. He was barely aware of the others as he combed the mountain, wanting now to be the first to make the discovery. Hunger evaded him as he lived on jerky, biscuits, and water. He forgot the warmth of the charcoal fire their first two nights. Sleep became a nuisance, not a necessity, because he felt he was missing valuable digging time.

Night bathed the Andes in black, halting Zane's emerald foraging. Long after the others were asleep, he stared at the sky, thinking the stars were close enough to touch. They twinkled at him. He raised his hand, pretending to clutch a particularly bright star. Suddenly he dropped his hand to his thigh. "You're a fool, Zane. Trying to find a lost emerald mine is like trying to pluck a star from the sky."

Then slowly he smiled. "But what an intoxicating adventure. No wonder J.C. loved this life. And Lilli, too."

For months Zane had gone along with Cold Tap's plans because he'd wanted the money Cold Tap was paying him. Ensnared by the illusion and the hypnotic lure of treasure, he'd left common sense back in New York. They were never going to find the source mine, he thought. The source had eluded men for centuries. It was time they admitted to themselves that although this had been a great adventure, they were on a wild-goose chase. Zane decided in the morning he would speak to Cold Tap.

Zane overslept the next day and when he awoke, Cold Tap was already hammering away at a piece of stone.

"Cold Tap, we've got to—" Zane stopped talking and peered at the deep green stone Cold Tap had chipped off into his hand. "What the hell?" Zane's eyes were incredulous as he looked at the rap singer.

Cold Tap hacked off another piece of green beryl. "Look!"

"I'm looking! I'm looking! We found the emerald mine!"

Topa, Silva, and Carlos turned around and carefully worked their way over to where Zane and Cold Tap were standing, being careful not to slip on the crumbling rocks, since there was a space of forty feet between them and the edge of the precipice. They moved closer to inspect the rock, then the emerald in Cold Tap's hand. They conversed in excited Spanish over the heads of the two Americans.

Zane's eyes were filled with wonder and awe. "This can't

be!" He looked at the mountain wall not a dozen feet from his left side.

"Why the hell not? If there're emeralds near Bogotá, why not up here? Somebody had to find them sometime. Why not me?"

Zane shook his head incredulously. "I never thought you'd find them."

"And I never thought I wouldn't!" Cold Tap laughed.

Zane turned toward the mountain wall and then walked over to it. He began chipping away at the dirt and rock beneath his hands. He hammered and chiseled, then hammered some more. He found nothing.

Topa and Silva inspected the ground around the original find and unearthed several more glistening green rocks. They spoke with so much excitement, Cold Tap merely stood and laughed at the scene.

Zane crossed over to Cold Tap, who watched him with suddenly serious eyes. "How does one go about digging out an entire mountain? I mean, who knows where the vein runs? This could be the top . . ."

"Or it could be the bottom, eh?" Cold Tap clutched his jaw between his forefinger and thumb. "It kinda boggles the mind, doesn't it?"

"Do you think this is really it? Or just these few stones here?"

"My guess is we got lucky and found a few rocks. But it's my bet these fellas tell all their friends and their friends' friends, and before you know it, the biggest part of the legend will be about me. And that's pretty special."

"Immortality has many guises."

"Precisely. Who's going to remember a rap singer twenty . . . a hundred years from now? But to be mentioned in a legend . . . now that's an accomplishment."

"It certainly is. I'm glad I was a part of this adventure. You know, there's only one other person I know who is as nuts as you are."

"Don't tell me it's that gal of yours."

Zane smiled proudly when he spoke. "Yeah. She'd do this—every day of the week if she could."

"My kind of woman. Maybe I should latch onto her."

Zane rubbed his thumb thoughtfully across the face of the

emerald and then handed it to Cold Tap. "Not a chance. She's one treasure I'm going to claim."

"Good for you." Cold Tap slapped Zane on the shoulder. "Well, I guess I'd better get this area surveyed, take our photographs and videos. Then we need to start back down."

Zane hastily unpacked the cameras and loaded the film and tapes. It took the rest of the day and all of the next to document everything they would need to verify their story. They made camp for the duration and mused over the adventure they'd had.

Zane worked all day with a smile on his face, because when he flew back to the States, he was going back to Lilli.

The moon hung full like a sterling silver disk above the Andes that night. Zane crossed his hands beneath his head as he stared up at it, wondering what Lilli was doing tonight back in Houston. Was she out with friends? Was she working late? Did she think about him as much as he thought about her? Did she miss him?

He closed his eyes and drifted off to sleep, knowing he could always find Lilli in his dreams.

Thirty-three

Zane was so excited when he walked into New Antiquities that he walked straight toward Lilli's office in the back, went up to Faith with a huge grin on his face, and without a customary greeting, just asked, "Where's Lilli?"

Taken aback, Faith simply stared incredulously at Zane and said, "She's not here."

"She's at home, right? Took the day off? Good for her. I'll just go over there." He started to walk away.

"Zane!" Faith finally said. "Wait a minute!"

"What's the matter?"

"Lilli's not there."

His disappointment was evident. "Where is she?"

"Peru."

Zane felt his jaw drop open. "What's she doing in Peru?"

"It was part of J.C.'s will. He wanted her to go there and find the lost rivers of gold."

Totally deflated, Zane sank into the chair opposite Faith's desk. "I can't believe this. I thought I'd go out of my mind on the flight back to New York. I had to pull some strings to get a flight out of Kennedy to be here. I really need to see her, Faith. When is she coming back?"

"I don't know."

Zane's eyes narrowed and he leaned forward in the chair. "You work for the woman, Faith, and you don't know when she's coming back? I don't mean to be too specific here, just a generality will do. This week? Next?"

"I don't know. She didn't say."

"Faith, have a heart. I'm not playing games here. I really need to see her." He clenched his fist. "Now, when is she coming back?"

"Zane, honestly, I don't know. She doesn't know. She told

me she wasn't coming back until she found the lost rivers, whatever the hell they are."

Zane slapped his forehead with the palm of his hand. "I don't believe this."

"It's true! She and Barry should arrive there later today," Faith said.

Suddenly Zane grew rigid. "Who's Barry?"

"Barry Whiteman. He's a real adventurer type. Just like J.C., she said. He's helping with her expedition. Lilli said he's been all over South America. He's helped her out a lot, Zane. She's in good hands."

Faith watched Zane's face as jealousy caused it to turn red. Her words had had precisely the effect on him that she'd hoped. She didn't give him a chance to respond. "They were flying to Cuzco and then trekking up to Machu Picchu. Boy! I've always wanted to go there. Haven't you? It's supposed to be a really spiritual place. But I suppose you've heard all those stories, huh? Yeah, they left yesterday. It took them a while to figure out all those squirrelly maps of J.C.'s. Man! He had more junk than I want to see in a lifetime. I just don't know how they figured it all out, but they did. Like minds and all that . . ."

Faith couldn't help baiting Zane. To her way of thinking, it was time he put his big-city ego on the shelf and realized how important Lilli was. Faith was tired of Lilli's spending her life pining over Zane. Any fool could see the two of them needed to be together. Sometimes fate just needed a little nudge, she thought. Or maybe even a real hard shove.

"You know, Zane," Faith said, keeping her tone nonchalant, "I think I've got photocopies of all her maps and itineraries in the office. I'll go look on her desk."

Faith rose and went into Lilli's office.

It took every ounce of Zane's self-control not to ask a million and one questions about Barry Whiteman. Who the hell was this guy who Lilli thought was the hero type? How long had he been around? There was always the chance that he was old, like her father.

"Here we are," Faith said as she placed a folder in front of Zane. "At least you can kind of keep track of where she's going and all. You can see, from that calendar, she intends to start up into the mountains tomorrow. No phones up there, I'm afraid. But she's at the El Presidente tonight."

"How old is this Barry?" Zane said, not lifting his eyes from the folder.

Faith grinned mischievously. "Your age, I'd guess. Kinda cute, too, if you like the type."

"What type?"

It took every ounce of self-control for Faith to keep a straight face as she shrugged her shoulders. "That Harrison Ford type. You know, Indiana Jones and all that . . ."

Zane bolted out of the chair and started for the door. "I'm going to Cuzco."

Faith didn't miss a beat. "Too rugged and sweaty for my taste. I like them a little less animalistic . . ." Faith was smiling as she lifted her arm and waved to him. He was halfway out of the store in four strides. " 'Bye, Zane. Have a great trip!"

Cuzco, Peru

Asleep in her hotel room, Lilli began to dream the sound of Zane's voice calling to her. He told her that he loved her as he held her gently in his arms and kissed her. They were teenagers in the dream and then, in a flash, they were older. There were no regrets between them and no room for animosity or sadness. Everything about their life was filled with love.

Then suddenly the dream turned dark as she heard Zane saying, "You always preferred the dead to the living, didn't you, Lilli?"

The words roused her and forced her to wake up. She remembered that Zane had once accused her of loving her father more than she loved him. Maybe he'd been right about that. After all, here she was, ready to climb a mountain for a dead father's wish when a very much alive and loving Zane was in New York City wondering if she could love him.

Lilli punched her pillow and sat upright as she brought her thoughts into focus. She was tired of blaming herself for their not getting together. She'd had ambitions of her own. She had learned to be independent, and she knew what it was like to please herself and take care of herself. She didn't *need* a man to make her feel worthwhile: She *wanted* Zane in her life because she loved him.

She remembered their last night together when she had wanted to make sweet love to him and resurrect his passion for her. She had let the moment slip through her fingers, thinking she had to put him off. Then he had gone back to New York and, despite his promise, hadn't called. When she was younger, she would have taken that as a sign he didn't love her. Now her intuition told her that something had happened to delay him and that they would get together when she returned. She was sorry, though, that he didn't know about *this* trip. They could have planned it together. Even though he did not have the same appreciation for nature that she did, he might have participated in the preparations; he would have done that for her.

Thoughts of Zane continued to plague her for over an hour. Finally she decided that since she'd embarked upon this road to fulfill her father's will, there was little that could be done about Zane at the moment. This time was meant for J.C.

How odd it was, she thought, that J.C.'s discovery had always evaded him. Could it be that the gods were always watching everyone and that they had deemed him not worthy because he'd robbed one too many ruin? J.C. had picked Lilli for this job . . . this all-important discovery that could possibly clear his name and give him the immortality he sought.

What if she failed? What if Barry's theory that the rivers of gold were in Peru was wrong? What if they were on the wrong track?

Exhausted, Lilli closed her eyes, and this time, sleep overtook her.

Thunderstorms had delayed the departure of Zane's flight to Peru. He'd read *USA Today* twice before the plane left the runway.

The flight seemed to last forever. The stewardess brought Zane a Bloody Mary and he thanked her politely. "Could you tell me when we'll be landing?"

"Another two hours, sir," the stewardess replied. "Would you like a pillow and a blanket?"

Sleep was the last thing on Zane's mind. "No, thanks."

"Very well," she said and walked away.

Zane was more than anxious to see Lilli. He wanted to tell her about his trip to Colombia and the thrill he'd experienced searching for the emeralds. He couldn't wait to describe the way the moon hung in the sky; the crisp, thin air of the Andes; the beautiful terrain; and the closeness he'd felt with nature. He hoped he could relate to her the connectedness he'd sensed with her. He had discovered he liked her kind of adventure, and because of his experiences, he understood her better than ever before. Most of all, he wanted her to know that he loved her with all his heart.

Thirty-four

T he next morning Lilli and Barry met for breakfast. Over steaming cups of the finest coffee she'd ever tasted, Lilli listened as Barry expounded about Machu Picchu.

"For centuries this city of sparkling granite shrines, fountains, lodgings, and steep stairways was hidden by thick emerald-green veils of jungle foliage. Not until 1911, when Hiram Bingham discovered the ruins, was anyone outside the Incan world privy to the magnificent sight," he said.

"Machu Picchu was built as a *huaca,* a holy place. It was there that the Incan lords began to call themselves the Sons of the Sun and worshiped Inti, the mighty personification of the sun itself. According to the latest excavations, it's been discovered that the majority of bones inside the citadel were female. Experts have theorized that the Incas were hiding their women from the invading Spanish. Others believe that the women were needed to tend the mummies of rulers and high priests who were buried here. Because of the humid atmosphere, every three days the women had to bring the mummies out of the crypt and put them in the sun to dry."

"How eerie."

"It is. The train up the mountain is always packed with visitors who are hoping to find their own spiritual enlightenment."

"I can't wait to start." Lilli's enthusiasm shone in her face.

"Good. I've got our train tickets, staples, cooking equipment, lanterns, digging tools, toiletries ... did I miss anything?"

Lilli laughed. "I don't think so."

"The best news is that I hired Adriano. He's considered the best guide down here," he said, biting into a piece of Peruvian corn bread. "When we were still in Houston, I telephoned Walter Alva, the director of the Bruning Archaeological Museum in Lambayeque—"

Lilli's eyes widened appreciatively. "The man who's doing all the excavations on the Moche people near Sipán, Peru?"

"Precisely. Anyway, he recommended Adriano. It took some doing, but I held out for him. This kind of cockeyed expedition is just the kind of thing that gets Adriano's juices flowing, or so he tells me."

Lilli detected the cynicism in Barry's voice. "You're not so sure about this venture anymore, are you?"

Barry stirred his coffee thoughtfully. "It's one thing being caught up in the excitement of the moment back in Houston. It's another when I'm here and seeing the enormity of our task."

"But you've done this kind of thing before, right?"

"Sure. But I realize now it was a bit different. We always knew exactly where we were going. When I look up at those mountains and down at J.C.'s map . . . I get this real sick feeling."

"I'm not surprised, but I trust my pop."

Barry put his hand over Lilli's. "I think the world of you, Lilli. I really do. But when it comes to J.C., I'm afraid you've had blinders on." He paused for a minute as if he were unsure how to proceed.

"Go ahead and say it. I can take it," she urged.

"Lilli, I made some calls. Especially a few down here. I understand from Walter and some other archaeologists that J.C. wasn't exactly a stand-up kind of guy."

"He was a *ladron de tumbas,* a grave robber," she offered apologetically.

"You know that, huh?"

"Yeah. It's taken me a long time to admit it. What else do they say?"

"That he was a dreamer. That he didn't have a clue about what he was doing."

"I know." She sighed heavily.

"We could be up there a long time, Lilli."

She shook her head. "No, we won't. I've already decided that we'll follow the map. I'll make you a deal right now. A river is pretty damn hard to miss, wouldn't you say?"

"Yeah, I'll go along with that."

"Well, Pop's journals tell us that from Machu Picchu we will have to travel northward and cross this spur here," she said, pointing to the map. "We should be seeing some signs of a river around there somewhere. If not, you can head back down immediately."

"What about you?"

"I'll stay up there with the rest of the crew. Adriano can come back up after he's seen you down the mountain. Fair enough?"

"All right," he said gamely, and stuck out his hand for Lilli to shake.

"So I think we'd better gather up our stuff and get going."

It took the better part of the day to load up all their supplies. Adriano brought two other friends with him who were experts at mountain climbing and, according to Adriano, had even woven a straw bridge high up in the Andes with their cliff-dwelling families. Both Merino and David were Quechua and spoke several area dialects. Lilli had already cleared government papers and permits with the local authorities and back in Houston had registered their small expedition with the proper archaeological officials.

Arrangements were made for four llamas to bring up supplies of food and water, blankets for the cold nights, medicines, including serums against snake and insect bites, and even tweezers to pull out the poisonous spines of the Black Palm, a plant indigenous to the area.

Lilli, Barry, and Adriano were contracted to ride to Machu Picchu on a bus similar to the tour buses that rode up the mountainside on a daily basis from the hotels. From there they would have to make their own trail through the jungle.

From Cuzco they took the train up the moutainside, which reminded Lilli of the railroads of the American West a hundred years ago. Devoid of a modern switching system, the trains would telegraph to one another at the various stops, alerting each other as to their progress so as to avoid train crashes. At each of the stops Lilli noted the children, who gathered around the platforms selling woolen goods and trinkets. She noticed that the children were dressed in their finest clothes and that they charged the tourists to have their picture taken with them. Lilli liked the unusual hats all the women wore. A fellow tourist told her that each village had a particular style and color of hat, which the women wove. Lilli tried to take their picture, but all the women refused, forcing her to snap shots of the back of the hats. Finally the train ride came to an end, and the group transferred to the bus that would carry them up the switchbacks.

The ride on the tourist bus was comical. All but three passengers were American, and every one of them, including the family from Rio de Janeiro, was coming to Machu Picchu because he or she had read about its spiritual importance.

Adriano took this time to tell Lilli and Barry about the amazing discoveries that Walter Alva and his wife, Susana Meneses, were making in Sipán.

"Not until 1987 did anyone know of the treasure of the Moche settlement at Sipán. At that time some grave robbers sold their bounty and it began appearing in the art markets."

Lilli cringed at the term "grave robber," which Adriano apparently noticed.

"Had it not been for these men, we would have none of the incredible insights into our past ancestry that have come to light in Sipán," he said to reassure her, and Lilli smiled back at him with heartwarming gratitude.

"I'm afraid I know little of the Moche, other than the fact that they predated the Incas," Lilli said.

"Yes. They date back to A.D. 100. Perhaps even before that. Corrosion has destroyed many of the Moche artifacts being discovered at Sipán—funerary masks, gold spools worn over the ears, fan-shaped rattles, and tumis, or knives. But through the use of recently devised Swiss methods, archaeologists are able to restore the gold pieces to their natural state. This is a great blessing. We have discovered that these people were very advanced, indeed, perhaps even more so than the Incas. There was an ancient fruit they used for medicinal purposes called the ulluchu. The theory is that the ulluchu is from the papaya family and was used as an anticoagulant. The Moche harnessed the mountain rivers into an irrigation system to water the arid coastal areas. This was accomplished at the same time that the Romans were irrigating their land. The Moche painted their pottery with the same skill and techniques as the Greeks. They invented their own form of gilding in order to make objects appear as if they were made of solid gold. They excelled at joining metal pieces by edge welding, crimping, and using tabs that projected through slits. The Moche used the same blowtubes for metalworking that the Spaniards were using, but the Moche did it a thousand years earlier."

As Adriano spoke about the Moche, Lilli found herself asking questions. How did a people suddenly rise to such a high level of civilization? Had intuition and experiment produced their remarkable ability to electroplate precious metals when no one else in the world was doing this? And what was within the soul of these people that spurred such artistic expression when most Indians in North and South America were content to raise corn and hunt for their evening's meat?

It was these kinds of questions that used to keep J.C. and Lilli up at night talking and supposing over huge mugs of coffee or drinking Coronas.

Just being there, listening to Barry and Adriano spar, rejuvenated Lilli. This kind of exploration was the thing that made her feel alive. Lilli liked it best when one question led to another and then another.

She glanced away from the two men beside her and looked out the open bus window at the thick green walls of vegetation that hid the rocky mountainside. The earth itself held the answer to so many mysteries, she thought, and even though man had been digging for centuries, needing desperately to find the answers, it seemed that Mother Nature always covered up the answers faster than man could dig them out.

Perhaps she was on an impossible mission. Perhaps she was half crazy to pit herself against a jungle that could easily swallow her up. She must have been crazy to believe in the dreams of a dead man.

As Lilli looked from Barry's sparkling eyes to the rapid, excited movements of Adriano's hands as he described a copper mask he'd seen that had been electrochemical-plated, she realized that she wasn't doing this for her father. She was here because she wanted to be.

She had come to Peru for herself.

She wanted to discover something all her own, just like Walter Alva and his wife were doing. She might not be the foremost expert on anything and she didn't have a string of degrees following her name, but that didn't matter to her. For once, she wanted to discover something on her own and then share it with the rest of the world.

For a long time she had felt that something in life was eluding her, but that time was drawing to a close. Lilli smiled. She was quite glad, indeed, that she had come to Peru.

The bus tour spent several hours at Machu Picchu as the guide showed everyone around the crumbling ruins and explained Incan life. Lilli was entranced with the multitude of colorful wildflowers that seemed to grow right out of the rocks. The fog spun around the precisely cut stones like whirling banshees. At quiet moments, Lilli thought she could hear the soft moan of ancient voices, but then she realized she was only caught up in a trancelike state produced by a slight case of altitude sickness. The tour guide continued on but most of his information Lilli had heard a thousand times. However, the drone of the guide's broken English filled the hours while they waited for their pack animals and the rest of the crew to arrive.

Lilli consulted with both Barry and Adriano about the best course to take. All three agreed that they would head to the south, around the small peak to their right, then traverse the west slope and over to the high peak on the west, which they all believed was the peak J.C. had indicated.

The tour guide moved the group along. Lilli heard him relate the story of the "hitching post of the sun." He told how the worshipers of the village had singled out a young man not of their tribe, and proclaimed him a god. Little more was ever known about this man or where he came from or what magical powers he possessed. The villagers tethered the young man to the hitching post, which was a long stone post secured down into an enormous boulder jutting out over the cliff. "They believed," said the guide, "that, so tethered, the god would not stray too far from their domain. Thus, their land would always be blessed."

Lilli wondered who this god could have been. Many believed that Machu Picchu was a refuge for the last of the Incan nobility when the Spanish were marauding their cities. The latest investigations had shown that it was indeed a military garrison

ut in the end none of that had mattered, since the nobles had
o empire left to rule. They melted away into the jungle and
en the foliage overtook the citadel in a way the Spaniards
ever could. Machu Picchu became the Incas' greatest secret
or centuries.

Lilli stared at the hitching post for the longest time. Nearly
hundred feet below was the Urubamba River. She couldn't
elp but wonder what had gone through that man's mind as
e was strapped to a rock, suspended between life and death.

David and Merino arrived by three o'clock. They all said
eir good-byes to the bus tour and headed toward the base of
e highest peak.

As the trail narrowed, the little band became engulfed by
oliage that soared from the jungle floor. The mountain peaks
ut off the sunlight long before the end of the day, making
urther exploration impossible. One of the pack llamas carried
nough dry firewood and kindling for a month. While David
nd Merino tied woven bed slings to the bases of huge trees,
illi prepared an evening meal of jalapeño chicken, one of
er favorite recipes. In a frying pan she sautéed onions and
reen, yellow, and red peppers until soft. Then she added
hunks of chicken, two cans of tomatoes, a large spoonful of
alapeño, and a can of frijoles negros. She served it over flat
orn bread. There was plenty of chicha, or corn beer, and she
as reminded of the times when she'd made similar meals
hile on exploring expeditions with her father.

The moon was only half full that night, but the stars were
o big and bright they seemed to light up the sky. She sipped
e last of her chicha from a metal cup and listened to the
oices around the fire as they spoke in Quechua to one an-
ther. Barry was already asleep in his sling, snuggled deep in-
de a down-filled bedroll.

There were no city lights this high above the world, but the
ounds of insects and birds, animals and wind, seemed nearly
s loud as the traffic must sound to Zane in New York.

How far away he was from her, she thought, and yet there
as a part of her that felt he was nearly within arm's reach.
he wanted desperately to pull him close to her. She remem-
ered what it was like to lie next to him and feel his body
ingle with hers just after they had made love. She remem-

bered the touch of his lips on her back and neck when the
would lie like spoons, one curled against the other.

Lilli looked down at the empty cup. She wished she coul
pick up a phone and call Zane. She wanted to tell him tha
she loved him and she wanted to know that he still loved he
She had a life to live for herself and it was about time sh
started living it. But in order to do that, she had to mak
amends with Zane.

Lilli carefully rinsed out her cup in a water bucket, the
placed the cup with the rest of the stacked tin cups and plate
they would use for breakfast. She went to her sling an
climbed in, then slipped her legs into the bedroll. She crosse
her arms behind her head and stared up at the night sk
again.

"Fine time to figure out your life, Lil. A real goddamn fin
time."

She fell instantly asleep.

Thirty-five

Z ane stared at the sleeping Lilli just as dawn gilded the emerald forest with light.

He had followed Lilli's journey to Cuzco, then to the hotel, and then had spoken with the tour guide when he'd come down from Machu Picchu that day. The guide was very informative and told Zane that he had overheard Lilli and her friends plotting out their pathway into the mountain. He told Zane he didn't know what they were looking for, but that Lilli had talked about the fact that there were few running rivers in the area.

"If she wanted to be on the river, I could have shown her that," he said with merry dark eyes. "For a fee, of course."

"Of course." Zane laughed along with him and tipped the man for the information.

Zane found another guide through the hotel who was willing to drive his old Volkswagen bus, still emblazoned with peace symbols and the words "Flower Power" on the side, up to Machu Picchu. Zane knew that he had to catch up with Lilli during the night while she rested; otherwise, she would have too long a head start on him and he might miss her altogether.

Because the sun had gone down early, Lilli and her group had not traveled far from the site of the famous ruin. Zane used his infrared binoculars, a gift from Cold Tap on his last expedition, to scan the area. To the southwest, he'd seen a trickle of white smoke rising above the treetops.

It was a simple matter to find Lilli after that.

Zane walked quietly into camp and stole up to the sleeping Lilli. He gazed down at her and his breath caught in his chest when he realized how much he'd missed her in only these few short days. Masses of dark hair spilled over the sleeping bag and through the wide holes of the woven sling. She wore not a speck of makeup, which made her appear very young and reminded him of the day they'd first met at her house. Her dark, silky lashes fluttered against her cheeks. Her sensuous mouth was slightly open, and suddenly she gave a small gasp. Then her brow furrowed slightly, as if she were having a bad dream.

What demons pursued her in her dreams? he wondered. Did she ever dream of him? He couldn't and wouldn't believe she had substituted this Barry for himself. Zane had to believe he would always be her one true love.

He touched her hair, relishing the silky feel of it as it slid through his fingers. With his forefinger he traced the edge of her jaw and then let his thumb rest momentarily in the nearly imperceptible dimple in her chin. She was his, once and always. That much he knew. Lilli's heart was steadfast. How could he have wasted so much of his life running away from her? Running away from himself?

Zane heard her moan and saw her face tighten as her head twisted from left to right.

"Zane . . ." Lilli cried out softly in her sleep.

It frightened him to think that she was having a bad dream about him. Tenuously, he placed his hand on her shoulder and gently nudged her, wanting only to ease her out of her reverie.

"Zane," she groaned, still within the dream.

"Lilli," he breathed.

She opened her eyes slowly. She knew she was still dreaming because she thought she saw Zane. She smiled at his face in the dream.

Zane smiled back at her. "Are you happy to see me?" he whispered hopefully.

"Oh, yes," she said and reached out her arms to him.

He leaned over and placed his head against her shoulder. She could smell the scent of him as if he were truly there. Then she felt the touch of his lips against her cheek. Then it hit her that this was no dream.

She gasped. "Zane! What are you doing here?"

"Looking for you." He laughed.

"But . . . but . . . this is the middle of the jungle!"

She tried to hoist herself onto her elbows, but they poked through the wide weaving of the sling, and she slipped awkwardly. She kicked at the bedroll, trying to make her escape, but she merely wound up looking as if she were backpedaling. She felt like an animal caught in some kind of trap. No matter how she moved and twisted, all she accomplished was further enmeshment.

"Here, let me help," he said and held the sling taut for her.

"I can manage," she said tersely, not used to someone giving her aid, though she found the act oddly comforting. She was overwhelmed by the fact that he had come all this way to find her. He was here, actually here. He would not vanish in the next three minutes. Even if they had an argument, he couldn't catch a cab from up here and leave her. And she couldn't leave him.

For Lilli, the jungle had always been a beautiful and exotic place, whose deadly secrets she respected. How odd to think that the jungle might finally bring them together. Here, they were forced to face each other and their own deep secrets.

As Lilli finally freed her elbows and legs, Zane smiled at her impishly. "I can see how well you manage all by yourself."

She planted her feet on the ground. The nearness of him almost knocked her over, and it still seemed impossible that he found her. "What are you doing here?"

"Looking for you."

His smile, his voice, the heat she could feel from his body, engulfed her and captured her mind and heart all over again. She was succumbing to him, and although she knew she should and that this might be her last chance for happiness, her mind wouldn't let her go without a fight.

"Goddamn you, Zane, you infuriate the hell out of me!"

"Ditto for you, Lilli." He grinned seductively and then pulled her into his arms. "Now show me how much you missed he," he said and kissed her with passionate and hungry lips. "I came here for you to finish what you started back in Houston," he breathed between kisses.

"Are you crazy?"

"A little. I've got to be, to go halfway around the world and nearly straight up to heaven to find you." He pulled her closer to him, crushing her breasts into his strong chest. He ran his hands down the length of her and grasped her buttocks with both of his hands, then pushed her pelvis into his quickly hardening shaft.

Lilli was breathless as the kiss overtook her. She felt as if she were falling off the side of the mountain. She lost herself to him as she always did when he kissed her. Their intensity was nearly too much to fathom and she trembled. She wanted him totally and she knew he was eager to take her, too. Their kiss deepened, and as it did, she took his hand and placed it on her breast, then covered his strong fingers with her own.

He groaned so loudly, the crew stirred in their sleep.

Lilli was so lost to Zane that she completely forgot where she was and what she was doing. Then she heard, in what seemed to be a very remote distance, the sound of Barry's voice.

"Lilli? Lilli? What the hell is going on? Who is this jerk?" Barry scrambled out of his bedroll.

Adriano didn't budge from his hammock but simply stared at them as if this were an everyday occurrence in the Andes. She heard the sounds of laughter from David and Merino.

Their voices blended with the cacophony of jungle animals waking with the dawn. Birds swooped out of treetops and chirped and cawed to one another. Rodents scurried under the brush.

Lilli was still as deeply into the kiss as Zane was. She never wanted to leave his arms.

Zane held her tightly, relishing this moment he had thought about, dreamed about, and orchestrated on the long plane flight to Peru. He couldn't believe he'd actually found her.

He finally heard the other voices around him, and in particular the male voice that belonged to Barry. He had thought he should be jealous of Barry, but he knew now, with this one kiss from Lilli, that no man would ever hold her heart except him.

Zane reluctantly pulled his mouth from Lilli's lips, even though his body told him it was going to be the most difficult thing he'd ever done. He smiled down at her.

His eyes were filled with love, Lilli thought as she gazed up at him. The morning dawn wove ribbons of peach-and-gold light through his blonde hair, and she couldn't help thinking that the sun god the Incas had worshiped so long ago must have looked like him.

She hugged him and then whispered in his ear, "You are crazy, Zane McAllister, to come all this way just to get a little."

He traced the outer shell of her ear with his tongue and watched her shiver. "I came for a Lilli."

Barry stomped over to the duo. "What the hell is this? Saturday night at the drive-in?"

Lilli smiled. "Barry Whiteman, this is Zane McAllister. Barry, this is Zane."

Zane stuck out his hand. "Glad to know you," he said winningly.

"Charmed," Barry growled. "You'll have to excuse me. I haven't had my coffee yet and I don't make it a practice to wake up to molesters."

"He's not a molester, Barry. He's . . ." Lilli looked at Zane quizzically.

"I'm her hero. I hope."

Barry looked from Lilli's obviously happy face to Zane's equally beaming face and dropped his attack. He shook Zane's hand. "Good luck, pal. I've got a feeling it's not an easy job."

Lilli was the first to join in the laughter. Then she introduced Adriano, David, and Merino. While the men packed away the bedding, Lilli set about making coffee and breakfast.

Over the meal, Barry briefed Zane on their intended passage and showed him the maps.

"Zane's never done anything like this, Barry, so I think we should both watch out for him, especially when we get up higher and encounter steep cliffs—"

Zane was quick to interrupt. "You know so much, Lilli Mitchell. I'll be fine."

"But, Zane—"

He stuck up a hand to stop her retort. "I'm getting to be an old hand at this now."

"What are you talking about?"

"The client of mine who bought the dagger from you took me to Colombia to help him find an emerald mine."

Lilli nearly dropped her jaw, though her eyes surveyed him suspiciously. "When was this?"

"Last week," he said triumphantly. "I made an incredible discovery in the mountains there."

"You mean you left me, went to Colombia, and then came here?"

"I did go back to Houston, trying to track you down. You aren't as easy to catch as you might think."

Lilli blushed with pleasure and then her eyebrows shot up at the thought that any new discovery usually cast new insight into Incan history. "What did you find in Colombia?"

Zane couldn't contain a satisfied grin. "I knew I'd pique your curiosity sooner or later."

"You're just teasing me."

He leaned very close to her face, his eyes dazzlingly blue in the dawn sunlight. His voice was low and filled with seductive promise. "I'll tease you, Lilli Mitchell, but with my body, not with my exploits." He took her hand and kissed the tip of each of her fingers.

Then he abruptly turned away and spoke to Barry. "Do you suppose I could put my backpack on one of the llamas?"

"Certainly," Barry replied.

Zane turned back to Lilli. "I'll tell you all about it later." Then he left her and followed Barry.

The midday sun rose full and hot over the Andes Mountains. Ribbons of steam curled along the jungle floor, masking important footholds and impeding progress. The air was still, the only movement caused by scurrying cuys or guinea pigs or an occasional puma. The higher they rose, the less animal life they encountered. The tropical vegetation began to graduate into thick mats of green grasses. Gone were the araucaria and coigue pines used for thatching; Lilli saw only cypress trees and shrub growing between the rocks.

Zane kept the group entertained with his own adventure story about Cold Tap and their discovery in Colombia. Lilli was quick to notice that Adriano and the others were pleased that Cold Tap had chosen not to exploit the emeralds, but rather had been content with the excitement of the hunt. Lilli was fascinated that Cold Tap and Zane had painstakingly pieced together bits and pieces of information, both legend and fact, to arrive at their conclusions.

Just like J.C., she thought. How many times had she and her father consulted old books, experts, and old stories to pick out the pieces they believed were real? How many times had J.C. told Lilli that he was guided by his intuition as much as his logic? That same intuition guided Lilli. She believed in her heart that only inspiration or some mystical guide had told Barry to make her stand on the chair and look down on the map. There was something beyond them all that pushed them along and prodded them to do things they did. Lilli had to believe they were on this journey for many reasons. Maybe J.C. was still standing next to her, his spirit invading her mind and giving her direction. Maybe it was J.C.'s spirit that had led Zane to his discovery in Colombia.

It boggled Lilli's mind to know that on his first venture Zane had accomplished more than most trained archaeologists and anthropologists. Maybe it was true what they said about beginner's luck. She believed it was more than just luck, though. He'd used his wits and intuition as his guides. Also, he had no ego, no reputation, no university position to uphold—all of which were pressures that could impede judgment.

Lilli's admiration for Zane grew a hundredfold that day as she listened to his stories.

The sun's rays shone through the wide-leafed palms and lushly branched trees and glinted off the steel machetes the guides used to slice their way through crisscrossed vines and twining greenery that obstructed their passage. Because this particular area was so dense, everyone was expected to work. Lilli's arm ached by midday, and by midafternoon her muscles were screaming from overuse. Her legs had turned to rubber and she felt as if she couldn't move another step. Perspiration streamed down her face and her T-shirt was soaked with sweat. Never had Lilli experienced such a difficult trip. Her expeditions with her father seemed like Sunday outings compared with this.

Often she glanced up at Zane and marveled at his stamina. He'd taken off his camp shirt long ago and now wore only an army-green sleeveless T-shirt. His well-defined muscles rolled easily with the rhythmic swing of each machete cut. His skin was covered in a fine film of sweat, but he seemed not to be bothered by the heat, the physical exertion, or the insects. In fact, he seemed incredibly at one with the jungle, as if he'd been born to this land.

Lilli was seeing Zane through new eyes. She found it difficult to imagine him as she'd last seen him in Houston, impeccably dressed like an advertisement out of *GQ*. This was a Zane she had not known before and she couldn't help but wonder how he felt about finding this side of himself.

Zane was whistling as he chopped away at an incredible wall of vegetation. He could feel the blood flowing through his veins, feeding his muscles as they worked at their full capacity. He remembered the nights when he would go to the club and work out on the machines forcing his body to the limit.

To his amazement, Lilli kept up with him. She never complained about the heat or the insects, though she did use nearly an entire can of insect repellent. Zane had come to understand what the jungle inspired: that engulfing need to tame the untamable. And for the first time, he understood Lilli in a new, deeper way that he never would have known if he hadn't gone there to find her.

It warmed Zane to know that he and Lilli were becoming one, evolving into a team. They were rising above the sexual side of their relationship. It was true that he still wanted to possess her sexually at nearly every turn, but now even those thoughts were infused with more emotion, more love, than he'd ever known.

By the end of the day they had come to the top of the peak that Lilli had determined was the point of origin for the river of gold. Although this entire section of the Andes, called the Cordillera Vilcabamba, was formed by the erosive action of rivers that cut deep canyons into the mountains, most of these rivers had dried up long ago.

Exhausted, they made camp for the night. While Zane fed the llamas and the rest of the crew set up the hammocks, Lilli made the fire and put a pot of coffee on to brew. She opened tins of beans and set them in a pot to warm. There were peach slices for dessert. She was warming bread near the fire when Zane crouched next to her.

He put his arm around her shoulder. "Don't look so glum, darlin'."

"What if J.C. was wrong and his calculations are off?" she asked in a worried tone. "We'll have come all this way for nothing."

"Lilli, I know you like I know the back of my hand. You wouldn't be here if you hadn't gone over every detail of J.C.'s work. Probably memorized every legend backward and forward. I trust you, Lilli."

She looked at him with her face cupped in her hand. "Thanks for the vote of confidence." She looked back at the fire. "However, I didn't trust my memory as much as you do. I brought along Pop's last journal. It's just a thumbnail sketch of a lifetime of work, but a couple of items have haunted me."

"Such as?"

"The legend about the sun god at Machu Picchu. I've never been able to understand why he underlined nearly the entire entry. Zane"—she raised her eyes hopefully to him—"would you read it and give me your opinion?"

Zane's smile was broad and pleased. He leaned down to kiss her gently. "I'd be honored," he said.

Supper was consumed hastily; then the group sat around the fire exchanging stories and information about various digs they'd been associated with. David was fascinated with Zane's tales of the lost emeralds, although they all agreed that no one would ever truly know if what he and Cold Tap had found was the one true "source" mine.

"This is what makes a legend a legend," Lilli said. "Century after century, man keeps searching for proof of the stories, and we come so close at times. Then we get frustrated and go back to our old lives."

Zane leaned over close to her ear. "I hope you never want to go back to your old life—at least not without me."

Lilli watched his face in the firelight and the flames making shadows on his cheeks. At that moment she realized how right it felt to be with him like this. They were well suited to each other in a way she'd almost forgotten. How full of surprises he was, this lost childhood love of hers. Lilli had been busy all day breaking down the false images she had built of

Zane in the same way she'd hacked her way through the jungle. He was not trying to take her father's dream from her; he was trying to help her fulfill his wishes. Here he was, sitting beside her, urging her to grow to her full potential. He demanded nothing of her, but only wanted to give her his heart. It was dangerous business, this art of loving, and yet, as she looked into his eyes, she saw only hope and caring, love and concern for her. Lilli felt her heart open to Zane as it had never opened before. She felt free and yet strangely safe. He truly wanted the best for her and he loved her enough to allow her to explore the world and her dreams without being tethered to him. As her heart welcomed him, she realized that she loved him in that same way. If he wanted to live in New York, she would follow him there. She realized now that nothing could stifle her love for him. She loved him unconditionally.

What amazed Lilli most of all was the knowledge that even as a very young girl, she had instinctively loved Zane with her entire being. She had known then that he was meant to be hers. She'd never questioned it at the time. Later, she had told herself she'd been a fool, that she had trusted blindly because of her youth. Perhaps it had been because of her youth that she had known things then that she later closed off to her heart, and *that* had been where she had gone astray. Her heart had always belonged to Zane; first, last, and always.

The best part of Lilli's discovery was that she trusted him implicitly, even with J.C.'s precious last journal. She was stunned at the thought. Not three weeks ago, she wouldn't have shared this cherished document with anyone, let alone Zane. Now she hadn't the slightest qualm about revealing to Zane what her father had written. She wanted him to see where J.C.'s head had been all the way back to the years when she was young romping ignorantly among the ruins at Tulum and Palenque. She wanted Zane to trace her past using these papers as his guide. To Lilli, this journal was like handing Zane a diary of her past.

"I'll get the journal," she said, eagerly jumping to her feet.

Adriano had placed the duffel bags and makeshift saddlebags in a pile not far from the fire. It was difficult to see in the dark, but Lilli knew precisely where she had placed the journal and retrieved it easily.

She raced back to Zane, who had just stoked the fire with an extra log. He pulled out a small, battery-operated flashlight from his own backpack and began to read.

Lilli noticed that Zane was concentrating intensely. He seemed unaware of Lilli or the crew, who now sat off by themselves, drinking their corn beer and exchanging jokes in Quechua.

Lilli allowed him the space, both physical and mental, that he needed. She watched from a distance as his fascination caught fire. Sometimes he would flip excitedly from page to page, tracking down an idea. He pulled a pen from his backpack and made notes to himself.

It was over forty-five minutes before he spoke to her.

"Lilli, I see this translation of the legend about the sun god. I've noticed that your father has made all kinds of marginal notes on every story, asterisked half this stuff, but he seems to have discounted this legend in his calculations. Yet it is so prominent in his journal. I'm inclined to think he may not have had enough time before he died . . ." He touched her knee. "I'm sorry," he said, seeing the grief in her eyes.

"I'm okay. So—what do you think? Any ideas?" she asked, turning her attention to the journal.

"Well, as you know, it's the whole story about this sun god for whom the Incas made the hitching post. I don't know who this fellow was, but he certainly wasn't Incan. It says here that he had hair the color of gold and his eyes were blue like the skies from which he descended . . ."

"Like you," she said lovingly.

"I never want to be a god, Lilli. Just a man. Always remember that. I've got a hell of a lot of faults. Just remember to love me in spite of them. Okay?"

"Okay." She smiled.

Zane turned back to the translation. "This poor guy. They left him tied to this hitching post like he was an animal. They must have fed him, because he stayed alive for a long time. He always kept his eyes on the heavens, both day and night. He told them that he would be taken away . . ."

"I never thought about that phrase before," Lilli said. "How odd. Why didn't they use the word 'escape,' I wonder?"

Zane shrugged his shoulders. "I don't know. Must be one

of those things that loses something in translation. After all, the original text is over a thousand years old. Anyway, we have this fellow who kept praying and waiting. At dawn he prayed to the morning star—that would have been Venus. And that makes sense, since the Incas worshiped the moon and Venus. But then the story goes on to say how he had kept his eyes to the southwest all day, and one morning the inhabitants went out to minister to him and he was gone."

"Do you have any thoughts about where he might have gone?"

"Well," Zane said, grinning boyishly, "my bet is that some young honey took a liking to him and cut his manacles and the two of them took off for the mountains."

Lilli smiled. "Interpreted that way, it's a wonderfully romantic tale, isn't it?"

"Um-hmm." Zane reread the legend.

As he read, Lilli noticed that he was frowning. "Zane, what are you thinking?"

"There's something here, but I can't figure out what it is. It's just a gut feeling I have."

They heard the sounds of Adriano, David, and Merino climbing into their bedrolls and sleeping slings. "I don't think we're going to figure out anything more tonight," Zane said. "We'd better get some shut-eye. What do you say?"

Lilli nodded as she yawned and stretched her arms over her head. "It has been a long and very tiring day."

Zane helped Lilli into her sling. He bent over and kissed her good night, then stood and looked down at her. "You have no idea how much I want to make love to you, Lilli Mitchell." He touched her cheek. "I could make love to you all night long, despite my exhaustion."

Lilli smiled impishly. "That's a rather scary thought. What's it going to be like when you're well rested?"

"You'd just better watch out!"

"Promises, promises," she teased and found her eyelids closing, despite her desire to listen to his voice.

"Good night, my love," he said, then bedded down close by and fell instantly asleep.

Lilli awoke the next morning and discovered that Zane had been awake for hours. The llamas were packed with all but the breakfast dishes. Coffee was already brewed, potatoes were baked, cornbread was warmed, and eggs were being fried. Zane hustled around the campfire, administering to the crew as if he'd been doing this all his life.

Lilli rose, rubbed her eyes, and walked over to the fire.

"Mornin', sunshine," Zane said. "How do you like your eggs? Fried, I hope."

"Just coffee is fine."

"We have a long day ahead of us. You need to eat. Here, I'll fix a plate for you."

Lilli blinked twice and wondered what kind of vitamins Zane was on. She felt as if she'd been dragged through the jungle by her heels. Every muscle in her body was sore. She wanted nothing more than to go back to bed. In a real bed . . . in a hotel with room service.

Lilli rubbed her aching shoulders. What had happened to her? She used to love this life. It had been all-important to her. She had been with her pop and she had wanted to please him.

The thought hit her like a thunderbolt and her eyes flew open. She sat down slowly and accepted a cup of steaming coffee from Zane. To please her pop. Had she done all this just for him? Or was any of it for herself?

Zane handed her a tin plate filled with food. "I hope the yolks aren't hard."

Lilli looked up at him. "We have to talk, Zane."

"Yeah, I know," he said quickly and sat down beside her. "I know this may come as a shock, but I want to go back down."

She breathed a sigh of relief. "Oh, Zane! I do, too!"

"You do?" He was shocked.

"Yes. I was silly to come up here, thinking that J.C. had found some stupid rivers of gold—"

"Lilli, what are you saying?"

"That—that we're going back to Cuzco and then take the next flight out of Lima back to Houston, of course." She put her plate on the ground and threw her arms around his neck. "I love you, Zane. I want us to make a real life together and stop believing in these foolish daydreams of mine."

Zane's face was filled with confusion, and he pulled back. "Lilli, you don't understand. I don't want to quit and I apologize for making you think I did. We're so close to it, can't you see? I got up in the middle of the night and had a real brainstorm. I think I've got it all figured out, and I can't leave here without testing my theory."

Lilli was astounded. "You sound just like my father. I don't want you to become a dreamer like him, Zane. He spent his life pursuing something that was simply a waste of time. Let's not waste our lives on things of the past. I want to make a future for us."

Zane slipped one arm around her waist. "I do, too, honey. But first, just indulge me in this one time. I'm a new hand at this, but it does get into your blood pretty quickly, doesn't it?"

"Yes," she had to admit. "That it does."

"Okay. Now can I tell you my theory?"

"We're going back to Cuzco . . ."

"No. Just back to Machu Picchu. It should take only half the time, since all we have to do is follow our own trail, and it's downhill all the way. Then tonight, after that last bus tour, I want you to tie me to that hitching post."

Lilli stood up and looked down at him. "It's the altitude, Zane. It's fried your brain."

"No, seriously. I think there's something in that story about the sun god. He saw something at dawn to the southwest, and I want to be where he stood so I can see it, too."

"You're nuts! Certifiably nuts!"

He stood, reached out for her, and pulled her into his arms. "Yeah. But you're nuts, too. About me, aren't you?"

Then he kissed her so deeply, so tenderly, that she nearly felt the earth move beneath her feet. "That I am," she said between kisses. "That I am."

Thirty-six

$\mathcal{Z}$ane's head bobbed forward onto his chest as the dawn broke. He would have missed the sunrise completely had it not been for the sound of a condor swooping overhead. And it was imperative for his experiment that he not miss the sunrise.

Sleepily, he looked over at Lilli and the others, who slept in their bedrolls on top of the ruins close by. Lilli had struggled to stay awake with him all night as he sat with his chin on his knees near the hitching post. However, when she finally admitted she couldn't stay awake any longer, Zane stood and had her tie him to the hitching post. Lilli protested this tethering with every argument she could think of, but Zane believed there was a correlation with his standing position and the early dawn. He wanted to re-create the morning of the sun god's disappearance.

"This is totally ridiculous, Zane," she had said as she fastened the hemp around his wrists. A large, precisely cut hole to match the end of the hitching post had been chiseled into the huge boulder on which Zane stood, and the post was anchored into the hole. The boulder jutted out over the edge of the cliff. Each time Zane looked down, he felt dizzy.

"Tie 'em tight, darlin'. It's a long way down there."

"I don't like this. Sometimes you can be so stubborn." She checked the rope to be sure it was securely fastened.

"I know, but the legend says—"

Lilli cut in before he could continue. "That story is a thousand years old. What do you think you can possibly see, anyway? Whatever it was is long gone. Even the mountains are shaped differently today than back then. More erosion, more vegetation . . ."

"Please don't use logic, Lilli. Besides, look at it this way.

389

If nothing happens, then we'll wait here for the tour bus and hitch a ride down with it. Adriano and the others can take the animals down to the city and we'll go on from there, just as you want."

"I'm too tired to argue with you tonight," she said, walking around to his side and standing on her tiptoes to kiss him. She placed her hand on his chest and let it slip slowly down to his flat stomach. "There are advantages to having you in this position," she said, grinning wickedly.

Zane gave her a sideways look. "Lilli, please. I thought you were tired."

"I was . . ." She kissed him again. "But I've decided to have mercy on you tonight, my love."

"Thank God. Now please, get some rest. You're going to need your strength."

"I think you're going to need yours, Zane McAllister," she teased and kissed him one last time before slipping into her bedroll.

Zane raised his head slowly and tried to blink the sleep out of his eyes. He was facing southwest and was witness to the sun's first rays as they dusted the vegetation with light.

At first he thought his eyes were playing tricks on him. In the distance he saw a light. Then the sun rose a bit higher and the light became brighter. He hadn't been mistaken!

Suddenly it was a beacon flashing a golden beam of light directly into his face. He found he had to close his eyes to it, the light was so intense. He lifted his lids slowly and then quickly lowered them. It felt like a laser piercing his retina.

"Lilli!" he shouted to her. "Lilli! Adriano! Come quickly!"

He could hear them scrambling out of their bedrolls behind him, but he dared not turn in case he missed the miracle.

"What is it, Zane?"

"What do you see, *señor?*" Adriano asked.

"Can't you see it?" He heard them rush toward him.

"My God!" Barry shouted excitedly.

"*Sancta Maria!*" David exclaimed.

Then a hush fell over the whole group as they watched the beam of light across the spur from them grow more intense and then slowly begin to fade.

"Lilli! Quickly! Get the map! Barry! Help her mark the place. Whatever that is . . . that's where we're going."

Barry went to his backpack and hurried back with the map and slid to the ground on his knees. Lilli quickly untied Zane's hands from the post.

Zane rubbed his wrists, but still he did not move. "Can you get a bead on it?"

"I think so," Lilli answered as Barry used a ruler to mark the spot. "From the looks of it, we were halfway there yesterday."

Zane watched in the distance as the light suddenly disappeared. He turned toward the group and saw the frightened looks on David's and Merino's faces. Adriano didn't look at all pleased. "What's wrong?" Zane asked.

Cautiously, Adriano glanced from his crew back to Zane, then at Lilli and Barry. "The others, they say they will not go back. Fools. They think you are fools. Up and down. Up and down."

Zane scanned David's pallid face and Merino's equally white one. "Bullshit," he said to Adriano. "They're scared to death. But I'm not going to make them do something they don't want to do. I'll take one of the llamas with enough supplies to last for a week. With the progress we've already made, I can get there in less than two days. Nobody has to go with me."

Lilli watched the hired crew as all three backed away. She was also quick to note that Barry said nothing. "What's on your mind, Barry?" she asked.

He hesitated for a moment, but when he looked at her, she could see defiance in his eyes. "This isn't what J.C. had in mind at all. I don't think this is anything. I mean, shit, Lilli, for all we know, it could be some old plane wreckage that the sun was just bouncing off for a minute or two. I think that the reason you found no notes on those sheets was because J.C. most likely had investigated this alternative and found it lacking. I believe in your father's work, Lilli, like you *used* to, if you can remember as far back as last week. I personally think this approach is about as harebrained as they get and frankly, I don't want any part of it. I've got a lot of other things to do. I'll be going back with the guys."

"I'm sorry you feel that way, Barry," she said sincerely. "I wish you all the best." She shook his hand.

"Same here," he said and tersely shook her hand. He pointedly did not shake Zane's outstretched hand.

In less than an hour Lilli and Zane were on their way back up the peak. They made very quick time following their own cleared trail. Infused with their new discovery, they both found that they tired less easily and were able to make even better time than before. As they moved on toward their destination, the jungle thinned and the going became much easier.

The air was cooler and the ground rockier, though covered with ground grass and vegetation. As the sun sank behind the mountains, Zane groaned with impatience.

"We're so close, Lilli. I'll bet we aren't but a stone's throw from the spot, but it's just so hard to see."

"If only there was a full moon, we could go on."

"Oh, well," he said. "Whatever it is, it's been there for a thousand years and one more day won't matter."

"No. I guess not."

"You're really tired, aren't you?"

"Yes, I am," she said, sinking down on the ground.

"We won't need the slings this high up in the mountains. I'll make a fire and fix us something to eat. You rest for a bit," he said, then fetched her bedroll for her.

Lilli barely remembered reclining her head, much less falling into a very deep sleep. It seemed only seconds before Zane woke her and handed her a plate filled with food. Her stomach growled as the aroma from the stew hit her nostrils. She sat up and took the plate gratefully. She sank her spoon into the chicken and vegetables. "This is really good. I didn't know you could cook."

"I can't," he said. "I hit one of those gourmet stores on the way out of Houston. It's amazing what they put in tin cans these days."

"It's delicious," she said, taking a big scoop and then washing it down with freshly brewed coffee.

"Lilli," he said between bites, "will you marry me?"

Lilli stopped in mid-motion. She turned to him. "I think the altitude has affected your brain."

He smiled. "I'm serious. Maybe I should have waited for champagne and roses—something more romantic . . ." He put his plate on the ground and scooted toward her on his knees. "How's this?" He took her hand and kissed each finger.

The light from the fire was low already and she could barely see his face, but the lovelight in his eyes shone bright as the moon. "I can't think of anything more romantic than a mountaintop. Are you sure, Zane?"

"Yes. Are you?"

"Yes. I'm more certain about you than I have been about anything in my whole life."

He was smiling now, not broadly or boastfully, but happily. "It took you a long time to come to me," he said a bit accusingly.

"It took us both a long time," she said and placed her plate to his. She held her arms out to him and embraced him.

"I love you, Lilli," he said with so much emotion that his voice cracked.

"I love you," she said and kissed the hollow at the base of his neck. "I've come to realize so many things about myself on this trip. I've done you such an injustice over the years, believing that my loyalty to Pop was more important than my feelings for you. I've fought myself for so long, I nearly forgot what it was to feel at all. Or maybe I felt too much. I thought I would die when you first went away to New York, and then you forgot about me. I hated you then. I tried so hard to let you go."

"Let's not talk about the past. Let's make a future, Lilli. I won't run from you anymore and you won't run from me. Is that a deal?"

"Oh, yes," she said and kissed him sweetly.

Slowly they sank to the grass-covered ground. Zane kissed Lilli tenderly at first, and as she kissed him back, she felt the emotions rise within her chest like molten lava. Lilli had held her love in check far too long. She wanted to laugh, cry, and shout with joy all at the same time.

Her arms tightened around him, pulling him closer to her. Had it been within her power, she would have found a way to fuse his body to hers. Never had she felt this close to anyone. Never had she known this kind of serenity, as if the pieces of life's puzzle had suddenly all come together.

As his passion surged through him, he plunged his tongue deeply into her mouth. She accepted the invasion and when she succumbed to his power over her, his urgency was replaced with an eagerness to please her. He slipped his hand under her camp shirt and unhooked her bra, then caressed her breasts.

"God, Lilli, what you do to me." His voice was deep and velvety and sent her senses reeling. He toyed with her nipples until they became hard and erect. She cried out in the night.

"Zane . . ."

He crushed his erection against her thigh as he pulled her shirt over her head. The firelight pirouetted across her skin, gilding it with burnished gold. He discarded his hiking boots, socks, shirt, and pants while she slipped out of her shorts, shoes, and socks. He placed her on one of the bedrolls and put the other beneath her head.

His eyes were open as he kissed her throat and then do the valley between her breasts, thinking that they had com this land to find the rivers of gold, and they had found s thing more precious than gold. They had found love.

In the firelight and the faint silvery beams from the waning moon, he looked like a golden god to her. She sank her hands into his thick blond hair and watched how it curled around her fingers like golden rings . . . like wedding rings.

Zane blazed a trail of exciting, tiny bites and kisses across her abdomen and then down farther to the triangle between her legs. He spread her legs apart with his hands and she obligingly opened herself to him. Lovingly and tenderly, he caressed her passion's bud with his tongue, over and over until Lilli was breathless.

Lilli felt fire shooting through her body, and Zane stoked that inferno with kisses, bites, and flicks of his tongue. He wanted her to want him, but even more than that, he wanted her to experience pleasures she had never known, not even with him. This time they would not turn away from each other. This time he would make his mark on her soul so that she would never want to live a minute without him.

Lilli clutched his hair as she reached her first orgasm and screamed his name until it echoed against the mountain walls. Love filled the air around her, and again she cried his name.

Zane gently entered her. She lifted her hips to him, accept-